Love in a Far Place

Rosie Mackenzie

ISBN 9780645733884

Ballynastragh Books

Step into the changing world of post-World War II Australia, where two sisters, bound by love and torn by choices, make new lives after Maria Vincento entices her sister, Angeline away from their home on the tiny Italian island of Procida. As Angeline reluctantly sets foot on the ship to their new beginnings, her heart carries the weight of a shattered dream.

At the Villawood Migrant Hostel on Sydney's outskirts, fate introduces them to Stewart Erskine, a gregarious Scottish immigrant destined for remarkable success. His presence sets in motion a series of events that will forever alter the course of the sisters' lives, pushing Angeline to confront an agonising decision.

Years later, Angeline's granddaughter, Emily, a celebrated Sydney model, grapples with her grandmother's failing health. When she stumbles upon the secrets of her late grandfather's enigmatic business dealings, Emily is more determined than ever to unravel her grandmother's past, which takes them to an apple orchard in Tasmania where a young Italian, Raphael Lombardi, worked as a prisoner-of-war.

Coming to terms with her grandmother's past, does Emily have the courage to follow her own heart and leave her old life behind?

From the beloved author of *The Homestead on the River*, comes a poignant narrative of lost loves, hidden family mysteries, and the enduring power of hope that will leave you captivated.

www.ballynastraghbooks.com.au

Dedication

To Rob and our precious family for all we have shared.

Procida

It's a well-known fact that Isola di Procida *is not as showy and glamorous as her sister islands, Ischia and Capri. Yet, in her own, quieter way she is just as beautiful. And, as many women are wont to do, Procida has made the most of her assets, dressing up in pinks, blues, reds, yellows and ochre. For centuries, the island's hard-working fishermen have spotted their homes from the sea by the colour of their houses perched below the church steeples.*

Two sisters grew up in a modest faded pink villa on this tiny speck of land in the Bay of Naples. To an outsider, one of the sisters was flashy and bold—like Ischia and Capri. The other sister was less so but, like Procida she was just as desirable.

When they migrated to a far place on the other side of the world, one of the sisters left her heart behind on Procida. It would be many years later before she found it again.

By then it was almost too late.

Chapter One

On hearing the knock at the front door, Angela Erskine jumped.

After her usual swim at the beach at Bronte, followed by the steep hike to her house on the hill, she rested under the clematis vine on the back verandah where she had soon dozed off. Standing up, she moved through to the hallway and opened the door. Outside was a man of about forty, tall, dark haired and quite attractive in a tousled sort of way.

'Mrs Erskine?' he asked, stepping forward.

'Yes,' Angela said. 'That's me.'

'Greg Ashton … from the *Sydney Mail*. Could I please have a moment of your time?'

Angela shot him a small smile. 'And why might that be?'

'I'm doing some research for an article I've been asked to write.'

'Oh!' Angela said, wondering why on earth he would want to interview her for an article. 'What are you writing about?'

'In the light of ICAC finding Harry Turner guilty of corruptly obtaining the lease to his mine in the Hunter Valley, there's a rumour circulating that many years ago your late husband, Stewart Erskine, may have obtained the lease to his Glasgow Mine in a similar sort of deal. A politician making a bit on the side: gifting the licence without a competitive tender and against departmental advice. I wondered if you'd like to comment.'

Although his statement startled her, Angela remained composed. She had followed this Harry Turner corruption case in the newspaper and nightly news with interest and wondered how it would pan out. 'I've nothing to say on the matter,' she said, holding his eyes steadily with hers before stepping aside and attempting to shut the door in his face.

'It's just that—'

'As I said, I've nothing to say.'

'Please, Mrs Erskine … maybe just hear me out—'

'No, I won't. And now,' she said firmly, 'I would really like you to leave.'

She moved back and closed the door with force. For a moment, she stood with her back against its hard surface, her heart racing. She wondered how he had found out where she lived. She wasn't in the phone book. And how long before his article involving Stewart might break in his newspaper? She really should ring her son, Gavin, but he was overseas on business. The same business he had inherited from Stewart, despite Stewart ranting and raving over the years that he wasn't up to the mark.

After checking at the window to see if the journalist had gone, she went to the kitchen to make a cup of tea, which she carried back to the verandah where she tried to calm her anxiousness. The afternoon was warm and clear, the late sun gentle on her skin: a touch of Indian summer, which normally would delight her.

Sipping from her teacup, she gazed over her garden to the sea beyond.

Ever since she was a child, known as Angeline on *Isola di Procida*, a tiny island in the Bay of Naples, she loved being close to the sea, delighting in all of its moods. Here at Bronte Beach, even if there was a howling wind and angry clouds sulking overhead, she found it difficult to be unmoved each morning when she came out of her bedroom and stood at the window to stare at the sand, ocean and sky. It was as if she was getting a fix before her day started. There had been many times when she needed more than an expansive view of the sea to get through each day, but that time had long since gone. Now her days were filled with things she *wanted* to do. Not things she was *supposed* to do as the wife of Stewart Erskine, the great restaurateur, businessman and mining magnate. Every newspaper and TV station in the nation had reported him as dying from a heart attack on a business trip to South Korea ten years ago.

And now, she thought anxiously, he was to be in the news again.

She took another sip of tea, felt it slide down her throat. Already she could imagine how it would be. Headlines and more reporters at her door. Stewart's face on the TV.

Taking a long, deep breath she looked at her watch and was surprised to see she had been sitting here for over half an hour. Time she put the journalist's visit out of her mind and had a shower. She was expecting her granddaughter, Emily, to pop in and Angela was still wearing her swimmers under her caftan. After her shower she padded to the bedroom, pulled on her slacks and top, rubbed her hair dry and ran a comb through the thin strands. She was not one to seek pity, but she found it difficult to relate the image in the mirror with how she felt. Inside she was no different than when she swam naked with her sister, Maria, in the warm cerulean waters off the sandy beaches on Procida Island. But the vision before Angela now was of a woman of eighty years of age. She sighed, smoothing a finger over her cheekbones, still high and proud, down to her neck, once so swan-like and a stage for Stewart's diamonds and pearls.

She picked up her lipstick and stained her lips a golden peach, opened her compact and added a dab of colour to her cheeks to make her look less like a ghost. Feathering her eyelashes with mascara, she then lined her lids with brown pencil. She always took time with her makeup, ever since Maria showed her how to enhance the best of her features.

'No matter how dismal you feel, my sweet Angeline,' Maria had said with a laugh, as Angela watched her applying mascara to her long, thick eyelashes, 'a girl must put on her very best face to the big wide world out there.'

Oh Stewart, she now thought. What would Maria think of the journalist's visit?

Leaving the bedroom, Angela went to the kitchen and poured herself a glass of *Pinot Grigio.* She was about to take it back out onto the deck when she heard a knock on the door. She was afraid it might be the journalist come back, but was relieved when Emily called out.

'Nonna? You there?'

'Coming, darling,' she called back, placing her wineglass on the bench.

As always when she saw Emily standing on her doorstep, she was taken aback at how lovely she was. She was wearing heavy makeup from a fashion shoot, for unless working as a top model, Emily needed little adornment to her beautiful face. Her eyes, a magnificent greeny-blue, were heavily made up and her tight tangle of black curls, which were usually loose and glossy around her face were tied up in a high ponytail. She had bronzer on her cheeks and her lips were stained a deep red.

'Ciao, my darling. How lovely to see you,' Angela said cheerfully, belying the angst she was feeling after the journalist's visit. 'Come ... I've just poured myself a glass of wine. I'll get you one as well.'

'Sounds wonderful, Nonna,' Emily said, throwing her handbag on the plump white couch in the living room as she followed Angela to the kitchen. A few minutes later they were sitting under the clematis vine on the verandah.

'I do love it here,' Emily said, as she sipped from her glass of wine. 'It's so peaceful with just the sound of the sea.' She sighed as she placed her glass on the table and picked up an olive from a small bowl. 'Mind you, *Mandalay* was peaceful too with all that land. Do you ever miss it?'

After Stewart died, Angela sold their house, *Mandalay*, in Bellevue Hill. In one way, she was sad to leave all that was so familiar. In another way, she couldn't wait to get out. And, of course, when she had seen this house she had fallen in love straight away. From the moment she first set eyes on it she loved it more than any other home she had lived in. It wasn't just that it was perched on a knoll overlooking the beach, it was the elegant curves of the walls painted a Mediterranean salmon pink and the rambling garden with its weeping willow, holm oak, elm and wattle tree which had convinced her it had to be hers. Even *Mandalay*, where she and Stewart lived for so long, didn't have a kitchen that appealed to Angela as much as this one did. Besides, *Mandalay* always needed maids and gardeners to maintain it. This house only needed Angela and the wonderful Brenda who came in once a week to keep it ship shape.

'At first I thought *Mandalay* was far too ostentatious,' she told Emily. 'When I got over that I enjoyed it.' She chuckled. 'After all, one would be hard put to not enjoy living in such a place, wouldn't one? Even so, for the first time in my life once I moved in here, I felt as though I was truly my own person.'

'You don't get lonely without Grandpa?'

'I have my books and my many interests. The garden, beach to swim at, and my friends.' She smiled. 'And I have you, darling and your brothers. Why would I get lonely?'

'You don't miss him?' Emily asked with a sad smile.

Angela did miss the Stewart she first met. He was an interesting man; learned in history like no other man she had known, and he had wonderful enthusiasm, charm and a terrific sense of humour. In fact, if they were at a party and she could hear a raucous group laughing out loud, she knew Stewart would be in the middle of it. Usually, telling a story with all around him in raptures.

In hindsight, she should not have agreed to marry him. Having done so, she was never brave enough to disentangle herself from the marriage. The 1950s were so different to nowadays. And then, she supposed, it became a sort of habit. A habit she was fearful to change, mainly as she had no idea how to change it. What she should have done right at the beginning was make a life of her own, maybe found a career. With Gavin to look after, and Stewart more or less demanding she be available at all times to accompany him to functions, it was impossible. So, instead, she had lost herself in her gardens, her books, charity work, bridge, and her cooking. Still, she couldn't help feeling the life she led with Stewart was an ill-fated one.

'I'm sorry, Nonna,' Emily said, saving her from having to answer. 'I shouldn't have brought Grandpa's death up, for I'm sure you miss him dreadfully. As do I.

Angela placed her hand on her knee. 'I'm sure you do, darling.'

They chatted for some time before Emily said, 'This afternoon I got a message on my phone to ring a fellow from the *Sydney Mail*. Wonder what he wants? Maybe they're doing a fashion magazine supplement.'

Angela felt her throat go dry. 'Did he say who he was?'

Emily looked at her oddly. 'He did, but I can't remember his name off hand. Why?'

'Check your message again and see if it was a Greg Ashton.'

Emily picked up her phone and pressed the message button and listened.

'That's him alright.'

Angela nodded. 'Then I know what it's about. Your name's out there … and he was looking for me. He must have found out another way to find where I live for he came to see me a little while ago.'

'What on earth for?'

'They're doing an article on Stewart. And wanted my input.'

'What sort of article?'

Angela waited a while before answering. 'Oh, just the usual. About his business dealings.' She wondered how much to tell Emily. 'Mainly about Glasgow Mine.'

'What about it?'

'How your grandfather got hold of the lease.'

'Oh. Why would they be interested in that after all these years?'

There was a long pause as Angela looked across the garden to where the night was closing in, silhouetting the trees against the sky as if they were cardboard cutouts. She knew what she was about to say might cloud Emily's opinion of Stewart, who she had been so fond of. But she felt she owed it to her to explain before she possibly read about it in the newspapers.

'A business acquaintance told him about the lease to the mine that became Glasgow Mine when it was coming up at a good price.'

'Gosh. And why didn't that business acquaintance get the lease himself?'

Angela coughed, fiddling with her glass. 'He didn't have the money. Besides, he was a politician in the New South Wales government. He was the one with the power to issue the lease. So, as you can imagine, it mightn't have looked good if he had been seen to have taken advantage of his position.'

Emily's eyes widened. 'Wow … so Grandpa took advantage of it instead? Kind of like insider trading?'

'Yes. You could say that.'

'Oh my God!' Emily tugged at her hair and folded a strand around her finger, something she had done since a child when she was upset. 'Bribes and crook politicians! A bit like the Harry Turner case in the papers right now.'

Angela nodded. 'Yes, a bit like that. We have a diligent reporter delving into the past, even though both Stewart and the politician involved have long since departed this world.'

'But Nonna, you and Dad still have shares in that mine!'

'We do. Though, if it's anything like what happened with the mine Turner was involved in, Glasgow's licence to mine may well be revoked if it's proved Stewart bought the mine as a result of corruption.'

'Have you told Dad the reporter came around? Oh, I forgot he's in Hong Kong, isn't he?

'Yes, and as you know he's long since distanced himself from the mine. Even,' she said with a smile, 'if he does receive a good dividend each year. As do I.'

'So, it's sort of corrupt money you and Dad are getting!'

'Not *all* your Grandpa's money was like that.'

'Gees, Nonna,' Emily exclaimed, pushing her chair back on the tiles. She gave her a penetrating stare. 'What do you mean? Not all?'

'He worked very hard in his restaurants to put himself in a good financial situation in order to be able to do his many business deals.'

'Shonky business deals?'

'As I said there were many deals that were well and truly above board.' Angela was reluctant to spoil Emily's memories of her grandfather. 'In fact most were,' she added reassuringly.

'But some that weren't. Like Glasgow Mine?'

'It was all a long time ago. And I'm afraid Stewart didn't always involve me in his business decisions. Some I got to know about. Others I'd no idea about at all. And I must admit I preferred it that way. My charity work, fundraising and committee positions kept me busy.' She glanced around the garden. 'And I like to think that I was able to buy this house with money from his restaurants, which Maria and I helped him start the first of in the *Erskine* franchise back in the 1950s. Not using money he made from possible inappropriate deals.'

'But his name could be splashed all over the newspapers,' Emily said, turning around, eyes even wider. 'Our name?'

Angela nodded. 'I'm afraid it could be, darling. But not *your* name. Stewart Erskine's.'

'Did you know at the time how he obtained the lease to Glasgow Mine?'

Angela nodded. 'I had some idea.'

'So, they could call you as a witness if they take it to court?'

'Yes, that's a possibility.'

'Gees, Nonna! They could use you to sully Grandpa's name.'

'Only if I choose to.' Angela smiled reassuringly. 'I'm an old woman. Old women's memories aren't what they used to be.' She paused. 'But in any case, nothing might become of it.'

'Do you think they've tried to contact Dad?'

'I've no idea.'

Emily sighed. 'What I can't understand is why Grandpa would do something suss like that? I mean, surely he wasn't that sort of person was he?'

Angela shook her head. 'No, he wasn't.' She held Emily's gaze for some time and then turned away, afraid she would detect the lie in her eyes.

'Would you like me to stay and see if you can get hold of Dad?' Emily asked. 'I was going to the movies with a couple of girlfriends, but I can easily put it off.'

'No darling … you head off. I'll be just fine.'

'Are you sure?'

'Absolutely.'

Emily stood up to take her glass inside. Before leaving, she leant down to give Angela a kiss. 'I'll give you a ring tomorrow, Nonna. I've got another shoot all day, but after that.'

'Thank you, darling. By then, I'm sure I'll have spoken to your father.'

After she left, Angela sat there for some time before getting up and heading inside. On placing her wine glass in the dishwasher, she wondered what to have for dinner. Somehow after the journalist's visit and having to tell Emily about Glasgow Mine she didn't feel hungry. Later, she might make a small bowl of pasta. Moving to the living room, she sighed deeply before stepping over to the sideboard where she picked up a photo of Stewart and Maria and wiped a speck of dust off the glass. Her sister was looking straight at the camera with her beautiful laughing brown eyes beneath thick lashes. Stewart had his arm around her. There was no doubt that he was an incredibly good-looking man. Although it was a black and white photograph, Angela could recall those eyes of Stewart so vividly, the colour of which she imagined a Scottish tarn would look like on a rainy day. She had seen the mood in them change so many times over the years. In this photo the corners crinkled at the edges, the pupils shone with pleasure. Angela had taken it down at Circular Quay before they all boarded the ferry for a day at Manly, not long after she and Maria had arrived in Australia and met Stewart at the Villawood Migrant hostel outside of Sydney.

A year later the joy that was in Maria's beautiful brown eyes had turned to torment and Angela was sworn to secrecy.

Don't tell. Ever.

Chapter Two

'Hold it, babe. Yeah … super … that's great. Look straight at the camera. Away. Back again. Terrific.'

It was the next afternoon when Emily posed against a sandstone cliff at Manly, a pair of sunglasses perched on her nose as she modelled a black and white dress.

'Now that great smile,' the photographer called out, throwing her a cheeky wink and running a hand over his tanned forehead.

Being a model was the last thing Emily had imagined she would be. She always thought she would be a writer. In fact, she had recently enrolled in an online creative writing course. She was determined when her modelling career slowed down, which it was bound to do at some stage, that she would take herself back to uni and finish the English Literature degree she started before she was discovered when she was walking through the Queen Victoria Arcade in the centre of the city one morning after one of her uni lectures. At first, Emily thought it was a scam. She'd heard of other girls being approached by a supposed scout for a modelling agency and it turned out to be nothing more than a sleazy bloke making a clumsy proposition.

But this scout wasn't like that at all. Close to six foot tall, she looked to be in her sixties with a mass of thick, grey hair hanging loosely about her shoulders. Even though she was casually dressed in blue jeans and a white button-up shirt she was one of the most elegant women Emily had ever set eyes on. Emily stared in amazement at the card she handed her and then at the woman's appraising eyes, the smoky colour of the sea on a stormy afternoon at Bondi.

'Hi, I'm Liz Falcon,' she had said to Emily with a wide grin, showing slightly crooked teeth. 'Would you believe I've been searching for weeks for someone like you to star in an advertising campaign for a client's new perfume. They want someone natural and unknown … and here you are, right in front of my nose. You'd be perfect.'

Even Emily knew that Liz Falcon was the well-known founder of one of Sydney's top modelling agencies, *Falcons*. She had seen her photo in the *Daily Telegraph* social pages and read an article in the *Women's Weekly* about her. She had been a successful model herself. When she retired she started her own agency.

And there began Emily's modelling career, meaning she had to put her studies at uni on the back burner.

Although she quite liked being a model, she was shrewd enough to know she was never going to make it to the top of the world ladder. In fact, she had no desire to try. She liked her food too much and loved living in Sydney. If she wanted to further her career and become another Miranda Kerr or Elle MacPherson she would have to diet within an inch of her life and live overseas. Both things she was loathe to do.

'This way,' the photographer called out, lifting his camera high and dragging Emily back to the present. 'Side on. Yep, great. Front. Super. Now let's see the back.'

He stepped over and planted a kiss on her cheek, which he left there for a second too long. 'That was terrific, babe. No wonder you're so successful.'

Another flirting photographer, Emily thought with a wry smile. It had been on a modelling assignment on Hayman Island when the photographer for the shoot, Mathew Abels, had literally swept her off her feet. They had been going out for over a year now and had even talked of getting a place together. After this shoot was finished, she was to meet him for a drink at a bar along Oxford Street. One of the reasons Emily felt she had fallen for him was that with his thick mass of gingerish hair and smattering of freckles he reminded her of photos of her grandfather when he was around that age. Since his death she had often looked sadly at that photo, which made it so much harder for her to come to terms with what Nonna had told her about him.

Although he wasn't one of those who spent hours reading stories to Emily, or bouncing her on his knee, she had been very fond of her grandfather. Sometimes they would go for walks through his vineyard, *Riverside,* up in the Hunter Valley, about fifty kilometres from Glasgow Mine, as he explained each and every grape variety. To Emily he seemed his happiest when pottering within the vines. Even though *Riverside* was one of the biggest and most successful vineyards in the Hunter, it was as though he was no longer the mogul he was known as, but a humble winemaker checking on his vines and telling Emily about them.

Emily loved *Riverside*. It was there where she learnt to ride when she was only very little on a Shetland pony called Monty, which her grandfather had bought for her and let her keep up there. To discover that he might be outed by the press as corrupt made her sad. And very angry.

It goes to show that you think you know someone when you really don't know them at all, she thought.

Now that Nonna had shared how he landed the lease to Glasgow Mine, Emily was even more grateful that she wasn't relying on Erskine money to make her way in this world. Well, that wasn't entirely true, for her father had paid her school fees and was helping her pay her uni fees when she was discovered by Liz Falcon. Now, she made enough money to not have to ask for any handouts from her father.

After the shoot wound up she changed back into her own jeans and top and helped the David Jones team load the clothes she had modelled into their station wagon and then walked to her own car parked under an elm tree.

Just as she was about to pull away from the curb her phone rang. She turned off the ignition and picked it up.

It was Chrissy, her best friend and flatmate. 'Where are you, Em?'

'On my way to meet Mathew. Why?'

'Because he's cheating on you, Em.'

Emily took a deep breath and felt the heat rise in her face. 'How do you know that?'

'I saw him with my own two eyes. He didn't see me, but I sure as hell saw him. He was with that blonde model. The one who became quite famous on that home reno show. Now seems to be everywhere.'

'Janice Mayer.'

'Yeah. That's her.'

'Maybe it was work.'

'Some sort of work. It was just the two of them sitting in a back seat at that coffee shop along McPherson Street.'

'*The Three Blue Ducks?*'

'Yeah. There. I was getting a coffee. They were holding hands across the table. Looking into each other's eyes all lovey-dovey. Just as I was about to leave he leant over and kissed her. It wasn't work, Em. As you know I've never really taken to him. This proves it.'

Emily thought for a moment. Two weeks ago, when she and Mathew had gone to a party at a friend's house in Bondi, Janice Mayer was there. She had been all over Mathew like a rash.

'Isn't Mathew the very best photographer in the world?' she had gushed to Emily, after sashaying over to join them with a glass of champagne in her hand.

Now, as she held the phone with Chrissy on the other end of the line she knew in her heart that her friend could be right. Emily had suspected something was wrong for a couple of weeks. Nothing she could really put her finger on—just a gut feeling she had. The smile he normally greeted her with wasn't as free and open as it used to be. And often he would make an excuse to rush off if they were having lunch or dinner. In fact, when he'd rung this morning to ask her to have a drink with him he had sounded a bit odd, insisting she come, despite Emily telling him she would be tired after the shoot. Had he seen Chrissy after all and wanted to explain?

'I'll ask him what's going on when I see him,' she said to Chrissy, trying to sound nonchalant, even though her heart was beating hard against her chest.

'Well make sure you do, Em.'

'Thanks, Chrissy. I'll catch you a bit later.'

Placing her phone in her handbag she sat there for some time, staring blankly out of the window to where a couple were walking across the street hand in hand. She couldn't believe Mathew would do this to her. Surely Chrissy had got it wrong. When she saw him he would explain.

Eventually, she pulled away from the curb and headed for the bar in Oxford Street. She found a park up a side street and for a moment sat behind the wheel, trying to work out how she would handle things. Would she accuse him straight up? Or would she wait and see if he said something? In the end, she decided to do that. After checking her face in the mirror, and wiping some of the excess makeup off from the shoot, she slid from behind the wheel and made her way to the bar. Mathew was already sitting at a table by the back window and saw her the moment she came in. As soon as she saw him walk towards her she suspected Chrissy was right. It was the look of uncertainty on his face as he held her eyes with his. When they sat down at the bar, with all her good intentions of letting him explain himself disappearing into mid-air, she rushed straight in.

'Chrissy saw you at the *Three Blue Ducks* with Janice Mayer,' she said, holding his hazel eyes with hers.

There was a long uncomfortable pause. 'Yes,' he eventually said. 'I thought she did.'

'Would you have told me you were there if she hadn't seen you?'

He took hold of her hand. 'I'm sorry, Em … sorry you had to find out that way.'

'So how long has it been going on?'

He looked embarrassed. 'Since that party at Bondi.' He fiddled with the coaster on the wooden surface of the table. 'I'm a cad, I know. I didn't mean to hurt you. It just happened …'

'Yeah, yeah. She seduced you. It wasn't your fault.' She shook her head in mock disbelief. … 'go on, tell me.'

'Well actually that *is* what happened.'

'Oh really!' She sighed, exhaling a deep breath. 'It takes two to tango, Mathew, so don't give me that.' She looked at him, long and hard. 'No doubt you've slept with her?'

He nodded slowly. 'I'll break it off, Em. It's you I love. Not her.'

Emily sighed and stood up. 'Sorry, Mathew. It's too late for that.' Her voice was stiff and final. 'You made your choice. As Nonna would say, "You've made your bed, now you go lie in it".'

She then turned her back and walked away, head high, shoulders back. It was only when she got behind the wheel of her car that she banged her head against the steering wheel and let the tears flow.

It was five minutes later when she sat back, wiped her eyes and started the engine. In the last twenty-four hours her faith in men had taken a beating.

First her grandfather. Now Mathew.

Chapter Three

'Hi, Mother,' Gavin said down the phone the next morning. 'I'm back early. Flew in last night.'

'You got my message?' Angela asked. 'About the journalist?'

'Yes, I did. A bit strange after all this time.'

'So …'

'I'll be around at eleven to talk about it. Okay?'

'Aren't you worried about what could come out?'

'Of course. But let's talk about it when I get there.'

Angela sighed. 'I'll look forward to seeing you. Will you have lunch with me?'

'Would love to, Mother. But I've promised Bianca I'd take her to lunch.'

'Bianca?'

'Sorry … my new lady. You haven't met her yet.'

'Oh!' She tried not to sound annoyed. 'I presume you'll at least have time for a coffee.'

'Just a quick one. I told Bianca I'd pick her up at her office at twelve.'

It was a month since Angela had seen Gavin. But she supposed a cup of coffee was better than nothing. 'I'll see you at eleven then. In the meantime, I'll wander down to the beach.'

After finishing the call, she stood there for a moment, looking out of the window to where a currawong was perched on a branch of the holm oak tree. She sighed. Gavin was forever changing his women friends. She could only imagine he was hoping to find the perfect one, one who would erase his ex-wife Samantha forever from his mind. Such a woman had not yet come along. Angela doubted she ever would. Unless it happened to be this Bianca. But she doubted that.

Being a weekday, the beach wasn't nearly as busy as the weekend when she wandered down the steps an hour later.

'*Ciao*, Angeline,' said her friend Elena in greeting, originally from Naples. Angela often enjoyed a coffee with her at one of the cafes across the road from the beach.

'*Ciao,* Elena,' Angela said back and they continued on in Italian for their conversation. Angela loved being able to speak her native tongue with this group of women. Like all the other women who gathered here on the beach, Elena called her by her childhood name, Angeline, which is how Angela had initially introduced herself, wanting to differentiate between Angela Erskine and the person she had become since Stewart's death. As time went on she cherished the memories using that name invoked.

'It is a beautiful morning,' Elena said, raising her plump, tanned arm to the sun.

Angela smiled. 'It will be lovely in the rock pool.'

'Absolutely. Now,' Elena added, throwing Angela a bright grin, which made her eyes almost disappear into the deep folds of her cheeks, 'I have that book I promised you. The one set in Naples. It needs to go back to the library in a couple of weeks, but I'm sure you'll have plenty of time to read it.' She rummaged in her beach bag and brought out a hardcover book. 'You know where I live. If we miss each other down here you could pop it in my letterbox.'

After admiring the glorious Mediterranean colours on the cover, Angela placed the book in her straw bag. 'Thank you, Elena. I'm sure I'll enjoy reading it.'

'But come,' Elena said. 'Let's have a swim in the pool to get our exercise, then I'll tell you my news.' She smiled mischievously, standing up and dragging her swimming cap over her head, pushing wiry wisps of grey hair inside.

'Your news?'

Elena needed no more encouragement. Plonking back down again next to Angela she leant forward. 'My cousin is coming from Naples to visit us. I've always liked this cousin. He was very handsome,' she chortled, her whole face wrinkling in unison with her dancing eyes.

'Oh,' Angela said. 'How exciting for you all. When does he arrive?'

'He's coming next week. He likes to swim so I'll bring him here to meet you.'

'I'll look forward to meeting him.' Angela smiled at her friend. 'Particularly if he's handsome.'

'Ah, time ravages us all. But last time I saw him he was indeed handsome.'

'How long ago was that?'

'Let me think. It would have to be twenty years at least. He was in his mid-sixties then.'

'Well, twenty years can't have caused too much havoc.'

But as she looked down at her own wrinkled legs, Angela wondered if that was true after all.

'Now, I'll go for that swim,' Elena said. 'Would you like to join me? Maybe we should try the surf first. It's calm now. Afterwards we can go to the rock pool.'

'Yes,' Angela said. 'That sounds perfect, Elena.'

And, as she followed Elena into the water, she thought how lovely it was that her cousin was coming from Naples. She wondered, if by chance, he would know of Raphael. They would be much the same age and there was a very long shot that they may have met. But that was silly. Naples is overflowing with millions of people and of course Raphael may well be dead.

As she sat on the sand after her swim, with the sun warming her salty skin, she remembered how it was Raphael who first filled the sisters with ideas of this vast and exciting country on the other side of the world when they were living on the vibrant, but small Procida. At times, Angela wanted to blame him for his wild tales, which had enticed the girls to come to this far land, but she could never find it in herself to do so.

*** *** ***

It was a blistering hot afternoon in the summer of 1939 when Angela first saw Raphael Lombardi, the only son of wealthy merchants from Naples who had a holiday house on Procida. Angela and Maria were swimming at the secluded Chiaiolella Beach not long after they had arrived from Naples to live with their much-loved widowed Aunt Sophia in her faded pink villa. Their parents had been tragically killed in a motor vehicle accident between their car and a truck, driven by one of Mussolini's dreaded Blackshirts on the steep winding road from Positano on their way back from a cousin's wedding.

Raphael had ridden his bike out along the winding dirt road, *Via Schiano,* between olive and prickly pear trees, which Maria and Angela had walked by earlier. The girls had watched him from the water as he propped his bike against a falling-down fence near to where a brown goat was tethered with a rope to a stake in the ground. After stopping to pat the goat, he traipsed through the long grass across to the dunes and jumped down to the far end of the beach where he took off his shirt and flopped in the water.

Hardly anyone ever came to this beach, so the girls, who had loathed their itchy woollen swimsuits which Aunt Sophia had made for them, had felt safe in removing their clothes and rushing naked into the water before he arrived. On Procida, it was regarded as a sin for women to swim on the beaches, let alone be naked. So even though Angela was only thirteen and Maria a few years older, if Aunt Sophia found out, or worse still, one of the nuns or priests, there would be hell to pay. Maria was already regarded with suspicion, having arrived from Naples and refusing to dress in the dower clothes so many of the female islanders wore: shawls, long dresses and dark stockings. And even after all the years since Aunt Sophia's husband had died, their aunt still wore the black of a widow.

That day the temperature soared towards 100 degrees and the water was so warm it gave little respite to the girls sweltering bodies.

'It's as if we're taking a warm bath,' Maria laughed, splashing Angela with water.

With alarm the girls watched Raphael swimming towards them. Both girls wrapped their arms over their bare breasts, shocked that someone had seen them swimming here, let alone naked. To Angela he looked to be about sixteen. His dark hair was longer than most of the other boys on the island and his skin was deeply tanned from the sun.

When Raphael saw with horror that they were naked, he made a hasty retreat out of the water, got on his bike and rode off. But a week later when Maria and Angela were making sand sculptures on the same beach, this time in shorts and t-shirts, Raphael arrived on his bike again and asked if he could join them.

'*Si,*' both girls said at once, beckoning him over.

When he sat down on the sand and pointed across to Aragonese Castle built on a volcanic rocky islet attached to the nearby island of Ischia and told them that the rock it sat on was where the mythological Typhon had laid his arms upon, the girls were more than impressed with his great knowledge. Before they left that afternoon Raphael had built a good replica of Aragonese Castle in the sand and shown the girls how to search for cockles in the shallow waves by using their feet to dig deep down into the sand where the cockles were. He also took them to the rocks to follow the tracks to where loggerhead turtles hid their eggs in the sand.

'They live off sea oats that cover the dunes,' he said, as they peered at what appeared to be a nest hidden under the sand. 'The female can lay up to a hundred eggs. And when she has done so she covers the nest up and disappears, never to come back.'

'That's not very nice of her,' Angela said, thinking what a waste of energy it was to lay all those eggs and then disappear.

'Much later, Angeline,' Raphael said, 'the young turtles break out of their eggshells and dig themselves out of the sand. But only about one in seven hundred eggs survive to grow up.'

'How terrible,' Maria exclaimed, shaking her head.

Angela gaped at Raphael in awe. 'How do you know so much?'

'I've been coming to this beach since I was little.' He laughed. 'Until you two came along I had it mostly to myself.'

'We thought it was *our* beach,' Maria had said with a laugh.

They then scrambled up the bank to where Raphael had left his bike and together they walked back along the track, pilfering handfuls of ripe juicy nectarines and figs along the way, until they came to the outskirts of the village where Raphael hopped on his bike and bade them farewell, calling a bright *arrivederci* over his shoulder.

Before Raphael returned to Naples that year he and the two girls were almost inseparable and often he would sit around the table enjoying Aunt Sophia's cooking, including the rabbit stews made out of the wild rabbits he had shown Angela and Maria how to trap. And skin. At first Angela had been horrified, but when she realised that it was the difference between being hungry or not, and seeing Aunt Sophia's beaming face when she put one on the table for her to make into *coniglio alla Procidana,* rabbit cooked with herbs and tomatoes, she knew it was all worthwhile.

'You are the best cook on the whole island of Procida,' Raphael told her often, making Aunt Sophia's face break into such a huge smile that the girls thought it might explode with happiness.

After dinner he would play them tunes on his ancient cane flute, which he told the girls a favourite uncle had given him when he was a small boy. Although Angela was no great music critic she thought the tunes he played were beautiful. And whenever he would finish playing, Aunt Sophia would clap her hands and say, 'More. More.'

Angela's favourite piece was *Tarantella.* When he played it she and Maria would get up and dance with Aunt Sophia clapping her hands in joy.

Other times he would arrive and dip his finger in the tasty pasta sauce bubbling on the stove, causing Aunt Sophia to smack him on the hand and berate him lovingly. 'You, Raphael, are a rascal.'

But then she would smile and give him a spoon to taste it. She even let him help her make the sauce one day and his very favourite cake, *torta caprese al limone,* made from almond meal and lemons.

When the islanders discovered with dismay that Mussolini had decided to join the war on Germany's side in June 1940, rationing became stricter and stricter and the black market for food was rampant. Raphael and the girls tried not to think of what was happening outside of their small world on Procida. Often, they would climb up to the oldest village on the island, Terra Murata, surrounded by desolate grey stone walls about ninety metres above the sea.

'It was settled in the middle ages and fortified in 1563,' Raphael said the first time they went up there, once again impressing the girls with his knowledge.

'It feels so eerie and bleak.' Angela shivered, wrapping her arms around herself to ward off the stiff breeze whistling through the dismal narrow street. She glanced towards the penitentiary on the hill with its small and barred cell windows and where she knew rats, owls and swallows lived in each and every scary crack. 'And imagine being locked up in there.'

'Maybe if the enemy comes to Procida they'll lock us all up in there as well,' Maria said.

'I'll protect you,' Raphael assured them.

'Fine lot of use you'd be against those monsters,' Maria scoffed. 'You'd probably be the first they'd kill.'

'Maria!' Angela exclaimed. 'Don't be so mean.'

'In wartime, people are very cruel. Just ask Aunt Sophia about the last war when her darling husband, Maurizio, was killed.'

'Surely, no one would be interested in our little island,' Angela said.

'You are right, Angeline,' Raphael smiled, trying to cheer them up. 'Procida is far too small for them to bother about.'

Yet, even at the young age she was, Angela wondered if he was right. Or would she one day look out of Aunt Sophia's window to see boatloads of marauders scurrying across the water from Naples to take the island of Procida as their own?

'Will you have to go to fight in the war?' Angela asked him worriedly.

'I might,' he said, putting down his flute and peering across the dark sea to where there was the outline of the island of Ischia.

'Maybe we should hide you here somewhere on Procida. In the caves. You must not go back to Naples.'

Raphael added another piece of wood to the fire, poking it under the hot plate they had made out of a piece of flat metal they had found on the beach. 'If I am called to duty I will go.'

'It will be over soon and you won't have to worry about that,' Maria stated with confidence, standing up and leaning down to turn the fish on the hot plate with a stick. 'I know it.'

But Maria was very wrong.

Raphael didn't come back to Procida that year. And the next year the girls were devastated to discover that, young as he was, he had been conscripted into the Italian Army. Many boys due to be conscripted had tried to hide; however, Raphael wasn't one of those.

'He is a brave boy,' Aunt Sophia said to the girls, after a friend told her down at the fish markets that her own son had been conscripted and that Raphael was with him.

'Where will Raphael go to fight?' Maria asked in horror.

'What if he gets killed?' Angela cried out.

'It is a dreadful war,' Aunt Sophia said. 'Many will get killed. All we can do is pray for him.'

And that's what Maria and Angela did, often lighting a candle for him and the other Italian soldiers in the church of Santa Maria della Pieta.

'Where all the priests have a connection with the sea,' Aunt Sophia told her, as she pulled a leaf from the red carnation growing in a milk can on the windowsill before they headed down for confession one Saturday afternoon, 'they are either sailors themselves or sons of sailors.'

Angela thought this sounded so romantic that it immediately became her favourite church on the island.

Otherwise, she and Maria would light a candle for Raphael and the other soldiers in the churches of Holy Annunciation or Madonna della Libera, where the chapel walls were covered with black and white photographs of Procida's missing sailors over the years, with their names, their ship and the year of the tragedy written alongside. Looking at these photographs made Angela wonder if Raphael was fighting the war on land or at sea, being taken to far off places.

As the war dragged on, living became harder and harder for the islanders on Procida. Maria and Angela were often hungry when the stored crops of fruit and vegetables, particularly artichokes, which even had its own *Festa del Carciofo,* festival of the artichoke, were all eaten or had gone rotten, and the seas were rough or there was no fuel and the fishermen couldn't go out in their trawlers. Sometimes there was no flour and the *pane* (pith) of the plentiful lemons was used as a substitute for bread. It was fortunate that Raphael had showed them how to catch and kill the wild rabbits on the island, although even they became scarce.

In the winter months, when the rain and strong winds whipped up the narrow streets, food became scarcer than ever. Even Aunt Sophia found it difficult at times to put a meal on the table, despite Maria and Angela pilfering what fruit and vegetables they were able to and trapping what rabbits they could hunt. There was no fuel for heating and to keep Aunt Sophia's fire going the girls had to scout around the hills for pieces of wood or on the beaches for driftwood. At school they froze in icy classrooms, their fingers and toes covered in chilblains. Many of the men were seconded from the island to fight in the war, so it was left to the women and elderly men to try and carry on. Both Maria and Angela read a report in the newspaper of the horrific carnage of the Battle of Sidi Barrani in Libya where so many Italians were slaughtered or taken captive.

'What if one of those men is Raphael?' Angela cried.

'Do you think we would have heard?'

'Who would tell us?'

'I don't know, but we must presume he is still alive. The alternative is just too awful to think about.'

'What if he has been taken prisoner?'

'If we knew where he was we could write,' Maria said, after she put down the newspaper and sat at Aunt Sophia's ancient sewing machine with a candle for light, mending a hole in one of Angela's dresses. 'Maybe his captives might let him have a letter, or,' she smiled at Angela, 'you could unravel the wool in that blue jumper that no longer fits you and make yourself useful by knitting socks to send to him.'

'Don't be so silly, Maria. If he's held captive somewhere I don't think they would let him have those sort of things. I bet he's not even allowed to play his flute if he was able to smuggle it in. And he's probably starving to death, or they're torturing him.'

'Angeline, stop that,' Maria scolded her, standing up. 'We don't even know if he was in that battle in Libya. Maybe he has a cushy office job somewhere.'

'I don't think so. Again, you're being really silly.'

'And you think awful things too much. We must not worry ourselves sick until we know some more.'

Two days later, a dozen Fascist soldiers landed on the island and interrogated many of the islanders.

'They are looking for young men in hiding who don't want to fight,' Aunt Sophia said, peaking out of the window as they stomped up the narrow street. 'They will search until they find them.'

'I met the Russo brothers up in the hills yesterday hunting for rabbits,' Maria said. 'What if the soldiers find them?'

'They'll have seen the soldiers arrive in the harbour. They will be hiding in the caves,' Aunt Sophia said. 'Hopefully, they'll not be found.'

'If they *are* found they will be shot,' Maria said.

Angela's eyes went out on storks. 'What if someone tells the soldiers where the caves are?'

'That is the problem,' Aunt Sophia lamented. 'Who of us islanders knows who can be trusted? Or who may be an informer? The fear of reprisal is overwhelming. If the Germans discover someone is hiding a fugitive and then discover someone knew about it they too will be shot.' She heaved a dark sigh. 'And if they confiscate any more trawlers, we'll have no fish at all.'

Gina, Aunt Sophia's neighbour, had a radio which Aunt Sophia and the girls were invited to listen to, together with a couple of the other neighbours. But the news was so bad that after a while Angela would make an excuse so that she didn't have to listen.

'And to think what we hear on the radio is probably censored anyway,' she said to Maria as they were getting into bed after Maria told her what she had heard that afternoon on Gina's radio. 'In truth, the losses are probably so much worse.'

It was on the 2nd May, 1945, when Angela was cutting up carrots she had stolen from an elderly farmer's vegetable patch, only just escaping over the wall before he rounded the bend in his donkey and cart, when Aunt Sophia came bustling through the door from listening to Gina's radio next door.

'It says on the radio the war is over,' she said, beaming from ear to ear.

'It is over?' Angela cried. 'I don't believe it.'

'It is true,' Aunt Sophia said, taking her in her arms and twirling her around, tears of joy streaming down her cheeks.

Angela cried tears of joy as well and thought of Raphael. 'Our soldiers will now come home.'

Many Italian soldiers did return home, but none were Raphael as far as Maria and Angela could find out. And the friend of Aunt

Sophia was of no help as her son had sadly been killed in Libya, so she didn't know where Raphael was. On Procida, everyone tried to resume some sort of normality, despite Italy's economy being in ruins, dire rationing in place, and the black market still thriving. Angela had held onto the hope that once the war was over things would be so very different, but in many respects they weren't.

It was in the summer of 1947 when Angela, having left school, was working behind the counter at the small, dark grocery store on *Marina Grande* near to where the steamer from Naples berthed in Procida's sleepy harbour, when the hanging beads over the door jingled, telling her a customer had come in. Lifting her head from the counter she saw it was a man, over six foot tall. When he stepped to the counter he smiled and pointed to the cigarettes, asking for a packet of *Carabelas*. Although cigarettes were still rationed in Italy there was a small selection behind the counter, which Angela knew the owner of the shop had rustled on the black market. As Angela got out the cigarettes she couldn't take her eyes off the man's face. Her heart missed a beat and she felt a warm shiver travel her body. There was no mistaking that smile. Or those dark, fathomless eyes, despite them not being as carefree as they used to be. Without doubt she knew it was Raphael. Although there was that something less carefree in his eyes, the war had been kind to him for his face was unlined, and even though he was slim, he wasn't thin.

'Raphael,' she exclaimed in disbelief. 'It is you.'

For a moment he looked perplexed. Which wasn't surprising as Angela had only been thirteen when he left. She was now eighteen. Even she knew she looked a lot different to what she had back then.

'Raphael … it is Angeline,' she said, handing him the cigarettes.

'Angeline,' he exclaimed, surprise written all over his face.

'*Si,*' Angela said. 'It is me.'

He laughed, flicking his floppy fringe back from his eyes. 'But you have grown so much.'

'It would be very odd if I hadn't,' Angela said. 'Even you have grown.'

'It has been a long time,' Raphael said, looking her up and down. 'When I left you were a child.' He eyed her bosoms, obvious beneath her silk blouse. 'Now, Angeline, you are a woman.'

'And,' she giggled shyly, her eyes shining from beneath thick eyelashes, 'you are now a grown man.'

'And Maria?' he asked. 'And Aunt Sophia? How are they?'

'They are good. When I finish here in ten minutes I could take you to them. They will be as surprised as I am.'

They chatted all the way up to Aunt Sophia's place where Maria was sewing napkins for the market on Sunday, which filled the streets with colourful stands.

When she saw Raphael she dropped what she was doing and jumped up and down clapping her hands. 'Just look at you,' she kept saying. 'We thought you may be dead. But here you are. As alive as could be and take a peek at the size of you.'

After he gave Maria a hug, Raphael hurried to the kitchen to find Aunt Sophia busily making the girls' favourite dish, *Braciole in Ragu Sauce*. Aunt Sophia put down her wooden spoon, wiped her hands on her apron, pushed a soaked strand of grey hair back over her forehead and gave him a huge gap-toothed smile.

'Raphael … you have come home!' she cried. 'You have come home.'

'I *have* come home, Aunt Sophia,' he said, dipping his finger in the sauce. 'And you haven't changed one bit,' he added, bestowing a kiss on her rosy cheek.

Aunt Sophia insisted on opening a bottle of her own homemade lemonade and they took their glasses outside, together with some small buns known as *a jontas*, which she had not long ago taken out of the oven, filling the air with the enticing aroma of hot bread, which Angela could never resist. They sat at the wooden table on the cobblestones next to the geranium bush, in the cooler air, where there were chairs set back against the wall so that Aunt Sophia could invite her neighbours to sit with her. Although many of the islanders kept to themselves behind high walls, Aunt Sophia still liked to socialise. It was here that Raphael told them how he was captured by the Australians in Libya and taken as a prisoner to

Australia where he was sent to work on an apple orchard in Tasmania, as most of Australia's workforce was fighting in the war.

'Australia!' Aunt Sophia exclaimed, shaking her head in wonderment. 'It is so far. I'm surprised you found your way back here.'

'Did the Australians treat you well?' Angela asked, looking at him worriedly.

'Yes,' Raphael said, 'on the whole they were very fair to us.'

For some time they sat there as Aunt Sophia and the girls filled him in on what had been happening on Procida since he had left.

'I missed it here. Particularly,' he said with a smile at the girls, 'Pozzo Vecchio and Chiaiolella Beach where we first met. In fact, I was thinking of going for a swim this afternoon.' He looked at Angela and then Maria. 'Would you like to come?' He grinned. 'It would be like old times.'

'I can't go,' Maria said. 'I must finish my sewing.'

'Will you come, Angeline?'

'*Si*, of course,' Angela said excitedly. 'I'd love to come.'

It was while they were sitting under the headland on Pozzo Vecchio beach after their swim in the still chilly sea, when Angela, wearing a new blue costume Maria had made for her, asked him about the war before he was captured.

'It must have been so awful. We thought we might never see you again. Aunt Sophia said so many more Italian men were lost in this war than were lost in the First World War when her Maurizio was killed.'

'I don't want to talk about the war,' he said. 'But I will tell you about Australia. Oh, Angeline, you have got to go there.' He laughed that wonderful free, naughty laugh she loved so much. He drew her a map of Australia with a twig in the sand, making a small dot at the bottom, which he pointed to. 'When I am rich and famous I will take you to Tasmania for a holiday. And I will introduce you to the family who owned the orchard. They were good to us.'

'I am glad to hear.'

'We worked very hard, but I didn't mind. I much preferred being in the orchard than the long hours in the sheds, sorting and packing the apples. I grew to love the smell of the apples, grass, and the cattle and sheep in the fields next to the orchard, mixed with the salty air of the bay and the Australian eucalyptus trees. Even in the cold and wet of winter when we pruned the trees I enjoyed working outside.'

'So, it was by the sea?' Angela asked.

'Yes. It was on a wide bay and when the tide was out we could search for cockles, or sometimes we were allowed to take the rowboat out and fish for little fish they called flathead or dive for shellfish. The farm had a big waterfall with the river starting high up in the mountains. Although the water was sometimes icy cold we often went up into the bush where there was a rock pool in a gully below the waterfall and where we could wash ourselves after work.' He grinned. 'We would light a fire and dry our clothes around it. The view from the top of the hill looked down over the farm and out across the bay to the islands.' He sighed.' When I was homesick I would walk up to that hill and sit there as it reminded me of the view to Ischia and Capri from here.'

'That would have been comforting,' Angela said, smiling at him.

Raphael nodded. 'Australia doesn't have buildings as ancient as we have in Italy, but there were many old brick buildings on the orchard farm from the times when convicts were sent there in the 1800s. We got paid one pound per week, but there wasn't much to spend money on anyway. Apart from *sigarettes.*' He laughed. 'The Australians call them "smokes". They fed us well off the farm with meat, eggs and milk. And we grew our own vegetables in an enclosed area to keep the native wild animals away—wallabies, kangaroos and possums. There are many trees in Tasmania, some thousands of years old. But there were no olive trees that I could see. Next to the old stone cottage we lived in was a thick grove of trees called wattle. When they bloom in spring it is as if they're covered in a gown of yellow gold. I've never seen a tree with such bright blossom.'

'Even brighter than the skin of a ripe apricot?'

'Oh yes. And it gives off a beautiful aroma of honey nectar. There are also many eucalyptus trees. They call them gums. The

Australians drink lots of tea and sometimes they boil a tin can of water on a fire and put a gum leaf in it.' He laughed. 'They call it billy tea.'

'No olive trees to make oil and they drink tea with gum leaves in it! Sounds as though they have very odd customs in this Tasmania,' Angela said with a smile.

'There was a small church on the hill where we could go to pray. On Sundays, a priest would come from far away to say mass. And there was a dance hall nearby and although we were not supposed to go there to dance we did.' He smiled. 'When I first got there I found some cane and made myself a flute. I used to play at those dances.'

'Tarantella?'

'Yes, they loved to dance to that. I also played the flute to my fellow prisoners as we sat around the fire at night. There were children living on the farm. They helped me learn English. In return, I made them toys out of wood.'

When Raphael had left for the war Angela knew she was far too young to be in love. Even so, she had felt something very much like love. And all the time when he was away and she and Maria talked of him and prayed for his safe return, that love grew inside of her until now sitting with him on the beach it threatened to make her heart burst with happiness.

***

49

Over that summer of 1947, Raphael and Angela were almost inseparable. Although the island was still poor and struggling after the war they were rich with love and joy. They swam at the beaches, lazed in the countryside, picked wild herbs and figs or sat under the pomegranate tree in the back laneway behind Aunt Sophia's villa where they patted the lazy cats in the fragrant heat of the afternoon when everyone else was having a siesta. Once they climbed down the steep cliff to *La Spiaggetta Degli Innamorati*, known as Lover's Beach, where they perched on the rocks below the cypress trees and devoured the oranges they had pilfered in a deserted villa's garden on the way. Raphael told her how he wasn't keen on joining the family business. He wanted to become a doctor.

'I saw what the doctors did during the war in Libya,' he said, 'I knew then I wanted to be one.'

'You will have to study hard,' she said, peeling her orange and throwing a long piece of peel into the sea.

'I know. It will take many years. But it is what I want.'

'Have you told your parents?' she asked, watching the peel float off as if it was a tiny orange boat heading out to sea. She took a bite of the succulent flesh and wiped the juice from her chin with her sleeve. 'What will they think of their son being a doctor? Surely they will be very proud. Or will they expect you to go into the family business instead?'

'I haven't told them yet,' he said, leaning over and giving her a long, arduous kiss, which made her tingle from head to toe. 'But I will soon.'

As the summer wore on and they spent more and more time together, Angela fell even more deeply in love as they talked of the future. A future she thought naively would involve her.

One afternoon, her world came crashing down in one clean swoop.

'But how could you?' she exclaimed in horror when he told her that he wasn't going to become a doctor after all and he was to join the family business and marry a girl from Naples his father had insisted he wed. They were at a table in one of the cafes that hugged the harbour at *Cala di Corricella*, sipping from glasses of icy cold juice, squeezed from the island's oranges.

'It is the way it has to be, Angeline,' Raphael said, holding her hand gently in his. He then lifted her hand to his lips. 'I'm so sorry,' he said, his earnest brown eyes moist with tears which threatened to trickle down his cheeks.

His voice seemed to be coming from a long way away, as though it was someone else talking. Angela sat immobile. Stunned. She thought her heart would split into so many tiny fragments that there was no way in the world she would be able to piece it back together again, even if she found the strongest glue. 'You were so keen to go to university and become a doctor,' she said. She tried to keep the heartbreak out of her voice, but she could hear it seeping through.

'I love you, Angeline, and I always will, but I have no choice,' Raphael said, lifting her face to his and stroking her cheeks. 'If I try to fight him my father will cut me out of our family completely and that would break my mother's heart. Maybe if the war had not come things would be different and I could have made my own way by now. But the war did come. This is the way it is. I must obey. It is my duty.'

'And the girl you are going to marry?'

'I've known her since we were children. She's the daughter of a proposed wealthy business partner for my father's business, which is floundering because of the war. It is all worked out. Part of the agreement is that our two families should intermarry so that the company can be passed down to both families. If I do not marry this girl my family will lose everything. I cannot take the responsibility for that.'

'But you love me?' Angela said, lifting her hand to wipe the tears from her eyes.

Raphael fiddled with his straw, taking it out, flicking it dry and placing it in the glass again. From up on the hill church bells rang out across the village, proclaiming the evening Angelus and they both crossed themselves and sat in silence honouring the religious moment.

Looking up after the chimes had ceased, Raphael held her eyes with his. 'I may not love her, but I will try to be a good husband.' He gently pulled her head to his shoulder and ran a hand softly through her tousled hair. 'Maybe … maybe I can learn to love her,' he said. 'And you, Angeline, will find someone to love, to make you happy. To marry.'

Angela was so upset that she thought she was going to burst out crying. She was also very angry.

'Learning to love is not the real thing, Raphael. But you go ahead and do just that,' she threw at him, standing up and moving away from their table to where a fishing net was thrown over a small blue boat and a flock of seagulls were frolicking in the shallows in front of it. Sitting down, she put her back to Raphael and played with the fur of a cat sunning itself on the fishing net.

'Angeline,' he said, coming over and disturbing the cat,' please don't feel like that.'

'I'm not upset about you marrying that girl,' she lied. 'It's just that you said you were going to become a doctor … and … now … well …'

'Life isn't always as one imagines, Angeline,' he said softly, taking her hand.

'No,' she said, removing her hand and picking at the fishing net furiously with her finger. 'It's not, is it?'

He placed his hand on hers. Angrily she pulled it away. 'Go,' she said. 'Go, Raphael. And yes, you're right, I'm sure I'll find someone to marry. And it will be someone I love. Not someone I will have to *learn* to love.'

She then stood up and walked away, leaving him there. Not looking back, she stomped up the steep stone steps and ran along the laneway, past the book stand, which she normally loved to linger over in case she spied a book she would like to read, to Aunt Sophia's place, where she rushed upstairs and threw herself on the bed. When Maria called out to say dinner was ready she said she wasn't hungry. And the next morning she said she was feeling sick and would stay in bed. It was two days later when she finally surfaced, having decided to put Raphael behind her. Obviously, that is what he had done with her. Even so, she couldn't help thinking of him day and night.

'He had no option,' Maria said, when Angela told her what had happened. 'You didn't really think his rich parents would let him marry you?'

'You don't understand.'

'Oh, but I do. Only too well. They are what my friends and I call the "*persone estive.*" On Ischia and Capri they come to their fancy villas for the summer and then go back to their even fancier villas in Naples, forgetting all about the islanders during the hard winter. Procida may not be as fancy as Ischia and Capri, but with the sort of family like Raphael's it probably still goes on.'

'Raphael is not like that.'

'But his parents no doubt are,' Maria said, placing an arm around her comfortingly. 'And you can't let what happened ruin your life. Raphael is right. You will meet someone else. You will forget him.'

Angela knew she was wrong. She would never forget Raphael.

***

Even now, with her features blurred and smudged with age, Angela often thought of Raphael, as she had done many times over the years she had been married to Stewart. She wondered what had happened to him in that far off place on the other side of the world. Was he still alive? Was he still playing his flute? He would be in his mid-eighties now.

Did he ever think of her?

Chapter Four

Gavin threw his keys on the hall table when he arrived fifteen minutes late for his meeting with Angela.

'Hi, Mother,' he said, leaning down to give her a perfunctory kiss on the cheek.

Stewart had prided himself on never being late for an appointment no matter how trivial it was. He often ranted and raged to Angela that Gavin would be late for his own funeral.

'What a hide that reporter from the *Sydney Mail* had in coming around to hassle you,' he said, as he stood in the kitchen nursing a mug of steaming coffee a few minutes later. 'I mean, what's the point? Dad's dead and so is the politician involved. Besides, Glasgow Mine's no longer in the family, is it?'

'As I said to Emily, we do still have shares.'

'If everyone who had shares in a company were responsible for how it works, there wouldn't be many people buying shares.'

'True, but your father *did* start the mine and procured the original lease.'

'And, because he's dead he can't be taken to task, can he?' He paused. 'Mind you, if he did get the lease illegally I wish to God he was here to answer for it.'

Angela noticed the bitterness in his tone, but before she said anything she heard his phone *bip*.

'Sorry,' he said, after checking the message. 'Bianca wants me to ring her.'

'Surely, it can wait. You *are* meeting her in a short while.'

'It sounds urgent. I'll go out on the deck to ring her.'

A few minutes later he was back.

'So, was it urgent?'

He looked sheepish. 'She wanted to know if it was dressy where we're going for lunch.'

Angela sighed. 'Oh! And that was urgent?'

'No need to get all huffy, Mother. I didn't know it was that, did I?'

'Why do you think they're trying to drag the Glasgow Mine lease up?' she asked, ignoring his comments.

'It has to be because of the Turner case with the ICAC. That corruption council is determined to get him.' He glanced at her. 'But, I tell you what, if something Dad did back then destroys our name. I mean after what his final—'

'Gavin!' she interrupted sharply. 'Don't go there.'

He stepped over to the window and stood with his back to her. When he turned around he looked at her closely. 'You look tired, Mother. You're not overdoing it, are you?'

'I didn't sleep much last night. Worrying about the journalist's visit.'

'Well, let's hope I can sort it out.'

'And how are you planning on doing that?'

'As you know, I do a lot of advertising with the *Sydney Mail!*'

'Yes, I realise that,' Angela said, noting the menace in his voice, but she imagined it would take more than a threat of advertising removal to shut down a story like that once a reporter got hold of it. 'Anyway,' she added, trying to put her worries to one side, 'how's business? With all that advertising you must be selling a lot.'

On Stewart's death Gavin had taken over his development company, SD Holdings. He had just completed a new block of prestige apartments down at Pyrmont, which he was selling off the plan. As well as Glasgow Mine, he had also taken over the *Erskine's* restaurant chain. Within a couple of years, much to Angela's annoyance, he had sold everything off apart from the development company he still owned and ran successfully.

'The last release of apartments walked out the door within a couple of hours,' Gavin said, shaking his head and chuckling to himself. 'Maybe we sold too cheaply.'

'Better a bird in the hand than two in the bush,' Angela said. 'Stewart always used to say that.'

'True. We're having a big launch for this lot. Hence the advertising.'

'Of course.' She watched him move to the sink where he washed his mug under the tap. He had put on a bit of weight lately and it didn't sit well on him. If he was taller he may have been able to carry it off better. 'Any news on the boys?' she asked him.

'Jonathon comes in now and then when he wants some money.' He sighed. 'He looks to be off the drugs, but who would know? I don't hear a thing from Allen.'

'Don't you worry about them?'

'I gave them a good education. If they want to stuff up their lives, that's their business.'

'I hear from Allen every now and then. He seems to be rather enjoying his life.'

'What! Spending all day surfing at Byron?'

'If you kept in touch you'd know that he's also working in a surf shop. He says he loves it.'

'And why would he want to do that when he has a perfectly good business here to be part of?'

Angela smiled. 'Like Emily, maybe he wants to try and make it on his own. Such a pity you don't keep in touch with them all a bit more. Particularly Emily. After I go, she'll need you more than ever.'

'And where are you planning on going, Mother?'

'You know what I mean … at my age it's obvious I won't be here forever.'

'I'll give her a call. Maybe ask her out for dinner with Bianca and me.'

Angela didn't like to say that she thought that was the last thing Emily would want to do. Meet another of her father's long line of women friends.

Again, his phone beeped. Looking at the screen he jumped up. 'Best be going. Or I'll be late.'

'And that was Bianca again?'

'She's said she's ready to be picked up out front of her office.'

'I thought she rang to see what to wear.'

'She did. There's a great boutique next to her office. I told her I'd buy her a new dress. That's why she wanted to know if it was casual or dressy. She wants to wear the new dress.'

'Oh.' She sighed. 'Well, I must say I'm relieved to hear that you're possibly on top of the *Sydney Mail* sniffing around. Now off you go,' she added, trying not to sound too churlish. 'You don't want to keep your Bianca waiting.'

Leaning down he gave her a kiss on the cheek. 'Make sure you get a better night's sleep tonight.'

No sooner had Gavin left and she had gone outside to the verandah to sit and read the newspaper when there was a knock on the door and Emily called out.

'I just saw Dad leaving,' she said, looking back at the road when Angela went to let her in.

'Did you speak to him?'

'No, he'd gone down the hill before I could attract his attention. What did he think about the reporter coming around?'

'He assures me he's going try and sort it out.'

'Oh? How?'

'He does a lot of advertising with them.'

'And?'

'Oh, I don't know, darling,' Angela said, not wanting to go into how Gavin may or may not stop the paper from writing about Stewart. 'Perhaps with all that advertising he has some sway. Anyway, let's forget about the reporter and come sit with me on the verandah. It's beautiful out there with the holm oak and elm tree starting to turn.'

They went to the kitchen where Angela took a jug of water from the fridge and poured them both a glass, which they took to the verandah. 'After they chatted for a while, there was a stretch of silence as Angela watched Emily fiddle with her handbag, open it and shut it again. It was as though she wanted to say something, but she didn't know where to start.

'Are you okay, darling?' Angela asked her.

'It's not just that I'm worried about Grandpa,' Emily said, sounding sad. 'I've broken it off with Mathew.'

Angela got a shock to hear this, but was inwardly relieved. She had only met Mathew on a few occasions and although he was pleasant enough she had never really thought he and Emily were suited. As far as Angela was concerned he seemed a bit too interested in talking about himself. Telling her of all the awards he had won as a photographer and how much he loved photographing Emily. To Angela, it was almost as though he regarded Emily as a prized subject of his photos rather than his girlfriend. However, she knew Emily was taken with him so had held her tongue.

'Oh, why was that, darling?' she asked, giving her a concerned smile.

'Chrissy found out he was cheating on me.'

Emily then told her the whole story.

When she had finished talking, Angela put a hand on her knee. 'I think you did exactly the right thing, darling.' She smiled. 'I never thought he was good enough for you.'

'You never said anything.'

'No. It was your decision to go out with him. I respected that.'

'Anyway, I've decided to get away for a while.'

'Oh. Where to?'

'I've asked a travel agent to look into a railroad trip through India. I've always wanted to go there. She's working on an itinerary for me.'

'Darling, that sounds wonderful. When will you go?'

'I'll need to check with Liz Falcon at the modelling agency. I'm seeing her shortly.' She checked her watch. 'In fact, I'd best shake a leg or she'll be waiting at the coffee shop where we've agreed to meet.' She looked at Angela. 'You look a bit whacked, Nonna. Are you alright?'

Angela smiled. 'I'm fine, darling. Just a bit tired.'

'And worrying about that journalist wouldn't help.' She checked her watch again. 'Well, if you're sure you're okay I suppose I'd best get a move on. Liz hates to be kept waiting.'

She leant down and gave Angela a kiss before taking her glass inside to the kitchen and running it under the tap. She then called out to Angela to say a final goodbye and soon Angela heard the front door bang behind her. Picking up her empty glass she went inside and took it to the kitchen.

She thought of turning on the news then changed her mind. She knew it would be full of the Turner case, but she didn't have the strength to watch. Besides, her hip was hurting so she needed to take a Panadol. What she hadn't told Emily was that she had made an appointment to see the doctor about the nagging pain she had been experiencing in her hip for some time. She hoped he could give her something to alleviate it. And yes, Emily was right. She was tired. She wasn't sleeping like she normally did.

In the morning she caught the bus from the stop fifty yards from her house into Bondi Junction and from there she took the train into the city. She had thought of asking Emily to come with her, but she didn't want to be a nuisance, particularly now that she had told her about breaking up with Mathew. There was no point in asking Gavin, as he was sure to be busy. Not only with work but his new lady, Bianca. Besides, if he heard Angela had a bad back the first thing he would want her to do was move out of her house.

'It's all those steps up and down to the beach aggravating it,' he would scold her. 'I told you that would happen.'

And before she knew it, Angela would be in a nursing home and there would be a 'For Sale' sign outside her house.

She had been going to Dr Wallace for over forty years. Both of them were getting on a bit now, and she knew it wouldn't be long before he retired. However, Angela was loath to make a change until he did so. She had first met him when Gavin had broken his leg playing soccer as a teenager and she had taken him to the Sydney Hospital for it to be x-rayed and put in plaster. Dr Wallace had not long been out of medical school and had been the doctor on duty at the Sydney Hospital. Angela was very taken with him and when he told her he was going to join a practice in the centre of the city she decided to become one of this first patients.

As she sat in his surgery she gazed out of the window to Hyde Park. One of Angela's and Maria's favourite spots to walk when they were living close by in the early 1950s was through the fig-lined avenue in the middle of the park. If her back wasn't giving her so much trouble she might have even walked there today. She liked to buy a sandwich from one of the small cafes bordering the park and take it with her and sit by the Archibald Fountain, donated by JF Archibald in 1932 in honour of Australia's contribution to the First World War in France. She also liked to sit in the Nagoya Gardens watching games of chess on the huge outdoor chess set near the entrance to the underground St James railway station.

'Dr Wallace will see you now, Mrs Erskine,' the receptionist said, indicating to the doctor's door.

'Thank you,' she answered, standing up.

'Good afternoon, Mrs Erskine,' Dr Wallace said when she entered his room. He always called Angela 'Mrs Erskine' and she always called him 'Dr Wallace'. 'And what can I be doing for you today?'

He always asked Angela that as well. One of the reasons Angela liked going to him was that he was very much to the point. None of this small talk that so many doctors went on with, taking up half the appointment time, which these days seemed to be charged by the minute.

When she told him what was bothering her, he asked her to step up onto the examination couch and told her to lie on her stomach. After prodding and poking her back where it hurt, he then told her to sit up and undo the buttons on her blouse so he could listen to her heart.

'All seems in order,' he finally said, after taking her blood pressure and feeling the glands in her neck. 'Though I think I might send you for an x-ray on that back. And we might do some blood tests as well. You're due to have some anyway. It might be just a bit of sciatica, but best to be sure.' He paused and looked at his phone. 'Downstairs there's a new medical centre that can do the x-ray and take a blood sample, I'll give them a ring.'

'Thank you,' Angela said. 'I would appreciate that.'

Half an hour later she was lying under an x-ray machine, being poked and moved from one side to another. When all that was finished and she'd given a sample of blood she hailed a passing taxi and soon she was home at Bronte, having a cup of tea on the verandah. Later in the afternoon she went for a long walk along the beach, letting the waves wash over her feet. As always walking along the beach, with the sand between her toes, it reminded her of the beaches on Procida. If Maria was alive, she would now be in her mid-eighties, but Angela doubted that age would have slowed her up one little bit. She could envisage her almost skipping on the beach in front of her, wearing one of her bright red or yellow dresses, with the hem floating in the water.

'Hurry up, you slow coach,' Maria would laugh. 'If you don't get a move on the tide will come in and swamp us both.' Swishing her long grey hair over her shoulder she would smile. 'So, my Angeline, what shall we have for dinner tonight. Why don't we cook Aunt Sophia's favourite *Braciole in Ragu Sauce?*'

Angela decided that's how she would cook the two small lamb cutlets she had in the fridge for her dinner. Turning around, she trekked back up to her house on the hill and went out into her garden where she collected garlic and herbs for her *ragu* sauce.

Lying in her bed that night, she tried to put her aching hip out of her mind. Unable to ease the pain she got up and went to the couch by the front window where she looked out to the dark night. More than ever, she wished Maria was with her. Angela prided herself on never being lonely in her own company; however, right now, with her hip aching and the worry of the journalist delving into Stewart's past, she felt very alone.

Chapter Five

Emily put her hand under the tap and splashed her face with cold water. She ran her fingers through her hair and then she applied a quick dab of lipstick and mascara. She moved to the bedroom where she dragged a white dress with a short skirt out of the wardrobe and pulled it over her head. One of the perks of being a model was that sometimes she was given the odd article as a gift, this sass & bide dress being such a case. Already she was regretting being talked into going out to the Coogee Bay Hotel for a drink with Chrissy and her friends. She still felt dreadfully sad about Mathew. He had tried to ring her a number of times and had sent a mass of texts asking her to ring. She had ignored them all, even though she missed him so much. But after what he had done, no matter what he wanted to tell her, she knew she couldn't trust him anymore, so there was little point in talking to him. What she had to do was close the shutters on a year of her life and try and move on. It was the same advice she'd given out last year when a girlfriend's heart had been broken by a cad who was two-timing her with a work colleague. But taking that advice herself was proving harder. She felt funny going out without Mathew, but Chrissy had been insistent that she join her and her friends. 'Gees, Em … you can't sit around home moping about that dickhead. Besides, there's a whole wide world out there filled with great guys, who'll fall at your gorgeous feet.'

She smiled with the thought of Chrissy's prediction, which was so far from the truth it was laughable. Even before she had met Mathew she knew some guys she liked were often put off by the fact she was a model with a high profile.

She glanced at her watch. Rather than drive she thought she would call a taxi and then it wouldn't matter if she had a few wines. But first she went to the fridge and took out the previous night's pasta and quickly heated it up, knowing she was unlikely to have much to eat later on.

After checking her lipstick again, she waited outside her flat for the taxi. As she waited she thought about Nonna. She really did look tired yesterday. She hoped this thing about Emily's grandfather rearing its ugly head was not getting her down, even if her father reckoned he was going to try and fix it.

When she arrived at the Coogee Bay Hotel the place was packed. Chrissy and her friends were already there. They had taken up a spot next to the window looking out over the corso to the beach where tumbling waves broke onto the white sand. Emily hadn't seen Chrissy leave the house this morning on her way to uni. If she had she may have re-thought what she had decided to wear, for Chrissy was dressed down in a pair of ripped jeans and a skin-tight white t-shirt.

'Over here, Em,' Chrissy called out. 'Glad you made it. Wow, I love that dress. Lucky you. sass & bide.'

'Thanks, Chrissy. You look great, but my God did you wear that top to uni?'

'God no,' Chrissy hooted, running a hand through her mass of streaked blond hair, which was falling over a mischievous blue eye. 'I went home earlier and changed before coming here.'

'Ah! Just as well.'

After being introduced to a couple of the group she hadn't already met, Emily looked around the busy room abuzz with chatter and blaring music. Everyone seemed to be enjoying themselves, some a little too much, she mused, as she watched a girl in sky high stilettos nearly topple over before grabbing the girl next to her in order to steady herself.

Now Emily pushed her way through the throng and ordered a glass of wine. She spent some time talking to a girl who was doing law with Chrissy. She had met her before and really liked her. In fact, most of Chrissy's friends were nice. For over an hour she mingled, sipping on the one glass of wine. And as the alcohol took hold she desperately wished Mathew was here. The Mathew before she discovered he'd been cheating on her. Even though she was in a room full of people she felt very alone. She was about to take her wine glass back to the bar and tell Chrissy she was going to grab a taxi when the girl she was talking to looked over Emily's shoulder.

'Have you met Angus?' she asked with a smile. 'The farmer in our midst, doing Agricultural Science on the same campus as us.'

'No, I don't think so,' said Emily, turning around and eyeing the man behind her. He was over six foot tall with a shock of brown hair falling over his forehead. Emily noticed he was wearing a pair of cream moleskins and a blue and white checked shirt: a farmer's outfit, which although it should, somehow didn't look out of place in these urban surroundings.

'Where's the farm?' she asked.

'The Southern Tablelands. Not far from Gundaroo.'

'Near Canberra?'

'Yeah. Not far at all.'

Emily Erskine,' she said, holding out her hand.

'Angus McBride,' he said with a wide smile, taking her hand in his.

She noticed he had a really firm handshake.

'Gosh, with that name you'd have to be Scottish?' Emily laughed.

'Way back. My ancestors came from a place in Scotland called Kilmarnock, which is what our property is called. McBrides have been there since the 1800s.'

'Really! Well, my grandfather was Scottish. He came out here in the 1950s.'

'I reckoned Erskine was a Scottish name.' He grinned. 'So tell me, what do you do with yourself when you're not standing in the Coogee Bay Hotel talking to a farmer from Gundaroo?'

Emily was chuffed he didn't know she was a model. She wasn't sure why she was pleased. But she was.

'Can I get you another wine?' he asked, not giving her time to answer and holding his hand out for her glass. 'Then you can tell me what you do.'

'Thank you,' she said, furnishing him with a grateful smile. 'Another glass of wine would be great. If you can get near the bar that is. It was pretty packed before.'

When he came back he also had a glass of wine for Chrissy who was talking to a group of her friends. Are they an item, she wondered? Chrissy hadn't mentioned him.

On bringing Emily's glass back to her, he smiled. 'So ... you and Chrissy flat together?'

'Yes. We went to school together and now we have a small place in Bondi. Not much bigger than a shoebox, but we like it.'

'Are you studying as well?'

'I was. English literature. I'm afraid I gave it up.'

'Oh. And why was that?'

'Because I'm now into modelling. And,' she said with a laugh, 'much to my surprise I seem to be so busy there isn't much time for uni. Mind you, if I really put my mind to it I could do both. But I suppose I'm a bit lazy and as modelling won't last forever I can always do uni later. I'm doing an online writing course to keep the brain from going too mushy.'

'I thought you looked familiar,' he said.

She blushed. 'Well, I'm on TV a bit. And in the mags. Not that you'd read those sort of mags.' Then she laughed out loud. 'But I am on the back of some buses and taxis. An ad for sunscreen.'

'Ah,' he said. 'Maybe that's where I've seen your face.' He chuckled. 'Once seen, never forgotten.'

If anyone else said that she would find it a bit cheesy. Somehow, coming from him it didn't seem like that at all.

'So, how long have you known Chrissy?' she asked him.

'Her brother Mike and I boarded together at school here in Sydney. As you'd know their parents live up in Brisbane. We both went to London to work in finance. He's stayed on there.'

'Oh Mike. Of course.'

'When I got back to Sydney and started at uni doing Agriculture, Mike told me Chrissy was there too. We caught up.'

'Wow … finance to agriculture … now that's a change …'

Before he had a chance to tell her anything more, Chrissy bowled over to join them. 'So, you've met the yummy Angus?' she asked, putting a friendly arm around him.

Emily smiled. 'I have.'

'I thought you two would get on. In fact, I'm surprised you never met when we were growing up.'

'I was always down at Gundaroo when not at school,' Angus said.

'Yeah, and that's where Mike used to love to visit on school breaks.' Chrissy looked at him and then across the room. 'Come, both of you. I'll introduce you to a couple more of my friends.'

And that was the last chance that Emily had to talk to Angus, for once in the group of Chrissy's friends they both started talking to other people. At eleven she and Chrissy called a taxi as Chrissy had an early lecture and Emily also had an early fashion shoot. This time down at Darling Harbour for Myer.

In the taxi, Chrissy turned to Emily. 'So, what you think of Angus, eh?'

'He seems really nice.'

'Yeah, it was all very sad. He and Mike were working in London and then his brother, Duncan, got killed in Afghanistan and Angus felt he should come home to support his parents. That's why he's doing agriculture … to take over the property, I suppose.'

'Gosh. How awful that his brother was killed over there.'

'Yeah, Mike told me Angus was pretty cut up over it, as you can imagine.' She looked at Emily and grinned. 'You know what, he'd suit you a hell of a lot more than Mathew ever did … you being into horse riding and all that farmer stuff when you were up the Hunter at your grandfather's place.'

'Chrissy! I don't need anyone else to suit me. I'll be quite happy on my own for a while. Besides, once bitten, twice shy.'

'All men aren't like Mathew, Em.'

'I know, but even so. As I said, I'm more than happy with my own company right now.' She smiled. 'Present company excepted of course.'

'Okay, have it as you like, but—'

'No but's. Anyway, if he's so yummy as you say, why don't you go for him yourself?'

'Nah. I'm not his type. But you … well …'

'Chrissy, stop! Please!'

'Sorry. Just joking.' She touched Emily's knee. 'Forgiven?'

'Yes … you are.'

'Anyway, a group of us are planning on having a picnic down at Mrs Macquarie's Chair on Sunday. You want to come? Angus said he'd be in it.'

Emily thought for a moment. She loved being down by the harbour. And she had nothing else planned.

'Sure. Why not?'

'Great. But tell me, how's Nonna? I really should pop in and see her more. I just adore her.'

Nonna had always been very fond of Chrissy, even though she often told Emily she was a total scatterbrain, particularly when they were growing up and Chrissy would come to stay at *Mandalay* for weekends (as her parents had moved to Brisbane and Chrissy boarded). She would leave her things strewn all over the place.

'Nonna's okay,' she said. 'Getting older of course.'

But, as they drove, Emily thought of Nonna and wondered if she *was* okay. Or was she still upset about that journalist coming around and the memories it had brought up. If it wasn't so late she might pop around and see, but she was bound to be asleep. Or at least in bed. She would give her a ring first thing in the morning. She thought of telling Chrissy about the reporter and her grandfather. However, Chrissy had had quite a few wines and even if Emily swore her to secrecy she might well forget and tell someone tomorrow. Maybe even Angus or one of the others there tonight. And that thought upset Emily. If anyone was going to hear about her grandfather it should come from Emily. Unless the papers got it out there first, and that was something she didn't want to think about.

Chapter Six

After waking on Sunday, Emily grabbed her phone and checked her messages, Facebook and Instagram, then her news app. She felt her heart pound as she scrolled down an article at the top of the news.

> *In the light of the ICAC inquiry into the illegal issue of mining licences the NSW Premier will use special legislation to tear up three coal licences in the Hunter Valley worth hundreds of millions of dollars issued by corrupt former minister, James Read, and deny the companies that own them any compensation.*
>
> *The Premier's announcement is likely to spark legal action against the government by listed companies Coal Sphere and Hadden Coal. Coal Sphere claim their investors are being punished unfairly and the company will aggressively pursue all legal avenues to obtain compensation. It has previously suggested it would seek at least $500 million damages if its licence was cancelled.*

Much to Emily's horror the article finished up by saying, 'The Premier also stated that the government is looking into the case of other licences issued corruptly going back as far as thirty years.'

She took a deep breath and scrolled through her phone to see if there was any mention of Glasgow Mine and her grandfather in other online news. She was relieved when she saw there was none.

She thought of ringing Nonna, then decided not. It was early and she might well be still asleep.

Just as she was about to get up her phone rang. It was her father, wanting her to come to lunch.

'I'd like you to meet my friend Bianca,' he said. 'I'm sure you two would get on well.'

Another woman friend, Emily thought wryly. She was glad she had Chrissy's picnic as an excuse as she was fed up to the teeth with meeting her father's new ladies, who only seemed to last a few months before there was another one on the scene. Emily was only a few months old when her mother, Samantha, who Emily inherited her height and fine features from, took off to Bali, more or less leaving Emily with Nonna to look after her.

When Emily was fourteen her mother left once more, this time to America where her father told her that Samantha's sick, elderly parents needed her. She had never come back to Australia and neither Emily or her brothers had ever heard from her since. Her father later told her they had got a divorce.

Many of Emily's friends' parents had divorced, but as far as Emily knew none of their mothers had decided to settle on the other side of the world like Samantha had, more or less disappearing into thin air. Sure, she understood that her elderly parents needed her. But after they died, which they must have by now, couldn't she have come home then? One might leave one's husband. But children? What sort of mother could do that? A mother, who put herself before everything else. There must have been times when Emily was a kid when she and her mother did things together, but she was hard put to remember such a time. It was always Nonna who Emily could remember doing things with. Maybe when she was a baby her mother loved her. Cuddled her. Sang to her. Before Emily was old enough to remember.

Again, she thought how lucky she was to have had Nonna. Without Nonna to nurture her all these years Emily wondered how she would have turned out. She had now more or less blanked her mother from her mind, refusing to dwell on what might have been if she had a mother who loved her enough to come and visit. But she did have darling Nonna.

'So Nonna told you about that reporter who came around snooping about Grandpa and how he got hold of Glasgow Mine,' she said, ignoring her father's request to meet Bianca.

'She did.'

'She said you're hoping to sort it out.'

'And she's right.'

'So how are you going to do that? I mean, there was a bit in the news online this morning saying the government's looking into shifty deals from way back.'

'Yes, I saw that.'

'Maybe they're talking about Grandpa.'

'They'd have trouble proving anything that far back with your grandfather long since dead.'

'But you suspected Grandpa got hold of that mine illegally.'

'Nothing was proved.'

'Nonna more or less said he did.'

'Well, don't you go shooting off about that to anyone. He may have got hold of it through the back door, but it was hardly illegal. After all, a member of the NSW government was involved.'

'So …'

'So what?'

'Gees, Dad. You've only got to read the article to know there's corrupt politicians around.'

'That may be true. But let's forget about your Grandpa and what may or may not have happened. What about lunch? I'd really like you to meet Bianca.'

'Can't, Dad. I've got something else on. Maybe we could get together another time.'

He sounded a bit peeved, but she didn't care. It was typical of her father to ring at the last minute, imagining she had nothing better to do on a Sunday than come and meet another new lady friend. Before he hung up he told her he was going to Auckland for a few days the following week. She thought of asking if he was taking Bianca with him, but then she decided she didn't care one way or the other.

She heard Chrissy rumbling around in the kitchen getting her breakfast. Emily had stopped off at the IGA on the way home last night and, among other things, had grabbed some olives, cheese and biscuits for the picnic. And a small packet of bacon. Sunday mornings were not Sunday mornings without bacon and eggs.

She looked out the window to where the sun was playing chasing games up and down the wall of the house next door. It seemed as though it would be a glorious day. Standing up, she took off her pyjamas and put on a tracksuit and her sneakers. She would go for a run while Chrissy was using the kitchen.

'I'm running to Coogee—won't be long,' she said, poking her head into the kitchen.

'Say hello to the sea,' Chrissy smiled.

'You don't want to come? I can wait.'

'Not on your life. See you when you get back.'

'What time are we supposed to be meeting up for the picnic?'

'Angus is picking us up at twelve-thirty.'

Emily looked at her watch. 'Need any help getting food ready?'

'I'll make a pumpkin salad while you're out tightening muscles that weren't on the wish list when I was created. And we've got your cheese and things.'

'Thanks, Chrissy,' Emily said, giving her a hug. 'You're a gem.'

'Did you see this?' Chrissy showed her the same article on her iPad which Emily had read before. 'Mighty glad they've got those bastards in their sights with those shonky mine leases. Sounds like one's as corrupt as the other.' She paused. 'And also sounds as though the powers that be have others in their sight as well. From way back.'

Emily felt her heart lurch. 'Yes, I saw that when checking the news before I got up.'

Chrissy looked at her with a raised eyebrow. 'Hope your cherished Grandpa got his Glasgow Mine through the right channels.'

Emily smiled as she went to the door. 'I'm sure he did.'

As she ran down the street towards Bondi Beach she tried to put her grandfather to the back of her mind. She had always been quite good at that. Otherwise, how would she have coped with her mother deserting her like that? Jonathon and his drugs? Her father and his many women? Breaking up with Mathew was proving harder, but she was getting there.

Once on the beach she sped along the shore then took the popular path up over the hill where she weaved her way through the throngs already out enjoying the morning. Over the hill at Tamarama she came to Bronte where she ran past Nonna's house on the cliff and over the next hill, past the huge cemetery, the bowling club on the point and down to Clovelly, up over the hill to Gordon's Bay and ended up at Coogee. After a short rest, she started home over the same track. She loved the wind in her hair and smell of the sea. No matter how she was feeling when she started this run, she always felt happy by the time she'd finished, even if her calves were crying out in agony. Today was no different.

She sighed. Maybe the Premier wasn't referring to Glasgow Mine after all. And, even if he was, there wasn't a darn thing Emily could do about it. In the meantime, she was looking forward to the picnic at Mrs Macquarie's Chair.

***

Dragging on her dressing gown, Angela moved to the front door and picked up the newspaper. Glancing through quickly she was pleased to see that although the ongoing case against Turner was on page three there was no mention of Stewart.

Moving to the kitchen she made a cup of coffee from the new Nespresso machine Emily had talked her into buying. She sat at the small table in the corner and checked the paper more thoroughly. Although it was *The Australian* she was reading, she felt sure that if the *Sydney Mail* had broken the story on Stewart it would be reported here as well.

After a walk to the shop on the corner to get some milk and bread, she then wandered down to the beach for a swim. Afterwards, she busied herself in the garden, pruning the roses and weeding around the petunias and under the willow tree, where she sat for a moment on the wooden bench when she was done, which she loved to do, before heading inside for a short siesta, hoping to alleviate the pain in her hip which the gardening had aggravated. At five-thirty she poured a glass of wine and with it in hand she walked around the garden, admiring her weeding. She loved this time of year when the deciduous trees were starting to turn. Even the wattle tree seemed to be looking extra spruce right now with its leaves shiny and bright after the previous night's rain. Although still warm, there was a crispness to the air as evening closed in. When it came time for dinner she couldn't be bothered cooking anything so instead she placed some olives and cheese on a small platter and took it outside to the verandah, where she sat and watched the light fade and the outline of a new moon appear along with a splattering of stars. Ever since she was a little girl on Procida, Angela had always imagined her parents as two of those stars, looking down on her and Maria.

Maybe it was because of her possible illness that her mind flitted back to the day when she last saw her parents. When she said goodbye to them both as they got in their car and drove out of their rented villa in Naples to the wedding in Positano.

Arrivederci, Mama. Arrivederci, Papa. Ti Amo.

Even now she recalled how beautiful her mother looked, dressed so elegantly in the lilac taffeta suit Maria had helped her make from material they had found at a market stall. Angela even remembered her mother's hat which was made out of left- over taffeta stretched across cardboard and interspersed with flowers she had crafted out of a piece of silk she had found in another market stall. And how handsome her father was in his dark suit, which he normally only wore for mass on Sundays.

'Be good for Maria and Senora Bianchi while we are away, Angeline,' her mother had said, leaning down and kissing her as Angela stood between Maria and their neighbour from the apartment next door. And then her father had come over.

'I'll bring you a present, my beautiful Angeline.' He kissed her goodbye and pulled her ear in fun as he always did, before giving Maria a hug.

But sadly, Angela never got to see if her father had bought her that present. All she could remember was her absolute desolation on being told by Aunt Sophia that both her parents had been killed so tragically in that car accident and she and Maria were going to live with her on the small island of Procida.

The week before her parents left for the wedding, the sisters and their parents had stood on a seaside promenade with many others to watch Hitler and King Emanuel III pass by in a motorcade after Hitler had had a meeting with Mussolini. Little did Angela realise then what was to happen so soon. Not only was she to lose both of her beloved parents, and she and Maria would go to Procida to live with Aunt Sophia, a year later World War II took over most of Europe. And then when France was about to fall and the war seemed virtually over, Italy joined in on Germany's side, with the Italian army snatching a young teenager called Raphael Lombardi into its desperate claws.

Angela closed her eyes, blocking out the stars and the memories they invoked. Standing up she picked up the platter, which still had half of the olives and cheese uneaten. She went inside, put the remainder of her meal back in the fridge and placed the platter in the dishwasher. She then went to her bathroom and had a shower.

In bed she picked up the novel Elena had lent her and started reading. Although it was set in the Naples of today there were many things that Angela could relate to: the magnificent pastel stone villas of the wealthy on the hillside draped in dazzling bougainvillea, the aroma of pizza and Nutella stalls on the corner of the city corso, washing hanging from one balcony to another across the alleyways where rubbish was strewn, the pungent, tangy stench of dead fish and urine along the seaside promenade and the vision of the mafia furtively extorting money from business and shop owners. The beggars and thieves. All so different to the little island of Procida where doors never needed to be locked.

Closing the book, she turned off the light and shut her eyes, imagining herself back on Procida with Maria and Aunt Sophia. And then the fateful day when Maria came rushing into the store on *Marina Grande* where Angela was working.

***

'Aunt Sophia … Aunt Sophia …' Maria spluttered.

'What about her?' Angela asked, feeling alarmed.

Maria could hardly get the words out. 'She fell down the front steps onto the street. Madame Agosti from across the road came and got me from work. When I rushed down the neighbours were all there. And Doctor Giovanni was there as well.'

Angela's stomach rose into her throat. 'Oh my God! Is she alright?'

Maria shook her head and came over and put her arms around her. 'The doctor thinks she has had a heart attack. He, Gina and Phillipe from next door have managed to get her inside and onto her bed. But the doctor says she is very ill, so you must come quickly.'

Angela took off her apron. 'I'll lock up and put a notice on the door.'

When they got back to the villa, Aunt Sophia was lying on her bed in the downstairs bedroom and the doctor was fussing about her. As Angela rushed over she opened her eyes slightly.

'I'm so sorry to cause all this fuss,' she whispered. 'So silly of me to fall down those steps.'

Angela took hold of one of her frail hands and Maria the other. 'Don't talk, Aunt Sophia,' Angela said. 'It will tire you out.'

Aunt Sophia smiled and closed her eyes. All that night the girls sat by her bedside as her breathing became more and more laboured.

'Shouldn't she go to hospital?' Angela asked the doctor after he had packed his stethoscope away into his black leather medicine bag and she saw him to the door early the next morning.

'She would have to go to Naples and she doesn't want to do that.' He paused and gave Angela a compassionate smile. 'Her heart is failing and being in hospital is unlikely to help. It's best she remain here with you two, who she loves so much.'

Over the next week the doctor came constantly to visit and Angela and Maria managed to organise their work hours so that they could take it in turns to sit with her.

One morning when they were both sitting by her bed their aunt opened her eyes and gave them a small weak smile. 'When … when I leave this world and go and join my Maurizio, this villa will become yours.'

'Don't talk of such things,' Maria scolded.

Aunt Sophia ignored her. 'I have made a will. In it I have left the villa to you as well as all of my possessions.' She smiled again. 'Including my jewellery box that you have always loved, Angeline. Whenever you open it you must think of me and how much I have loved you.'

Angela looked over to the dressing table and saw the white wooden jewellery box sitting there with glittering crowns and butterflies on the front, and with a mirror and small compartments lined with pink velvet inside. She had coveted it since Aunt Sophia had shown it to her when she first came to the island and she was trying to cheer her up as she missed her parents so much. Thereafter she often sneaked into her aunt's bedroom to watch the ballerina swivel and twirl to *Fur Elise* when she wound the key in the back.

'Please hand me the jewellery box,' Aunt Sophia said weakly.

Silently, Angela got up and picked the box up, brought it over to the bed and opened it, surprised to see only one piece of jewellery inside.

'During the war I sold all my pieces of jewellery to buy food for us, except for the gold lira pendant inside this box,' Aunt Sophia said, holding out her hand for the pendant. 'This lira is from the time of Vittorio Emanuele II in 1861, commemorating him as the first king of a unified Italy.' Her voice became weaker with each word as she fondled the gold lira. 'It was passed down through Maurizio's family for generations and he gave it to me as a wedding present. It is for you, Maria,' she said, handing the pendant to her. 'Vittorio Emanuele's first child was also called Maria. Having this pendant has kept Maurizio in my heart all these years and now it will keep me in your hearts when I am gone.'

'Aunt Sophia, you are going nowhere,' Maria said with tears sprinkling her cheeks as she held the gold lira pendant in her shaking hand. 'Now you must sleep to get your strength back.'

'Yes,' Angela said, her own eyes welling. 'Please Aunt Sophia, do as Maria says.'

Aunt Sophia closed her eyes, but Angela knew she wasn't sleeping. 'You should go and explore the world,' Aunt Sophia said, opening her eyes and looking at each of the girls in turn. 'There's nothing for you here on Procida. Use the money you'll get from my villa to go somewhere where there's a future for you. Much as I love this island it is like a tiny, enclosed closet, one that is trapping you inside as if you were two beetles unable to escape. You need to fly off … spread your wings …'

Suddenly Aunt Sophia's breathing became ragged and both girls looked alarmed. 'You must rest,' Angela said again, stroking her arm. 'It is an order, Aunt Sophia.'

'Yes, Angeline, I will now rest,' she whispered, closing her eyes and folding her hands across her bosoms.

Three days later after receiving the last rites from her favourite priest, Father Alphonso, Aunt Sophia died peacefully while sleeping with both Maria and Angela by her side. Although both girls were devastated they were also relieved that she was no longer in pain, for as time went on she had found it increasingly hard to breathe. Listening to her trying to grasp for air was heart-rending.

Three days later, after Father Alphonso said a Requiem Mass at the church of Santa Maria della Pieta, where many of the islanders attended, they buried her at the *Cimitero Comunale di Procida* on a sunny morning with birds flitting from branch to branch and knocking down acorns from the ancient oak tree above where they stood.

And as her coffin was lowered into the ground, Maria and Angela held onto each other tightly.

'We will always remember you, Aunt Sophia,' Angela sobbed.

'And how kind you were to us,' Maria added, stroking Angela's hair and fondling the gold lira pendant around her own neck.

In those next few weeks at the villa the girls were heartbroken as they sorted through Aunt Sophia's clothes and possessions. Angela took the jewellery box up to her bedroom and put it on her own dressing table. Every night she would wind it up and watch the ballerina twirl as she listened to *Fur Elise*. Maria never removed the gold lira pendant from around her neck. Quiet and gentle Phillipe and his caring wife, Gina, from next door, were a great comfort to the girls. Gina often bustled in to help sort out Aunt Sophia's belongings, encouraging them to give away items that the girls were loath to be parted from, or she would cook a tortellini soup or one of the girl's favourites, lasagne with tomato, basil and aubergines (if they were very lucky Gina would have topped it with parmesan cheese, which was still hard to get hold of on ration cards). She would then leave her offerings on their kitchen table for the girls to find. Otherwise, she might invite them in for dinner with her and Phillipe where they would sit around their wooden table in the kitchen and talk about Aunt Sophia.

'I miss her so much,' Angela bemoaned one evening as they sat with Gina and Phillipe after finishing a haddock and pea risotto, which Gina had served with some delicious *ciabatta.*

'We all do,' Gina said. 'But she wouldn't want us to be sad. She would want us to remember the happy times.'

***

As Aunt Sophia had predicted every time Angela opened that jewellery box she thought of this beautiful, caring, laughing woman who had taken her and Maria into her home, enveloping them in her love.

Standing up now she went to the cupboard in the corner of her bedroom and pulled out the jewellery box. Opening it up she looked at its contents. There was a small colourful gemstone nestled in the corner: beside that there was the gold lira Vittorio Emanuele II pendant, which Aunt Sophia had given Maria and which many years later Maria had made Angela touch and make a promise: *Don't tell. Ever.*

Angela took the colourful stone and gold pendant out and went to find a soft cloth to polish them. When Emily was little she used to play with the box and loved to watch the ballerina dance. As they both listened to *Fur Elise,* Angela would hand her the gold lira pendant and tell her tales of Maria.

'This pendant has always kept me close to your grandmother, Maria,' she would tell her. 'When I depart this world it will come to you.'

She smiled as she remembered how Emily, eyes wide open in alarm, had once exclaimed, 'But Nonna why would you do that? Depart this world and leave me here? That's silly. In any case, where would you go?'

Walking over to the cupboard, she placed the jewellery box back inside. She then went to the bathroom and ran a long, hot bath to which she added a scoop of lavender bath salts, reminding her of the wildflowers which in spring and summer covered the fields running down to the sea on Procida. It was as if those fields were carpeted with hundreds and hundreds of Monet paintings, which she and Maria would scamper through.

Angela missed those happy, carefree days.

Chapter Seven

At twelve-thirty there was a knock on the door and Emily heard Chrissy welcome Angus McBride.

'You ready?' she hollered to Emily as she rushed back to the kitchen to fetch the picnic basket.

'Coming.'

Emily had settled on a pair of light blue cargo pants and a white t-shirt to wear. Over her shoulder she threw a yellow sweater. Although the sun was out, there was a cool breeze which she knew would be stronger down by the harbour. The wind would be blowing through the heads and unless they found a sheltered spot it would be quite cold.

As she passed the front door she stopped and greeted Angus with a happy smile.

He was wearing a pair of dark blue jeans and an open neck shirt and looked as though he had not long ago washed his hair, as it was still wet.

'Hi, Emily,' he said. 'Chrissy told me you were coming.'

Heading to the kitchen to give Chrissy help, she called over her shoulder, 'Thanks for giving us a lift.'

'Not a problem.'

When she came back out and Angus offered to carry the basket she raised an eyebrow: 'How's it going down Gundaroo way?'

'Haven't been back home to *Kilmarnock* for a few weeks. I've had a number of long assignments to finish and I work some nights at a bar in the city. Next weekend I'm rostered off so reckon I'll head down then.'

'I bet it's getting cold down there now.' She handed him the basket, indicating to take care of the bottle of wine sticking out. 'Do you get snow?'

He laughed. 'A few times when I was a kid we could toboggan on the back hill. Hasn't been much snow lately. Droughts are the main concern at the moment. We haven't had a drop of rain in months. Reckon this climate change thing might have something to it.'

Emily smiled. She had had more arguments about climate change with Mathew than you could poke a stick at. He didn't believe it existed. No matter how much information Emily bombarded him with, he had still refused to give in to her arguments. 'Well, there sure is something happening to the planet out there,' she said to Angus as she followed him to his Jeep parked out the front. 'And we can't be throwing out emissions like we are without it doing some damage. China might be the worst, but Sydney's got a problem as well.'

Angus glanced up at the sky. 'Mind you, it looks pretty clear today.'

'That's because there's a bit of a breeze. On a windless day it can really stink at times. All those cars, including this one,' she said with a laugh, patting the Jeep on the boot before opening it for him to put the basket in, 'have gotta clog up the atmosphere, let alone our arteries.'

'What about our arteries?' Chrissy asked, as she joined them by the boot, carrying a tartan rug.

'Climate change! Emissions!' Emily said.

'Don't get me started on climate change,' Chrissy said, hopping in the front seat next to Angus. 'We could be here all day.'

'My father reckons there's nothing to it,' Angus said, starting the engine and pulling away from the curb. 'We have some strong arguments at times.'

'Send him up my way,' Chrissy said with a giggle. 'I'll soon put him on the right path.'

Emily had the back seat to herself until they stopped off in Paddington and picked up two friends of Chrissy's. It took them a while to find a park close to Mrs Macquarie's Chair, but eventually they got one near the Botanical Gardens and soon they were throwing Chrissy's rug under the shade of a huge oak tree close to the actual Mrs Macquarie's Chair. It was one of Emily's favourite spots around the harbour. Only last year she had done a photographic shoot there for *Elle* magazine. Momentarily, she stood and admired the view. She never got sick of it. The Opera House and the Harbour Bridge were as clear as a bell on this day and a number of yachts tacked to and fro in the choppy water. Manly ferries chugged from one side of the harbour to the other, and across on the far shore she could make out Luna Park and Taronga Park Zoo.

Angus came and stood beside her. 'It's a view you'd literally die for, isn't it?'

Emily laughed. 'Just about.'

'I wonder what your grandfather thought of it when he first saw it?'

Straightaway Emily knew he had looked her up on the Internet. She wasn't sure whether she was happy with that or not. After all, everyone googled everyone in this day and age. Except Nonna, that is. The previous night when she was lying in bed, unable to sleep, she had actually googled her grandfather herself. She was relieved when nothing showed up about how he had obtained Glasgow Mine. She read the Wikipedia entry, which she had read many times before, saying how he was a successful restauranteur and business mogul who had tragically died of a heart attack in Korea. It listed all his achievements from when he had first arrived in Australia from Scotland and opened his first *Erskine's*. How on his death he had left a widow, Angela, and a son, Gavin.

Turning around, she smiled at Angus. 'I can't ask him. But I can ask my Nonna. She came over from Italy in the same year. On a ship called *The Toscana.*'

'Oh. What part of Italy?'

'A small island in the Bay of Naples. Procida. She and my grandfather met at Villawood Migrant hostel.'

'And your grandfather had a vineyard up the Hunter. And a coal mine called Glasgow. Being Scottish I couldn't forget that.'

'You *have* done your research,' she said lightly, trying to hide her angst.

'I was interested, that's all. When you told me he was Scottish.'

Emily laughed. 'I'm afraid I haven't been nearly as diligent. I haven't googled the McBrides of Gundaroo at all.'

'Well,' he said, 'come and I'll go get you a glass of wine from the esky. Then I'll tell you a bit about them. They're certainly not in the same league as the Erskines. All the same, there were some interesting characters in our distant past.

'I'd love to hear more about them,' she said. 'And your place at Gundaroo.'

As she watched him go over to the esky, she picked a pebble up off the ground and played with it in her hand. She smiled as she eyed a small lizard sunning itself on a sandstone rock not far from where she was sitting and she could hear the sound of birdsong from the nearby trees. It was as if it were an outdoor symphony.

Down on the harbour a gun went off, heralding the start of a yacht race. When Emily was only little, her grandfather had taken her out on his yacht on the harbour a few times, which she had loved. Nonna never came as she said she got seasick. Emily's mother, Samantha, often went out on the yacht but her father rarely did. To Emily, her grandfather seemed to have plenty of glamorous women to keep him company. It was only as she got older that she realised some of the women were not crew, but were in fact there to entertain her grandfather and his friends. She had never seen her grandfather behave inappropriately while she was around; however, now that she had heard what he supposedly did in gaining that lease for Glasgow Mine she wondered if he had always been faithful to Nonna. Even though he was in his seventies when he died, Emily remembered him as being a good-looking man. His red hair had gone grey, but it was still thick. And unlike a lot of men of that age he wasn't in the least stooped over. He looked after himself and dressed well. So, she presumed there were many women out there who had found him attractive. Not least because he was well-known, powerful and with plenty of money. Whether he was a womaniser certainly wasn't something she could ask Nonna about. Poor Nonna would have a heart attack herself if Emily brought that up.

When her grandfather built his huge racing yacht, *Pride of Erskine*, which he entered in the Sydney to Hobart and Hamilton Island Race Week, he never asked Emily to come on board, despite the fact he had a number of female crew members. Even Emily's mother had gone out a few times. Emily had only been fourteen when he died, so she was far too young to crew in big races, but she would have liked to go out on the harbour when they were practicing. By the time she would have been old enough to crew on *Pride of Erskine* he was dead. Soon after, her father sold the boat.

As Angus came back with her wine, she banished thoughts of her grandfather from her mind as they sat down on the grass.

'You two want something to eat?' Chrissy asked them, bounding over and pointing to where the food was laid out. 'I've put it all out on that flat rock over there and it's just a matter of helping ourselves. If we don't do it soon the bloody flies will make off with the lot.'

'Thanks, Chrissy. I'm famished,' Angus said, standing up and placing his bottle of beer on the ground. 'And then I can tell Emily about the McBrides of *Kilmarnock*.'

Sitting back down a few minutes later with their lunch on their knees, Angus told her how his family had held onto *Kilmarnock* ever since his ancestors arrived there back in the eighteen hundreds from Scotland. His father was now in his sixties and wanted to buy a yacht in the Med before he got too old, hence he was hoping that Angus would more or less take over the place when he'd finished his degree.

'And what do you think of that idea?' Emily asked, fiddling with the salad and piece of bread on her plate.

'I've always loved the land. Even if it's a bugger at times. Fortunately, it's not doing too badly at the moment, so I won't be tied there all the time. I can get away now and then.'

Emily waited a moment before giving him a compassionate smile. 'Chrissy told me your brother was killed in Afghanistan. I was so sorry to hear that.'

Angus glanced away into middle distance, picked up his beer, taking a long sip. He then took a bite of the piece of steak on his plate, chewing thoughtfully for some time. Swallowing hard, he brought his gaze back to her and gave a sad sort of smile. 'Yeah, he wasn't interested in the land. The army was always his first love. He went to ADFA and Duntroon in Canberra.'

'Yes, Chrissy told me.'

'He was seconded to the war over there a couple of times.' He let out a long, deep sigh. 'The poor bugger only had a week left on that last posting. Another bloody week and he would've been home.'

Emily held his eyes with hers. 'I'm so sorry,' she said. 'It must've been awful for your parents. And you as well.'

Angus nodded. 'Don't reckon the old man's ever got over it. My mum's not so bad. Or if she is she doesn't show it as much. But it knocked Dad around no end. Mum reckons she's got to get him away from *Kilmarnock* or he'll drop dead. Too many memories of Duncan there. It was Dad who taught him how to shoot. Wallabies and kangaroos. "Let 'em be and they'd eat everything in sight," was Dad's favourite saying. But he reckoned if he hadn't taught Duncan how to use a gun, he mightn't have chosen the army as a career.'

'And you?'

'Rabbits. And kangaroos where necessary. In the drought it's the most humane thing to do with the starving livestock. And with those poor bastards that get charred to pieces in the bushfires.'

'No. I mean how did you cope when Duncan died?'

'Ah. That. He and I got on pretty well.' He laughed, but it had a wretched tinge to it. 'That's when we weren't killing each other as kids.' Another long pause.' He was a good bloke. Too young to die in that bloody war, which has gone nowhere anyway. The Afghans will go back to doing what they've always been doing. Destroying themselves and their damn country.'

Emily could understand why he felt so angry. Without realising what she was doing she put her hand on his arm. 'They say time heals most things. Maybe in a few years it won't be quite as raw. For you and your parents.'

Angus placed his bottle of beer back down on the ground. 'Yeah, I've read that. Anyway,' he said with a grin, 'enough of maudlin talk. As I said before I'm headed down that way next weekend. The Yass Picnic Races are on. They're usually a bit of a hoot. So, I'll see how they are.'

'How who are?' Chrissy asked, romping up with a glass of wine in one hand and a sausage in bread in the other, which Emily pointed out was dripping tomato sauce down her white shirt onto her blue jeans.

'My parents,' Angus said.

'I'd love to meet them,' Chrissy said, wiping her shirt and jeans with a paper serviette. 'Mike always reckoned they were lovely to him.'

'I just told Emily I'm headed down there next weekend for the Yass Picnic Races. If you felt like getting out of the city you might like to come and meet them.'

Chrissy looked at Emily and then back to Angus. 'Both of us?'

Emily cast her eyes to heaven. 'Chrissy!'

'Well, you always say you miss going up to *Riverside*. This is a chance to become a country bumpkin again for the weekend. So, what you say? Why don't we take Angus up on his offer?'

Emily smiled. Good old Chrissy. She's got it all worked out. She thought for a moment. Why not? She really would like to get out into the countryside and smell clean, fresh country air. And it might take her mind off Mathew and what he may or may not be doing.

'The place could do with a bit of life,' Angus said. 'My mother's always telling me to bring some young ones home. Somehow after Duncan's death, up until now, I haven't felt like it. But it would do them good. Might cheer them up.'

Emily had a modelling stint at Myers on Friday, but the weekend was free. She was going to meet Gina, a girlfriend, for coffee but she could put that off. Gina would understand.

'What day are you thinking of going down?'

'Late Friday afternoon. It takes about three hours. A bit longer if the traffic's bad getting out of the city. If we leave by three-thirty we'd be there by six-thirty. In time for drinks and one of my mother's great roasts.'

'I won't finish my modelling gig until three-thirty.'

'Where's that?'

'Westfield at Bondi Junction.'

'That's not a problem. I'll swing by and get Chrissy and then come and get you.'

Emily fiddled with a piece of pine bark on the ground, picked it up and threw it into a nearby bush. 'Why not,' she said, turning around to them both. 'I've always wanted to go to a picnic race meeting. But, gosh, Angus, are you sure your parents won't mind? Two strange women landing on their doorstep?'

'Reckon they'll be chuffed. As I said it's a bit maudlin with just the three of us there. You never know, I might even talk them into coming to the races as well. Do them both good to get dressed up and head out for a bit. They'll know a hell of a lot of people there. People they've more or less shunned since Duncan died.'

Emily smiled and nodded. 'I'd really like to meet them. And I'd love to see your *Kilmarnock*.'

'Me too,' Chrissy said. 'It'll be a hoot, won't it, Em?'

Emily smiled. 'I'm sure it'll be great fun.'

Chapter Eight

It was just after noon the next day when Dr Wallace rang Angela. 'Good afternoon, Mrs Erskine,' he said. 'I got your x-ray and blood test results.'

'That was quick,' Angela said, feeling a slight apprehension.

'These days it doesn't take long at all. A couple of things showed up in your blood test and something on the x-ray I'd like to discuss. Perhaps Gavin could come in with you. Drive you in.'

Angela's blood rose. 'I'm quite capable of catching the bus and train as I normally do. And if there's something you want to tell me, which is so bad that I need someone else to be there, I'd much rather it be Emily than Gavin.'

'Oh, nothing like that at all. I just thought it would save you the bus trip.'

'I can quite afford a taxi,' Angela said, knowing she sounded cross, which was unfair to the doctor. 'I prefer the bus.'

'Well, let's say tomorrow at ten.'

'That soon?'

'I happen to have a free appointment. A cancellation.'

'Oh! In that case I'll be happy to see you then.'

After she put down the phone, she sat looking out of the window. Never before had Dr Wallace suggested she bring someone else in with her. She hoped the news he was going to give her wasn't bad. But, if it was, she was quite capable of coping with it herself.

Later, Emily popped in on her way to a barbeque at a girlfriend's place in Clovelly.

'It's an all-girls do,' she said. She shook her head and laughed. 'I think they're trying to cheer me up after Mathew.'

Angela decided not to tell her about going back to see Dr Wallace. Once she had seen him there would be time enough.

'That sounds lovely, darling. Thank God for girlfriends. But how was the night at Coogee?'

'It was fun.' Emily smiled. 'I met a friend of Chrissy's brother, Mike.'

'Oh, really! How lovely!'

'His name is Angus McBride. His family have a farm at Gundaroo. You might remember Mike used to go down there every now and then during the holidays.'

'Oh yes, I do remember that. He said it was a great place. Mind you that was a number of years ago. Now with the drought everywhere it mightn't be quite as good. But what on earth was he doing at the Coogee Bay Hotel?'

'He's at uni. Doing an agricultural course.' She paused. 'He was overseas with Mike, but then his brother got killed in Afghanistan. He came home to support his parents.'

'Oh, how very sad. It's such a tragedy that our young ones have to fight over there.'

'He was an officer. Went to ADFA. So, he chose it as a career. Even so ...'

'Tragic all the same.' She gave Emily an inquisitive smile. 'Is Angus nice?'

'Yeah, he is. He came on a picnic to Mrs Macquarie's Chair with us on Sunday. He's asked Chrissy and me down to stay at their farm next weekend.'

'And you're going?'

Emily nodded. 'I can't believe I didn't meet him when we were growing up.'

'That does seem extraordinary. And does he have a girlfriend?'

Emily laughed. 'I reckon Chrissy's trying to match us up. But I don't want matching up right now. Besides, as you know I'm planning on going to India.'

'You can't go fretting about what happened with Mathew forever. He really isn't worth it.'

'I know, I know, darling Nonna. It just takes a bit of getting over, that's all. Anyway, Dad rang on Sunday. Wanted me to go out for lunch with his new lady.' She grinned. 'I was pleased I had that picnic on and couldn't go. I asked him about Grandpa. He gave me a bit of a brush off.'

'Oh!'

'I was worried because there was a bit online about the Turner case and how the government might be going to delve way back, looking at shonky deals that politicians were involved in. But like you, Dad reckoned they'd have problems proving anything with everyone now dead.'

'I don't always agree with your father, but in this case I'm sure he's right,' Angela said, trying to sound positive, even though she had her own doubts. There could well be someone still around that might remember what had gone on. And possibly papers to prove it.

'Let's hope so, Nonna.' Emily stood up and looked at her watch. 'Anyway, I'd best be off as I'm picking my friend Jane up on the way.'

And then she was gone and it was silent, except for the *thump, thump* of the pounding waves down on the beach. Once again, as she thought of Stewart, she asked herself how different her life would have been if she and Maria had never come to Australia and met him, even though over the years she had learnt that the answer to that question was best not dwelt upon. They had come and that was that. She walked over to the bookcase and picked up a photo of herself and Maria, which Aunt Sophia had taken. She liked to keep many photos of her sister on display to remind the young ones of her. In this snap they were standing in Aunt Sophia's doorway next to the geranium bush and Angela had a flower behind her ear.

'Look, Angeline, this matches your pink blouse.' Maria had laughed, picking a flower from the geranium bush and playing with it in her hand before handing it to Angela.

Although the photo was black and white Angela could still remember the vivid pink of that geranium bush and the pink blouse that Maria had made for her as a birthday present. She wore that blouse with so many things, including a white, flouncy skirt Maria had also made her and which she loved. She had even brought it to Australia after Maria announced to Angela that was where they were going to live.

***

'I've made a decision,' Maria said to Angela with fervour on a cold and wet winter's evening when she had come back to Procida on the steamer from Naples after seeing Aunt Sophia's lawyer to finalise her will. The girls were huddled by the fire with the wind howling up *Via Flavio Gioia* from the harbour and rain pelting against the windowpanes.

'What decision?' Angela asked, leaning forward and poking a piece of wood in the fire.

'We're leaving Procida.'

'Leave here? Why would we do that?'

'We must take Aunt Sophia's advice and sell this villa. We need to go somewhere exciting, Angeline. A place where there's song and dance. Not like here where even a guitar or mandolin is looked down upon in case they corrupt the mind. They even used to look disapprovingly at Raphael for playing his flute. Most of the young

108

men who live here are boring and the whole island is, as Aunt Sophia said, one big suspicious busy body of a closed closet, gossiping and knowing everyone else's business. Apart from Gina and Phillipe of course.'

'It's not *that* bad.'

'Yes it is. Anyway, I saw an advertisement in a window today in Naples. It said how the Australian government is desperate for migrants. That it would cost us very little to go there by boat, as they would subsidise our fare.'

'Australia!'

'Yes, Australia.'

'Don't be so ridiculous, Maria. It's the other side of the world. You saw so when Raphael showed us on the map.'

'He liked it, and he was a prisoner! There's no future for us here. If we stay we're sure to end up like all the other women on the island: dressed in black, gossiping and being miserable.' She sighed. 'I too will have to wear black. I don't like any of the men so I'd be sure to end up killing my husband.'

'Maria! That's a dreadful thing to say.'

'Well, maybe not kill him. But you know what I mean. We have to get out into the world, Angeline. As Aunt Sophia told us there's so much to see.'

'Why don't we go to Rome or somewhere else here in Italy. Naples?'

'No. We will go to Australia. I have decided.'

Angela felt like saying that Maria made all of their decisions from when they were very little, like where they would sit on the bus in Naples if they were going on an outing or what dress Angela would wear to a birthday party. However, she was now an adult and could make her own decisions. And she had no intention of sailing to the other side of the world, even *if* Raphael had said it was good. But then, when she tried to come up with an argument as to why they shouldn't go, she was unable to find one.

In the end, after Maria came back from another visit to Naples carrying brochures which showed how enticing Australia looked with its wide open spaces, eucalypts, wattles, blue skies, white sandy beaches, kangaroos and koala bears, Angela gave in.

'You are doing the right thing,' Gina and Phillipe told the girls when they showed them the brochures. 'We will miss you, but as your aunt said, there is no future for you here.'

However, it took many visits to Naples and much paperwork back and forth to the island before they were approved by the immigration authorities and told they would be leaving by ship in six months' time. During that period, they were able to sell Aunt Sophia's villa to a lovely couple from Naples who were moving to the island to be closer to his elderly parents, which gave Angela and Maria enough money to start their new life in Australia.

When it came time to leave, Gina and Phillipe came over with the girls on the steamer from Procida to Naples and were at the docks when they boarded the huge black Lloyd Trestina ship, *The Toscana,* for Australia.

'*Arrivederci,* my beautiful girls,' Gina said tearfully. 'Please take care.'

'We will always remember how kind you were,' Maria said, hugging her tightly and wiping her tears with her hand. 'Always.'

***

It was a bright sunny day when Maria and Angela sailed into Sydney Harbour from their long voyage from Naples. They had stopped off along the way in Messina, Port Said, Colombo and Djakarta, each place's colours, smells and people so different to the island they had left.

Both girls were overcome with awe at the sight before them, with yachts and ferries chugging under the huge expanse of the Sydney Harbour Bridge and the magnificent mansions with verdant gardens perched on the shore. The city centre spreading up from the harbour was something Angela imagined New York might look like, with tall buildings dotting the skyline.

But her elation soon turned to despair when she saw where they were to live in the dry, dusty, fly-ridden bushland around Villawood Migrant Hostel, where they were off-loaded from clunky buses after driving through the frenzied city and sprawling suburbs.

'My God,' Maria exclaimed the second day they were there. She looked in despair at the rows of long, low-line Nissen style huts set in a dustbowl. 'It looks like a concentration camp.'

'Oh Maria, what have we done?' Angela moaned, tears filling her wide brown eyes.

The girls were told that this part of the country was in the midst of a severe drought. There had been no rain for months and the sun burnt high and brazen. The fields (paddocks, as they were called in Australia) around Villawood were parched as if they were acres of crinkled brown cardboard, and the waterhole below the camp was almost empty with its sides cracked and crater-like. It was so different to Procida's height of summer heat where the tangy aroma of fish, sea salt, lemons and mandarins filled the air. Angela could smell the dust and eucalyptus the moment she woke up in the morning, and during the worst part of the scorching day her skin wept with sweat and her hair, thick with dust, stuck to her head as if it was plastered there with a messy runny paste. Unlike on Procida, there was nowhere to go to get relief ... no beach, no sea, no vines or leafy trees to sit under. She remembered Raphael telling her of the native wattle trees with glorious golden blooms and a delicate aroma, but as it was the height of summer the ones round Villawood looked forlorn and haggard in the heat. She longed for a shady tree, but even if there was one she suspected the blowflies would be seeking relief there as well, getting in her eyes and crawling on her skin. She had even swallowed one, making her gag.

Despite the excitement of being in a new country and making an adventurous fresh start, it wasn't at all what they imagined they'd left Procida for. Particularly when they discovered that there were deadly snakes and hideous poisonous spiders ready to pounce at any moment. But it was the dust, flies and magpies that Angela hated most. She'd seen very few sheep before, as mostly there were goats on Procida. She'd certainly never seen a flyblown one, but at Villawood most of the sheep were flyblown. The girls and their fellow migrants from Poland, Germany, Italy and other European countries, and even a few from the United Kingdom, had to queue everywhere: the longest being to use the showers and toilets in a fibro-cement block, with a towering corrugated iron water tank on stilts attached to its side, a long way away from the sleeping quarters. To get their meals in the cavernous dining hut they'd often line up for over an hour.

'We'll be dead of starvation before we get to the end of this line. And when we do there'll be nothing left anyway,' Maria pooh-poohed aloud, as Angela tried to quieten her before any of the staff heard. For she was sure they would be sent back to their rooms without any food if they thought Maria was making fun of them.

Although there were many stoic immigrants at Villawood with their sights set on the future in their new land, there were others pining for their loved ones back home and wondering what on earth they were doing there. A number of the men had gone further afield to find work wherever they could, many on the Snowy Mountain or other hydro-electric schemes. Or if they were lucky they might have found employment in industry around the suburb of Bankstown close by, many of their families remaining at Villawood until suitable accommodation could be found.

'We'll soon get out of here,' Maria consoled Angela one night when she was lying on her bunk crying because one of the other migrants had pushed and shoved her when she was queueing for the shower. 'In the meantime, Angeline,' Maria added plonking down on the bunk beside her, 'do stop crying. It's bound to give you wrinkles. We might as well accept our lot and get on with it.'

And in the end that's what both girls did, realising they had no option. They soon made a few friends with the other women, Maria even giving sewing lessons on the Singer sewing machine set up in the small hut used for children's activities and card and board games for the adults at night. There was a game called Bingo, where someone called out numbers and you had to see if you had the same numbers on the piece of paper you were given. If you had all of the numbers you won a prize, which might be a handkerchief or a scarf. One of the women told Angela that around Australia many played bingo for money.

Both girls were fit and strong, so often helped with carting the wood and chopping it up for the boiler, otherwise there would be no hot water for showering. They also helped in the laundry and peeling vegetables in the kitchen, which Angela liked, as there was a gregarious Italian cook, Franco, with his Humpty Dumpty stomach bursting out of his blue and white striped apron, who had lived in Australia for many years and who helped her with her English.

She and Maria had been there a few weeks and on the way to have a shower, when they saw a tall man with a mop of red hair and a face dotted with freckles heading to the men's shower block.

'Ooh la la ... take a peek at that one,' Maria had said with a giggle, pointing him out to Angela. 'He looks like a tall giraffe among a field of us brown cattle.'

Maria's description was quite apt. Compared to many of the other migrants who were mostly from central Europe with olive skin, Angela couldn't help but notice him.

'And listen to him sing that *Waltzing Matilda* song,' Maria said as his voice drifted across the barren ground. 'He sounds like an Australian already.'

Once a week there was a singalong for the migrants in the main hut. *Waltzing Matilda* was one of the first songs Maria and Angela had learnt the words to as they valiantly tried to master English by going to classes, as well as listening hour on end to English-speaking records and talking to Franco and other staff.

As he passed the girls the man stopped singing and bowed, holding his hand in an exaggerated way in front of him. 'And good morning to you two bonnie lassies.'

He had a strong Scottish brogue and Angela thought he was very handsome. As he continued to smile at them she blushed with embarrassment. But she noticed Maria fiddled with her newly washed hair and smiled seductively. 'And good morning to you,' she answered in broken English.

'And who might Stewart Erskine be having the pleasure of meeting?' he asked the girls.

'Maria and Angeline Vincento,' Maria told him, tossing her hair back over her shoulder and treating him to another smile.

'Angela,' Angela said crossly. 'My name is Angela.'

Maria laughed out loud. 'My sister has this silly idea that if she is to be a *real* Australian she must change her name to Angela.'

'And Angela it shall be,' Stewart said, taking Angela's hand and raising it to his lips. He then turned to Maria, lifting her hand to his lips also. As he did, Angela couldn't help noticing how he held her hand just that little bit longer.

That evening as Maria and Angela were having dinner at a long trestle table in the corrugated iron dining hut with a cement floor covered in faded linoleum with deep, jagged cracks, which a few scraggly weeds were poking through, Stewart came over to where they sat below a large Union Jack and a photo of the Queen.

'And may I be allowed to join you two beautiful lassies for dinner?' he asked with a broad smile.

Angela saw the disapproving look of the other women at the table. Although it wasn't a set rule, it was usual for the single men and women to sit separately. Just as Maria had flaunted the rules of dress on Procida she did so now, shifting in her seat and making room for Stewart to sit down beside her.

'But of course,' she said to him with her most beguiling smile.

And that's where Stewart sat each evening from then on. At first, Angela was jealous that he was monopolising her sister. But when she saw how happy he was making Maria she soon got used to him being around. And it was good to have him close by. Villawood was an intimidating place with plenty of bullying and brawls, particularly in the dining room where tempers often flared. Somehow, although the migrants weren't allowed to cook for themselves, which had caused quite a bit of angst, Stewart had wrangled his way into Franco's kitchen and managed to add a bit of spice here and there. And on the pretext of helping to serve out the meals he was able to secure tastier options for the girls without the others really noticing.

'Bonnie lassies like you need a wee sprinkling of spice thrown in here and there,' he would whisper, as he handed them their plates and gave Maria a secretive wink.

Watching Maria giggle behind her hand Angela had a feeling that Stewart was talking about more than just the spice in the food.

As a bonus he became friends with the camp's noted bootlegger, who ensured that there was always a bottle of good wine to share on a Saturday night when the three of them would take their glasses down to where there was a small dry creek bed and sit on a log of wood listening to the sound of crickets. And as time went by and Angela saw how close Stewart and Maria were becoming she came to accept him as a part of their lives. He told the girls he had applied to come to Australia, as like in Italy, the Australian government was crying out for migrants.

'I'm one of three bonny lads, so I'll hardly be missed at all,' he had said with a laugh.

'But don't *you* miss your family?' Angela asked, imagining leaving brothers and sisters behind in Italy.

'When I make my great fortune here in Australia I can go back to visit or bring them over here.'

It was on seeing how he manipulated the staff at Villawood to his own benefit, and how adamant he was that he was going to make his great fortune here in Australia, when Angela had the first inkling that Stewart Erskine would be a very successful businessman, no matter what it took.

It was later when the restaurateur Cesare Carpani came into their lives and events took such a tragic turn that she realised how true that was. By then she was sworn to secrecy.

Don't tell. Ever.

Chapter Nine

When Angus pulled up outside *Kilmarnock* homestead a Scottie Terrier came belting out of the garden gate, barking madly.

'G'day old fella,' he said, giving the dog a pat on the head.

He turned to Emily, who was sliding out of the back seat. 'This's Rex. I got him as a pup for Mum.' He chuckled. 'When I left for overseas, and Duncan was in the army, I figured she might feel a bit lost without her sons making a racket around the place. I think she and Dad cursed me at first, but they wouldn't be without him now.'

Emily leant down to pat the dog and was rewarded with licks all over.

'The working dogs aren't allowed in the house, but Rex isn't much of a working dog, so he gets to have a few privileges. Dad reckons it's not fair on the others, but Mum won out.'

'Lucky you, Rex,' Emily said, watching the dog jumping around in joy.

She was pleased to find it was quite warm. The sun was still out and there was no breeze at all. For a moment she stood staring in fascination at the bluestone homestead with a galvanised iron roof and white plantation shutters on the windows. She loved the vine-covered wide verandah with French doors opening out to it and was amazed at how many English-style trees surrounded the house. Oaks, elders, beech, all blended with the natives. The garden beds were a riot of colour and clusters of rose bushes dotted the lush green lawns, neatly mowed with the edges trimmed.

Gosh, Nonna would adore this, she thought. I must take lots of photos on my phone to show her.

'Wow!' Chrissy said, coming to stand beside her and patting Rex. 'What a place!'

'You like it?' Angus asked.

'It's terrific,' Emily said. 'Like something out of *Country Life*. Though so much better.'

'My mother spends most of her time in the garden. We've got a bore, so she gets water from there, which also feeds the dam. It gives her huge happiness.' He paused, as there was the sound of footsteps on the gravel path. 'Talking of which, here she comes now.'

'You made good time,' said the woman walking towards them. She was wearing blue jeans and a yellow polo neck jumper, and her greying dark brown hair was tied back. Her skin was marked from the sun and there were deep lines around her blue eyes. Yet, in a no-fuss country sort of way, she was a very handsome woman. 'I thought the traffic might be horrendous and you'd get held up,' she said, smiling at her son. 'It seems to be getting worse by the minute in Sydney.'

Angus stepped forward. 'Hi, Mum.' He gave her a kiss on the cheek and turned around. 'I'd like you to meet Chrissy. She's Mike's sister.'

'Oh yes, Mike did mention you. How wonderful to meet you, dear.' She moved forward and took Chrissy's hand.

'Hi, Mrs McBride,' Chrissy said. 'You're very good to have us arrive on you like this.'

'And this is Emily,' Angus said. 'A friend of Chrissy's.'

Emily moved forward and took her hand. 'It's lovely to meet you, Mrs McBride. And the same as Chrissy, I'd like to thank you for having us stay.'

'Not at all. And the first thing you must both do is call me Betty. My name's Elizabeth, but no one's called me that forever.'

Emily looked around. 'You have the most beautiful garden imaginable. You must spend a lot of time in it.'

'Far too much time my husband tells me.' She laughed heartily. 'He says if I spent as much time looking after him as I do my garden, he'd be flourishing just like the garden is. Mind you, he doesn't do too badly. Does he, Angus?'

Angus smiled. 'Where is he?'

'In his study. He probably didn't hear you drive up. Come,' she said, beckoning to Chrissy and Emily, 'and I'll show you where I've put you both. You're sharing, so I hope that's okay.'

'Of course,' Chrissy said.

'We flat together,' Emily said and then winked mischievously at Betty. 'I'm used to her chaos.'

Betty smiled and as she did Emily thought what a gorgeous smile she had. Some people's smiles didn't quite reach their eyes, but Betty's did, which made her all the more attractive. 'Well, I hope you'll find it comfortable where I've put you.'

They followed her into the garden, down the path and onto the wide verandah surrounding the house on three sides. To one side of the doorway was a green wrought iron setting and further along, as the verandah widened in the corner, there were a couple of heavy wooden and canvass deck chairs with a round table between. In the centre of the table was a pot of petunias.

Inside the front door they entered a long hallway lined with portraits and paintings. An Indian runner ran the length and the furniture was dark and heavy.

I bet it's been here forever, Emily mused.

When they came to the third door on the right, Betty opened it and showed them into a bright and airy room with French doors opening to the verandah. There were two single beds, a chest of drawers and a wonderful cedar wardrobe. The beds were covered with brightly coloured bedspreads, which matched the material of the curtains. To Emily, who imagined the morning sun filtering through those curtains, it was a room she would happily spend a lot of time in.

'It's just beautiful,' she said to Betty. 'You've decorated it so tastefully.'

'Thank you,' Betty said. 'I only did it up recently.' She paused. 'It used to be Angus's brother's room. Duncan loved it so much I thought it was a pity to close it up after he died.' Another pause. 'Angus said he'd told you how he was killed.'

'Yes, he did,' Emily said. 'I'm so sorry for you all.'

'Thank you, dear. It was his choice to join the army and I respect that choice, even though we would've liked him to take over here. There was always a risk that he'd be killed once he went to Afghanistan. I've had to learn to live with that. Sadly, Bill hasn't taken it so well.'

Chrissy sighed. 'Bloody government of ours shouldn't go messing about in other people's problems. We've got enough of our own.'

Emily could see Betty bristle. 'Duncan thought it was a cause worth fighting for. As I said, it was his choice. Unlike those conscripted for the Vietnam War.'

'Oh, I'm sorry, Betty,' Chrissy said, looking devastated she'd upset their hostess 'I didn't mean to be so insensitive.'

'Of course you didn't, dear. I'm afraid I'm a bit touchy where's that's concerned.'

'Even though it was his choice,' Emily said, 'I'm sure it doesn't make it any easier for you to bear.'

At that moment Angus came to the doorway. With him was a much older man, nearly as tall as Angus. His hair was thinning and quite grey. His rugged face was that of a farmer, tanned and creased. It was obvious by his strong features that he had once been very handsome, but grief had taken its fair share of him.

He was wearing a pair of cream moleskin trousers, an open neck checked shirt and a well-worn pair of RM Williams on his feet.

When Angus introduced him they all went to the back of the house where there was a large glass conservatory.

'We might as well enjoy the last of the day's sunshine,' Betty said. 'It'll soon drop down behind the hills.'

The view through the glass was of the garden and beyond that to a paddock where three horses grazed. To the right of the paddock there appeared to be a creek as the land dropped away and Emily could see a thicket of willow trees. Close to the conservatory was a lily pond where a barbecue had been built into a wall of rocks with a clematis vine tumbling over the top. Next to the barbecue was a weather-beaten wooden outside garden setting.

'Now, Angus,' Betty said, turning to her son with a broad smile. 'Why don't you get us all a drink and afterwards we can light the barbecue and throw on some of those steaks I've got in the fridge?' She looked at the girls. 'I was going to have a roast. However, with this unusually warm weather I thought we'd barbecue. The men can get it going while we have a chat.' She looked at Chrissy. 'Angus tells me you're a vegetarian, so I've got a couple of salads and a potato dish which will hopefully fill you up.'

Chrissy smiled. 'Thank you.'

'A vegetarian, eh?' Bill said. He laughed heartily and Emily could see a look of relief on Angus's face. 'How the dickens do you reckon a poor bloke can make a living from his sheep and cattle if the whole world turns into goddamn lettuce eaters?'

'I'm sorry,' Chrissy said. 'It's just something I feel strongly about.'

'Well, when we've got a drink you can tell me how you got started on such a path that could destroy the livestock industry in one swoop.' He then looked at Emily. 'Thank God for people like your grandfather. We supplied our fair share of lamb and beef to *Erskine* restaurants over time.' He laughed again, looking at Chrissy. 'Mighty glad it wasn't a vegetarian franchise he was running, eh!'

Emily could see he was trying his best to put on a brave face in front of his son's friends. She also realised that Angus must have told him about her family. Thank God nothing had come out in the papers, otherwise it would have been embarrassing, or worse still, everyone would have hedged around it.

She smiled. 'It's fun to think I've been on the property that supplies the meat to *Erskine's,* even though the family no longer owns the restaurants.'

'Not any more we don't. Sadly, after many years of supplying them they stopped taking it a while back.'

'Oh!'

'Business decision they said. But not to worry ... *Grazings* Restaurant in Gundaroo reckons it's the best. And so they should. We give it to them at a damn good price. As we do with *Crowe's* down the road from there. Mind you, that lot aren't so much into the grain fed beef as they are into a whopping hamburger and chips. So, tell me who owns *Erskine's* now? I believe it went out of the family not long after your grandfather died.'

'A friend of my father's. Dimitri Carpani. My grandfather worked for his father, Cesare, back in the fifties.'

'Yes, of course, I remember now … Dimitri Carpani. It was him who stopped taking our beef. I recall reading that his father was murdered way back. A robbery, I believe.'

'So I was told by my father, who was only a teenager when it happened. He and Dimitri have been friends since about that time.'

'Is that so?' Bill then turned to Chrissy. 'Now, young lady let's go get that drink ... and,' he chuckled, 'explain to me this "no meat" policy of yours and how you think it's going to save the animal kingdom.'

As Emily watched him steer Chrissy to the door, she thought she was going to like Bill McBride. Just as much as she liked his wife, Betty.

Later, watching Angus chatting with his parents as they sat in the garden with the last of the fading light disappearing behind the far tree-covered hills, and with the smell of newly mown grass, eucalyptus and wattle permeating the crisp evening air, she threw Chrissy a happy smile. She hadn't realised until this weekend how much she missed the country. If her grandfather were still alive she would have *Riverside* as her getaway. But, then again, if he were alive he might be facing prosecution. At least death might have saved him from that. Although it may not save the Erskine name, she thought with a pang.

During dinner, as Bill poured her a delicious glass of Cabernet Sauvignon from a local winery, *Tallangria Hill*, he told her how he still liked to ride around the paddocks, rather than checking his stock on a motorbike like a lot of farmers do these days.

'The day I can't ride a horse, is the day I'll be pushing up daisies in my grave,' he said with a chuckle, giving her a wink across the table. 'You ever ridden?'

'Many years ago. My grandfather had a place up the Hunter Valley. He bought me a pony. I used to go up there a lot, and I even rode in some of the local gymkhanas. I loved it, but when he died, Nonna sold *Riverside*, which was what the property was called. I kept my pony down in Sydney for a while at the riding school in Centennial Park. When I got too big for him, I sold him to the school. I've never got another, which I regret.'

'I believe your grandfather was into mining up the Hunter as well.'

Emily's heart missed a beat. 'Yes, that's right.'

'I always thought it was incongruous that he had that mine, when he was such a big player in the wine industry,' Bill said.

'I know. But *Riverside* was quite far away from where Glasgow Mine was. However, that's what some people complained about. Not having the mine in his own backyard.'

And they'll complain much more it they hear how he got hold of the lease.

'The mines are spreading more and more these days,' Bill said. 'I wonder how long it'll be before the vineyards have to close down?' He picked up his glass of red wine and took a sip. 'I'm mighty glad that the Premier's decided to do something about that bloke Turner getting his licence through the back door.'

Emily took an inward breath. 'My main memories of the Hunter,' she said, hoping to change the subject from mining, 'are riding through my grandfather's vineyard down to the river, where I'd tie my pony up and swim. My brother Allen and I had made ourselves a sort of swing down there tied to a gum tree. We loved to swing out into the river and flop in.'

Angus laughed. 'Duncan and I built one down on our river. Bloody good fun.'

With the mention of Duncan's name there was a silence before Bill stood up and went over to the fire where he added another log, giving it a poke before turning around and looking at Emily.

'Well, we'll have to get you on a horse tomorrow, young lady. See if you've still got what it takes.'

'I'd like that very much,' she said with a grateful smile.

Sitting there with Chrissy, chatting to the McBrides, she was so glad she'd decided to come down to *Kilmarnock* for the weekend.

Chapter Ten

When Emily woke up the next morning, the sky was overcast and she thought it was about to rain. Although she would be disappointed for the picnic races, she was pleased for the McBride family to get some water on their drought-ridden property.

She got out of bed, grabbed her cotton dressing gown and crept to the door so as not to wake Chrissy. She needed to pee and was grateful Betty had showed them the bathroom before they went to bed. Even though it was seven-thirty, the rest of the house seemed to be in silence, even Rex was nowhere to be seen. She wondered if Angus had got up earlier and gone for a walk and taken the dog. Or for a ride with his father.

Leaving the bathroom, she padded along to the kitchen. Betty had shown her where the teabags were in case she wanted to make a cup of tea. Deciding to make herself one, she picked up the electric kettle and felt that it was still warm. So someone was up, she noted. She boiled the kettle again, filled her cup and walked to the back door, which was ajar. That was when she saw Betty in the vegetable garden. She looked to be weeding.

'Good morning,' Emily called out. 'You must've got up early.'

Betty lifted her head and smiled. 'I don't sleep as much as I used to. The moment it's light I'm up and out here. It's the best part of the day.'

Emily glanced up at the sky. 'Could rain by the looks of it.'

'Much as I'd like it to rain, let's hope it holds off until after the races.'

'You still not coming?' Emily asked. 'Haven't changed your mind?'

'Bill's not keen. And I don't feel like going without him. It wouldn't be the same.'

'What if I convinced him to come?'

Betty stood up and knocked the mud off the trowel in her hand. 'I think that's unlikely, dear. Once Bill's made up his mind, he's loath to change it. He's been like that from the first moment I met him.'

Emily smiled. 'Where did you meet?'

'At the Sydney Royal. He won the show jumping.' She laughed. 'I was *Miss Royal Easter Showgirl* and had to present him with the prize.'

'Gosh, how extraordinary,' Emily said. 'But I can quite imagine you winning that.'

'It was a joke really. I got roped into it by a girlfriend. As you can see, it had its rewards. Otherwise, I'd never have met Bill. Or got to live in this lovely place. And,' she said with a small smile, 'had two such great sons.'

Emily nodded. 'Quite true.'

'Anyway,' Betty added, 'you can try to get Bill to go, but I doubt you'll have much success.'

'It'd do him good.'

'You'll have to wait until breakfast to broach it with him. He and Angus have gone for a ride to the far paddock, the one down near the river. There was a cow down there about to calve yesterday. They've gone to check on her.'

'I wondered if they'd headed out for a ride.'

'Bill thought of waking you. You could've ridden my mare, Jess. She's quite old now, but's still a good ride.'

'I'd love to ride her later if that's okay.'

Betty smiled and then gave her an appraising look. Emily noticed her warm, caring eyes. 'I'm sure you're a very successful, model,' she added, causing Emily to blush.

'Thank you, Betty. It's not forever. Still, it pays well and I'm saving up for my first house.'

Emily could see Betty eyeing her oddly. The same as everyone did when they heard Emily Erskine was saving to buy her own house. Surely, with all that Erskine money floating around Emily would have no need to save.

'I like to be independent,' Emily said, before Betty had a chance to comment.

'Well done for you,' Betty said.

'That's what Nonna says.'

'Tell me about your Nonna. Angus tells me she came out from Italy in the 1950s.'

'You'd love her, Betty. She's very down to earth. And she loves her garden too. It'd be great if you could meet her one day. She's eighty, but very spritely. Hardly had a sick day in her life. And she's great fun.'

'Well, I'd love to meet her.'

'I hope you can. Anyway, I'll leave you be and go take a shower.'

'You do that, dear. Then we can have breakfast.'

'That sounds lovely.'

Emily leant down and picked a small sprig of parsley which she put in her mouth. She could certainly tell that it was straight from the garden. She then went inside and back to the bedroom where she grabbed her towel and woke Chrissy up. In the bathroom she only ran a short shower, in case she used too much water. One thing she knew was that water was a scarce commodity on a farm.

I'd best warn Chrissy, she thought, or she's sure to take her usual ten minutes or so, washing her hair and scrubbing herself from top to bottom.

At eight-thirty they were sitting around the kitchen table having breakfast.

'Wow,' Chrissy said, seeing the colour of the eggs Betty served up, with bacon and tomatoes, missing Chrissy's plate with the bacon. 'You don't see eggs this colour in Sydney.'

'They're our own,' Betty said. 'The chook yard is down by the sheds.'

'You haven't changed your mind about the races?' Emily asked Bill, who, after tying their horses to the back fence, had come in earlier with Angus, with Rex bounding behind them. After removing their boots on the verandah, they had thrown their Akubras onto the stand by the back door, washed their hands under the tap in the kitchen sink and were sitting at the table.

'Nah,' Bill said. 'You young ones head on into Yass. I've had my fair share of race days. I'll get on with a bit of bookwork. Keeping the bloody taxman off our backs is a full time job.' He glanced at Betty. 'But you go love if you like. No need for you to stay and look after me.'

Betty shook her head. 'I've had my fair share of races as well. I'll look forward to hearing all about it when you come back.'

'You sure?' Angus asked, glancing from one to the other. 'There'll be lots of your friends there. Always is.'

Betty glanced at Bill and Emily could see a private look pass between the two. She wondered how long since they first met at the Easter Show. It must be over thirty years. Angus had told her he was twenty-eight and his brother had been eighteen months older.

'We can catch up with our friends at other times,' Bill said in such a way as to indicate the conversation with his son was closed. He looked at Chrissy. 'I believe you don't ride.'

'No. I should have learnt. I remember Mike telling me how he learnt to ride down here.'

'And he was a very good rider,' Betty said. 'Wasn't he, Angus?'

'Yeah. He caught on pretty quickly, that's for sure.' He laughed. 'But there wasn't much call for it over there in London.'

'Do you think he'll stay over there, Chrissy?' Betty asked.

'Who would know? I'm afraid we don't keep in touch as much as we should.' She looked at Angus. 'What you think, eh?'

'He's got a pretty good job there in finance, so reckon he'll stay a while.'

Betty smiled. 'Angus was enjoying it there too, weren't you. Until …'

'I'm happy to be back,' he jumped in quickly.

But, as he said that, Emily did wonder if he wouldn't have preferred to stay on in London for a while longer at least.

Bill turned to her. 'If you'd like a quick ride before you go dolly yourself up for the races, Angus and I have to head back down to the river with a pair of pliers. We saw a young ewe caught in the brambles down there. Need to get to her before the crows do. You could join us if you like. We can catch Jess in a moment. She's in the home paddock.'

Emily gave Chrissy a quick glance. 'You go, Em. I'll help Betty clean up. I need to iron my outfit anyway.'

'I'd love to have a ride with you,' Emily said to Bill. 'Just show me where Jess is and where I'll find her saddle and bridle.'

'When we've finished here I'll show you,' Angus said, taking a bite of the crispy bacon on his plate.' He checked his watch. 'I reckon we'll need to leave for Yass round twelve, so we've got plenty of time.'

'That'd be great.' Emily picked up her china teacup and sipped. 'It's such a beautiful tea set,' she said to Betty. 'It must be very old.'

'It is. Nevertheless, I like to use it all the time. It was Bill's mother's. She always kept it in the china cabinet. I could see no sense in that. And,' she said with a laugh, 'I hope whoever comes after me will use it as well.'

'It's so delicate,' Chrissy said, fondling the fine china. 'I get sick of drinking tea out of a mug.'

'Talking of tea, would anyone like another cup?' Betty asked, standing up and going to the kettle to fill the china teapot.

'Thanks, Mum,' Angus said, 'but if we're to be back here in time for Emily to get ready, perhaps we should get going.'

'True,' Emily said, taking her plate over to the sink. 'Thank you so much for breakfast, Betty. It was great.'

***

Fifteen minutes later, Emily was mounted on Jess, a fourteen hand bay, and riding towards the river with Bill, Angus, Rex and two working dogs, a Blue Heeler and a Kelpie. She was wearing a pair of Betty's leather boots and a wide-brimmed hat. She had forgotten how much she loved being on a horse. The movement of her body beneath the saddle. The whiff of Dubbin polish on the leather and the tangy smell of horse sweat mixed with the aroma of dust, grass and eucalyptus. She didn't even mind having to constantly swish the flies away. As she trotted between Bill and Angus, she felt more exhilaration than she had done in years. Much more so than when she saw a photo of herself gracing the cover of a magazine. Somehow this felt real. Watching Angus on his horse she thought how natural he looked, which was probably understandable, as he'd been riding since a kid. And the way Bill sat astride when they broke into an easy canter, she could easily imagine him as a show jumper.

'Betty told me you won the show jumping at the Sydney Royal Easter Show,' she called to him. 'That's how you met.'

'And a lifetime ago that was.'

After five minutes or so they pulled up as they came to a gate, which Angus opened from horseback. After they rode through Bill took off in a canter across the paddock and Angus and Emily followed. Jess was light in the mouth and had a comfortable gait. It wasn't long before they came to another gate, which Bill opened this time. Once through it was obvious they were close to the river, as the land started to drop away and there was a bank of weeping willows just ahead. It was then that Bill pulled his horse to a halt and dismounted. Angus followed suit.

'The ewe's just over there,' Bill said to Emily, pointing to a bush of brambles. 'You can go for a ride along the bank if you like while we disentangle the poor bugger.'

'You don't need any help?'

'Nah,' Bill said. 'There's a path leading down to the river further along. Jess will show you where it is. It's her favourite spot. Just be careful she doesn't do her party trick.'

'Oh! What's that?'

'Flopping down in the water, saddle and all. Make sure you hold the reins tightly. That'll stop her.'

Emily laughed. 'My pony at my grandfather's place in the Hunter tried to do that as well. He nearly drowned me once.'

'Well, you'll know how to stop her then.'

As Emily watched the two men step across to the bramble bush, she turned Jess's head into the sun and they trotted along the bank. It was the silence that she couldn't get over. After Sydney's traffic it was as if she was in a padded box with the gentle sound of birdsong and the hum of crickets being softly piped trough. It reminded her so much of *Riverside*, when she used to ride down to the river, often on her own, as her brothers weren't keen riders. Allen was always breaking his neck to be fishing and Jonathon usually lazed in bed reading or was on his computer. Her mother, Samantha, wasn't keen on the land and Emily's father and Grandpa seemed to clash so often that they didn't spend much time together. Yet, Emily had never been lonely. Again, despite her father's assurances, she thought of the scandal possibly waiting to break about her grandfather and found it difficult to know where to file those thoughts. If he was here now maybe she could look into his eyes and discover what was going on behind them. It was at *Riverside* where she got to know him best. When in Sydney he was often busy and she rarely remembered him being at *Mandalay*. Searching her mind as if she was groping for a particular coin in the money tin he had given her for her tenth birthday, she couldn't really put a finger on anything that might have alerted her to the fact that he was a man who carried out shady deals. But back then she wasn't looking, was she? If he was here now and she knew what she did it would be so different. Surely, she would be able to make up her own mind as to whether he was an honourable or dishonourable man.

Flicking the flies away from her face, she told herself to fill her mind with the present. Not the past. Or the future for that matter. Right now, she was doing what she loved to do. Riding a horse in the countryside. She patted Jess on the neck. 'I could get used to this,' she whispered, leaning forward and fondling her ear.

Clambering down the bank to the river, Jess was startled by a rabbit scuttling out of the bushes and shied. 'Steady, old girl,' Emily soothed her, balancing herself in the saddle and patting her on the neck. 'It's just a silly rabbit.'

When they got to the water's edge she let Jess's reins loose so that she could put her head down and drink.

'But we won't risk going in for a swim,' she chuckled to her.

Across on the other bank a herd of cows had wandered down for a morning drink. Lifting their heads in curiosity they gazed across the river. Amongst the cows, egrets pecked in the dirt. And above their heads a couple of red and pink rosellas were sitting in the branches of a gum tree overhanging the water. Emily nearly jumped out of her skin, as just above her head a kookaburra started to cackle so loudly that it sounded like it had a loudspeaker attached to its beak. Jess didn't move an inch, as she slurped at the water.

She's obviously used to the sounds of the bush, Emily thought, even if she is frightened of rabbits darting out between her legs.

'How's it going down there?' she heard a shout from the bank above. 'We've released the ewe and are ready to head back.'

She looked up at the two men. 'It's just glorious. I never want to leave.' But as Jess started to pound the water with her hoof, she laughed. 'However, if I don't want to get dunked, perhaps I'd best.'

She then tightened Jess's reins and turned her head towards the bank. After clambering up again she smiled at Bill. 'Coming down here on a motorbike wouldn't be the same.'

'Nah,' he said. 'Mind you, Duncan had one. Drove me bonkers it did. All that noise disturbing the peace.'

'I'd love to see a photograph of him,' Emily said to them both. She had been surprised there were no photos of him back in the homestead, at least, none that she had seen.

"I'm afraid I made Betty put them away,' Bill said. 'Looking at them made me too bloody maudlin.' There was a long pause as a flock of noisy galahs flew overhead. 'If you'd like to take a look, I'll show you. There's plenty stacked away in drawers and in albums.'

Emily saw Angus smile at her gratefully. When she first met him at the Coogee Bay Hotel she wouldn't have imagined him as he was here at *Kilmarnock*. Somehow, this setting suited him so much better. It was the ease with which he sat in the saddle, managed the dogs, and his obvious affinity to the country and stock. She also saw how caring he was with his parents, who were in such pain. As Angus must be as well, particularly coming back here to where he had spent his childhood with his brother.

***

At twelve, they were dressed and ready to go to the picnic races. Emily had initially decided on an outfit from a small boutique in Paddington to wear. Then when she modelled one of the outfits at Myers, an orange pleated skirt with a blue, white and orange top, she had changed her mind and bought that. Chrissy looked gorgeous in a black and white dress, which she had found online.

When it arrived and fitted her like a glove she had been so excited. She found a wonderful black hat with multicoloured feathers at the Paddington markets to go with it. Emily had decided to go hatless with her hair lose around her shoulders.

'You both look lovely,' Betty said. 'You're a lucky man, Angus.'

He grinned. 'There's no doubt about that.'

When Betty saw them off out front of the house, Emily felt sad. If Duncan hadn't died maybe she and Bill would be joining them. Then again, if he hadn't died, maybe Emily and Chrissy wouldn't be here in the first place.

Driving through Gundaroo, Angus told them that the aboriginal name for Gundaroo was *Candariro*.

'Supposedly means blue crane. Governor Macquarie bequeathed a fellow called Peter Cooney the land in 1825.'

'Wow,' Chrissy said. 'Lucky bloke.'

'The first non-residential property was called the Harrow Inn.' Angus then pointed out the Colonial Inn, otherwise known as *Matt Crowe's Wine Bar*, where people were drinking and dining on the verandah.

'I've downed a few there with the old man and Duncan,' Angus said. 'During the Gold Rush it was known as *The Commercial Hotel*. I reckon a few nugget finds were celebrated there.'

'Or the sorrows of those who failed to pan a damn thing were drowned,' Chrissy said with a laugh.

'True.' Further on past the lovely stone church he pointed to *Grazing's* restaurant. 'It's got a great reputation,' he said of the restored 1865 Royal Hotel with a red corrugated iron roof. 'They grow most of their own veggies out the back. Lots of people come from Canberra to dine there.'

When they got to the racetrack in Yass the place was packed. Lining the track were dozens of cars and farm utes with their backs to the railing. On the rear tray of each ute people perched sipping glasses of champagne. Angus drove around for a while before he found a spot and then he backed in and lowered the tailgate. When they got settled, he took out an esky with a few bottles of champagne. Filling three glasses, he handed one each to Chrissy and Emily.

'Cheers,' they all said at once, clicking glasses.

'Let's have this, then go place some bets,' Angus said. 'Then we can attack Mum's picnic.'

Betty had insisted on packing a cold chicken, salad and some bread rolls in a picnic basket, which was on the back seat.

'Sounds great,' Chrissy said.

Looking around, Emily thought everyone had made a huge effort with their outfits. A lot of the women wore hats or fascinators. Many of the men were in suits, although like Angus there were a number in moleskins and jackets. A group to their left had obviously decided it was a great idea to make it into a fancy dress party. There were all sorts of hilarious get ups; one girl as a cowgirl and a fellow as a cowboy, and two girls were wearing bunny outfits. Most seemed well and truly on their way to having a good time, swigging champagne from the bottle. But in total contrast to that lot there was a group of older people dressed sedately, adorned with Panama hats and pearls, and sitting in a circle on deck chairs with a table set up with a white tablecloth in their midst. And over at the members stand it was packed. Everyone seemed to be out to have a good time. Although Emily was sure the farmers here would have gladly welcomed rain, it had held off and the sun was trying to poke through the clouds.

'Come,' Angus said, putting his glass down on the Jeep's tray. 'Let's go place our bets.'

Around where the bookies were loudly working the crowd, it was absolute mayhem as bets were laid. Looking at the bookie's board, Emily had no idea which horse to bet on so went by how she liked their name. When she had placed three ten dollar bets, she stopped, but Chrissy was determined to have a wager on every single race and outlaid seventy dollars with Angus's help.

'Not that I know much about any of the horses, but Dad gave me a few tips as he follows the races,' he said.

With their betting slips in hand, they walked over to look at the group of horses getting ready for the first race. Although it was a country meet there were some fine looking thoroughbreds. Emily wondered what they thought of it all. Were they caught up in the excitement, or were they dreading the race ahead? A number of them were certainly prancing around as though they were enjoying being the floor show. And the jockeys in their colourful silks all looked so serious. But, then again, to them it was serious business. Their livelihood depended on riding winners. Many a jockey started their careers at country meets like this. Many horses too. Perhaps one of these might end up as a winner of the Melbourne Cup.

As they wound their way through the crowd back towards the Jeep, Angus was stopped numerous times by people he knew. Quite a few came over to chat as the afternoon went on. Emily thought what an easy-going lot of friends he had. She also couldn't help noticing that some of the women were giving him a lot of attention.

'Gees,' Chrissy said, as she watched one particularly pretty one, wearing a tiny miniskirt, monopolising him as they leant over the railings watching the action, 'if she leans in much closer she'll push him right over. Heaps of these local women seem to fancy him.'

'Well, he *was* brought up around here.'

'And he has that great property coming his way one day.'

'I don't think it's just that. He's a nice guy.'

'Yeah, you're right … he *is* a nice guy. So …?'

'Chrissy!'

'Sorry!'

After Chrissy went over to the member's stand to go to the loo, one of the horse trainers who Angus knew through his parents came over to say hello. When Angus introduced Emily to him he grinned.

'Ah. I've met your father. He and his friend, Dimitri Carpani, the fellow who took over your grandfather's *Erskine* franchise was with him. They're looking to buy a racehorse together. Came and had a look at a mare in my stables at Randwick.' He grinned. 'Like two peas in a pod they were. Must say, you don't look a thing like your father.'

'I take more after my mother. She's American. I haven't met Dimitri Carpani, but he's probably very Italian looking like my Dad who resembles his Italian mother, rather than my Scottish grandfather.'

'Ah! Well, I'm very pleased to meet you,' he said. 'Say hello to your father.'

He then left them to join a group nearby. And, after the last race had run, Chrissy, Emily and Angus had about as much money as they started with. But Emily didn't think Chrissy's voice would ever be the same with all her screaming, trying to get her horses over the line first. Emily felt quite hoarse herself. As they got into the Jeep to drive home, she thought what a great afternoon it had been. She looked forward to telling Nonna about it.

On the way back to *Kilmarnock* they stopped at *Crowe's Wine Bar* in Gundaroo for a hamburger with a group of Angus's friends.

As they sat out on the verandah in the fading light, Angus smiled at the girls. 'If you'd like to come down again, I'll take you to *Grazing's* for a fancy meal, rather than just a hamburger.'

Emily thought how much she liked that idea, as the sun started to set. Not only had it been a great weekend, she also really liked Angus McBride and his parents. She bit into her delicious hamburger, which was no doubt made from *Kilmarnock* beef, and she thought she might tell her father about *Erskine's* not taking the McBride's produce any more. He could ask his friend, Dimitri Carpani about that.

Chapter Eleven

'I'm not happy with your blood count,' Dr Wallace said to Angela, looking at a piece of paper on his desk. 'And, these x-rays show a shadow on your hip.' He put the x-ray down and looked at Angela. 'I think we might need to explore a little more, so I've asked St Vincent's Hospital to book you in for more tests. We can get it sorted out then.'

'Do you think it could be serious?' she asked, feeling an anxious lump in her throat.

'It's difficult to say at this stage.' He fiddled with a pen on his desk. 'Best to be sure.'

'Yes, of course,' Angela said. 'I quite understand.'

'As soon as I get a day and time at St Vincent's I'll let you know,' he said.

'Thank you. That would be good.'

She then got up and smiled at him before moving towards the door.

'Would you like me to ring Gavin?' he asked. 'Or Emily?'

'I'll ring Gavin,' she lied, 'so don't worry.'

She then bade him farewell, paid the receptionist and made her way out into the sunshine in Hyde Park. Finding a bench under a tall fig tree, she sat down. Despite blinking hard, tears watered her eyes. She wiped them away with force. Although she knew there were more tests to be had, in her own mind she suspected she was ill. How else to explain why she had been feeling tired and her hip hurt so much? She tried to console herself with the thought that no matter what the tests showed up it was unlikely she was going to die straight away. She could just as easily be hit by a car or drop dead from a heart attack. After sitting for some time, watching the people coming and going and shuffling the fallen autumn leaves in a million different directions, she decided she might as well try to cheer herself up with a treat. Rather than go straight home to an empty house, she would take herself to lunch. She always liked the David Jones food bar and at this time of day she was likely to get a seat. As she had done on a number of previous occasions, she would order a dozen oysters and a glass of wine. With any luck they would be those delicious Tasmanian oysters she loved so much.

***

'I'm so glad I went,' Emily said when she came around later to tell Angela about *Kilmarnock.*

'It was good fun, then?'

'It was wonderful, Nonna. You should've seen *Kilmarnock.* You'd have loved it. Angus's mother's garden is just glorious. Every imaginable flower and shrub. And her vegetable garden is to die for. I think they only use what veggies she grows in her garden for cooking and they kill their own meat and have chickens.' She handed her half a dozen eggs Betty had insisted she take home. 'They used to supply their meat to *Erskine's* but now that Dad's friend, Dimitri Carpani owns the franchise they don't take it anymore.'

'Oh,' Angela said. She tried to hide her annoyance at the mention of the Carpani name. 'I daresay Dimitri had to make many business decisions like that when he took over.'

'Yeah, probably you're right. Anyway, Betty and Angus's father are lovely,' Emily said, 'but they are still hurting heaps over Duncan's death.'

'Such a sorrow for them. They'll find it hard to get over it.' Angela sighed, thinking of Maria who was younger than Duncan when she died. 'But the place sounds wonderful, darling. And the races? How were they?'

'They were great.'

'And Chrissy? Did she enjoy it?'

'Yes, she did. At the races she bet on everything in sight. The McBrides are obviously very fond of Mike, so they were thrilled to meet her.' She stopped and looked at Angela worriedly. 'Are you okay, Nonna? You look pale.'

'Darling, I'm fine. Just a bit tired, that's all.' She gave a small cough. 'But I do need to go into hospital for a few tests. I'm sure it's nothing important. At my age all sorts of things show up on scans and blood tests.'

Emily stared at her in horror. 'You've had scans and blood tests? And you didn't tell me?'

'Darling, you're busy. And you were going away. I didn't think it was necessary.'

'Nonna, anything to do with you is necessary as far as I'm concerned. Tell me what's going on.'

When Angela told her what Dr Wallace had said, Emily stood up from where they were sitting in the lounge room and went over to the window.

On turning around, it was obvious she had wiped tears from her eyes. 'When are you going into hospital?'

'Next week. St Vincents. I believe it's very good there.'

Emily nodded. 'It's supposed to be the best.' She gave her a small smile. 'So, what day are you going in?'

'Monday.'

'I'll come and pick you up and take you in.'

Angela smiled gratefully. 'That would be lovely, darling. As you know your father's in Auckland on business. Now, let's forget about my tests … come sit back down and tell me more about your visit to *Kilmarnock.*'

Before sitting down, Emily leant over and kissed her on the cheek. 'If something should happen to you I don't know what I'd do.'

'Nothing will happen to me, darling. I'm a tough old bird.' She smiled and changed the subject. 'Now, I was going to cook a veal casserole with some wonderful fresh mushrooms, onions and tomatoes I picked up from the veggie stand on the way home.'

'The yummy recipe with sage and cream in it?'

'Yes. Would you like to stay and have some with me?'

'Yes, please. I always love that dish.'

'On Procida, Aunt Sophia used the wild mushrooms from a field on the way to the beach. Maria and I used to scavenge them for her. I think it was one of Maria's favourite dishes. I still remember the night when Stewart commandeered the kitchen at Villawood, she gave him the recipe then.'

'You must miss her so much.'

Angela smiled. 'Yes, I do.'

'I wish I'd known her.' Emily walked over to a photo of Maria on the small coffee table in the corner. 'She really was beautiful, wasn't she?'

'Yes, there's no doubt about that.'

'And you said she made most of her own clothes.'

'And mine too.'

Emily ran her finger over the photo. 'This dress looks gorgeous.'

'Actually, that's one of the few she didn't make herself. She saw it in a shopfront in Naples and saved up to buy it. You can't see in that black and white photo, but it was yellow and white.'

'Did she always wear her dresses showing her figure off like that?'

Angela sighed. 'Yes, she mostly did, no matter how much I tried to tell her to be less "out there".'

Emily smiled. 'I bet the men loved it.'

Angela paused. 'Yes, they did.'

'Well, just as well Grandpa snapped her up when he did.' She smiled. 'They were very much in love, weren't' they?'

Angela nodded. 'They were indeed.'

'It was so sad what happened.'

'Yes, it was.' She placed a hand on Emily's knee. 'She would have loved to meet you, darling,' she said, as the photo was placed back down. 'But let's not be maudlin, come help me in the kitchen.'

After dinner, Emily sat with her for a while watching television. But when they both started to tire of the programme, and Angela could feel her eyelids becoming heavy, she suggested Emily should go home and she would go to bed.

'Would you like me to stay the night?'

'Darling, I'll be fine. You head off and I'll see you on Monday morning.'

'Well … if you're sure.'

'Yes, I am. I'll be sound asleep before you even reach home.'

Before Angela turned off the light after slipping between the cool sheets, she opened the drawer by her bed and took out a bottle. It was last year when she had told Doctor Wallace she was going through a period of not sleeping and he had offered the prescription to her. As he had done the year before. And the year before that. Under her bed was a small suitcase where she had stored a cache of unused pills. Although she had willingly taken the prescription from the doctor, gone to the chemist and had the prescription filled, she had rarely used them. In her mind, she had thought that one day they may be useful if she decided she might like to end it all because of old age and pain. She wondered if that time was coming sooner than she thought.

But rather than take a pill, she returned the bottle to the drawer and turned off the light.

***

Emily was desperately worried about Nonna, trying to disguise her fear when she drove her into St Vincents. She looked very fragile when she walked away with the nurse who took her for tests. When Emily asked if she could stay, the nurse said the tests would take most of the day, so she was best to go and they would ring her when Nonna was ready to be picked up.

Earlier, before they left Nonna's house, Emily asked her if there was anything she wanted her to do while she was in hospital.

'As a matter of fact, there is something I'd be grateful if you could do, darling.' Nonna went to the coffee table in the centre of the room and picked up a book. 'I promised my friend, Elena, who I sometimes meet down on the beach, that I'd give her back this book she lent me. I keep forgetting to give it to her and last time I saw her she said it was overdue at the library. I'd hate for her to get fined. I've got her address here. She lives just behind the cafes down by the beach.'

'Of course I'll do that,' Emily said. 'I've heard you talk about Elena. She sounds nice.'

'Don't tell her about me going to hospital. Maybe just say I've gone away for a few days and asked you to do this for me. If you say I'm in hospital next thing she'll be in and fussing around like only Italians can fuss.'

Back in her car, Emily took out the book and address from her handbag.

She navigated Sydney traffic and was soon outside a small iron gate opening to a neat garden where an astonishing array of stone gnomes of all shapes and sizes and outfitted in dazzling costumes perched among the garden beds or peeped from under leaves. There were elves, sprites, goblins, trolls, leprechauns, fairies, brownies, pixies and fays, all looking as proud as punch to be the keepers of such a garden. Near the front door on the verandah, where wooden shutters painted a Mediterranean blue contrasted with the white walls of the modest bungalow, smugly stood the largest and proudest of all the gnomes, a bearded elf holding a sign that read *benvenuto*, which Emily knew in Italian meant *welcome*. The verandah was a riot of red geraniums and roses in pots, and at the side of the house there was a vegetable patch where every conceivable variety of vegetable was growing. In its midst, an elderly man wearing a red shirt and looking much like a garden gnome himself, was squatting down to weed between rows of carrots and beans.

Opening the gate, Emily called out. 'Hi, there.'

He lifted his head. And, as he did, his face broke into a broad smile.

'I'm after Elena,' Emily told him. 'My Nonna borrowed a book and she wanted me to return it.'

The man straightened up. Even though he was quite elderly, he was tall and stood straight, and his face, deeply lined as it was, was strongly boned. She could imagine that once he was very good-looking. His crinkled dark brown eyes shone behind thick eyelashes, and although his hair was grey it was still quite dense.

'Elena is not here,' he said in a thick accent. 'She has gone to do some shopping. I am her cousin from Naples. I arrive here one week ago.' He laughed. 'Her garden, it is overrun like a jungle. I fix it for her.'

'Oh,' Emily said, holding up the book. 'I'll just leave this here on the verandah. Perhaps you could give it to Elena when she comes back. Can you tell her that Angeline's granddaughter dropped if off.'

She knew that Nonna's beach friends called her Angeline, which Emily thought was cute.

'I will tell her,' the man said, walking towards her. 'She will be back before too long.'

'How do you like Australia?' Emily asked.

'It is good,' the man said. 'I was here many years ago. I have always wanted to come back. It has changed a great deal.'

'How long ago were you here?'

He smiled broadly. And as he did his whole face creased, resembling one of the Flake chocolates Emily loved so much. 'Many, many years before you were born.' Wiping his head with a handkerchief he stepped over to where Emily stood. 'Many, many years.'

Emily grinned. 'It's changed a heap since I was born. So I'd imagine it's like a different planet since you were here. How long are you staying?'

He ran a bony hand through his hair. 'I am here one month.' He grinned mischievously. 'That is if Elena will have me stay that long.'

Emily remembered Nonna saying that Elena's husband had died many years before and she lived on her own. 'I'm sure she'd be glad of the company. Particularly if you're turning her vegetable patch into a market garden like you seem to be doing. Anyway,' she added, glancing back towards her car. 'I'd best be off. But it's been great meeting you. Enjoy the rest of your stay.'

He looked up to the sky. 'With sunshine like this, how could I not enjoy?'

'That's very true.'

She then left him and went back to her car. She looked forward to telling Nonna how she had met Elena's cousin. Hopefully that might cheer her up. She had a thought. When she brought Nonna home from hospital, she might ask Elena to come around for a glass of wine and bring her cousin. The cousin could tell Nonna about the Naples of today. Perhaps he might even know the island of Procida. He could even have been there.

She had freed up the day with Liz Falcon at the agency in order to be with Nonna, but seeing as she had been told to leave her on her own at the hospital, she now had time to kill. Normally, she would relish this time to do her own thing, but with the worry of Nonna utmost on her mind it no longer looked that attractive. She would have preferred to have a modelling assignment to keep her busy and take her mind off things. She thought of ringing Chrissy to see if she was free for a coffee, but then she remembered that she was having a day in a legal office as work experience. And her other girlfriends would all be at work as well. In the end, she decided to go for a bike ride around Centennial Park. She took her phone in case the hospital rang.

After doing two circuits she bought herself a sandwich at the kiosk for a late lunch. She ate it sitting on the bank by the lake where she watched the ducks and geese in the water, which she always loved to do. Now she lay back on the grass, relishing the warm sun on her bare legs. She tried to imagine Naples, where

Elena's cousin came from. What it would have been like when Nonna and Maria lived there before their parents had been tragically killed in a car accident? And with that sadness clouding her mind she thought of Mathew. Hard as she tried to dispel it, barrels of hurt and fury burnt inside her like a raging volcano. At times it threatened to erupt and she required all of her self-control to stop picking up the phone and abusing him. She wondered, what if Chrissy hadn't seen him that day? Would he have gone on as though nothing had happened? After all, he did say he only loved Emily. But hard as she tried to believe him, it didn't ring true. She sat up, picked up her phone and looked at the last three text messages from him asking her to ring. For a second she thought of doing so. Despite what he had done to her she still missed him. With the phone in her hand, she watched two black swans glide under the bridge from the pond next door. They looked so graceful and contented. She knew they mated for life, which made her sad for her own predicament. She put the phone back down firmly on the ground.

Rather than dwell on what might have been with Mathew, she made herself think of her weekend at *Kilmarnock*. She liked Angus and his parents and going horse riding was great fun. This made her think of *Riverside* and her grandfather. She wished he were here to give Nonna support if it proved she was ill. But, then again, would he have been any support? Emily had noticed that he and Nonna were fairly distant with each other. She lay back down on the grass and must have nodded off, as when her phone rang she had trouble remembering where she was.

Sitting up, she checked the number, but it wasn't one she knew. 'Hello,' she said.

'Emily Erskine?'

'Yes, that's me.'

'This is Dr Wallace. Your grandmother's doctor. I wonder if you could come into the hospital at four this afternoon, to be there when the specialist speaks to her.'

'The specialist?' Her heart gave an anxious extra beat. 'So it's serious then?'

There was a long pause. 'The specialist will talk to you when you come in. But yes, it is serious. Particularly at her age.'

She swallowed hard. 'Are you saying it's cancer? Or something like that?'

There was another pause, longer this time. 'I'm afraid it looks like it might be ... but as I said, we'll talk to the specialist when you come in.'

'Yes ... yes, of course,' she said, tears threatening to trickle down her cheeks.

When she hung up, she looked out over the water to where the swans were gliding back under the bridge to the pond they had come from. A wave of fear ran through her, causing her to shiver. She should have guessed Nonna was ill, as she had been looking worn-out lately. She glanced at her watch. It was two-thirty. By the time she rode home and had a shower she would be cutting it fine to get to the hospital by four.

Back at the flat, the tears that had threatened to spill since Dr Wallace's phone call flowed down her cheeks and she wept as she had never wept before. She hadn't even been this distraught when her grandfather had died. Not even when she realised her mother was not coming back from America. Not even when she found out what Mathew had done.

It was close to five minutes before she could make an effort to pull herself together. Crying like this wasn't going to do anyone any good. Not Emily. Or Nonna.

She wiped her eyes and went to the bathroom to have a shower. Under the scalding water, she made a decision. There was a friend of Chrissy's called Libby at uni who had been desperate to find accommodation. The flat she was renting was going on the market and the owners wanted her out. Only yesterday, Chrissy asked if Libby could sleep on the couch in the living room until she found somewhere else to rent. She could have Emily's room while she moved in with Nonna to look after her. Suddenly, she felt a dreadful sadness for Nonna. And, selfish as it was, she feared for herself. Despite Nonna being quite old, Emily always imagined her being a part of her life.

And the rest of the family's.

Chapter Twelve

Angela lay on the hospital bed, staring up at the ceiling. It had been a busy morning. First, she had been wheeled in for a cat scan and, after that an x-ray, and then what seemed like a multitude of tests. As yet, no one had come back to let her know what the results had been. She gazed around the sparse room, clinically clean, clinically lacking in any feeling whatsoever. Last time she had been in a hospital was when she discovered that she was unable to have children of her own. For many years, when they were first married, she and Stewart had tried, but to no avail. Eventually, she did fall pregnant, but sadly lost the baby very early on in her pregnancy. After that she never fell pregnant again. There were many times when Angela had wondered how things would have been if she and Stewart had had a child. Although Angela had brought Gavin up, he never really felt like her own.

Now the door opened and Emily came in. Angela was surprised to see her, for as far as she knew the nurse hadn't rung to tell her to come and get her.

'Hi, Nonna,' Emily said, leaning down to give her a kiss. 'I wasn't busy, so I decided to come in and see how you're getting on.'

'Oh darling, you shouldn't have bothered,' Angela said, focusing on her lovely face. 'I haven't heard from any of the doctors as to how the tests went.' She looked at her watch.

'Goodness me … how time has flown. You'd think someone would have been in by now.'

'I bumped into Dr Wallace in the corridor.' Emily smiled at her. 'He said he's coming in shortly with the specialist who did your tests this morning. They've got the results back.'

'Oh. That's good,' Angela said, lifting herself up on the pillows. 'I'll be able to get out of here sooner than I thought.'

'Let's wait and see what the specialist tells us.'

Angela held her eyes. 'Emily Erskine, I know you well enough to suspect there's something wrong. What is it, darling?'

'Nothing. Nothing at all. In fact, I was just going to tell you that I went by Elena's house and dropped off her book. Her cousin from Naples was there. He seemed really nice. He was working in her veggie patch. He said he'd been in Australia many years ago.' She paused, smoothing a crease in the bed sheet. 'I had a thought that when you come home we might ask Elena and him around for a drink, coffee or something. Maybe he could tell you about Naples. What it's like now.'

'*We* could invite …?'

At that moment, Dr Wallace and the specialist arrived. Although Dr Wallace was wearing a dark suit and tie the specialist was in what looked to Angela like painter's white overalls and he had his hair curtailed under a red and white bandana. He didn't look much older than Emily.

'What a pleasure to meet you, Mrs Erskine,' he said, moving forward. 'I'm a great fan of *Erskine's* restaurants. I know the family's no longer involved in the running of them; however, I read how your husband started the chain back in the 1950s. What a legacy he left behind.'

Angela smiled. 'Yes, he did, didn't he? Now, young man, what have you got to tell me?' She looked at Dr Wallace. 'Such an entourage must mean serious business.'

The specialist glanced at Emily. 'You must be Mrs Erskine's granddaughter. Dr Wallace told me you were here.'

Emily nodded. 'I brought Nonna in early this morning.'

The specialist paused, looking to Angela as though he was searching for words. 'I'm afraid a few things showed up in your scan and blood tests, Mrs Erskine,' he eventually said. 'Of most concern is the tumour on your left hip bone, the one that's being giving you trouble.'

Angela felt her heart lurch. 'A tumour?'

'Yes.' He paused. 'Normally when that happens, it means you've a primary tumour somewhere else. We took the liberty of doing more tests when you were in the theatre.' He looked at Emily and back to Angela. 'Unfortunately, it appears the primary tumour has metastasised and spread.'

'The lump on my breast?'

Emily looked aghast. 'I didn't know you had a lump on your breast, Nonna!'

'Nor did I until this morning when I was getting dressed and noticed a dimple on my left breast. When I felt it I could feel a lump nearby. I hadn't noticed it before.' She smiled at the specialist. 'At my age, one doesn't spend a lot of time admiring ones breasts in the mirror.'

Angela could see the colour rising in Dr Wallace's face. 'It was remiss of me. I should have suggested you have a mammogram a few years ago.'

'And if you had suggested it, I would've refused,' Angela said, 'so no need to go berating yourself. I thought if I'd reached the age I had I was more likely to die *with* breast cancer, rather than die *of* it.' She took a deep breath and Emily stepped forward to hold her hand. After a lengthy pause Angela gave a nervous cough, but then she decided there was no point in beating around the bush. 'How long are you giving me?' she asked the specialist.

He shook his head. 'It's hard to say. There are many options you can consider for treatment, but what I would suggest at this stage is chemotherapy and radiology. We can make some appointments for you to come back in next week to start. In the meantime, I'll get the radiologist to come and see you in the morning to go through the programme. After that, you can go home.'

Emily took hold of her hand. 'I'll move in with you and look after you, Nonna, while you have the treatment.'

'And what about your overseas trip? The one to India.'

'It's not for a while yet. And I'd gone off the idea quite a bit,' she said, unconvincingly. 'I was thinking of putting it off.'

'Darling,' Angela said. 'You're not a nurse. You're a model.' She glanced at the specialist. 'And a very good one, I might add.'

The specialist smiled. 'I'm sure she is. In any case, there's a lot of home care options these days, so being a nurse is neither here nor there.'

Emily smiled. 'See, Nonna? We'll cope just fine.'

'I can make a few phone calls and get the right people to contact you,' the specialist said.

'Thank you,' Angela said, giving in. 'That would be very good of you. Now,' she added, feeling very tired and knowing she was close to tears, 'leave me be.' She looked at both doctors. 'No doubt you have other patients much sicker than I am. Younger too, who need your care. Emily, you be off too.'

'Can't I stay for a while?'

'No, darling. All of a sudden I feel very tired. A sleep will do me good.'

After they had all gone, Angela turned over with her face to the wall. When she'd discovered the lump on her breast, she had almost decided herself it was cancer. So although she'd got a horrible shock when she was told the news, it wasn't as much a shock as Emily had thought. What had surprised her most was how quickly the doctors had come to their decision. In the olden days she would have waited weeks for such a diagnosis.

She wasn't sure which was worse.

Knowing straight away, or holding onto the hope that there might be nothing wrong. Tears trickled down her cheeks onto the pillowcase. She was glad Emily had left and couldn't see her crying.

After a moment, she pulled herself together and wiped her eyes with her sleeve. On the whole, she had had a good life. It wasn't as though she was young like Maria was when her life was taken so suddenly. Angela was an old woman. She was very sad it had come to this, but laying there feeling sorry for herself was a luxury she wouldn't allow herself. Whatever lay ahead she would manage to cope with. One way or another.

****

At three the next afternoon, Emily picked Angela up from the hospital. After dropping her home, she told Angela she would pop up to the chemist to have the prescription for the strong painkiller prescribed by the specialist filled. While she was out, Angela went to her bedroom and took off her earrings, which were hurting her lobes. As she put them in the drawer of her dressing table she noticed the jewellery case Aunt Sophia had given her. She opened it and for a moment fondled the colourful gemstone in the corner. Putting it gently back inside, she pulled out Maria's gold lira pendant. Holding it in her hand, she could almost see Maria laughing down from up above.

'And about time too that you came and joined us up here. Mamma, Papa, Aunt Sophia, Stewart and I've been waiting so long. Now you're on your way. When you come you can leave Aunt Sophia's gold lira pendant with Emily to keep her close to all of us.'

She sat down on the bed, all the time fondling the pendant. Up until now she had never worn it. She was too terrified she might lose it or forget to take it off when she was swimming at the beach. But now that she knew she was likely to join her sister, she decided to slip the pendant around her neck. She would leave it there until she died and it became Emily's. And as she fondled the crown on the delicate gold lira with her finger she made a decision. She wouldn't have any treatment. If she were much younger she wouldn't hesitate to have chemo, radiation and such, but she could see no point. All it might do was prolong her life a few more months at the very most. She wanted to make the most of the time she had left, not be so ill from the treatment that she couldn't function. She would let the cancer run its course. Let it have her, until she could bear it no more. Then she would decide what to do. Although she was frightened of the pain that would undoubtedly come, she wasn't afraid of dying. She was no longer religious, but at times she did wonder about the afterlife. She would continue to pretend there was somewhere up above where she would be welcome.

She was still thinking of this when Emily came back in with the painkillers. They were sitting in the lounge room, nursing a cup of tea when Angela turned to her. 'I've made a decision, darling.'

'Oh! What sort of a decision?'

'I've decided I'm not going to have treatment. I'll let it run its course …'

Emily looked aghast. 'But Nonna … why on earth not? The doctor said it will give you more time, and you never know it might even cure you.'

'Highly unlikely. And one thing I know is that it will be very invasive. I would rather spend the time that I've left enjoying my life, not visiting hospitals and coping with the aftermath of treatment.' She picked up the packet of painkillers Emily had laid on the table beside her. 'And I'm sure these will give me relief from pain.'

Emily paced the room, glancing at her anxiously. 'Nonna, you've at least got to try the treatment. What if it works quickly and then you're just fine?'

'And then what? It comes back in a few years and I have to go through it all again. No, I've made a decision and that's it. I don't want to hear another word about it. It's my life, so I can decide.'

'And what about me?'

'Darling. You are young. When I'm gone you'll still have a whole life ahead of you, and hopefully I'll always be in your memories. Now,' she said, standing up. 'Be a dear and take the teacups to the kitchen and I'll put this lot of tablets in the drawer of my bedside table. And no more maudlin talk. Promise.'

Emily smiled sadly, standing up to pick up the teacups. 'Okay, Nonna, I promise. But why don't you have a rest on your bed now? You must be tired after all those tests and everything.'

'I don't feel in the least like lying on my bed. I've been doing that in hospital.'

'I just thought—'

'I may have been given a death sentence, but physically I feel no different to what I did before that sentence was handed down. As I said, what we'll do is make the best of the time I have left. Now,' she grinned, heading to the bedroom, 'how about when I've put these away we both have a glass of wine and then think what we might have for dinner.'

'Gosh, Nonna, are you sure you should have a wine? I mean—'

'Mean what?'

'I just thought …'

'Well, put that thought to good use and decide what we'll have for dinner.'

Emily smiled. 'I got some delicious looking flounder from the fishmonger when I went up to the chemist.'

'Flounder sounds wonderful, darling.'

Later, as Emily sipped from her glass of wine after they had finished dinner she looked at Angela sitting across from her. 'Nonna, are you absolutely sure you won't have any treatment?'

'Yes, I am,' Angela stated firmly.

'But what about Dad?'

'What about him?'

'Surely he'll insist you have chemo or something.'

'It's not his body, so he has little say in the matter.'

'What about Jonathon and Allen?'

'Darling, I'm sure they'll accept whatever I decide. Now, no more talk of it. No more at all. Off you go home and leave me be.'

'Actually, Nonna, I thought I'd stay the night. I've had a couple of glasses of wine, so I'd best not drive. And I'd really like to stay.' She told her about Libby possibly moving into her room to share the flat with Chrissy. 'In the morning, I'll go and get some things and put them in the spare room.'

Angela looked at her watch. It *was* getting quite late and Emily had had a couple of glasses of wine. 'That would be lovely, darling,' she said. 'After all, the bed's made up so you'd just have to slip between the sheets. We can have a nice breakfast in the morning, using the eggs you brought back from *Kilmarnock*. I even have some bacon.'

'Yum!' Emily said, licking her lips. 'That sounds delicious.'

On kissing her goodnight, Emily pointed to the gold lira pendant around Angela's neck.

'I've never seen you wear that before, Nonna. It's always been in your jewellery box.'

Angela smiled. 'I was going through my jewellery box just now and thought how silly it was not to wear it. As you know it's supposed to keep one close to those who leave us. Now that I'm not well I've been thinking of Maria and Aunt Sophia more often.'

Emily touched the gold lira. 'It really is very beautiful isn't it?'

Angela smiled. 'I remember when Aunt Sophia gave it to Maria as if it was yesterday.' She fiddled with the pendant. 'No doubt this twenty lira is worth quite a bit more than it was when it was minted to commemorate the unification of Italy back in 1861.'

Emily laughed. 'I bet you're right there. Maybe we could look it up.'

Angela shook her head. 'No matter what it's worth it couldn't be more valuable than the memories it invokes.'

Chapter Thirteen

Before she went to sleep in the spare bedroom, Emily rang Chrissy to tell her about Nonna and that she was spending the night with her.

'Oh, Em. I'm so sorry. Poor Nonna.'

'Yes, I know it's hard to believe. I've decided to move in with her full time for now. So you can tell your friend Libby she can have my room for the time being.'

'Gosh, Em. Are you sure? I mean …'

'I need to be with Nonna, so it'll be great if Libby takes my room. It'll take the pressure off me. I'll get my things tomorrow morning.'

'I can help you pack. A few of us are meeting for brekky at Ralph's Café at uni. I only have one lecture after that so should be home by eleven.'

'Thanks, Chrissy.'

'Are you okay, Em?'

'Yeah. Sad. But I'm okay.'

'Well, give darling Nonna my love. And a big hug.'

In the morning, Emily awoke with a sick feeling in her stomach when she thought of Nonna being so ill. And choosing to die rather than having any treatment! In a way, she was angry with her for refusing. Yet, on the other hand, she could understand her not wanting to do so. As Nonna said, it was her decision and hers alone. Even so, Emily felt she was giving in too easily. Over time, Emily hoped that she might be able to change her mind. Or her father might. She knew Nonna might be angry if she rang him and told him before she did, but it would be good to forewarn him and when Nonna told him he could pretend he didn't know. Emily felt she had to try to get him on her side in coaxing Nonna to have treatment. She looked at her watch. Auckland was two hours ahead. She didn't want to ring him from Nonna's house, in case Nonna heard, so she decided to go for a run to the beach. Nonna's door was still closed so she silently let herself outside. Down on the beach she dialled her father's number.

'Nonna's got cancer,' she told him when he answered. 'And she's refusing to have any treatment.'

There was a long silence on the end of the line as Emily listened to the waves crashing on the shore. 'I'm very sad to hear that, Em,' he eventually said. 'I thought she looked tired when I last saw her.'

'She's more than tired, Dad. She's dying.'

Another silence. 'How do you know that?'

Emily told him how she had been in St Vincent's when the specialist gave his diagnosis.

'Oh! And she's adamant not to have any treatment at all?'

'She won't listen to me, but she might listen to you.'

'I doubt it. As you should know by now my mother is a woman of her own mind. Once she's made it up about something that's it. Believe me, I should know.'

'When are you due back?'

'In a few days.'

'Well, when you get here, please see if you can talk her into having treatment,' she pleaded. 'Dad, please, I beg—'

'Do you want me to ring her now?'

'No. She doesn't know I've rung you. Just come around when you're back. I'm sure she'll tell you about it then.'

She was going to tell him how she had met a Sydney horse trainer at the Yass races who knew him and Dimitri Carpani, and also about *Erskine's* not taking *Kilmarnock* produce any more, but she decided to wait for another time. Nonna was her priority right now.

When she finished the call, she sat there for a moment, watching the early morning swimmers in the surf. Further out a number of board riders were waiting for a wave to catch. Across on the rocks fisherman were risking their lives trying to snare a fish with long lines whilst balanced precariously close to the raging sea. Before heading back up the hill to Nonna's she decided to ring Liz Falcon, who she knew would be up and about.

'I need to slow down bookings for a while,' she told her when she answered.

'Gosh, Em, I was only saying yesterday how many bookings are coming in for you right now. You seem to be the flavour of the month.' She laughed down the line. 'Don't tell me. You're pregnant!'

Emily sighed. 'No, Liz, nothing like that. Nonna's been diagnosed with cancer, so I need to spend more time with her. I'm moving into her house to be with her.'

'Oh, I'm so sorry, Em. I know how close you are to her.'

Emily swallowed. Somehow just telling Liz about Nonna made her want to cry.

'It's okay, Liz. As Nonna says it's not as though she's a spring chicken.'

'Yes, I know, but even so …'

'I'll still do as many shoots as I can, just don't go signing me up for any too far away, anywhere I may need to spend the night.'

'What about the Tasmanian gig? At Port Arthur. For the tourist board down there? We promised them you'd be available.'

Emily had clean forgotten about that. She hated to let people down when she had promised to do something. 'Can you leave it with me, Liz? Maybe I can get Chrissy to move in with Nonna while I'm away.'

'Well, let me know as soon as you can. Otherwise I'll have to scout around for someone else in a hurry.'

'Sorry, Liz. Yes, I promise.'

***

'Are you sure you still want to do this?' Chrissy asked later as they packed Emily's things in her room at her flat. Chrissy went over to the window and swatted a fly hovering on the glass. 'I can always ask Libby to hold off. Or you can leave most of your stuff here.'

'I reckon I'll be with Nonna for some time, and there's plenty of room for my things there. Not only is there the spare room, there's also a huge storage area underneath that's hardly got anything in it. Not that I want to take anything other than my clothes and a few small bits and pieces at this stage.'

'Well, if you're absolutely sure you're happy with Libby taking over.'

'Yes, I am. Now,' she added, handing Chrissy a cane basket overloaded with her shoes, 'how about carrying these out to the car? I'll get an armload of my clothes from the cupboard.'

'Angus came for brekky this morning at Ralph's Café,' Chrissy said, struggling with the weight of the basket. 'I hope you don't mind, but I told him about Nonna. He asked for your number so he could give you a ring.'

Emily nodded, but she refused to let Chrissy see that inwardly she was pleased that Angus was going to ring her. If she did look pleased, Chrissy was sure to go on about it and try and make more out of it than what it was—Angus being caring and friendly. 'That's nice of him,' she said, nonchalantly, 'but don't go telling anyone else about Nonna. She wouldn't want the whole world to know.'

Later, as Emily was unpacking her things at Nonna's, her phone rang. It was Angus, who told her how sorry he was to hear about

Nonna. He then asked her if she was free to meet him for a cup of coffee, as he had to go to Westfield for a haircut. Apart from wanting to see him again, she needed to get some things from the supermarket so they arranged to meet at the Coffee Club. In the meantime, she finished putting her things away and after checking the list of bits and pieces to get at the supermarket with Nonna, and seeing if there was anything else she needed, she drove to Bondi and parked at Westfield.

Angus was already waiting for her when she arrived at the Coffee Club.

'Again, I'm so sorry about your Nonna,' he said, getting up from his chair. He was wearing the same outfit he had on when she first met him at The Coogee Bay Hotel. Checked shirt, moleskin pants and boots. She wondered briefly if he had worn this outfit when in London, or was it just since he'd been back in Australia and up and down from *Kilmarnock*.

'Thanks, Angus. It was certainly a shock.'

'What's say I order us a coffee? Then you can tell me about it.'

'That'd be great.'

When he sat down again and they waited for their coffee to be brought over, Emily told him how Nonna was refusing to have treatment.

'Sad as it is for you, I reckon I understand where she's coming from,' he eventually said, compassion filling his eyes. 'My own grandmother was faced with much the same. She opted for treatment for ovarian cancer, but it was useless. All it meant was that the last year of her life was spent in one hospital after another. She lost all her hair and most of the time felt absolutely dreadful. More, I suspect, from the treatment than from the actual cancer, which they could control the pain of to a certain extent. Then the chemo played havoc with her heart and she could hardly walk without getting breathless. Before she died she said to me she would have been better to have spent the last year of her life doing things she wanted to do. Spending more time in her beloved garden and with her family.'

'But at least she tried …'

'It didn't get her anywhere, Emily. Perhaps if she'd been much younger it might have been worthwhile. But like your Nonna, she was in her eighties.' He paused. 'I watched her go through all that treatment for nothing. She was a great old bird and I would have much preferred it if she'd spent her last months without all that invasive treatment.' He smiled. 'So, as I said, I can understand how your Nonna feels.' He moved aside to let the waitress put their coffee down on the table. Picking up the spoon, he stirred the froth on the top. 'Don't go making it harder for her, Emily. If she's decided she doesn't want treatment, let it be. Try and enjoy whatever time she has left. That's what I wish I'd done with my grandmother, but I felt so sorry for her when she lost all her hair and was so sick from the treatment. I couldn't really see past that.'

'How old were you?'

'It was quite a few years ago. Before I went to England.'

'So she wasn't here to see Duncan killed.'

'No, at least she was spared that. She adored us kids. It would have killed her anyway to hear about Duncan.'

Emily smiled compassionately as she fiddled with her own spoon. 'You've had a tough few years.'

He laughed. 'Nah. It hasn't all been bad. Anyway, what does your Nonna love the most in the world?'

Emily thought. 'The beach and her garden.'

'Well, why don't you take her down to *Kilmarnock*? She can see my mother's garden. Maybe get some cuttings. I reckon it'd do my parents the world of good to have you both there. Cheer my father up.'

'I couldn't ask your parents to have us stay. After all they've been through so much.'

'Nonsense. Besides,' he winked, 'they really liked you.'

She felt herself blushing. 'How do you know that?'

'Mum told me. In any case, you don't have to ask them about going down. I will. When do you reckon you could go?'

Emily mulled this over. She was sure Angus was right. Nonna would love it down at *Kilmarnock*, and a trip out of Sydney would do her good. Maybe take her mind off things. And now that Emily had had a taste of the country again, she loved the idea of riding down to that lovely river again. 'Before it gets too cold,' she told him. 'The nights are really closing in now.'

'How about a couple of weekends away?'

'Would you be there?'

'I'm on weekend shifts for the next month or so. And uni during the week. But you go down, Emily. As I said, they'd love to see you both.'

'Well, if you're sure.'

'I am.' He looked at his watch. 'But now I'd best get my haircut and then I'm off to work.'

She gave him a warm smile. 'Thank you, Angus. I really appreciate you meeting me. And for giving me that advice about Nonna. I daresay in the long run I've been thinking more about me than Nonna, and what I'll lose when she's gone. She's been my rock for so long.'

She told him how her mother now lived in America and they never heard from her, trying to make it sound as though it was the most normal thing in the world.

'You'll always have your memories of your Nonna,' he said, giving her an understanding smile. 'Besides, no one knows how long she's got. It might be quite a while.'

'At least I'll have time to prepare myself. Unlike you and your parents with Duncan.'

He stood up. It was as if he didn't want to talk about his brother. Now. Here. She was sorry she had brought it up.

Standing up beside him she gave him a kiss on the cheek. 'Thanks again, Angus. It really has been great to talk to you.'

'I'll ring you when I've spoken to Mum and Dad. But plan on the weekend after next.'

After they parted she went to the supermarket. Walking down the aisle she thought what a lovely man he was. And even though she wasn't looking for him to be any more than just a friend she was pleased Chrissy had introduced her to him.

That night, as she and Nonna sat on the verandah in the fading light, she told her what Angus had suggested.

'I'd really like to go down there again,' she said, making it sound as though Nonna would be doing her a favour by coming. 'And, as I said before, you'd really love it, Nonna. Angus reckoned it'd cheer his parents up to have the company.'

'What? An eighty-year old woman on her last legs? I doubt I could cheer up a clown, let alone anyone else.'

'Nonsense. I'm sure they'd be delighted to meet you.'

Angela smiled. 'Well, I daresay it would give me something to look forward to. Maybe we could just pop into *Kilmarnock* for afternoon tea or such, rather than put them out by staying the night, and go onto Canberra. Autumn there is such a lovely time when the trees are turning, as they would be on the drive down. I've always loved those poplars that line the road past Goulburn. They should be spectacular at this time.'

'Let's see what Angus comes back with, but I suspect they would like us to spend the night there.' She smiled. 'Anyway, before that, what do you think about my idea of asking Elena and her cousin around for a drink sometime?'

'Oh yes. You started to tell me about her cousin and then the doctors arrived. What is he like? Elena told me he's handsome.'

'He does have a lovely look about him. Seems fun too. I thought it might cheer you up to hear about Naples.'

'Gosh, all this cheering up you've got organised for me, darling.' She smiled. 'I'm actually fine, but I do appreciate your sentiments. However, I'm not sure I want to hear about the Naples of today. Although it's probably a great improvement on the Naples I knew before the war.' She sighed. 'I bet it's still dirty and smelly, but you'd think if her cousin comes from Naples he must know Procida. It's not far across the bay. And I do like Elena.'

Emily saw the moment she gave in.

'If you promise not to tell her about my illness it might be quite fun. Just for an hour or so.'

Chapter Fourteen

Emily had no sooner left in the morning to go to a short photographic shoot than Angela heard a knock on the door. When she opened it, the same journalist as before stood on the step. She was about to close the door when he said, 'I'm sorry to disturb you again, Mrs Erskine; however, I wonder if you could spare me a moment to tell me about your time working for Cesare Carpani at his restaurant, *Cesare's,* in Stanley Street, Darlinghurst in the 1950s when you first came to Australia.'

A shiver darted up Angela's spine. 'Oh, why?'

'I believe you and your sister worked for Cesare and his wife, Bettina. And your late husband, Stewart worked there as well. After the three of you left Villawood Migrant Hostel.'

Angela nodded. 'Yes, we did. Why is that of interest to you?'

'I was researching an article about the emergence of Italian restaurants in inner Sydney and your husband's name came up in an article about *Cesare's* restaurant in Stanley Street on the website, Trove from the 1950s. There was a review in the *Daily Telegraph* at the time which said Stewart Erskine was the chef there. It also said that you and your sister, Maria, newly arrived migrants from Italy, were the "charming waitresses".'

Angela remembered such an article being written when she and Maria first went to work at *Cesare's.* Both girls had been excited to see their name in print. However, after Maria died and Angela came across the article, she had torn it up into little pieces. In a dark fury she hurled it in the fire, watching it turn to cinders.

The journalist smiled. 'It was after he worked at *Cesare's* when Mr Erskine opened his first *Erskine's* restaurant, wasn't it?' Another smile. 'The beginning of his restaurant empire, you might say.'

'Yes, you could say that. But why are you so interested in my late husband?'

'I'm a journalist. Naturally curious.'

'I thought my son had …'

'Shut us up?'

'Yes, well …'

'He may have managed to get the story about Glasgow Mine crushed for the time being in our newspaper, but if ICAC take it further, which they may well do, that might be a different matter. In any case, I'm still fascinated by the story of how a bloke from Scotland did so well after coming here as a migrant to *Villawood* with more or less nothing.'

'There are hundreds of migrants who came to Australia who have done well. That's how Australia has thrived.'

'Yes I know. In fact, my grandparents came here from Ireland after the war. Maybe that's why the subject of migrants of that time is of particular interest to me. Also, I'm a great fan of *Erskine's* restaurants. Only last week I had a very good meal at the one down at Rushcutters Bay. I even met Cesare Carpani's son

Dimitri there. Amazing to think he now owns the *Erskine* franchise, isn't it?'

'My son sold the franchise to him on my husband's death. He wasn't interested in that part of the business.' She looked him in the eye without wavering. 'Now, if you don't mind, I really am very busy.'

'So you don't want to tell me how it was working at *Cesare's* all those years ago with your sister? It was also about that time when the popular *Beppi's* opened in Stanley Street. A fascinating time in the emergence of Italian restaurants in inner Sydney.'

Angela looked at her watch. 'Yes, it was. I'm really very sorry, but I must go. I'm expecting an important phone call,' she lied. She offered him a half-smile. 'Good luck with your article.'

She then stood back and shut the door. Bile rose in her throat and she thought she was going to be sick. It was the same biliousness she felt whenever she thought of Cesare Carpani, whether it be in the middle of the night when she couldn't sleep or if a thought of him invaded her mind during the day. She went to her bedroom where she pulled out a cardboard box. It was here that she kept many papers, including a few newspaper cuttings. Holding one in her hands, she looked down at the rumpled, pillowy face of Cesare Carpani gracing the front page of the *Sydney Mail* as it reported how he was murdered in a robbery outside his restaurant, *Cesare's,* in Stanley Street. She had no idea why she still kept this cutting, except that in some perverse way it was proof that he was no longer part of this world. Tearing the page into tiny pieces, she watched his face disappear, piece by piece. She picked up the scraps, stood up, and went to the kitchen where she threw them in the rubbish bin. If only it was that easy to erase him from her mind. But, hard as she tried, his noxious face was etched there clearly, ever since she first set eyes on him over sixty years before.

***

'God, how I hate him,' Maria spat with venom when the sisters had only been working at *Cesare's* for a month and Signore Carpani had gone outside for a cigarette.

'I've got a good mind to tell Bettina what he's like. Last night when we were tidying the tables away he actually got me up against the wall and tried to kiss me.' Maria glanced over at her sister. 'You were outside getting the sign in.'

Angela looked at her in horror. 'I was only outside for a moment!'

Maria nodded. 'I know. As soon as you went out the door he pounced.'

'My God! Did you tell Stewart?'

'God forbid! If I did he'd kill the man with his own two hands.' She laughed, her bright tinkling laugh. 'He doesn't have that red hair for nothing.'

Maria and Angela were living in digs above the restaurant at the far end of Stanley Street and Stewart was in a hostel in Woolloomooloo. Usually, when the last customer had left the restaurant, they would clean up and then Angela would go upstairs to bed. Maria and Stewart often went for a drive in Stewart's Holden, which he had bought second-hand while still at Villawood, or they might go for a walk.

'I'm taking my bonnie wee *signorina* for a stroll,' he would say with a laugh, taking Maria's hand in his and leaning down to give her a kiss. 'Aren't I the lucky man to have such delightful company?'

Angela was sure that sometimes they would end up back at Stewart's hostel, with Maria in Stewart's bed. A couple of nights Maria hadn't got home until the birds had started their early morning concert in the jacaranda tree outside their window and the soft dawn light was breaking through the thin muslin curtains above her bed.

Angela loved seeing her sister and Stewart so happy together. They were so much in love, sharing secrets and laughing and joking with each other; cuddling together in the Holden under the jacaranda tree lit up by the streetlights, as Angela watched from the window above. Walking down the street, hand in hand. At times, she felt a pang of jealousy that she and Raphael were denied the chance to have that same happiness. However, those pangs only lasted a short while. She worshiped Maria so much that she was very happy for her. And for Stewart.

One evening as they were getting ready for bed, Maria sat in front of the mirror at the dressing table, brushing her hair.

'Stewart has leased a place in Castlereagh Street,' she said, turning around on the stool and crossing her slim legs encased in nylon.

'What on earth for?'

'He's going to open his own restaurant. He inherited some money from a distant cousin in Scotland. He'll use that. He's asked me to go with him to set it up. He wants to call it *Erskine's*. Of course, I said you had to come with us.'

'He's going to open his own restaurant?' Angela exclaimed in disbelief.

'Yes. He only told me today. Franco, the cook from Villawood is going to work with him there.'

'Rolly polly Franco, who helped us with our English?'

'That's him.'

'But what if it doesn't work?'

'It will work. Stewart will make it work.'

'Signore Carpani will be furious. And Bettina will be too.'

'I know. When Stewart told him, Cesare stormed out of the kitchen, banging the door on the way. He then stormed back in and told him to leave straight away.'

'My God! And what about us?'

'Stewart said we should give Cesare a week's notice. Otherwise, we'd be leaving him and Bettina totally in the lurch. I don't worry about him, but I do like Bettina.'

Although Bettina was polite to the girls over the next week, Signore Carpani was darn right rude, picking fault with everything they did and telling them he would be glad to get rid of them.

'With you two working at your boyfriend's fancy new restaurant it's bound to fail,' he told Maria as he followed her around the dining room, huffing and puffing and straightening the already straight cutlery and serviettes. 'And if it doesn't,' he spat with virulence, 'I'll make sure to destroy him anyway.'

Both girls put that threat down to his many bursts of anger, which they had often been a witness to when he threatened to destroy a supplier who might have given him a bad order of meat or fish. Or worse still, none at all, when he would really fly off the handle, causing Bettina to rush out from the kitchen to try to calm him down.

When it came to their last night working there, Cesare told Angela she wasn't needed. It was a Tuesday and often this was their quietest night. The girls had decided to move into the YWCA hostel the next morning, which was close to where Stewart was opening his new restaurant.

As Maria was working, Angela decided to go to the cinema. She would have liked someone to go with, but she didn't really know anyone well enough in Sydney to ask to accompany her. She had been dying to see *A Streetcar Named Desire,* as she loved Marlon Brando. After putting on a tweed skirt and a new blue twinset she had bought for two pounds with her first pay cheque, she caught the tram and as it was raining after the movie she went into a café next to the theatre and bought herself a hot chocolate. As the rain cleared she caught the tram back. When she got off outside the restaurant, it was just before midnight and the restaurant and their room upstairs were both in darkness. After letting herself in downstairs, she crept upstairs in case she woke Maria, put her key in the lock and went into their room. That was when she found Maria lying on her bed curled up against the wall, sobbing out loud.

'What in heaven's name's the matter?' Angela exclaimed, moving quickly to her bed.

'Nothing,' Maria murmured in a muffled voice, though it was obvious there was something *very* wrong with her.

Angela had never seen her lie in this position before. And Maria never sobbed. Not even when she fell off her bicycle in Naples and broke her arm. Not even when their parents had died or when Aunt Sophia had passed away. Crying she may have done, but sobbing was not in Maria's nature. So why would she be sobbing like this unless something awful had happened to her?

'Don't be so stupid. Something's got to be wrong,' she said to her as she sat on her bed. 'Have you and Stewart had a fight?'

'No,' Maria sniffled.

'So what's happened to make you cry like this?'

Maria turned around and wiped her eyes with the sheet, which she pulled tightly around her chest.

'I will tell you, but you must swear to secrecy.'

'How can I do that if I don't know what you're going to tell me?'

'It's a risk you take. If you tell we're both ruined.'

Maria took Angela's hand and after sitting in silence for a good two minutes she finally revealed what had happened to her.

She told Angela that she was putting the rubbish in the bin outside the back door when Signore Carpani came outside to have a cigarette. As Maria went to go back inside he lurched towards her.

'He then grabbed my arm and threw me up against the wall.'

'Oh my God,' Angela cried. 'Where was Bettina?'

'She had gone home to bed.'

'So what did you do?'

Maria shook her head and let out a deep, ragged sigh. 'I couldn't do anything. Although he was drunk, he was still very strong. He whacked a hand over my mouth and yanked my dress up. Even though I scratched his face and kicked and screamed like a tiger he wouldn't let me get away.' She took a deep breath and let it out again and looked in desperation at Angela. 'He threw me on the ground.'

'Oh Maria how awful,' Angela said. She then noticed a dark bruise on Maria's forehead. 'Is that how you got that awful bump?'

'Yes.'

'And … and then what happened?'

'He … he …' Maria tried to control her breathing. As she looked at Angela, tears spilt over her cheeks and onto her hands, which were twisted together like a tight ball of twine.

'He what?'

'He–he …'

Angela felt a rush of nausea surge through her. She wanted to cover her ears so she wouldn't hear what she dreaded might come next.

'He … raped me,' Maria spluttered.

Angela gagged and her stomach rose to her throat. 'No, no, Maria. No,' she cried, swallowing hard to stop herself being sick. She took her sister in her arms and caressed her beautiful hair. 'It can't be true, tell me it's not.'

'It is true,' Maria said, turning her desolate brown eyes to her sister's. She wrapped her arms around her shaking body and touched her hair. 'I've tried to scrub every part of me clean in the bath, but I can still smell him.'

Fury raced through Angela, flooding her veins as if it was a raging torrent, threatening to drown her. 'I'll kill him,' she eventually said. 'With my own two hands.'

'What good would that do?' Maria said, wiping her nose with her sleeve. 'You would go to hell.'

'But, Maria, what about Stewart? You'll have to tell him.'

'No. If we do that he's the one who's sure to kill Signore Carpani. And then he'll be in jail.'

'Oh, Maria,' Angela said, sitting up straight and looking into Maria's eyes, which looked the most desolate Angela had ever seen them, 'surely we should tell the police. Signore Carpani should go to jail, not Stewart.'

'There's no way in the world the police will believe me against a fine, upstanding member of the Italian Catholic community with a lovely wife. They'd scoff at the very thought of him being accused by a newly-arrived migrant from Italy who supposedly dresses provocatively. They'd laugh me out of the police station.'

'They wouldn't. Not if I tell them about how awful Signore Carpani is. How he tried to kiss you before.'

'You only know what I told you. In any case, if we tell the police Stewart will then know, and, as I said, he's sure to kill Signore Carpani. I know he would.' She paused and stroked Angela's hair. 'Besides, Stewart and I have been talking of marriage. If he knows what happened he may think I'm soiled goods.'

'Oh Maria, it wasn't your fault. He wouldn't blame you. Surely he wouldn't.'

'I couldn't blame him.'

'So has he definitely proposed?'

Maria sat up in the bed further and slowly swung her legs over the side. She went over to the window where the streetlights glowed in the darkness outside. The moon had now disappeared altogether, which didn't surprise Angela, for if it had shined through the window she would have wondered how it could be so uncaring.

'We've talked of marriage, but we thought we'd put off getting engaged until we've got *Erskine's* up and going.' She turned around. 'It's not as though I've got a father that he'd have to ask my hand for.' Grief was written all over her lovely face. 'After this, I'll have to think about it. If I don't tell him about Signore Carpani, I'd be starting our married life off as a lie.'

She came over and sat down on the bed again. As she lay on the pillow, she pulled Angela down close to her. Together, they lay side by side, with Angela stroking Maria's hair. When she thought of that awful, horrible man raping her beloved sister she put her face into the pillow to stop Maria from hearing her sobs.

Angela didn't sleep a wink that night and she doubted Maria did either. The next morning, they were up early, well before Cesare or Bettina arrived, and they rang a taxi and moved their belongings into the YWCA hostel. When Angela broached the subject that night as they lay in their narrow beds, Maria shut her down.

'I don't want to talk about it. To do so brings it all back and makes me want to die. Please don't mention it ever again. Do you understand? Never.'

It was the first time Angela had heard Maria speak so angrily. And there was such a hard look in her eyes that it frightened her.

After a moment she nodded. 'Alright, I won't mention it. But—'

'No buts. That's how it is. Put it out of your mind, as I will. Now, let's turn the light off and go to sleep.'

Over the next month, Angela tried to do what Maria said and put what had happened out of her mind as both girls helped Stewart and Franco paint and decorate the restaurant premises. It was an old building, but it had good proportions and many attractive features, including intricate ceiling roses, two open fireplaces with ornate mantlepieces and large windows with deep sills, ideal for placing vases of flowers on. Once painted brightly and with colourful tablecloths covering the wooden tables it all came together. The final touch was the navy blue door with a shiny brass sign proclaiming *Erskine's.*

'We've all done a great job,' Stewart said proudly when it was ready to open. He put an arm around Maria and smiled at Angela. 'Aren't I the lucky one to have two such bonnie lassies to help me.'

Looking at Maria and Stewart, and then at Franco putting the finishing touches to the kitchen, Angela felt very happy. She had nearly succeeded in putting out of her mind Cesare Carpani having raped Maria. And standing at the front door on the very first night *Erskine*'s welcomed diners, well, it was almost as though that unspeakable, abhorrent attack on Maria was a bad dream, which she had imagined.

At least, it was until one evening when Maria came into their bedroom at the YWCA hostel and told Angela she was pregnant.

'How many weeks?' Angela exclaimed, sitting up straight on her rickety iron bed and placing the book she was reading down by her side.

'The doctor said it's hard to tell. Maybe eight.'

Angela did a quick calculation. 'Oh my God, Maria! About the time you were raped by Signore Carpani?'

Maria walked over to her bed and sat down. She pulled off her shoes and lay back, looking up at the ceiling where the paint was peeling off and a large water stain marked the area around the dim electric light. 'Yes, about that time.'

Angela took a deep breath and threw her legs over the side of the bed onto the linoleum floor. Standing up, she stepped over to where Maria was lying and sat down beside her. 'Oh Maria. I'm so sorry. What on earth will you do?' A taut silence stretched out as Maria lay on the bed as still as a statue. 'I know it's against our religion and all that, but surely you'll have to have an abortion.'

There was a further stretch of silence as Maria fiddled with the edge of the frayed blanket, playing with a piece of loose wool. She pulled the piece out and scrunched it into a tight ball in her hand.

'There's no way I could have an abortion,' she said. 'What if the baby is Stewart's? I made love to him the week before it happened. And we made love the week after as well. I thought I wouldn't be able to do it, remembering that hideous night … but … well …'

'And?'

'I managed to block what happened out ... and ...'

'It could well be Stewart's,' Angela noted.

'Even if it isn't, I couldn't possibly kill a tiny being within my womb.' She let out a deep sigh. 'I've thought about it on the way home on the tram from the doctors. I'll tell Stewart I'm expecting his child. He'll then insist that we get married straight away.'

'But what if the baby doesn't look a smidgen like him? You know what I mean … red hair and—'

'It took after my side of the family. We Vincentos have strong genes.'

'Maria! You said you'd never start your marriage living a lie.'

'Yes, I know I said that. But what option do I have? Whose ever child it is, it deserves to have a good life. It wasn't its fault that what happened, happened. Besides, Stewart will be delighted we're getting married. And even more delighted that I'm carrying his baby. We've talked about having hordes of little children.' She laughed. 'He wants a whole clan of them.'

Angela shook her head at Maria's forced bravado. In a way it was none of her business, but she desperately hoped that her sister was doing the right thing. She wondered what she would do if she were in the same situation. But hard as she fretted over that thought, she couldn't decide what she would do. So who was she to berate Maria for the charade she was playing at?

'What if people guess you got pregnant before your marriage? I mean—'

'Plenty of babies are born premature. We'll have one of those.' She touched her stomach with barely a hint of a bump. Then she touched her breasts. 'The beauty of being Italian is that people expect us to be curvaceous. And with you and me working in the restaurant with all that tempting food around a girl is bound to put on a bit of weight.'

And, despite the cloud hanging over Maria and Angela's head in regard to the baby, a month after the first banns of marriage had been announced at Sunday Mass, Stewart and Maria's wedding was a joyous occasion. Stewart wanted it to be a grand affair, but Maria insisted on it being simple.

'I hate big weddings,' she said when the three of them were discussing it. 'A small one is much more intimate and romantic.'

And that is what it was. Just a priest, Maria, Stewart, Franco and his wife, and Angela on a bright Wednesday morning in the side chapel of St Mary's Cathedral in Hyde Park. As Angela took a photo on the steps outside the cathedral afterwards of Maria and Stewart, she thought how beautiful her sister looked in a simple white dress with flowers in her gleaming hair cascading over her shoulders and down her back. And how happy Stewart was standing proudly by her side.

Over the next seven months as Stewart, Maria, Angela, and Franco made a great success of *Erskine's,* turning it into one of Sydney's most sought after restaurants (helped by a great review by a well-known food critique in a leading Sunday newspaper brought queues to their door), Maria never once mentioned Cesare Carpani and what he had done to her.

One cold and overcast morning when she and Angela were on their own, sitting around the table in the kitchen at *Erskine's,* Angela was reading the newspaper and she told her sister there was a photo on the social pages of Cesare and Bettina at a function for Archbishop Gilroy at the Italian Club.

'Look at him standing there, as smug as can be, next to the Archbishop,' she said, folding the paper in two to show Maria.

'Don't you ever dare mention that man's name in my presence,' Maria spat with the venom of a hissing snake, pushing the paper away 'As far as I'm concerned he's as dead to me as those monsters Mussolini and Hitler are. They all deserve to rot in hell.'

She then got up and went over to the sink where she poured herself a glass of water. Turning around she touched her belly.

'There's not a day that I don't think of what he did to me. Every morning when I awake he's there. Every night when I go asleep he's there too. How can he not be, with this baby in my belly.'

'But Maria, it may well be Stewart's baby you're carrying.'

'That's the only thing that keeps me going.'

As Maria's belly grew, Angela could see her becoming more and more anxious.

***

When Maria's waters broke in the middle of the night, Stewart rushed her to St Margaret's Maternity hospital in Darlinghurst.

From the hospital, he rang Angela at the flat she was now renting in East Sydney. 'I'll ring as soon as it arrives,' he said, sounding excited.

But the next morning there was no news so she went into work at *Erskine's*. When she rang the hospital to see what was happening an officious nurse said she couldn't tell her anything but would get Stewart to ring her.

It was three hours later before he rang.

'So?' Angela asked excitedly. 'Has it arrived?'

A slight pause. 'Yes it has, a bonny wee boy. Doing very well.'

'And Maria … how is she?'

This was a much longer pause and in it she heard Stewart swallow. 'She's very weak, Angela. And she's asking for you.'

'She's probably exhausted. I mean having a baby is—'

'It's not that. It was a very difficult birth. She haemorrhaged and lost a lot of blood. They've given her a transfusion, but it doesn't seem to be working. It's as though she's given up.'

Angela felt her heart lurch. 'She's not—I mean … she's —'

'Get here as soon as you can.' Another pause. 'As I said, she keeps asking for you. Come quickly.'

'Oh my God!' She took a deep breath. 'I'll be there straight away. I'll catch a taxi.'

'I'll tell her you're on your way.'

At the hospital, Angela rushed down the hallways until she found the ward where Maria was. The nurse at the desk told her to wait and she would check if she could see her. A few minutes later, she came back out.

'You may go in now.'

When Angela entered the room she couldn't get over how many machines there were around Maria and how they all seemed to be beeping at once. Maria appeared to be asleep. Sitting next to her was Stewart.

'How is she?' she asked, stepping towards him.

Stewart shook his head, stood up and came over, guiding her away from the bed. 'Not too good,' he said, quietly.

'Where's the doctor? Shouldn't he be here? Or at least a nurse.'

'The doctor was here until a moment ago. He said he'd be back shortly. The nurse has gone to get some more water. I'm to press the button if anything changes.'

'And the baby?'

'They have him down in the nursery.' He moved back to the bed and picked up Maria's hand and Angela was surprised when she didn't react. 'As I said, she's lost a lot of blood,' he whispered behind his other hand, which she noticed was shaking. 'She's very weak. Exhausted. But she needs to fight.'

He looked exhausted himself. 'Why don't you go and get a coffee,' she said. 'I'll sit with her.'

After a moment, Stewart let go of Maria's hand and nodded. 'Yes, I need to go to the bathroom. I won't be long.'

When he left, Angela stepped over and looked down at Maria. She was so beautiful lying there, her long dark hair spread out on the pillow, her lovely lips slightly apart, her thick lashes touching her pale cheeks.

'Maria,' she said. 'It's me. Angela … Angeline.'

Maria slowly opened her eyes, but it took some time before she focused them on Angela's face. 'Where … where's my baby?'

'In the nursery being looked after,' Angela soothed her, taking hold of her hand and holding it within hers.

There was a long, long pause as Maria cast her eyes around the room. 'Where's Stewart? He was here?'

'I know… he's gone out for a moment.'

Maria clenched Angela's hand. 'The baby … the baby … it doesn't have red hair,' she managed to get out.

Angela shook her head. 'I haven't seen him. But even if he doesn't have red hair, we have our own ancestry to blame.' Angela listened to her laboured breathing.

'No matter who the father is … he's my baby.' Maria took a deep breath and let it out again. 'If anything should happen to me—'

'Maria, nothing will happen to you. You're very weak, but that's to be expected. You've got to fight. For Stewart. For the baby. For me.'

Maria opened her mouth to speak again, but was unable to get the words out. She struggled with another breath. 'Angeline … promise me you'll look after the baby. And … and … promise me too that you'll look after Stewart. He's a good man and I love him so much. But please … please,' she whispered, 'don't ever tell him that the baby … my son … may not be his. And never, ever tell my son. Never.'

Angela squeezed her hand tightly within her own, now clammy with fear, and nodded as tears trickled down her cheeks onto both of their hands. 'Maria, you're going to be just fine… and the baby…well, the baby is most likely Stewart's. We both know that.'

'It may not.' An agonising silence stretched out as she fiddled feebly with the sheet. 'You know that as well as I do!'

Angela touched Maria's face with her hand, wiping the tears from her smooth skin. 'It makes no difference, he'll be loved. By you and Stewart. By us all.'

Maria coughed, trying to get her breath, and her eyes looked pleadingly at Angela. 'Don't tell. Ever …'

Angela held her distraught eyes with hers. It was as if they were wide, dark chasms of dread and fear. So unlike the beautiful, fathomless, shining ponds of laughter and love they used to be. Before Cesare Carpani came into their lives. As Angela held her sister's hand in hers, she could feel their shared anguish in the sticky moistness of their intertwined fingers.

'Never … ever tell …' Maria begged her. She touched the gold lira pendant around her neck. 'Put your hand on this gold lira and make me that promise. Please, Angeline.'

Angela looked at Aunt Sophia's gold lira pendant, which she knew Maria had never removed from around her neck and felt like weeping, but she somehow stopped herself.

'I promise,' she eventually said, touching the polished surface of the pendant. And as she held Maria's eyes with hers, she was sure her beloved sister knew that the baby she just bore was not the son of her much-loved husband. Did that somehow affect the birth, causing her to lose so much blood leading to her present weak state? She thought of her parents up above in what she was sure must be heaven. Of Aunt Sophia up there too.

'Please, please,' she beseeched them, 'Please look after Maria.'

'Thank you, Angeline,' Maria said, placing her hand on Angela's, which was still touching the pendant. 'I know you will keep your promise.'

She closed her eyes and a small smile appeared on her pale lips.

Stewart came back in with the nurse, who asked them both to leave Maria to sleep and go to the waiting room down the corridor.

'I'll come and get you if there's a change,' she said, ushering them to the door.

Hours went by. Day became night as Angela and Stewart nodded off in the hard chairs in the waiting room. They dared not leave, apart from when Angela walked along the corridor to where behind a glass partition new babies were lined up in bassinets. It took her a little while to work out which one was Maria's baby, but then she saw the name. Erskine. It was impossible to see what he looked like, for all that was visible was a mop of dark brown hair peeping out of the swaddling clothes. As she stood there, Stewart came up alongside of her and together they gazed at the tiny being.

'Thanks be to God he doesn't seem to have my red hair,' he said with a smile.

If only he had, Angela thought sadly. If only he had.

Just as dawn broke through the window another kindly nurse brought them both a cup of tea and some Arnotts' biscuits.

When Stewart asked if he could go and see Maria, she said. 'The doctor said not to disturb her.'

'But how is she?'

'She's weak but sleeping. When she wakes I'll ask the doctor if you can go to her.'

It was two hours later when Angela heard bells ring and saw a flurry of nurses and a doctor fly past their door. She hoped desperately that it wasn't to Maria that they were rushing. It was a busy hospital and there were bound to be emergencies.

But an hour later when she looked up and saw the doctor standing in the doorway … he didn't have to say anything for Angela to know what had happened. His eyes said it all.

He went up to Stewart and held out his hand. 'I'm so very sorry,' he said. 'Your wife haemorrhaged again and lost too much blood. We did all we could, but we were unable to save her.'

Angela heard Stewart let out a loud, piteous cry, and saw tears flood down his cheeks. He shook his head. 'NO … NO!'

She rushed over to him and despite her own terrible anguish she held him in her arms and let him sob, feeling his tears run down her arm and onto the floor. As they clung to each other, Angela's heart shattered like a broken pane of glass with shards piercing every fibre of her body. She found it impossible to believe how Maria had gone from life to death so quickly. Angela had no idea how she would cope in this world without her. How could she live, not seeing her beautiful laughing smile; her passionate brown eyes; hearing her tinkling laugh; seeing her love of life until that fateful day when that love of life was shattered by a monster.

She asked herself again how much Cesare Carpani was to blame for her sister's death. Surely, if she had had a normal pregnancy, knowing that the baby she was carrying was that of the man she loved, it would have been enough for her to come through the birth. As it was, her pregnancy was filled with fear and apprehension caused by the monstrous man who raped her.

Walking slowly from the waiting room, she moved down the hallway to the glass window overlooking the nursery. And, as she gazed at Maria's baby, she wondered at the huge responsibility that lay ahead for her. She had promised Maria that no matter who the father was she would look after him. And that she would keep her secret forever.

Don't tell. Ever.

***

It was Father Duncan, the Irish Catholic priest at St Canice's Church in Rushcutters Bay, which Angela and Maria often frequented for mass and confession, who said a Requiem Mass for Maria, where a few friends and some of the staff from *Erskine's* came and paid their respects. The priest then arranged for her to be buried under a beautiful eucalyptus in Waverley Cemetery overlooking the sea. When it came time for the pallbearers to lower her beloved sister into that grave with a southerly wind funnelling up the coast, Angela felt such sadness as she hadn't imagined possible. And, as the wind whipped against their faces, she took hold of Stewart's arm and held onto him for support. After a moment, she realised that it was her who was supporting him.

As they walked back to the car he turned to her. 'Thank you again for saying you will come and look after the baby when he's released from hospital.'

'Stewart, I'm pleased to be able to do that.'

'Maria would have wanted it,' he said, touching her on the arm.

'Yes, I know. She would have.'

A week after the funeral they went to the hospital together and brought the baby home to Maria and Stewart's house. And, as Angela tucked him into the bassinet with yellow netting that she had helped Maria buy, she touched his forehead with her hand and tears trickled down her arm onto his tiny face. Wiping them away, she promised herself that she would never look at this baby, wondering who his father was. If she did she would be unable to cope.

All she would allow herself to see was Maria.

At times, Stewart frightened her so much with his grief. Melancholy moods and dreadful drinking seemed to overtake him. The moment he got home from work he'd head to the drinks cabinet in the corner of the living room and pour a whisky. Then another. And another. And he seemed to have little interest in the baby. Seeing him as he was, Angela suggested that he should take time off work at *Erskine's* and return to Scotland for a while, to see if he could shake off his grief and catch up with his family.

'And who would run *Erskine's*?' he asked.

'You have Franco and good staff. And I can keep an eye on things.'

What she didn't say was that if he continued to grieve like he was doing he was better to be away from the restaurant for a while, as one of the waitresses had told Angela that his melancholy demeanour was starting to rub off, not only on the staff, but also the patrons. And, quite frankly, Angela felt she could care for the baby far better without him being there to look after as well.

'Maybe you could go for a short time,' she said. 'A change of scenery would do you good.'

Eventually, with much persuasion from Franco and after the christening of the baby (who Stewart had decided to call Gavin Mario Erskine in memory of his grandfather and Maria), he did decide to go. And in a way, Angela's life became much easier. Now she only had Gavin to cope with. And although her days were filled with washing nappies, boiling bottles, feeding and burping him and rocking him to sleep, she somehow found a sort of contentment in her daily routine.

When Stewart returned from Scotland he seemed to be in a better frame of mind.

'You were right,' he said to Angela. 'It was good to get away and see the family.'

During the next year or so they settled into a companionable routine where Angela looked after both Gavin and the household and Stewart worked hard in his restaurant. Stewart paid her a salary and she got her board and keep. In the evenings when he came home they sometimes sat by the fire in the living room, Stewart cradling a glass of whisky and sometimes Angela would have a glass of sherry.

It was one evening, fifteen months after Maria's death, when Stewart coughed nervously and put his drink down on the table by his chair. 'I've been tossing things over and over for some time,' he said, looking across to where Angela was sitting, knitting a jumper for Gavin. 'Would you consider marrying me, Angela?'

Angela gasped. She hadn't seen this coming.

He looked over at the baby in the playpen. 'Then you could adopt Gavin as your own. I know how fond of him you are and how much he loves you. And needs you.'

When she got over the shock, Angela took a deep breath to steady herself. For quite some time she sat in silence, looking into his earnest eyes as she tried to come to terms with his proposal. Stewart was right—she *had* become very attached to Gavin—and having promised Maria that she would look after him forever, one of her worries was that Stewart would meet someone else and Angela would lose touch with Gavin.

She was immensely fond of Stewart, but she wasn't in love with him. What she felt for him was unlike what she had felt for

Raphael, and she was certain that Stewart was not in love with her, although she suspected he was very fond of her. Maybe love could come later. For both of them. But could she marry Stewart knowing she had to keep Maria's secret from him? Forever?

She stood up, put her knitting down and picked up Gavin's rattle, taking it over to the playpen where she knelt down to hand it to him. For some time, she watched him play with it. Taking an inward breath, she made a decision. It wasn't just her who was worrying about Gavin's future. Stewart, too, would worry as to what would happen if Angela left him on his own to bring up the baby. Of course, if he did meet someone else that woman may well be prepared to take on that responsibility, but in the meantime he needed someone here who Gavin loved as a mother. Besides, Maria had asked her to look after them both. By marrying him she would be doing just that. And yes, she could keep her sister's secret from Stewart. To tell him what Cesare Carpani had done to her would destroy him. Totally. Forever. And with Maria now sadly dead, what possible good could it do for him to know?

Eventually she turned around. 'Yes, Stewart,' she said, giving him a warm smile. 'I will marry you, and together we can look after Gavin. It's what Maria would want.'

Six weeks later they were married by Father Duncan at St Canice's Church in Rushcutters Bay, with Franco and his wife in attendance.

It was only much later, at a time when Gavin was a teenager, that she wondered if she had made the right decision to marry her sister's widower.

Chapter Fifteen

It was one of those perfect Autumn evenings where there was a slight chill in the air, but not enough to preclude having drinks on the verandah. As Angela finished getting ready to receive their guests, she decided to try to put the journalist's visit and the tragic memories it invoked to the back of her mind. She was looking forward to seeing Elena and her cousin. Emily was in the kitchen, putting the finishing touches to the antipasto platter, when Angela heard a knock on the door.

I'll get it,' she called out to Emily, straightening her skirt and checking her lipstick in the mirror.

When she opened the door, Elena was standing there with her cousin. Inwardly, Angela smiled. He had made such an effort. His thick grey hair was neatly brushed and he wore a white shirt and a red tie and his shoes were highly polished. Elena was also dressed up. Her blouse and skirt were immaculate and on the lapel of her blue jacket she wore a beautiful broach. She even looked as though she had been to the hairdresser for her hair was wonderfully coiffed. To Angela, who mostly saw her in swimmers, it was as though she had stepped straight out of the 1950s. Her legs were encased in shiny, thick mesh stockings and on her feet she wore a pair of patent leather shoes, much like the ones the Queen always wears. She also carried a handbag just like the Queen's.

'*Ciao,* Angeline,' she said beaming a radiant smile which lit up her whole face.

'*Ciao,* Elena,' Angela said, moving forward to greet her.

'This is my cousin, Marco,' Elena said, turning to her cousin.

'It is good to meet you, Angeline,' he said in faulting English and holding out his hand. 'Elena has told me much about you. She said you are from Naples.'

'I was born in Naples,' Angela said, taking his hand, 'but I spent a number of years on the island of Procida.'

'Ah, Procida. I know it well.'

Angela smiled. 'Well, I look forward to hearing all about it.' She pointed to the verandah. 'We should take advantage of this weather before the winter settles in, so let's go sit down outside.'

'Yes, let's do that,' Emily said, moving forward and giving both Marco and Elena a welcoming smile. 'You head out and I'll bring our drinks. Nonna insisted I get a bottle of *Prosecco* from the Veneto region for the occasion. Would you like a glass?'

Marco smiled and Angela thought what a good-looking man he must once have been. '*Grazie.*'

'And Elena?'

'*Si. Si.*'

'You said you've been here in Australia before,' Angela said in Italian as she smiled at Marco when they took their seats on the verandah. 'Many years ago.'

'It was during the war,' he said. 'I was taken prisoner in Libya and brought to Australia.'

'Oh! And whereabouts was that? Where you were held as a prisoner in Australia?'

Marco laughed. '*Siamo fortunate.*' He looked at Emily who had now joined them, handing the drinks and nibbles around. 'In English, I think you say: we lucky. We go to Tasmania. We work on the orchard. There be five of us.'

'That's funny,' Angela said, thinking how extraordinary that Marco should have been in Tasmania when Raphael was there. 'I knew someone many years ago on Procida who ended up there.'

'There were quite a few of us Italians there in Tasmania. What was his name?'

'Raphael Lombardi,' Angela said.

Marco's face burst into a huge grin, the wrinkles at the corner of his eyes radiating in happy abundance. He smacked his leg with his hand and jumped up. 'Raphael Lombardi. I remember him. *Lui nomo buono.* Good man. He used to play the flute. He was very good.'

Angela's face flushed with excitement. 'Yes, that would be the same Raphael. He played very well.' She raised an eyebrow. 'He was on the same orchard with you in Tasmania?'

'He be in Tasmania, but not where I be,' he said, sitting down again and cutting a small slice of Fontina cheese off the platter Emily handed him and placing it on a biscuit. 'I meet him on the

ship going back to Italy after the war. We become good friends.'
He chuckled. 'Even if I say so myself, I hold a tune back then. We good team, Raphael, me.'

Angela smiled. 'Did he ever play *Tarantella?*'

'Ah! *Tarantella*! Many times.' Marco laughed again. 'It a good tune to drink to.'

'I can quite imagine,' said Angela, smiling. 'But tell me … where in Tasmania was Raphael sent as a prisoner?' She thought for a moment, trying to recall the conversations she had with him about being held prisoner there. 'He said something about convict buildings.'

Marco scratched his head. 'He tell me where he was, but I forget. I in the Huon Valley, but he not there.' He smiled and again looked at Emily. 'Sorry for my English. It is not that good.'

'You are doing very well, Marco.' She smiled at him and topped up his glass.

He nodded and took a sip of *Prosecco*. 'There was much orchards there. Many of the workers, they were serving overseas. We replace them.' He shrugged. 'I lost touch with Raphael when we get back to Italy. My parents, they die and I go live with a cousin in Cinque Terra. When I marry a girl from Naples, I go there to live. But I never see Raphael again.' He paused. 'So … you know him well?'

Angela smiled. 'Quite well.'

'After the war?'

'Before ... and afterwards.'

'So you know where he be now?' Marco asked her, placing the pip from an olive in a small bowl on the table.

'No,' Angela said. 'I haven't seen him since I left Procida.'

'That be a pity,' Marco said. 'I like to see him again. I like to sing to his flute. But, my voice, it not be what it used to be.'

Angela smiled with the mental picture of Raphael and Marco making music together.

'I would have loved to have heard you together,' she said.

'Oh, yes, so would I,' Elena said, lifting her glass towards Marco in a toast. 'The flute has always been a favourite of mine.'

For over an hour they chatted on the verandah. When Emily went to the kitchen to get more drinks they lapsed into Italian, but as soon as she came back out Marco spoke his broken English, which Angela thought was very caring of him. She enjoyed his and Elena's company so much so that she totally forgot she was ill. When they got up to go, she was disappointed that the visit was over. Having Marco in her house somehow brought Raphael closer to her once more.

After they left, she and Emily were clearing up when Emily said, 'What a coincidence that Marco should know your friend Raphael.'

'Yes,' Angela said. 'It is quite amazing really.'

'Tell me more about him.'

'There's not much to tell, darling. Maria and I met him when we first went to the island. We more or less grew up together. Island children.'

'Did you see much of him when he came back after the war?'

'Of course we did. Procida is a small island.'

'He must have missed you when you came to Australia?'

Angela smiled. 'We were childhood friends. The war made adults of us all. We were leading different lives by the time it ended.'

'Oh! Anyway, I'm so glad we asked them around. Aren't you?'

Angela nodded. 'It was lovely to see them both.'

After Emily left to meet up with Chrissy for the movies, Angela sat on the white couch in her living room. How incredible it was that Marco knew Raphael, and that they should have been a musical item together on the ship sailing back to Italy! Raphael's flute must have been a great comfort to him during those war years, and to all those who listened to him play. Even now, as she sat here all these years later, she could almost hear the notes floating out into the Bay of Naples as he played to her on Procida.

Standing up, she went to her bedroom and took out her jewellery box. Hidden amongst other things, including Maria's gold lira pendant, was the small gemstone she treasured, often taking it out and polishing it. It was a tourmaline stone. She picked it up and played with it in her hand. So many times over the years she had done just this. When she first came to Australia she thought she might have it made it into a pendant. In the end, she had left it in the jewellery case where she knew it was safe. Nobody but Angela ever knew it was there. Not even Maria. At times she had almost told her about it. In the end, she decided to keep the stone a secret. And that is where it had remained all these years. Yet she remembered the moment she had received it as if it was yesterday.

***

When Raphael, now married for some time, heard Angela was leaving for Australia he came to see her. With the merging of his wife's family's wealth into their business, Raphael's father had been able to hold onto their villa on Procida, which they still used during the summer months. When he turned up at Aunt Sophia's villa, Angela didn't want to see him. She was excited about going to Australia and felt that if she saw Raphael all those feelings, which refused point blank to flee her heart no matter how much she tried to banish them (even going to the new small cinema and swimming on the beach with other boys hadn't done the job) would ruin that excitement. She had heard his wife gave birth to twin boys the year before. Sometimes, she knew he was on the island, and once she had even seen them all on Pozzo Vecchio—Angela, Maria's and Raphael's beach. When she had recognised them, despite having an aberrant desire to see what his wife and

219

twins looked like, she had hopped back on her bike and ridden home to Aunt Sophia's villa where she and Maria had been living after her death. She ran up the stairs and threw herself on her bed in floods of tears, the wrenching pain in her heart like a tight cord strangling her chest.

'You are a stupid girl not to see him, Angeline,' Maria scolded her, standing in the doorway of their bedroom with her arms folded in front of her crossly.

'I might be a stupid girl,' Angela blurted out, 'but I'm not going down.'

'He has been good enough to come and say goodbye,' Maria said, going over to the wardrobe and grabbing a cardigan for Angela to put on. 'The least you can do is go say goodbye to him as well.'

In the end, Angela gave in. She walked down the stairs and saw him standing there. A little older, but just as handsome as ever, his brown hair flopping over his familiar liquid brown eyes. He was wearing a pair of blue jeans and an open-neck shirt, beautifully ironed. Ironed by his wife, Angela thought with anger, but soon that anger dissipated when he gave her his Raphael smile and asked her to come down to *Cala di Corricella* with him.

'I am very glad you are going to Australia, Angeline,' he said, holding her eyes with his as they sat at their favourite taverna, sipping lemonades. He paused and kicked the ground with his heel. 'But I was very sad to hear that Aunt Sophia had died. I'm afraid I was away in Milan and didn't hear about it until much later. After she was buried.'

'I wondered if you knew.'

'She was a very lovely woman. You must miss her.'

'It's very hard to live at her villa without her. That's why, in a way, I'm glad we've sold and are going to Australia.'

'I'm sure you will be very happy there.'

'And you, Raphael? Are you happy?'

Raphael stood up and looked out to the bay where a number of trawlers and colourful *paranza,* traditional fishing, boats bobbed up and down in the choppy sea. Along the shore, smaller fishing boats were tied to pylons or pulled up on the rocky beach and the fishermen were repairing their nets in readiness for their next expedition. Children played in the shallows, splashing each other and crying out in joy and a mangy dog scavenged in the rubbish further along the corso. Above their heads, Angela could hear the rustle of people getting ready for the evening, with the windows thrown open to the cooler air, and she could just make out the sound of a radio.

'I'm happy enough,' Raphael said, turning around. He paused and gave her a lopsided grin. 'And now I have the children.'

'They must be so cute,' Angela said, not letting on for a second that she had seen them there on the beach.

He came over and sat down again. 'Yes, they're very cute. I'm a lucky man.'

'And they can take over the business when you're old and grey,' she said, touching his arm with her hand. She was taken aback by the sharp current of desire that shot through her body when her skin touched his and her face burnt bright red. She imagined she looked much like the scarlet paint on the fishing boat along the shore.

Raphael took hold of her hand and put it to his lips. For some time, they sat in silence, Angela's eyes never leaving his. 'I won't make them give up their dreams if they want to become a doctor or whatever they wish to do.' He paused and held her eyes with his. 'Nor will I stop them marrying someone of their choosing,' he said. 'They will follow their hearts and marry someone they love.'

It was then that Angela realised Raphael loved her as much as she loved him. They sat in silence before Raphael, trying to shift her mood, pointed to a *paranza* fishing boat coming in from the sea with its colourful sails flapping in the warm breeze and trailed by squawking seagulls.

'I didn't see boats like that in Australia,' he said, trying to sound cheerful.

'That's because the sharks would turn them over in a second,' Angela said, also endeavouring to appear cheery. 'How we will survive would be anyone's guess. Between sharks, snakes and poisonous spiders ...'

'You will have this to keep you safe,' he said, fiddling in his pocket and pulling out a tiny black velvet sachet with a drawstring on the top, which he opened. He took out a glorious polished gemstone, a three-sided prism of pinks, red, light greens, blue and yellow, which danced in the sunlight.

Angela gasped. 'It is exquisite.'

'It is called a tourmaline stone. It is believed to arouse feelings of joy, love, and most of all,' he said, holding her eyes with his and handing her the stone, 'forgiveness. It is also known for its protectiveness. I hope it keeps you safe, Angeline.' He smiled at her. 'Particularly, with those dreadful snakes, spiders and sharks in Australia. When you look at it I hope you think of me. And our island.'

He pulled out another stone, equally as exquisite, from his pocket. 'I have one too, Angeline. When I look at it I will think of you.'

Angela felt tears dribbling down her cheeks. Hurriedly, she turned away. She wiped her cheeks with her hand and looked back at him. 'Thank you,' she said, fiddling with the stone. 'It is beautiful. I will always treasure it.'

Raphael stood up and Angela could see that there were tears in his eyes. 'I will walk you back to the villa,' he said, blinking hard. 'I just had to come and say goodbye and give you that gemstone. I will miss seeing you around.'

She looked at him in surprise. 'You have seen me?'

He nodded. 'Every time I come to the island I see you. I have kept my distance. Until now.'

And then he stepped forward and kissed her on the cheek.

'*Arrivederci, Angeline*. I will never forget you,' he said when they arrived back at the villa. He stopped. 'In Australia when you see a wattle tree with its golden bloom, smile happily and think of me when I was in Tasmania and loved those trees.'

And then he was gone, not turning back, and she watched his tall frame disappear around the bend in the street. Standing there for some time, Angela clasped the stone in her hand and wept, not just for the fact that he was gone, but for what he had given her. The happiness she had known. A happiness she suspected she would never know again.

***

Placing the stone back into the case, Angela closed the lid. Her back hurt and she felt nauseous. She wondered if that was the cancer doing its hideous job. She looked out into her garden to where the branches of the wattle tree were shifting in the breeze. Every spring when it came into bloom she thought of Raphael telling her how lovely the golden blooms were. And that every time she looked at them she would smile happily and think of him. Even now, despite the tree not being in bloom, she smiled. One of the reasons she would never willingly go into a hospice to die was because she couldn't take that tree with her.

Chapter Sixteen

'You're deep in thought,' Emily said to Angela, as they whizzed past the turnoff to Bowral on their way to *Kilmarnock*.

'I was thinking how lovely the countryside looks,' Angela said. 'There's been such a lot of rain lately it all looks so green.'

A large truck whizzed past with a roar. This road had changed so much over the years, she thought. When she came this way with Stewart, it had been a dirt road. If one got stuck behind a truck, the dust was horrendous, but there was nothing one could do until there was a flat stretch of road with no one coming the other way. Now it was a four-lane highway with special shady places to pull over and rest. Every now and then there were busy, garish petrol outlets selling soft drinks, sweets, pies or sandwiches and offering Internet. Or there might be a McDonalds or KFC franchise. In the old days, one packed a thermos and sandwiches in a basket and pulled over to the side of the road, throwing a picnic rug on a farmer's land. If they ran low on petrol Stewart always had a spare can in the boot.

'Angus said they've had a fair bit of rain at *Kilmarnock*,' Emily said. 'The dams are full and the creek's running madly.'

'I'm so glad you organised this weekend, darling. Already it's doing me the world of good to get out of the city. I just hope we won't be a burden to Angus's parents. It's so kind of them to offer to have us stay.'

'They wouldn't hear of anything else.'

'It's such a pity Angus isn't going to be there.'

Emily threw her a sideways glance. 'He's really busy at work and had to get some assignment in. But he was very happy you and I are going to visit his parents. His father has been even more down lately, and his mother is finding it difficult. Must say, I can't blame her. She's trying really hard to move on from Duncan's death, but Bill seems to be dwelling on it all the time.'

'Death is sad at any time, particularly when it's someone so young.'

'Even when they're older it's still sad. Like Grandpa.' She looked at Angela. 'You must know this road so well. All those functions in Canberra which Grandpa used to go to. He really was well thought of, wasn't he? I mean … to be wined and dined at The Lodge and Government House. It makes it so much harder to think he may have done something suss like getting hold of Glasgow Mine lease in such a way.'

Angela didn't say anything, she just put her hand on Emily's knee and gave it a gentle squeeze. Would Stewart have been wined and dined like that, she wondered, if he hadn't made huge donations to political parties over the years and entertained so many politicians at *Erskine's* restaurants, *Mandalay, Riverside* and on his yacht, *Pride of Erskine?* She remembered one particular lunch at *Mandalay* when she and Stewart entertained a prominent New South Wales politician and his wife. It was not long after that lunch when Stewart gained the lease to set up Glasgow Mine. Although nothing untoward had been discussed at that lunch, Stewart had invited the politician and a number of his friends out on *Pride of Erskine* for a day's sailing. When Angela had queried why he was spending so much time with the politician Stewart had shrugged.

'He's a good bloke. Besides, I owe him a favour.'

Angela wasn't stupid, so it wasn't long before she put two and two together when Stewart told her he had gained a sought after lease to mine up the Hunter. And with much pomp and ceremony, that same politician had opened Glasgow Mine. Afterwards, there was a reception at *Riverside*.

She had said nothing.

But in her own mind, Angela knew that didn't clear her from being a party to what Stewart was up to.

'Your grandfather was certainly feted by the high and mighty,' she eventually said to Emily as they passed the row of poplar trees that Angela had always loved. Even though it had been years since she'd seen them on that last visit to Canberra with Stewart, they looked magnificent, their autumnal colours a resplendent display of red, yellow and burnished gold.

'Chrissy told me her father reckoned he was regarded as a real mogul.'

'He was certainly a good businessman.' Angela smiled. 'And yes, I suppose you could regard him as a mogul.'

'What sort of business was he doing in South Korea?'

Angela fiddled with the scarf around her neck, pulling it tighter and loosening it again. 'It was to do with Glasgow Mine.'

'Oh! In what way?'

'I didn't go into it too much, but having Glasgow Mine, Stewart was keen to work with the South Koreans. See how they managed their power.'

'Wow. And that's what he was doing when he died.'

'Yes, that's right.'

'And you didn't go with him.'

'No. I had no desire to go to South Korea. I read enough about the Korean War to put me off the place. Although, I gather it's now quite a tourist area.'

'Was he on his own when he died? I mean, who found him?'

Angela looked out of the window to where a few alpacas grazed on a small hill and another couple hovered around a half-full dam. 'When he didn't turn up for a meeting his assistant went looking. That's when they found him.'

'Poor, Nonna. It was bad enough for me when he died, but you must have been devastated to lose him that way and not be with him.'

Angela nodded. 'It was a great shock to us all.'

***

228

When they arrived at the gates to *Kilmarnock* and rattled over the cattle grid, Emily pointed ahead. 'Here we are, Nonna. The homestead's not far up over that hill.'

Since Emily's visit, the paddocks had greened up and the cattle and sheep looked fatter. It's amazing what a bit of rain can do, she thought. We might hate it in the city, but to the farmers it's manna from heaven. No sooner had she pulled the car to a halt under a flowering cherry by the garden gate than Betty came rushing out with Rex by her side. When they got out of the car and Emily introduced her to Nonna she looked so pleased to see them that Emily was immediately glad they had come.

'What a pleasure it is to have you here at *Kilmarnock*, Mrs Erskine,' Betty said to Nonna, taking her hand. 'And you too, Emily. Bill and I've been looking forward so much to your arrival.' She laughed. 'He even had a haircut for the occasion.'

Nonna smiled. 'Goodness, there was no need for that.'

'He insisted. Now,' she added, looking around for the luggage. 'Let me take you inside and settle you into your room, Mrs Erskine. No doubt you'd like a short rest before dinner.'

'Please call me Angela. And no. I'd much rather you show me around your lovely garden. That would be far better than wasting a moment having a rest.'

Emily saw Nonna rest her eyes on the wattle tree in the corner.

'Such a beautiful tree,' she said, flashing a broad smile at Betty.

Betty returned her smile. 'It never fails to lift my heart when it blooms, no matter what.'

Nonna leant down and patted Rex on the head and was rewarded with licks all over her hand. 'What a lovely dog,' she said. 'I've always loved Scottie Terriers.'

Emily smiled. 'He's called Rex, Nonna. And yes, you're a cutie,' she said, patting the dog on the head.' She turned to Nonna. 'Why don't you and Betty look around the garden and I'll take our things inside.' She glanced at Betty. 'Where would you like me to put everything?'

'I put your grandmother in Duncan's room. And I've put you in Angus's room. I hope that will be okay for you, dear.'

'Absolutely.'

Emily watched Betty take Nonna by the arm and together they walked through the small gate into the garden. Going to the boot of the car, she took out her small case and then Nonna's.

Inside, she met Bill walking down the hallway.

'Hello there, Emily,' he said, moving forward to greet her. Although he smiled warmly, she couldn't help but notice that the smile didn't quite reach his eyes, which looked somewhat haunted. And he'd lost more weight, making his trousers hang loosely. 'And where is your grandmother?'

'Out in the garden with Betty. She couldn't wait to see it all.'

'Well, I'll go and join them.' He paused and smiled again. This time his eyes were part of that smile. 'In the morning, what's say you join me for a ride to check the stock. I haven't been round the paddocks in a few days.'

'I'd like that very much.'

'Angus said to make sure you take his Cassidy for a run. It will do him good.'

'Yes, he told me to do that. But do you think I'll be able to manage him?'

'Of course you will.' He paused. 'However, if you'd prefer you could ride Jess.'

Emily thought for a moment. It'd be good to test herself. And she had told Angus she would take Cassidy out.

'No, Cassidy is fine. What time were you thinking of going?'

'What's say after breakfast? I know Betty has bacon and eggs planned.' He grinned. 'We wouldn't want to miss that, would we?'

When he had gone, Emily put Nonna's case in Duncan's room, stopping for a second at the window to watch Betty showing Nonna around the garden. They looked to be in deep conversation. She then saw Bill walk up and join them, and watched him take Nonna's hand in greeting. She saw the smile on his face, and once again she was pleased they had come.

Further down the hallway she went into Angus's room and put her things on the bed. She hadn't been in here before. On the table by his bed was a framed photograph of two young boys. She picked it up and immediately recognised Angus. She presumed the other boy with an even wider smile than Angus was Duncan. On the chest of drawers was another photo of them. This time as teenagers. And next to that was a photo of Duncan in his army uniform. His parents mightn't be able to cope with photos of their son on display, but Angus did. She felt tears threatening and took out a tissue to wipe them away. On the wall there were various rugby photos and even a couple of riding trophies. She picked one up and read the inscription. 'ACT Cross Country Champion, 1999'. And underneath was Angus's name. Although she knew he was a good rider, she had no idea he had won trophies for it.

Moving to the bedside table she picked up a book. *Birdsong* by Sebastian Faulks. Despite the gruesome war scenes, it was one of Emily's favourite books. Yet she couldn't help feel that for someone who had lost his brother to war it was a tragic book to read. Playing with it in her hand she moved to the window. Outside, she could see the horses grazing in the home paddock. In the centre of the paddock was a dam where a family of ducks swam towards the reeds on the far shore. Further out, a flock of sheep huddled under the eucalyptus trees and to her right a herd of cattle were happily doing their own thing, grazing or chewing the cud. Close by were the cattle yards and further on the shearing shed. These were scenes that Angus and Duncan would have seen every day when they were growing up here. In a way, she wondered how either of them ever wanted to leave. But of course they would have wanted to do so. There was a whole wide world out there waiting for them.

Until the day Duncan was killed.

Since then, it would have become a lonely scene for Angus— seeing his brother in every blade of grass in those paddocks; on every fence; at every gate; under every tree, particularly the one they used to swing off into the river as kids. And with his father retreating into himself it would have become even lonelier for him.

She moved away from the window and went to her bag to get out the present she had brought for Angus's parents. She and Nonna had wondered what to get. In the end, they had settled for a couple of bottles of good wine, one Riesling, one a Pinot, and a box of chocolates. Probably a bit boring, but safe. She smiled as she thought of her grandmother, Maria, and what she might have brought for a present. The way Nonna always described her she was obviously quite out there and great fun, so she would have possibly brought something much more exciting. A dazzling scarf for Betty, a bright, fun tie for Bill. As she had often wished over the years, she wished again that she had met her grandmother. How sad it was that she died having Emily's father. Emily's grandfather must have been distraught to lose his wife like that. But how lucky he was to have Nonna there to look after both himself and her father.

One day when she was up at *Riverside* and they were walking through the vineyard, she asked her grandfather to tell her more about her grandmother. She watched him look across the vines to where the hills rose brown and grey up to the horizon. After some time, he turned his eyes to her. 'Maria was totally different to any girl I had ever known. Her beauty was admired by everyone who met her. Her love of life was a joy to watch.' He then turned away, but not before Emily saw his eyes fill with tears. After a moment he turned back and smiled, however it was a painful sort of smile. 'But come,' he said, taking her hand, 'let's not be maudlin. We should go see what's happening up at the house.'

'Do I remind you of her at all?' she asked him. 'I mean ... I know I don't look a lot like her, but is there anything else maybe?'

He never answered her. It was as if he hadn't heard. And, as Emily could see talking about her grandmother upset him, she let the subject drop.

Now, heading for the door, she went to the kitchen to put the wine and chocolates on the bench and then stepped out through the back door to the garden to join Nonna and their hosts.

***

That evening Bill cooked lamb cutlets on the barbeque.

'They're our own,' he said proudly, as Nonna complimented him on how tender and juicy they were.

'And the salad is delicious,' she said to Betty.

'Thank you, everything is from my garden.'

'You can certainly tell the difference,' Emily said, meaning it.

Afterwards, they moved inside to a roaring fire in the front drawing room, where Bill insisted on serving ports with their coffee.

'I could get used to this,' Nonna said. 'Quite easily.'

'So your son, Gavin, took over the family business when your husband died,' Bill said to her. 'Emily's Dad.'

Emily watched Nonna take a sip from her coffee cup. 'Yes, but he's more into developing. Glasgow Mine and *Riverside* were sold many years ago, as were *Erskine's* restaurants.'

'Yes I remember that,' Bill said. 'Sadly, they stopped taking our beef and lamb when there was a change of ownership. Not a hint of an apology, even though we'd been supplying them for decades. Just a phone call one day to say they had another supplier and wouldn't want *Kilmarnock* beef or lamb anymore.'

'Oh,' Nonna said. 'Emily did tell me, and I was sorry to hear it.'

'That's business I suppose. Anyway, I heard that fellow Dimitri Carpani now owns the whole *Erskine* franchise.'

'Yes, Dimitri bought the franchise from my son, including the original *Cesare's* which Stewart had bought from his mother after his father, Cesare's, death back in the 1960s.'

'I gather he was murdered in a robbery outside his restaurant.'

'Yes, that's quite right,' Nonna said. 'The night's takings from his restaurant were stolen.' There was a slight pause before Nonna went on. 'After my husband passed away, Dimitri made Gavin a good offer for the entire portfolio of *Erskine's* restaurants, including the original premises of *Cesare's* and also *Erskine's,* which my sister and I helped Stewart set up. After much deliberation, Gavin accepted.'

'You must have been sad to see the *Erskine's* franchise go out of the family,' Betty said.

Nonna nodded. 'Yes, I was. However, it was Gavin's decision.'

Emily remembered Nonna and her father having a number of heated exchanges about this. In fact, one day when she stood outside the living room at *Mandalay* she was surprised to hear her father speak so sourly about his own father's legacy. It was as if he couldn't get rid of the *Erskine's* franchise quickly enough. She got a dreadful shock when she heard him almost shout at Nonna. 'I'm surprised, Mother, that you're not happy to see them go out of the family as well. After what he did to both of us.'

When Emily had approached her father as to why he was so keen to get rid of the restaurant franchise he told her it was a business decision. And Nonna had said much the same when she'd asked her. It was only just now, hearing Betty ask Nonna if she had been sad to see the *Erskine's* franchise go out of the family that she wondered about that conversation she had overheard all those years ago at *Mandalay.* Was her father referring to how her grandfather had got hold of Glasgow Mine, or was he referring to something else when he told Nonna she too should have been pleased the *Erskine's* franchise had been sold after what Stewart had done.

236

Now she saw Nonna smile at Bill. 'I'm afraid Dimitri upset quite a few of our suppliers by dropping them. Many of them had been with *Erskine's* for many years. In a way, I wish Dimitri had changed the name from *Erskine's* to something else.'

Emily now remembered another conversation with her father. When she said she was pleased her grandfather's legacy was to be kept on by Dimitri Carpani using the name *Erskine's,* her father had shrugged and said Dimitri had paid good money for the name so he had every right to keep it on, but as far as he was concerned he'd be happy if Dimitri changed the whole franchise to the name *Cesare's.* When she told Nonna this she was furious and got up and left the room. Now, as she listened to Nonna, Betty and Bill talk together she sympathised with Nonna. To see someone else owning what she had helped her husband and sister set up must have been distressing.

'We were sad to hear of your husband's death,' Bill said to Nonna, interrupting Emily's thoughts. 'Such a tragedy. His heart, I gather. And being in South Korea wouldn't have helped.'

Nonna put her cup down. 'Yes, it was very sad, but not nearly as sad as the death of your son.'

'Thank you,' Betty said. 'It doesn't seem to get any easier with passing time, does it, dear?' she added, glancing at Bill, who sighed and looked towards the window.

Nonna smiled. 'Stewart was of a good age, but even so ...'

'It still hurts,' Betty said.

'Yes,' Nonna said. 'When I lost my sister, Maria, who was Emily's grandmother and married to Stewart at that time, she was only very young.' Emily saw Nonna's eyes water up and wondered if it was because of Nonna's own illness that she now felt so dreadfully sad about Maria. 'She died in childbirth with Gavin,' Nonna went on. 'I still miss her dreadfully.'

Betty nodded. 'So you brought Gavin up when you married Stewart. Your sister would have been pleased you did that.'

Nonna smiled. 'Yes, I think she would.'

'All very sad,' Bill said. 'If anything, the pain of losing someone seems to get worse.' He paused, stood up and went over to the window where he stood for some time, fiddling with the glass of port in his hand. Eventually he turned around. '*Kilmarnock* has been in the family for a number of generations. We're looking forward to Angus coming back home and taking over from us, aren't we, Betty?'

'We shouldn't put pressure on him,' Betty said.

'Of course there's pressure,' Bill said, taking a long sip of port. 'He has to. We don't want it going out of the family.'

'It'll be lonely for him on his own,' Betty said.

'We're not talking about tomorrow. Unless, of course, we go sailing like we were thinking of. And in that case it would only be temporary. He'll have plenty of time to find a wife.' He looked at Emily. 'What about that lass, Chrissy, who he brought down with you last time? Mike's sister. The one who lives on a lettuce leaf, causing us farmers to go broke?'

'Bill!' Betty exclaimed. 'Who Angus chooses to go out with is his business.'

Bill laughed. 'Well, he better sort himself out sooner, rather than later. You and I won't be around forever. Then he'll need to hightail it back here quick smart.'

Betty smiled. 'Give him time, Bill. He's doing that agricultural course. He knows it's his duty to take over here.'

Bill went over to where the carafe of port sat on the sideboard and offered it around. When everyone shook their heads he poured himself another glass and took a sip. 'I reckon Duncan would have come to his senses and got out of the army and taken over. But now that he's gone, well, it's up to Angus …'

'Bill,' Betty said. 'You're starting to sound all maudlin, and poor Angela and Emily don't want to hear about all of this.'

Emily was sure she saw tears in Bill's eyes and she watched Betty look at him worriedly. Was she afraid he was going to break down?

'I'm sure Angus will make the right decision,' Nonna said. '*Kilmarnock* is such a lovely place. Now,' she added with a warm smile as she picked up her shawl from the arm of the chair, 'if you'll excuse me, I suddenly feel very tired, so I think I'll call it a night.' She looked from Bill to Betty. 'Thank you so much for such a wonderful evening. Sitting outside under the stars like that was glorious. And dinner was delicious.' She smiled again. 'It's a long time since I've enjoyed myself so much.' She then looked at Emily. 'Be a dear and see me to my room. Then I'll use the bathroom and fall into bed.'

'Of course, Nonna,' Emily said. And then she too glanced from Bill to Betty. 'I think I might head off as well. But thank you so much. It was a lovely evening.' She picked up her coffee cup and then Nonna's.

'Leave those dear,' Betty said. 'I've got the tray. I hope you both sleep well,' she added, standing up to see them to the door. 'Please sleep in late in the morning. Emily knows I get up with the birds, but I won't serve breakfast until you're up and ready.'

'Thank you,' Emily said. She smiled at Bill. 'I look forward to that ride after breakfast, Bill.'

***

When Angela said goodnight to Emily and shut the door behind her she went to the window and looked out. Unlike her home at Bronte, with its twinkling lights and the sound of the surf, it was pitch dark and silent outside. She wondered about that silence. How Bill and Betty coped with it, now that Duncan was dead and Angus only came home fleetingly. Of course, there would be the station hands here during the day, but when they had long since gone home for the night it would be just Bill and Betty left to deal with their grief together. She had enjoyed talking to them both and hoped they had enjoyed her and Emily's company. It was obvious they were fond of Emily. One only had to see the look in Bill's eyes when he was talking to her to know that. And Betty was much the same. She wondered about Angus. In a way she felt sorry for him, as Bill had made it perfectly clear they hoped he would take the place over whether he liked it or not. There's more in that man's face than sadness, Angela thought. He's suffering from deep depression and is trying his darndest to drown it in alcohol.

Now, as she gazed out of the window, she wondered if Angus was given the chance would he choose this life, for the lot of a farmer was often a hard one. Sure, there might be good seasons, but there would be dreadful ones as well with droughts, bushfires, and stock and wool prices often dropping, while the cost of running the farm could increase hugely depending on the conditions. Then there was the isolation. Canberra was forty kilometres away and Sydney a good three hours' drive. It would take a special girl to want to live out here, despite it being a magnificent property. A girl like Betty had been when she took *Kilmarnock* and Bill on.

She was annoyed with Dimitri Carpani for ceasing to take their beef. Although she knew it would only be a small part of Bill's overall output, restaurants were notorious for doing that. Promising a farmer a regular order, then when they changed a recipe cancelling that order willy nilly, whether it be beef or a particular vegetable, or in the case of fishermen, fish.

Moving from the window, she sat down on the bed. Her hip was aching badly and she felt exhausted. Not just from the pain, but also from the angst the mention of Cesare Carpani's name had invoked. Even after all of these years the very thought of him brought back so many unwanted memories, sealing them in her mind no matter how much she tried to dislodge them. She remembered how furious she had been when Gavin told her he was going to sell the *Erskine's* franchise to Cesare's son, Dimitri. For days and days, they'd argued loud and furiously. In the end, Angela realised she was wasting her time trying to get him to see sense. Besides, she wasn't involved in the day-to-day running of the business, so unless she disclosed to him about Cesare she had a weak argument. Dimitri had offered a very good price, and, as Gavin pointed out time and time again, it was a sound and profitable business proposition.

Gavin had come around the night before they left and attempted to change her mind about treatment. Both he and Emily had spent ages trying to persuade her, but she was adamant she wasn't going to be bullied. It was something she felt very strongly about.

But how long before things became unbearable? When would she decide to put an end to it all?

But here, right now, despite the pain, she felt a calmness she hadn't felt for some time. She accepted her fate. Bill and Betty had been hit by a far bigger tragedy. After watching Bill, she wondered if he would ever get over it. If Angus had thought it would cheer his parents up, she was glad that she and Emily had decided to come here for the weekend before going onto Canberra for a night, where they would stay at the old Hotel Canberra, now known as the Hyatt.

She sighed and stood up. Moving over to the small case by her bed she took out her nightie. After brushing her hair and taking off her makeup she climbed between the crisp, cool sheets, the silence of the night lulling her into a deep sleep.

Chapter Seventeen

The next morning, after a leisurely breakfast on the side verandah with the sun filtering through the splendid autumnal Virginia creeper, Emily and Bill left Nonna and Betty talking roses and geraniums and went to catch the horses.

'We won't be long, 'Bill said. 'When we get back, I'll take you ladies for a drive into Gundaroo. We might even see if they've got a spare table at *Grazings*.'

Emily was happy to see that Bill wanted to go out for lunch. Last time they were here it seemed he was loath to leave the place. Perhaps he was trying to make up for his maudlin mood the previous night. She was pleased that Angus hadn't been there to see his father talking like that. Then again, if Angus had been there maybe it would have been a different scenario.

On catching Bill's horse and then Cassidy for Emily, they saddled up. When she knew they were coming down here again, Emily had found herself a second-hand pair of RM Williams boots at Vinnies and had accepted the offer of Betty's Akubra so she felt quite the part. Once they were mounted, with both horses eager to head off, they cantered through a couple of empty paddocks to check the cattle huddled together in the far one. Emily loved the feel of being back in the saddle. And although Cassidy was harder in the mouth to what Jess was, she was able to manage him fairly easily and he had a good, easy gait. She felt a certain pride in being able to tell Angus that she had managed him well. After checking the cattle, they trotted to another paddock to check some sheep, and then they headed down to the river. When she reined Cassidy in next to Bill's horse they walked along the riverbank before stopping to breathe in the view of the gnarled red gums, weeping willows and tall poplars, still a deep burgundy, but about to lose their autumn leaves.

'What a wonderful scene,' she said to Bill as they pulled the horses to a halt.

She let Cassidy's reins loose so that he could graze on the long river grass.

'Autumn's my favourite time here,' Bill said. 'Not much wind and the colours are good for the soul.' He paused. 'Sadly, it was autumn when Duncan was killed, but even so ...'

Emily thought that it may have been autumn here, but it would have been spring in Afghanistan with wildflowers sprouting in the mountains and fields amid the bloodshed. How desperate Duncan must have felt over there as he took his last breath away from his family and country. From all that was familiar.

All of a sudden, Bill's horse jinked to one side, snorted loudly and reared up on his hind legs.

'It's a snake,' he said, as he tightened his reins.

And sure enough, Emily saw a snake right in front of them, hissing and lashing out. She pulled Cassidy's reins tight and yanked him away.

'Woah now, young fella,' Bill soothed calmly, patting his own horse on the neck.

But his words were to no avail. His horse reared up again and with dread, Emily saw him somersault backwards on top of Bill. The horse got up and galloped off but Bill lay there. Motionless.

She checked where the snake was and seeing it slither away into the bushes she jumped down from the saddle, tied Cassidy to a branch of a tree and rushed over to where Bill lay. She knelt down over his still form and touched his face. 'Bill, are you okay?'

Nothing.

She called his name again, but he was out cold. With horror she saw blood oozing out of a gash on the side of his forehead. Oh my God! She felt ill. Not from the blood. With fear.

'Bill!' she tried again. 'Can you hear me?

Still nothing. She felt his neck and his pulse was still beating. She didn't dare to move him, fearing he had damaged his spine or neck.

Not sure what to do next, she ripped off her jumper and gently put it under his head.

She fumbled for her phone in her back pocket, but when she dragged it out there was no signal.

Oh no!

Making sure he was comfortable and was lying in a position to breathe, she spoke softly. 'Bill, I'll go back to the homestead and get help.'

With a final desperate glance at him she rushed over to Cassidy, jumped up into the saddle and urged him into a full gallop back to the homestead to raise the alarm. The whole time, as she coaxed Cassidy on, all she could see was the sight of Bill lying there out cold, his head bloodied, and Betty's distraught face when Emily would tell her what had happened.

Last year her son! Now her husband!

'Oh my God,' Betty exclaimed in horror with the colour draining from her face when Emily leapt off the horse and rushed to where she was in the garden sitting on a bench with Nonna drinking a cup of tea. 'Where is he?'

When Emily explained where Bill was she nodded. 'Yes, I know where you mean. You ring the ambulance and wait here for it. I'll go to Bill. There's a track along the side of the river that the ambulance should be able to follow. It will take you to where he is.'

'Shall I ring Angus?' Emily called out to her as she mounted Cassidy.

'Not until the ambulance arrives and we know how he is.'

Emily and Angela now watched her gallop at full speed towards where Bill lay in the river paddock. Emily knew Bill was a good horseman, but she had no idea that Betty was also.

When the ambulance sped up the driveway half an hour later, Emily rushed across and asked if she could get in with them to show where to go. After rattling over the paddocks they came to where Betty was sitting beside Bill with her hand on his head.

'I haven't dared move him,' she said as the paramedics tended to him. 'Every now and then he comes to, but then he seems to lose consciousness again.'

Emily looked at her distraught face and suddenly a vision of her as Miss Royal Easter Showgirl handing Bill his prize for show jumping flashed through her mind. Oh, Bill, she sighed, please, please pull through.

After the ambulance left with Bill inside, Betty beckoned for Emily to get up behind her on Cassidy. 'Duncan and Angus often double dinked on him,' she said, moving forward in the saddle and offering Emily a stirrup to heave herself up.

Once up, she held on tight as Betty urged Cassidy over to get Bill's horse. Leaning down, she took hold of the reins and handed them to Emily. He seemed to have calmed down, so was easy to lead. Soon they were back to the homestead where Betty rang Angus, who said he would come straight down.

'He sounded very upset, so I hope he drives carefully,' she said to Emily and Nonna when she got off the phone.

'I'm sure he will,' Emily said, putting her arm around her. 'I'll drive you to the hospital. Angus will have his car, so you won't want yours as well.'

'No. I'll drive myself,' Betty said. She looked at Nonna. 'I'm so sorry this has ruined your visit here.'

Nonna gave her a warm smile. 'Please don't even think that. It's Bill we've got to think of now.'

***

'It all happened so quickly,' Emily said to Angus as they waited to hear news of Bill at Calvary Hospital two hours later after she had dropped Nonna at the Hyatt where they had their booking brought forward. 'One minute we were enjoying the view of the river and then that snake freaked your father' horse out. It leapt out of nowhere to try and strike him.'

'That's what they do.' There was a long pause. 'I'm not sure what it would do to Mum if he doesn't pull through. She's been stoic about Duncan … but this … well …'

Emily placed a hand on his arm. 'I feel so much for you both.'

He turned to her and she saw tears in his eyes. 'He's a great Dad. Duncan's death has almost destroyed him. If he was his normal self, I'm sure he'd have controlled his horse. When you and Chrissy were down last I thought he was pulling out of it a bit.' He paused. 'What was he like yesterday when you came down?'

She smiled. 'He was fine. This morning he even suggested we should all go into Gundaroo for lunch.'

'Mum said he's been drinking quite a bit. What about last night?'

249

Emily waited before answering. She didn't want to tell him how maudlin his father was after he'd had a few ports. 'We all had a few wines and a port after dinner.'

'Port always makes him maudlin.'

'It's obvious he's hurting heaps, Angus. But really, he was fine. And he was great this morning. We had a terrific ride, up until the snake came from nowhere …'

He put his hand on hers.' I'm sorry you had to witness it all. You're already doing it tough with your Nonna so ill.'

'Angus I'm okay, really I am. It's you—'

She stopped when they saw a doctor approaching along the hallway. She tried to read his face.

'We're keeping him in a coma,' the doctor said. 'As a precaution. There's quite a bit of swelling in the brain.'

Betty, who had just returned with steaming coffees from the cafeteria rushed up when she saw the doctor. 'Will he be alright?' she asked, anxiously. 'Oh please God, I hope so.'

'He has a strong heart,' the doctor said, putting a reassuring hand on her shoulder, 'however, time will tell with his head injury.'

'So there could be brain damage?' Angus asked, warily.

'Again, time will tell. Let's hope for the best. But no matter what happens, we'll need to keep him in here for some time.' He looked at Betty. 'I believe you live out Gundaroo way. Maybe you could go home and get some rest. We'll ring you if there's any change.'

'No,' Betty said. 'I'll stay here. Close by.'

'Mum,' Angus said. 'Let's go home. We've got the phones and can be back within forty minutes if needs be.' He looked at Emily. 'Will you be okay?'

'We'll be just fine at the Hyatt,' she assured him. 'Will you ring me?'

'Yes, of course. The moment we hear anything.' He paused. 'Emily, thank you for coming here. I really appreciate it.'

'Yes,' Betty said. 'Thank you dear.' She smiled bravely. 'I'm sure he'll be alright.'

Emily nodded slowly. 'Yes, I'm sure he'll be just fine.'

But, as she said that, she wondered anxiously if he really would be. His head must have got one hell of a knock. The only saving grace was that the horse hadn't crushed him to death when it toppled back on him.

She kissed Betty on the cheek and said goodbye. She then looked at Angus, but when she came to speak she found she could find no words. Instead, she gave him a gentle smile, nodded and left him there. In the crowded lift, she tried to curtail the tears that were threatening. However, the moment she got outside and sat behind the wheel of her car she could contain them no longer and put her head on the steering wheel and sobbed. How had such a lovely day become a nightmare?

Angela sat in the *Tea Lounge* in the lobby of the Hyatt Hotel. It seemed like a place often frequented for the hotel's advertised 'high tea.' Around her tables were crammed with people from all walks of life, some in casual dress, others seeming as though they had dressed up for the occasion. Among the tables a waitress weaved a wooden trolley offering all sorts of cakes and sandwiches beautifully presented on silver tiers. As she sat there, Angela thought of the fragility of life, not only her own, but also Bill's, who was fighting for his in hospital. She thought back to the previous night and how sad he was about Duncan, who he had obviously adored. This made her sad to think of the fraught relationship Gavin had endured with Stewart over the years, culminating in the dire circumstances of his death in South Korea.

Although she had tried to put journalist Greg Ashton's last visit out of her mind, it was proving impossible. His delving into Stewart's dealings with Glasgow Mine still might mean a lot of bad publicity for the family and could destroy Stewart's legacy. Although, she was much more frightened of what the journalist might uncover if he dug deep enough into the relationship between Stewart and Cesare Carpani. It could be far, far worse.

It could shatter Angela's family forever.

It was at one of Stewart's restaurant openings, this time *Erskine's On The Sand* at Rattan Beach to the north of Sydney when Angela came face to face with Cesare Carpani, the first time since she and Maria moved to the YWCA hostel the morning after he brutally raped Maria. It was a Sunday lunchtime function and as the restaurant opened onto the beach, Angela suggested Gavin and his friend, Dave, come along to surf on the beach, which was notorious for having great waves to catch, while she and Stewart entertained the guests. When they arrived, there was a fine array of cars, ranging from MG sports to large Jaguars parked along the side of the road. Angela was never too keen on these occasions, as she felt compelled to make chit chat with Sydney's social set, who she felt were trying to outdo each other with what their money could buy, whether it be fancy cars or the latest jewellery or fashion. Despite the fact that she, herself, arrived in Stewart's black Mercedes, was dressed in an elegant white dress from Mark Foy's and wore a diamond necklace from Prouds around her neck, it wasn't really her ideal scene. She much preferred to wear denim jeans and a sloppy Joe while walking her dog, Safron, or popping down to the local delicatessen. Even when she took Gavin to his games of sport, where she could talk to the other mothers, she dressed down, although many of the other mothers wore twinsets and pearls.

When they got out of the car at Rattan Beach, Gavin and Dave scampered down the embankment to catch the waves. Dave was so blonde and Gavin so dark. It was 1965, when the Beatles were at their peak, and despite Angela and Stewart objecting, Gavin had let his hair grow into a thick, floppy mop imitating the boys in the band. His skin was tanned from the summer's son and although he wasn't that tall he was well built and muscular from all his sport.

When Angela felt she would no longer be missed at the function, she wandered down to the beach to see how the boys were getting on. After taking off her shoes and stepping onto the sand she noticed there was a third boy with Gavin and Dave as they ran across the sand to her. He was a bit younger, but Angela had immediately been struck by how similar he looked to Gavin. Not only was he of much the same height, he was obviously of Italian descent and his features had an uncanny resemblance to Gavin's. It was the same high forehead, slightly Roman nose and deeply set dark brown eyes.

'We caught up with Dimitri while swimming,' Gavin said to Angela, flicking his sodden hair back over his forehead. 'Dave and I have played soccer against him. His parents have a place further along the beach. Dimitri's asked us back to play snooker. Can we go, Mum?'

'I daresay you can; however, I'll come along to make sure it's okay with his parents.'

When they arrived at the house and Dimitri showed them through a small iron gate off the sand dunes and into a lush garden, a riot of colourful bushes and flowerbeds, and showcasing manicured lawns, Angela gazed at the large house sitting well back on the block. Somehow it looked out of place in this setting. Where most of the other houses had rambling slightly overgrown gardens and were built of weatherboards, appearing more in keeping with the beach setting, this one was built of rendered brick and was painted in apricots and blues like many houses in Naples. She was wondering what sort of people Dimitri's parents could be when her eyes settled on the one man she never wanted to see again in her life, Cesare Carpani. She thought of fleeing. If the boys weren't with her she would have.

Cesare was lazing by the pool, a cigarette in his mouth, a glass of wine on the table beside him and his thinning hair was greyer. But there was no mistaking it was him. He was possibly even portlier than when Angela had last seen him nearly fourteen years before. Angela knew that his restaurant, *Cesare's,* was still very successful and this house was no doubt his reward. The cost of property on this stretch of the coast was expensive and becoming more so every year. This was one of the reasons Stewart had decided to open an *Erskine's* restaurant here. Angela looked around for Bettina, but then she remembered hearing on the restaurant gossip grapevine that Bettina had divorced him soon after Maria and Angela had left Cesare's. At the time, Angela had wondered if Bettina somehow knew what he had done to Maria. Angela had also heard Cesare had got married again to a young waitress who had come to work for him and who had become pregnant. So even if she didn't know about Maria's rape, maybe this pregnancy was the catalyst for Bettina to divorce him. Dimitri was obviously the result of that pregnancy.

'*Ciao,* Papa,' Dimitri called out to Cesare, who lowered his sunglasses to eye the party. 'This is Dave and Gavin. Is it okay if we play snooker? Gavin's mother has come along to make sure it's alright.'

In an instant Angela knew Cesare recognised her, for his eyes fleeted knowingly across her startled face. She then saw him quickly glance from his own son to Gavin and back again. Undoubtedly he, too, had noticed the strong resemblance. Without so much as standing up he shook his head at Dimitri. 'I'm sorry, son,' he said in a strong Italian accent, taking a long drag of his cigarette before putting it down in the ashtray by his side. 'We're heading out soon. Your mother was about to go looking for you. You have to get changed.' He turned his eyes to Angela and although he still didn't acknowledge that he knew her, she had absolutely no doubt that he did. 'Perhaps another time your son and his friend can play snooker with Dimitri. Now, if you'll excuse me, I must go and get changed.'

'Dad!' Dimitri exclaimed. 'Can't we at least give them a cool drink?'

'Not now, Dimitri. You heard what I said. We're going out.'

'I'm sorry,' Dimitri said to Angela, looking mortified.

'It's not a problem at all,' Angela said, not wanting to embarrass the boys. 'In any case, we must be getting back to your father, Gavin. He'll be wondering where we are.' She then looked hard and long at Cesare. 'No doubt you've heard there's an opening of another *Erskine's* restaurant along the beach. I'm sure it'll be a great success. You should try it sometime.'

She then turned on her heels and walked along the garden path to the gate and climbed down the dunes to the beach with Gavin and Dave following. Trying to control her emotions, she took a deep breath and let it out again. She felt her heart race and for a moment she thought she might collapse onto the sand.

'You okay, Mum?' Gavin asked. 'You don't look so good.'

Angela gave a small smile. 'I'm fine, darling.' She touched her forehead. 'Just the heat.'

'That man wasn't very friendly,' Gavin said.

'Sounded like a real dickhead if you ask me,' Dave said. Then realising Angela was in hearing distance he apologised. 'Sorry, Mrs Erskine, but you know what I mean. He could've at least offered us a cool drink. Dimitri looked really embarrassed his father was so rude.'

Although Angela thought Dave's 'dickhead' description of Cesare was far too polite for how Angela felt about him she tried to sound nonchalant. 'You heard him say they were going out. So it was quite understandable.' She beckoned towards the surf. 'Anyway, you boys go have a final swim. The waves look great.

I'll head up to see what's happening at the restaurant and I'll give you a holler when we're ready to leave.'

She then clambered up the steep bank, put her shoes back on and smoothed down her dress before she went to find Stewart, who undoubtedly would be in the midst of a bevy of gushing women paying homage to the 'great restaurateur'.

As she made her way into the still crowded room, she felt a huge lump rise in her throat. Seeing Dimitri's strong resemblance to Gavin had confirmed what she had suspected for so long. Gavin was not her husband's son, but the son of Cesare Carpani.

He was Dimitri's half-brother.

***

'Hi, Nonna,' Emily said, bringing Angela back with a jolt to where she sat at the Hyatt. Emily threw her handbag on a vacant chair and ran a hand through her tangle of messy hair.

'How's Bill?' Angela asked anxiously.

'Not too good. He's still in a coma. Angus said he'd ring if there's any change at all. Oh Nonna,' she cried, plonking down on the chair next to her, 'it's just so awful.'

'Darling, I'm sure he'll be alright. They keep people in comas these days to ensure that the brain can heal or to encourage the swelling to go down.' She put her hand on Emily's knee and smiled, trying to cheer her up. 'Let's have some tea and then you can have a rest. Later, if you feel up to it, maybe we can have dinner in the restaurant. The waitress tells me they do a good smorgasbord.'

'I'm not sure if I feel like eating.'

'Starving yourself will do no one any good.'

Emily nodded. 'Even so, I think I'll skip the tea and go straight up. You're right … maybe if I have a short rest I'll feel better. What about you?'

Angela looked around. 'I think I'll stay down here. Somehow, having the people coming and going takes my mind off things. I'll come up in an hour or so.' She looked at her watch. 'It's now four-thirty, so what say I tell the waitress to book us in for dinner at seven. That will give you plenty of time for a rest and maybe a bath.'

'Thanks, Nonna,' Emily said, smiling gratefully.

'And maybe there'll be news about Bill before that.'

Chapter Eighteen

Emily left her then and went up to the room, which was at the back of the hotel looking out over the lake towards the Brindabella Ranges, an undulating blaze of gold and crimson in the late afternoon sun. In normal circumstances she would relish that view. Instead, she lay down on the bed staring blankly up at the ceiling and going over the events of the previous few hours. She couldn't believe that this time yesterday she and Nonna were happily driving into *Kilmarnock* and today Bill was fighting for his life. She pulled herself up off the bed, went to the sink and poured a glass of water to try to calm her anxiousness. With glass in hand, she stepped back to the bed and sat down. She looked at her mobile. Willed it to ring. She thought of ringing Angus to see what was happening, but if he had gone back to *Kilmarnock* as the doctor had suggested he might think it was the hospital if she rang. After a while, she lay back down and closed her eyes, trying to erase the last few hours from her mind.

When the phone rang half an hour later she thought she must have drifted off to sleep, as it took her awhile to register where she was.

'He's come out of the coma,' Angus said when she answered.

'Oh my God! Thank goodness. Where are you?'

'We decided to wait another couple of hours before heading back to *Kilmarnock*. They allowed us to sit with him. Just before we were to leave he stirred. Seeing us there, he asked what had happened. When we told him he couldn't believe it. The doctor said that although he's still a very sick man he should come through.'

'Oh Angus. I can't tell you how pleased I am.'

'Thanks, Emily, for being there at the hospital. It meant a lot.'

'It's the least I could have done.'

A long pause. 'Thank you all the same.' Another pause. 'I reckon we'll head home to *Kilmarnock* shortly. And I'll stay on there for now. Even when Dad comes home he'll need help.'

Emily smiled to herself. So Bill has got his way after all. Angus will be back at *Kilmarnock*.

'But what a dreadful way to get his own way,' Nonna said, when Emily went down and told her what had happened. 'However, I'm so glad he seems to be pulling through, darling.'

'Yes, thank God for that,' Emily said.

Nonna put her hand on Emily's knee and gave it a squeeze. 'Now that we can relax a bit … let's go and freshen up for dinner. I must say the smorgasbord menu looks very good. The waitress tells me they even have wonderful oysters from Tasmania. And I do love a good oyster.'

Later, as they sat in the restaurant relishing the Tasmanian oysters from the buffet, Emily put her wine glass down.

'I need to go to Tasmania to do a gig with the Tasmanian Tourist Bureau there. Why don't you come with me? It'd be fun to see if we could find where Raphael, that friend of yours and Maria's, worked on an orchard during the war, the one Marco told us about.'

'Oh, darling, that was all so long ago.'

'It may well be, but don't you think it'd be fun to see where he worked? And some of the other prisoners as well, including Marco. Until the other day I'd no idea Italian prisoners of war worked on our farms and orchards.'

'Not many people of your age would know.'

Emily slid an oyster into her mouth, relishing the salty taste. 'Anyway,' she said, buttering a piece of brown bread, 'we could hire a car. By all accounts it's very pretty.'

Angela sighed. 'Yes, I know. I went to Hobart many years ago with Stewart for the opening of Wrest Point Casino. But I don't think so, darling.'

'Why not?'

'As I said before, it was all so long ago when those Italian prisoners of war were there. And at my age and in my condition it's probably not practical.'

'I'd be with you. I'd look after you.'

'Thank you, darling. That's very lovely. But no.'

'It's a good opportunity.'

'Quite true, darling. And thank you for the suggestion.' She finished the last of the oysters on her plate. 'I must say, these Tassie oysters are everything they're made out to be. And more.'

Emily smiled. 'Well, if you come to Tasmania with me we can eat as many Tassie oysters as we like. Now,' she added, standing up, 'I'm going to get some of those prawns and Tassie scallops. Can I get you some?'

'That would be lovely, darling.'

When they had finished eating, Angela put her serviette on the table and picked up her wine glass. For some time, she looked at Emily as though thinking something through, before taking a sip of wine and placing the glass on the table. 'I must admit,' she finally said. 'I'm rather seduced by those Tassie oysters and scallops.' She threw Emily a mischievous grin. 'Do you think at my age I'm allowed the liberty of having a change of heart?'

Emily raised an eyebrow in an amused fashion. 'Of course you are, Nonna, but in what regards? I mean ...'

'Well,' Angela said, her grin broader now. 'When you were collecting these delicious morsels at the buffet I did some thinking. If you do feel you could have me drag along I might just consider coming to Tasmania with you.'

Emily leant over and took her hand in hers and gave it a squeeze, the smile on her face radiant. 'Nonna, that would be absolutely wonderful.'

'Wouldn't you have to ask Liz Falcon at the modelling agency?'

'No. Why?'

'Well, I might get in the way.'

'Darling, Nonna. Of course you won't get in the way. All the same I'll tell her you're coming. She's organising accommodation. It's just a matter of adding another room.'

'Which, of course, I will pay for.'

'Oh Nonna, it'll be great fun. Now, all we've got to hope for is that Bill makes a speedy recovery, which I'm sure he will.'

And as Emily walked Nonna back to her room, she felt a huge relief. She wouldn't have to let Liz Falcon down, nor would she have to leave Nonna on her own.

***

When Angela folded up the newspaper back at her house in Bronte a few days later, like every morning since Greg Ashton had landed on her doorstep, she was relieved when there was no article on Stewart. In fact, she couldn't find any article by Greg Ashton at all. She was wondering anxiously if he was still trying to delve into Stewart's connection with Cesare Carpani, when Emily called out.

'Are you ready, Nonna?'

'Just give me a couple of minutes.'

The previous night she had told Emily she would like to go into the library this morning and see if she could find out anything on Italian prisoners in Tasmania during the war.

'If I'm going there,' she said, as they sat in the living room after turning the television off, 'I might as well do a bit of research to see if anything shows up.'

When Emily dropped her outside the library on her way into town to see Liz Falcon to finalise details of the trip, Angela insisted she would catch the bus home, which she often did from the library.

'Good afternoon, Mrs Erskine,' said Cecily, one of the librarians when she saw Angela come in the door. 'How lovely to see you again.' She smiled. 'You look well.'

'Thank you, I am,' Angela said with a smile, belying the fact that when Emily asked how she was this morning she had lied and said she wasn't in much pain, when actually she had taken an extra dose of painkillers to counteract the persistent ache, which had kept her awake a lot of the night.

'Is there something special you're after today?'

'Well, yes. I'm on a sort of mission you might say. I'm doing a bit of research,' Angela said.

'How exciting. What are you researching?'

'Italian prisoners who were here in Australia during the Second World War working in the rural sector.'

'Really? I had no idea.'

'Not all that many people are aware.'

'Is there someone special you are researching?' she asked.

Cecily knew Angela was Italian because sometimes she would take out a novel written in Italian.

Angela chuckled. 'It's just a whim really. There was a friend of our family in Italy who was sent to Tasmania to work on an apple orchard. I'm going to Tasmania with my granddaughter and we thought it might be quite fun if we could visit that orchard. He made it and the family who owned it sound rather nice.'

'How interesting. Well, all our books on the war are in that aisle,' she said, pointing over towards the window. 'However, I can't remember seeing any on Italian prisoners here during the war. But you're quite welcome to go and have a look. In fact, I'll come with you and see what we can find.'

But when they scanned the shelves together the only book that was remotely close to the subject was Thomas Keneally's *Shame and Captive* and that was a novel and seemed to be set mostly in New South Wales.

Have you tried Wikipedia?' Cecily asked.

Angela looked blank.

'It's an online site that covers just about every topic you can think of.' She smiled. 'If you like, I'll see what shows up on that. Come back to my desk and we can see what we can find.'

'That's very kind of you, Cecily, but I don't want to take up your time.'

'You've got me quite fascinated now, so let's see what we can unearth.'

Back at the counter she gestured for Angela to wait as she typed some details into a search engine.

'Nothing much in Wikipedia or anywhere else for that matter,' she said. 'But there is this.' She turned her computer to where Angela stood. 'It's an article from *Centre for Tasmanian Historical Studies.*

Angela looked closely at the computer.

ITALIAN PRISONERS OF WAR

Italian Prisoners of War, captured in 1941 during the North Africa campaign of the Second World War, were evacuated to India, Ceylon, South Africa and Australia due to Egypt's political instability. Faced with a shortage of rural labour, the Australian war cabinet decided to employ these men in rural industry. Costing £1 per week plus keep, prisoners were an attractive source of labour to many employers, and a limit of three per farm was imposed.

From September 1943, shortly after the allied invasion of Italy, 950 prisoners were allocated to Tasmania out of some 13,000 nationally. The scheme proved very successful and many close relationships developed between prisoners and their hosts, continued in some cases after the war. Owing to a shortage of transport ships, many prisoners were not repatriated back to Italy until early 1947. Some later returned to Tasmania.

'Well, that tells us that there were certainly some Italian prisoners of war in Tasmania as you knew,' Cecily told her. 'But sadly, it doesn't tell us where exactly they were. Maybe when you go to Tassie you might be able to find out more.'

After thanking her for her time, Angela caught the bus home, where she went to the kitchen and made herself a tuna sandwich. As she sat on the verandah, eating it slowly, she wondered if she was being ridiculous to think of going to Tasmania with Emily. But unless she became so much sicker in the next week or so it would be petty to refuse. Emily obviously wanted her to go. And if she didn't go, she suspected that she would pull out of the shoot for the Tasmanian Tourist Board, rather than leave Angela on her own. Besides, trying to find out where Raphael was during the war gave her a purpose for the trip.

And it might be the last trip she would take anywhere.

***

'I think it's wonderful that your Nonna's going to Tasmania with you,' Liz Falcon said to Emily as they sat in a coffee shop in Martin Place with a noisy flock of pigeons drinking from the fountain nearby. She put her coffee cup down. 'And how romantic to think she'd like to find where that friend of hers had been a prisoner of war.' She sat back and smiled. 'I'd forgotten she was from Italy, but of course seeing as you call her Nonna I should have guessed. I don't think it was ever mentioned in articles about your grandfather when he was alive. Nor on his death.'

'She's always tried to stay in the background.'

'Can't say I blame her.'

When they finished their coffee Emily went back to Liz's office and they finalised the itinerary for the trip to Tasmania. It sounded fun. A couple of nights in Hobart and then down to Port Arthur. After that, if Nonna was up to it, they would drive up the east coast.

After leaving Liz she walked back to her car, thinking of what Liz had said about Nonna not being mentioned in any articles about her grandfather. She tried to remember back to what had been written about him when he died. She was only fourteen and not much interested in newspapers. Nor any news for that matter, unless it involved horses, clothes or music. To her, he was her grandfather, so she didn't need to read about him in the newspaper. As far as she was concerned, she knew *all* about him. As it has now turned out, she didn't know *all* about him at all.

She remembered the funeral as being a huge affair. Mostly, the day had been a blur. She had sat at the front of St Mary's Cathedral with Nonna, her father and brothers. All the way through the service she had held Nonna's hand tightly as tears streamed down her cheeks. And as her father, Jonathon and Allen, together with other pallbearers, carried her grandfather's coffin out of the church she was so desolate that Nonna put her arm around her and held her tight. Not once did Nonna cry. Now she wondered if Nonna's stoic demeanour might have had more to do with knowing that her grandfather wasn't that 'knight in shining armour' Emily had thought he was. Again, the conversation she had overheard at *Mandalay* between Nonna and her father all those years ago came to mind. It was when her father said he was surprised Nonna didn't want Dimitri Carpani to change the name on the *Erskine's* franchises when he had bought them … after what Emily's grandfather had done to both he and Nonna.

If Nonna wasn't so sick right now she might ask her what her father had meant. But all it was sure to do was bring back memories of her husband, which might make her sad and affect her health. In any case, it was all so long ago Emily wasn't quite sure why she was thinking about it now. Blow that reporter at the *Sydney Mail,* she thought angrily. If he hadn't come around upsetting Nonna and threatening to write things about her grandfather, none of this would be crowding her mind.

She had read once, in a self-help article, that it was useless to dwell on things one couldn't change, particularly the past. She would try to make herself take that advice. Mathew being a prime example. The previous night she lay awake imagining what he was doing and wondering for the umpteenth time if she could have handled things differently. It was a pointless exercise. What she would do now was try to concentrate on the future and how lovely it would be to take Nonna with her to Tasmania. Despite her illness, Emily would ensure they had fun. She owed her that. Nonna had been more of a mother to Emily than her own mother had ever been. She thought again how odd it was her mother didn't come back to Australia for her grandfather's funeral. That she hadn't come back to Australia at all as far as Emily knew. Surely if she had she would have come to see her family. She'd asked her father once if he ever heard from her, for Emily hadn't. Nor had her brothers, as far as she knew.

'We're divorced, Emily,' her father said. 'Why would I hear from her?'

'It's just that I thought she might have wondered how we all are. I mean, she is our mother after all.'

Whenever she broached the subject with Allen he told her to live in the present and not the past. She smiled as she thought of him doing just that, living in the here and now, surfing by the sun and wind in Byron Bay. Jono had told her he didn't much care either way what their mother did or didn't do, as he had never been that close to her. If she wanted to live her life without them that was her choice. Yet when he said that to her she did wonder if her mother had been around would Jono have taken to drugs like he did. Or would their mother have noticed his personality change, as only a mother would, or *should*, and got onto it straight away.

Thinking of all that now she was sadder than ever that Nonna was ill. Nonna, who had not only taken the place of their mother, but also their grandmother. Just as she got to her car she heard her phone ring. She fumbled in her handbag and pulled it out.

'Hi, Em,' Allen said, when she answered. 'I got your message about Nonna. I tried to ring her at home but there's no answer.'

'She's at the library.'

'Oh. So how is she?'

'Not well. As I said on my message, the breast cancer has spread. But for someone who's so ill she's amazing really.'

'I thought I'd come down tomorrow to see her. I've got a few days off.'

'Oh Allen, that would be great. I'll ring Dad and Jono and see if they're free for dinner.'

'How's Mathew?' he asked.

Last time Allen was down in Sydney he had come out for drinks with her and Mathew in Bondi. He and Mathew had got on well and Mathew had even said he would drive Emily up to Byron for a weekend. It was just two months later when Emily found out he was cheating on her.

'We broke up,' she said to Allen. 'Chrissy discovered he was cheating on me.'

'Oh.'

'Yeah, that's what I thought. Oh!'

'Well, you're best out of that sort of a relationship,' he said in the matter of fact sort of way that Allen always talked. 'Anyone else, then?'

'No, not really. And you?'

'A few dates. Nothing serious.' He laughed. 'All too difficult.'

And that's pretty much how Emily felt too. After she hung up, she rang her father and Jono. It would be good to have the family all together. She wished they could do it more often. They mightn't be the model family, but they *were* family. And, now that Nonna was ill, it was important they spend as much time with her as possible.

Chapter Nineteen

As Angela sat on the verandah with her family, she looked around. It wasn't often they all got together. It had taken her illness for it to happen now. She looked at Allen, who she had always had a soft spot for. From the moment he could walk he'd loved the surf and now with his long hair bleached from the sun and tanned skin he was the epitome of an Aussie surfer. As soon as he had left school he took off around Australia with his surfboard, finally ending up in Byron Bay. It was a life that obviously suited him, for he looked relaxed and happy. Jono, on the other hand, seemed somewhat uptight. He didn't look as though he was still using drugs, but one could never be sure. When he was in the depth of addiction he was pale and wan and looked almost derelict, now he was smartly dressed in a suit and his hair was newly cut. Gavin had told her earlier on now that Jono was supposedly clean he was going to take him into the business, which she was pleased about.

'I can only stay for a short while,' Gavin had said to her, leaning down to give her a kiss when he first arrived. 'I totally forgot I've got a dinner at the yacht club with Dimitri Carpani and his wife.'

'Couldn't you have changed it?' Angela asked, annoyed once more the Carpani name had come up.

'Sorry, Mother. We're looking at buying a racehorse together. The trainer, a friend of Dimitri's is dining with us: a New

Zealander who came over here and has made good. He got a second place with a two-year-old in the Golden Slipper and has won quite a few Group One races with other horses. Dimitri asked him to keep an eye out for a good horse. Evidently, he's found one coming up for sale.' He grinned. 'Perhaps I shouldn't have sold Dimitri *Erskine's* after all. He seems to be doing so well he's got plenty of spare cash to throw around.'

'So you still see a lot of Dimitri?' Angela asked, ignoring his comment about the sale of *Erskine's.*

'We catch up every now and then. Why?'

'Oh, nothing really. He stopped taking beef from the property, *Kilmarnock,* which Emily and I were visiting last week. Without so much as an apology. They'd been supplying meat to *Erskine's* for decades.'

'I'm sure it was a business decision.'

'There are certain ethical ways of doing business. And that's not one of them.'

'Maybe it was his mother who insisted. She did most of the accounts until she retired.'

'I knew Cesare's first wife, Bettina. Not this one.'

'Oh yes, I forgot. When you and Dad worked for Cesare, Bettina would have been there too.'

'Yes. She was. So what's Dimitri's mother like?'

'I've only met her a couple of times. Why?'

'Just curious, that's all.' She paused. 'That reporter from the *Sydney Mail* came back again. Said he was doing an article on the emergence of Italian restaurants in Sydney in the 1950s.'

'Oh. Did he mention anything more about Glasgow Mine?'

'I gathered the newspaper were shelving it for the time being, but it would be a different matter if ICAC took it further.' She sighed. 'Which of course might be happening right now and we wouldn't know. However, in researching his article on the restaurants. Greg Ashton came across something in Trove. A review of *Cesare's* back in the 50s, saying how Maria, Stewart and I worked there. He said it had piqued his interest.'

'Beppi's won some industry award recently and as you know the family have been running it there since the 50's. Maybe that's what got him interested in restaurants back then.'

'Yes, you're probably right.' Angela smiled lightly, belying the angst hovering like a dark, threatening cloud in her mind. She beckoned for him to sit down. 'Anyway, come have a drink before you have to rush off.'

He nodded and threw her a bright smile, his brown eyes crinkling at the edges. For a second Angela could see Maria reflected in those eyes and smiled at him warmly. For not the first time. Angela wondered how Maria would have coped with Gavin if she had lived. How would she have been able to look at him and not think of the night she had been raped by Cesare Carpani? Would she have kept the truth a secret from Stewart? Or would she have weakened and told him? And if so, how would Stewart have reacted? Before she had a chance to answer any of her own questions, Gavin handed her a glass of champagne and Allen came over to join them, putting his arm around her and hugging her to him. She had no doubt that Maria, with her wild and adventuresome spirit, would have loved Allen dearly.

It was a fun evening with everyone laughing and talking companionably and with Gavin only leaving just in time to catch up with Dimitri and his wife. Angela had relished cooking a large pot of spaghetti marinara earlier on and Emily had made a tossed salad and heated a loaf of ciabatta in the oven. There wasn't an ounce of pasta left on anyone's plate after they'd mopped it up with the crunchy bread. When the young ones cleaned up, Jono and Allen persuaded Emily to go out for a drink at a bar in Bondi and now Angela sat by herself on the verandah watching a sweep of twinkling stars and the outline of a half-moon in the black sky. She really had enjoyed her time with the family and yet she couldn't help feeling anxious. All the harmony of this evening could so easily be destroyed in a heartbeat by that journalist with the *Sydney Mail* digging deeper and deeper into the far, distant past, which was as clear to Angela today as it was back then.

***

Standing on her own a few weeks after Stewart's restaurant opening at Rattan Beach, watching Gavin play soccer against the team that included Dimitri Carpani, Angela heard *his* voice behind her.

'They look alike, don't they?'

Turning around she faced Cesare Carpani.

'Dimitri and your son,' he said. 'Funny that, isn't it?' He smirked. 'A pity your husband isn't here to see the resemblance. I wonder how he'd feel if I was to let him know the boy he thinks his son and heir is most likely mine.'

Angela shook her head and muttered between gritted teeth, 'And how would you manage to explain that?'

'Easy. His precious girlfriend, later wife, approached me for sex and I obliged.' He threw her a nasty smile. 'You told me when we last met how well *Erskine's* restaurants are doing, so your husband must be feeling pretty happy with himself. I can't imagine how he would feel knowing you've kept your sister's secret all these years. And I daresay your son would find it somewhat traumatic as well.'

The final whistle blew and the boys sauntered off the field together towards where Angela and Cesare were standing. As they approached, Cesare said again. 'Yes indeed, no mistaking ... a huge resemblance ...'

'Remember Dimitri? From when we were at Rattan Beach,' Gavin said when he plopped down in front of where Angela and Cesare were standing. He dragged off his soccer shirt and ran it over his face covered in sweat. 'We beat the socks off you, didn't we?' He laughed at Dimitri.

Dimitri grinned. 'There's always a next time, mate.'

Cesare patted him on the back. 'You played well, son.' He then smiled at Gavin. 'And congratulations to you and your team. Now, we'd best be off.' He looked at Angela. 'It's been very nice to catch up again, Mrs Erskine. You should bring your husband for a meal at *Cesare's* one day. For old time sake.' He glanced at Gavin. 'Did you know your parents once worked for me there?'

Gavin looked startled. 'I had no idea.'

'And your mother's sister, Maria, worked there as well.'

'My mother who died?'

'That's right,' Cesare said. 'Get Angela here and your father, to tell you about it one day.'

'Wow, that's cool, Mrs Erskine,' Dimitri said. 'You and Mr Erskine working for my dad.'

Angela smiled. 'It was a long time ago.'

'Yes,' Cesare said. 'A long time ago.'

'Before I was born,' Gavin said.

'Yes, that's quite so, son. But now, Dimitri,' he added, pointing to a black car parked under a tree, 'we really must be going. Your mother will be waiting for us to pick her up in the city.'

'Can Gavin come surfing tomorrow, Mrs Erskine?' Dimitri asked. 'A group of us are going down to Bondi.'

'What a good idea,' Cesare said. 'Maybe I could pick him up on the way through. I believe you live in Bellevue Hill. A very nice house by the sounds of it. Your father has done very well, Gavin. It'd be good to catch up with him again. I see him occasionally round town, but to have a chat would be great.'

Angela felt cold inside. Was that a threat? She looked across to Gavin.

'I'm afraid we have other plans for tomorrow, so you won't be able to go surfing.'

'What plans?'

'We'll talk about it later, Gavin.'

'Mum!'

'I said we'll talk about it later.' She glanced at Cesare. 'So you're still at *Cesare's* in Stanley Street full-time?'

'Every night except Sundays when we go up to the beach. Until the last guest leaves.'

'Well, it was good to see you again,' she said to Dimitri, trying to avoid Cesare's eyes. 'Maybe you and Gavin can catch up another time.'

All the way home Gavin complained about not being able to go surfing.

'It's got nothing to do with Dimitri,' Angela said. 'However, I would rather not encourage his father's friendship.'

'Why not?'

'Because when we worked for him he wasn't very nice.'

'Is that why he was so unfriendly up at Rattan Beach?'

She nodded. 'Yes, possibly.'

That night Angela lay awake tossing and turning. Would Cesare disclose his suspicions? Knowing the man, she felt it was a real possibility. Just for spite's sake. She had no doubt that Cesare still held a huge grudge against Stewart for starting a restaurant in opposition to him all those years ago. A restaurant that was the beginning of his successful *Erskine's* empire.

With Stewart away up at *Riverside* she decided to take things into her own hands: confront Cesare at closing time in Stanley Street. She was pretty sure she would probably get him on his own at closing time as he got in his car to drive home.

***

At 10 p.m. on Tuesday night she checked that Gavin was in his room asleep and drove her car to Stanley Street where she parked across from the restaurant and waited. It was pitch dark, the only streetlamp being about twenty yards away and so dim that it showed up little in the street. She saw him come outside and walk towards his car. He placed the bag with what she presumed was the night's takings on the ground and took out his car keys to open the door.

She slid from behind the wheel and stepped across the road to where he stood. 'Good evening, Cesare,' she said.

At first he seemed shocked to see her, but then his lips curled into an unpleasant smile. 'Mrs Erskine, surely it's a bit late for you to be out roaming the streets like this alone.' There was a pause as he fiddled with the keys in his hand and held her eyes with his. 'But let me guess. I think I know why you're here. After our meeting at the soccer, you're worried I might spill the beans! That one day your husband and his supposed son, Gavin, will find out the truth … and where will that leave you, eh! Having kept your sister's secret all this time. I have no doubt that if you had told your husband what happened that night, resulting in the birth of his bastard son, I would've heard from him by now.'

Angela shook her head. 'Surely you must have regretted what you did to Maria.'

'Like what?'

'Attacking and raping her that night at your restaurant as she put out the rubbish—'

'Rape is it? I told you! She wanted it. Had been teasing me for weeks in those fancy clothes.'

'You trapped her. Raped her. Killed her. Make no mistake about that.'

'Killed her? I didn't kill her.'

'You might as well have.'

'Because she knew the baby she carried and then bore was not her husband's.'

'She guessed, that's what killed her.'

'As we both know, you've only got to look at young Gavin to see he's from my sperm. I'm surprised your fancy husband hasn't worked that out.'

Angela stepped forward and poked him in the chest. 'You really are one ghastly, horrid man, aren't you? Maria and I should have reported you to the police back then when it happened.'

'So why didn't you, eh? Why?'

'Because—'

'Because there was no way in the world that she could have proved anything other than the fact she was a tart asking for sex and got what she wanted.'

'Don't you dare say that,' Angela spat. 'Maria didn't have a chance. You cornered her. Raped her.'

He pushed her away and went to open the car door. 'I should be congratulated. I did your husband a favour. Stopped him from spending his life with such a slut.'

As he reached for the handle Angela grabbed his arm and hissed, 'You absolute monster. You deserve to rot in hell.'

Again, he tried to push her away and she had to steady herself from falling over.

'Take your filthy hands off her. NOW, YOU BASTARD!'

With a jolt, Angela realised that the voice behind her belonged to Stewart. She spun around and saw him in the shadows.

'So here we have the cuckolded lover,' Cesare sneered. 'And you've heard that the boy you thought was your son is not your son after all. Your precious Maria was having it off behind your back—'

Before Angela had a chance to take in what was happening, Stewart rushed forward and took a swipe at Cesare, knocking him clean off his feet. When he was on the ground he grabbed him by the collar and pulled him back up, with his face close to his. Again, he punched him so hard that this time blood covered his face.

'Stewart, stop!' Angela shouted. 'STOP!'

But it was as if Stewart had turned into a complete mad man. The more Angela shouted, the more he punched. Stunned as Cesare was, he was unable to respond. Besides, Stewart was at least six inches taller than him.

'Don't, Stewart. You'll kill him!'

'It's what the lowlife deserves.'

Cesare staggered and fell backwards, and whacked his head on the ground. Angela heard him groan. He lay there unmoving, trying to get his breath.

'We should call the ambulance,' Angela cried, her eyes wide with horror.

'Leave him be,' Stewart said, dragging her towards her car and opening the door for her to get in.

'But we can't leave him like that.'

He waited before answering. 'No. You're right. I'll go to him.'

When he came back to the car a few minutes later he was holding the bag of money.

'Wh–why have you got that?' she asked in alarm.

A pause. 'To make it look like a robbery. I'll ditch it in the harbour.'

'But we've got to call the ambulance.'

'Too late for that.'

Angela felt a terrifying wave of panic wash through her. She thought it would burst her veins. 'Oh my God, Stewart. He was breathing when we left. So *was* he dead when you went back? Or did you just kill him?'

He didn't answer.

'If anyone ever finds out we were here, as far as you're concerned it was an accident,' he said hurling the bag of money in the back of his car. 'We got in a fight. Now, go. Go.'

Angela was in such a state of shock she nodded and started her car. In a daze and shaking from head to toe, she somehow managed to drive home and put the car in the garage.

Upstairs, she opened Gavin's door. With all that had happened she was incredulous to see him sleeping soundly. She closed the door and went to the kitchen and poured herself a glass of water. Lifting the glass to her mouth her hand shook so much she had to put it down in case she dropped it. She told herself she should pick up the phone right now and ring the police. Tell them what had happened. But if she did that they would arrest Stewart on the spot.

An hour later, he came into their bedroom where she was lying on the bed staring up at the ceiling, trying to control her breathing.

Shutting the door behind him he moved to the bed.

'You knew all along that Maria had been raped,' he said, looking down at her on the bed and pointing his finger at her. 'You kept it a secret from me. How the hell could you do that?'

'She begged me not to tell you. Made me promise.'

'And you suspected Gavin was not my son right from the beginning. Right from the moment we looked at him together through the glass in the hospital.'

She nodded slowly and wiped her nose with a tissue. She was grateful Gavin's bedroom was at the other end of the house with the door shut. 'I suspected, but I wasn't sure until I saw Cesare's son, Dimitri, with him at Rattan Beach on the day of your restaurant opening there. And then at the soccer—'

'And you said nothing!'

'I told you, I promised Maria I wouldn't tell. Ever.'

'And what about me? Where did that leave me, eh?'

'I thought I was protecting you from knowing the awful truth.'

'You obviously know all the God-awful details of how it happened. So tell me, word for word, everything you know.'

It was some ten minutes later when Angela finished talking. She told him how she had come home from the movies and found Maria sobbing on her bed. How she had told her then what had happened. And how she found out from the doctor that she was pregnant when they were living at the YWCA hostel. How she decided to tell Stewart it was his baby she was carrying, when in fact she really didn't know whose it was.

'But she loved you so much Stewart. She was frightened if she told you what had happened you wouldn't want to marry her.'

Stewart took a deep breath to try to control his emotions. 'Why didn't she tell me? I would have killed that Cesare bastard back then.'

'That's what she was afraid of. And you would have gone to jail for life.'

'Maybe that would have been preferable to letting that lowlife get away with it for so long. And, if I'd known what had happened, I would have made Maria have an abortion. If she had, she would still be here.'

'I know, but she wouldn't hear of it.'

Angela got up from the bed and went over to where he was standing by the dressing table. She touched his cheek with her hand. 'I'm sorry, Stewart. So very sorry …'

He removed her hand from his cheek and stepped over to the window. After some time, he turned around. 'You were right. Having that bastard's kid did kill her.'

Angela gasped. 'It's not Gavin's fault.'

'If she had given birth to my kid it wouldn't have killed her.'

'Stewart, don't think like that. Please.'

'Well, how am I supposed to think? Tell me that.'

'It's nothing to do with Gavin. You can't make him pay for what that man did to Maria.' She went over to the bed and sat down again, frightened she was going to faint if she didn't. 'What are we going to do about Cesare?' she asked, looking up at him in despair.

'Nothing. As I said, they'll pass it off as a robbery.'

'What if someone saw what happened?'

'That's a risk we've got to take, but I don't reckon there was anyone around. When I drove up I saw no one else there. Just you and him.'

'How did you know I was there?'

'I had to come back early from *Riverside* for a meeting tomorrow. As I came up the street I saw you head out and followed. You never drive out on your own like that at night, leaving Gavin by himself. Maybe it was instinct. And,' he said, staring at her with the coldest look she had ever seen in his eyes, 'if you do tell anyone about what happened, I'll be sent to jail. My business closed down and my assets frozen. You'll have to bring your sister's son up on your own with no money. No house. I strongly suggest this is a secret you and I keep between ourselves.'

With that he stomped out of the bedroom and shut the door behind him.

Three days later it was reported in the *Sydney Mail* that Cesare Carpani, a well-known restaurateur, had been murdered. It was presumed it was a murder/robbery. The night's takings from his restaurant, which his wife said he always brought home in a bag, were missing.

Night after night, at three am when she tossed and turned, Angela agonised as to whether to tell the police what had happened. In the end, she justified not doing so by telling herself Cesare Carpani had more or less killed Maria.

The next year, Stewart obtained the lease for Glasgow Mine and using cash and some shares in the mine bought Cesare Carpani's widow out of *Cesare's* restaurant and added it to his portfolio of *Erskine's* restaurants, ensuring the name died with the man.

And as time went by, Angela could see Stewart was making an effort with Gavin, but he failed and they became more and more distant with each other. As Gavin left school and then went to university, it was only Angela's begging that dragged Stewart to Gavin's important milestones.

'He's Maria's son,' she said to him when he said he was tied up with business and couldn't go to his school graduation.

But even though he attended she could see it was a real struggle for him. As other fathers looked on proudly at their son's achievements, Stewart fiddled with his cufflinks and looked off into middle distance when Gavin won the prize for Italian. After university, Gavin went overseas for a year and when he came back and asked to go into the family business Stewart at first refused. Again, it was only Angela's persuasion that made him change his mind. Over the years, as she saw them both struggle with each other, she wondered if she had been wise to do so.

Never once did Stewart or Angela mention the night Cesare Carpani died, Stewart was a changed man after that, a man who Angela didn't recognise.

Don't tell. Ever.

***

With Emily still out on the town with her brothers, Angela got up from where she was sitting on her verandah and went inside. She was preparing for bed when the phone rang. She was surprised to hear Gavin on the other end of the line. He sounded as though he'd had a fair bit to drink, for although his words weren't garbled he did sound unusually excited.

'I had the strangest conversation with Dimitri,' he said.

Angela's heart missed a beat. 'Oh! What about?'

'He went to the loo and gave me his credit card to split the bill. When I went to pay, I realised he hadn't given me his credit card at all. It was his Red Cross blood donor card he'd given me by mistake. And guess what? He's exactly the same blood type as me. You know how everyone always tells us it's such an unusual blood group.'

When Gavin's leg had become infected as a child, Angela remembered taking him to hospital where they told her his blood type was AB negative.

'It is an unusual type,' the doctor said. 'I presume either you or your husband have the same.'

'Actually, Gavin is the son of my sister who died in childbirth,' she told him. 'However, we shared the same blood type, A positive. I married Gavin's father after her death.'

'And your husband's blood type?'

When she told him without thinking that Stewart was O positive, he said, 'it's unusual for a child not to share one of his parent's blood types.'

Hurriedly, Angela had said. 'Maybe I've got my husband's wrong. I'll check when I get home.'

But, of course, she never did, as she knew without doubt Stewart was O positive. After Maria died, he had decided to donate blood to the Red Cross. 'That transfusion in the hospital might have saved her,' he said. 'Sadly, it didn't but my blood type O positive might save someone else. It's a common blood type, so it might be very useful.'

'Dimitri told me it was the same blood type as his father's,' Gavin said to her now.

Angela caught her breath. 'Really? And how did he know that?'

'Because when his father was attacked outside his restaurant he didn't die straight away. The milkman found him the next morning and somehow got him to the hospital where they needed to give him a blood transfusion. Dimitri had to give him some of his.'

Angela's heart missed another beat and almost stopped. 'I thought Cesare died outside his restaurant.'

'Evidently not. And before he died, Dimitri's mother told him Cesare muttered something about knowing who it was who attacked him.'

Angela's body went icy cold and she found it difficult to breath. 'Goodness,' she managed to utter, 'and was it someone he knew well?'

'Don't know. He died before he could get the name out.'

Angela's heart fired up again.

Thud. Thud.

'So his mother never took it any further.'

'It'd seem not. Dimitri said his father had a hell of a lot more on the go than just his restaurant. Black market grog, drugs and other things. His mother was frightened if she told the police she suspected it wasn't just a robbery gone wrong they'd uncover some of his shady dealings. Muddy his name and go after his assets, more or less throwing her and Dimitri out on the street. As it was, he left a shit load of money, probably mostly gained illegally, which Dimitri inherited. Hence, his wealth.'

'Gosh, and she told Dimitri all this about his shady dealings?'

'Only recently. One night when she was in her cups.'

Angela heard Gavin hiccup. He must have had a lot to drink.

'But talking of shady deals,' he went on, his voice sounding slurred now. 'I've been thinking about Glasgow Mine and that licence gained through the back door. Dad probably had lots of those sort of dealings going on back then. I mean, after what his ultimate final act was—'

'Gavin,' Angela jumped in, 'we agreed never to mention that again. Besides, your father wasn't always like that.'

'Oh! So what happened to him, eh?'

Angela looked at the photo of Maria on the sideboard. 'Something that changed him from a happy, gregarious, righteous man to a man who was capable of doing anything as long as it was to his gain.'

'What the hell was that something?'

Angela regretted telling him so much. 'It was all so long ago and I really don't want to go into it. He felt I let him down, although I had no choice. I should have told him something that happened when we were young, but I didn't.'

'Like what?'

'As I said it was all a very long time ago, so forget it, Gavin. I'm going to bed and by the sound of your voice I suggest you do the same. Goodnight.'

She then hung up and stood looking out to the dark sky where the moon had now disappeared and the stars seemed to have gone into hiding as well.

How could she ever tell him what it was that had changed Stewart so much? To do that would mean Cesare Carpani had won.

Who could blame Gavin for being bitter about Stewart? Not after his 'final act' as Gavin called it. Although she tried to shoo it off, a wave of bitterness penetrated her own mind as it reeled back to the night she found out Stewart had passed away. When she told Emily no one knew he had passed away until he didn't turn up for a meeting the next day and his assistant went looking for him, she had lied. Angela knew only too well there was someone with him when he died. And who that someone was.

***

'I'm so sorry, Mother,' Gavin said, taking deep breaths down the phone from Seoul where he'd been summoned urgently by Stewart's assistant. 'I'm afraid Dad has died.'

'Oh my God,' Angela exclaimed. 'How?'

'A heart attack.'

Angela gulped hard. Even though she and Stewart were not close she couldn't believe he'd died just like that. Her first thought was of Maria. Stewart had gone to join her.

'Was anyone with him?' she stammered. 'Or did it happen during the night? When he was on his own?'

There was such a long silence down the line that Angela thought they had lost the connection. 'Gavin. You still there?'

'Samantha was with him,' he eventually said.

'Samantha! What on earth was she doing there? Isn't she in America with her parents?'

'That's what I thought.'

'So why for God's sake was she with Stewart?'

Another silence stretched out. 'I'm afraid she and Dad were having an affair,' he stammered. 'It turns out they'd arranged to meet up here in Korea.'

Angela caught her breath. 'Samantha and Stewart! You've got to be joking.'

'No,' Gavin said. 'I'm not.'

'And you had no idea?'

'No. As you know, Samantha and I have had our problems. We don't really communicate that much. I had my suspicions she was seeing someone, however, I'd no idea who it was. As far as I knew, she'd gone to America to be with her parents. She obviously stopped off in South Korea on the way.'

'Hardly on her way.'

'Yes, I know. But Jesus,' he fumed, 'how the hell could she do that to me? And even though he's now deceased and I should respect the dead … to do what my father did must be one of the most despicable acts I know. Basically, he's not only screwed my wife, but our entire family as well. His grandchildren for God's sake. You too.'

Angela tried to control the emotions churning round and round in her stomach, making her nauseous.

'He evidently had a heart attack after they had sex,' Gavin said. 'Maybe it was the Viagra he took.'

Angela was so disgusted all she could splutter was, 'Oh!'

'They reckon it can cause a heart attack or stroke. Particularly if you take too much.'

Stewart, you silly, silly man, she thought, as tears rolled down her cheeks. What would Maria think of you? A vision of her sister and Stewart both so much in love, laughing, kissing and flirting flitted into her mind. Rage tore through her very being, curdling her blood, pounding her head. If Cesare Carpani hadn't come into their lives Stewart would not have died having sex with his daughter-in-law in Korea. He would have been with Maria. She pulled out a handkerchief and wiped her eyes. But no sooner had she wiped the tears away than another lot flooded down her cheeks. Her tears were for the death of a man who she and Maria had first met all those years ago at Villawood. A happy, gregarious, caring man full of love and hope for the future. Yet that man died many, many years ago. Once when Maria died. And again on that cold dark murderous night when Stewart found out that Cesaire Carpani had raped Maria and Gavin was her rapist's son. And that Angela had betrayed him by not disclosing her secret to him.

Was this how he got back at Gavin for being the son of that rapist mongrel he had murdered?

Eventually, she pulled herself together. 'No one should ever know Samantha was with Stewart when he died,' she said to Gavin down the phone. 'Least of all the family.'

She heard Gavin take a deep breath as if trying to control his anger. 'Yes, I agree. The boys might cope, but it would destroy Emily.'

'So where is Samantha now?' Angela asked.

'She's still here in Seoul. Needless to say, she's distraught and full of regret.'

'For having an affair with her father-in-law? Or that he's died while having sex with her?

'Both, I suppose. She says there's no way she could go back to Australia and face you. Face the children. So we've agreed she should continue onto America where her parents are waiting for her. As you know, her father has dementia and her mother's not well either.'

'Will she stay there?'

'Yes. We've agreed to divorce. I'll give her a settlement. She says she'll stay there for good. Make a life there.'

'She'll just walk out on Emily and the boys for good!'

'Be realistic, Mother. She was never a great mum at the best of times, so I don't think they'll miss her that much. And I'm sure they'll understand that being the only child she needs to be with her elderly parents.'

After Angela hung up, she sat there in a daze, finding it difficult to come to terms with what she had just learnt. She remembered when Gavin brought Samantha home the first time. Undoubtedly she was pretty, but straightaway Angela could see by her 'look at me' demeanour that she was selfish and spoilt. Gavin had been so besotted he didn't see past her beauty. Yet to Angela it was a brash sort of beauty. Tanned, toned, manicured and coiffed to an inch of her life. And yes she flirted with Stewart, and he flirted back. But Angela had thought it was all fairly harmless. Until now. She doubted love came into it. Angela had known for many years that Stewart had numerous mistresses. And she was pretty sure this wasn't Samantha's first affair by any means. To both Samantha and Stewart, Gavin was the pawn in the middle. Stewart wanted to avenge that Gavin was sired by Cesare Carpani and his birth had killed Maria. Samantha that her husband hadn't turned out as she had imagined. Stewart often belittled him in front of her, even though Angela chided him for doing so.

Angela had thought of leaving Stewart for many years, particularly after what happened that night with Cesare Carpani. Why she stayed, she wasn't sure. Perhaps it was because Maria had asked her to look after him. Or afraid to throw in the towel, so to speak. Start again. And in all fairness to Stewart, he provided for her very well, as he did for the rest of the family: Gavin, who wasn't his son; and Emily and her brothers, who unbeknownst to them weren't his grandchildren. Never once did he shirk his financial responsibilities or seek a divorce. Even as recently as the last year before he died she thought of seeking a divorce, but then she thought of how much Emily loved Stewart and how upset she would be if Angela started divorce proceedings against him. She could imagine all her questions as to why Angela would want to do that.

One of Angela's greatest sorrows was that Maria never had the chance to meet Emily. If she had, Angela had no doubt that she would love her to bits. There was something about Emily that reminded Angela of her sister. Not in looks, although they were both very beautiful, but more the way she held her head and the expression in her eyes. There was absolutely nothing in Emily at all that could be put down to anything she had inherited from Cesare Carpani, which Angela was eternally grateful for. Jonathon had very little of Maria in him, but every now and then she could see something lovely in Allen that came from Maria.

In the end, she decided to run with her marriage. Leave things as they were. Both she and Stewart led separate lives, but they came together for family events, social functions, weddings, funerals and where necessary. She wasn't consumed by jealousy of the other women in his life, which allowed them to have a friendship of sorts.

When Gavin arrived back in Sydney with Stewart's body, Angela was there to meet the plane. At first she was going to have a private funeral; however, she was talked into having it at St Mary's Cathedral, where other than family, friends, past and present employees, and customers of *Erskine's* and his other business associates, there were also many dignitaries and politicians who attended. As Angela stood at the front door of the cathedral after the service, thanking them all for coming, she held such a fixed smile on her face that she was sure if the wind changed it would stay with her forever.

One of the last people to leave the church was Bettina, Cesare Carpani's first wife. When she came up to Angela she took her hand in hers. 'I'm so sorry, Angela,' she said with deep compassion in her dark eyes. 'For your loss now. And for your loss of Maria all those years ago.' She shook her head sadly and took off the black mantilla she was wearing, all the time holding Angela's eyes with hers. 'I've never forgiven myself for not preventing what happened.'

Angela was taken aback. Bettina must have guessed Cesaire had raped Maria. Was *that* why she had divorced him? 'Thank you for coming,' she eventually said, smiling compassionately at the older woman.

'Ultimately, Cesare got what he deserved,' Bettina said. 'Sadly, it was Stewart and Maria who suffered the most.' She squeezed Angela's hand in hers. *'Dio vi benedica, Angela.'*

'God bless you too, Bettina.'

As she watched her go, Angela was sure Bettina had her suspicions it was Stewart who had murdered Cesaire, but had kept it to herself.

Ten days after the funeral, Angela placed *Mandalay* on the market and the next week Gavin put his own house on the market as well. Both of them wanted a new start away from the memories of Stewart and Samantha, which those two houses invoked.

Much to Samantha's credit she wrote to Angela and apologised for the tragedy in South Korea and also for getting involved with Stewart. She also agreed to keep it a secret from Emily and the boys as to what had happened and not to contact them again. Of Stewart's descendants it was Gavin who was left with a bitter legacy from the man he thought was his father. Cesare Carpani's vengeance now complete.

To Angela it was one more secret that needed hiding.
Don't tell. Ever.

***

When Angus rang Emily, after she left a message to see how his father was, she was pleased to hear his voice.

'Overall, he's not too bad. He and Mum have gone up to the Gold Coast to stay with her sister. If he came back here there's no way he'd rest. Unfortunately, he's suffering from dizzy spells, which could be permanent, meaning he can't drive. Nor ride a horse.'

'Oh, how awful,' Emily said.

She remembered Bill saying the only thing that would stop him riding a horse was if he was in the ground, pushing up daisies.

'How do you think he'll cope? I mean, if he can't drive or ride a horse?'

'He'll find it hard. But hopefully we'll manage. Anyway, he was asking after you.'

'That's lovely. And how are you coping on your own down there?'

'I'm sort of enjoying having the run of the place to myself, apart from the station hands. They're a bunch of good blokes and hard workers. By the end of the week, they sure earn the beers we down together. And I'm managing to do a bit of study, sending assignments in online.'

'When do you think your parents will come back?'

'Hopefully, they'll stay there for a few more weeks. And Dad can have a good rest. He paused. 'I had to pull a calf yesterday.'

'Pull a calf?'

'The mother was having trouble delivering it. One of the blokes had to give me a hand to pull it out. Not a great job, but I'm pleased to say both mother and son are doing well.'

'That's wonderful.'

'And I've got the shearers coming in again in a few weeks.'

'You're enjoying it, aren't you?' Emily asked.

'Yeah. I am as a matter of fact. But enough about me and *Kilmarnock.* 'How's your Nonna?'

Emily told him how they had had the family get-together.

'I think it really cheered her up. She adores Allen. And my other brother, Jono, was there as well.' She was going to tell him about Jono's past drug problems, then decided not. 'Dad was there too, but he had to rush off. He's got a new girlfriend and was off to have dinner with that fellow, Dimitri Carpani, who now owns *Erskine's.* We were talking about him when I was down with your parents. You might remember that his father, Cesare, got murdered way back when my father was a teenager.' She looked outside to where Nonna was pruning the roses by the front gate. 'I'm taking Nonna to Tasmania when I go down there to do a modelling gig for the tourist bureau. It's quite amazing, but there was a fellow, Raphael from the island, Procida, where she lived in Italy, who was in Tassie as a prisoner during the war. He was friends with Nonna and Maria.' Angus seemed interested, so she told him how Maria was her real grandmother but had died when having her father.

'How sad,' Angus said.

'I know. It must've been dreadful.'

She told him how Nonna had married her grandfather and brought her father up. 'That's how she became my darling Nonna.'

She smiled inwardly. 'As you can imagine, it would be fun if I could help her find out where Raphael was held as a prisoner.'

And so the conversation went on until Emily realised she had been speaking to him for over half an hour. He was easy to talk to and she loved hearing about *Kilmarnock*.

Chapter Twenty

Angela gazed out of the window as the Qantas plane flew low over Pittwater Bay towards Hobart. She had little recollection of the last time she had flown into Tasmania and wondered if that huge stand of pine trees was there then. What surprised her was that she remembered the countryside as being lush and green, but the fields below the plane were as brown as the leather handbag by her feet. She had heard that Tasmania had been in a drought and there were dreadful bushfires the previous year, but she hadn't imagined it like this. Even so, it was a pretty sight looking at the endless blue bay stretching out below the plane's wing.

Emily was also surprised at how dry it was. 'Somehow, I imagined it like Ireland,' she said, glancing at the view below.

'It was certainly greener than this when I flew in with Stewart for the casino opening in 1973. But I must say, I'm excited to be seeing it all again.' She touched Emily on the knee. 'Thank you for organising it, darling.'

'I hope you like the Henry Jones IXL Hotel we're staying in. It's right on the docks. Evidently the building was an old jam factory.'

Angela chuckled. 'Let's hope they've managed to get rid of the pungent smell of jam cooking.'

An hour later, after picking up a hire car and heading into the city on the road, which took them past sprawling suburbs and over the Tasman Bridge, spanning the Derwent River and then past Government house, she was amazed to see cattle grazing in the grounds. Angela stood at the window of her hotel room. It was such a lovely view over the fishing boats in the docks with the last of the sun casting a golden tinge across their decks where fisherman busily tidied away their nets, reminding her of the busy fishing harbour at *Cala di Corricella* on Procida. Across the docks was the large expanse of the Derwent River and up beyond the city the towering outline of Mt Wellington stood majestically aloof, yet seemingly enfolding the sprawling city below in its expansive embrace. She tried to remember it from when she was here with Stewart all those years ago. But seeing as they had flown in the day of the casino opening and out the next day, she didn't see much at all apart from the extensive view from the casino's revolving restaurant atop the magnificent circular edifice perched on the edge of the Derwent. She moved away from the window, unpacked her small case and hung her jacket and a couple of shirts in the wardrobe. She then lay down on the soft bed for a short rest.

That evening she joined Emily for oysters and crayfish in a cozy waterfront restaurant with the wonderful name, *The Drunken Admiral*. 'I've got an early morning shoot round Hobart,' Emily said, putting her mobile down from a call from the photographer as they finished their wine at the end of the meal. 'It's to show tourists what there's to do in Hobart before they head down to Port Arthur. Will you be okay on your own, Nonna?'

'Of course I will. I shall go exploring.'

'Well, don't tire yourself out.'

Angela slept well that night, and after a leisurely breakfast in the sunny atrium courtyard at the rear of the hotel, she decided that she would suss out the library and see if she could discover anything more about Italian prisoners stationed in Tasmania during the war. Collecting her handbag from her room, she headed outside and pulled out a map, where the receptionist had marked the library with an asterisk. She walked along the docks, past the fishing boats and a few fish punts with long lines of patrons. She smiled as she passed a young couple sitting on a bench trying to shoo the seagulls away from their fish and chips. Although the sun was out, there was a chill to the air, so she pulled her woollen scarf around her shoulders. After passing an old sailing ship called the *May Queen* she turned right. It was quite a steep rise to the library, a nondescript grey building at the edge of the city. The walk had tired her out somewhat, so she sat for a moment in the foyer. When she got her breath back she approached a young woman behind the information desk to see if she could help her find what she was seeking.

'Gosh, were there Italian prisoners here in Tasmania during the war?' she asked, looking blank.

Angela nodded. 'There certainly were. Mostly working in the apple orchards.'

'I had no idea. But wait a sec and I'll go see if anyone else might know.'

When she came back she shook her head. 'The only suggestion Jane, our head librarian, had was to try the Tasmanian Museum. It's down near the docks. We don't have many apple orchards left anymore, but there's sure to be some history down there of when we were known as the Apple Isle. Would you like me to ring and see if they have anything at all?'

Angela gave her a grateful smile. 'Thank you, that would be wonderful.'

Sadly, her enquiries drew nothing. 'I'm so sorry to be of absolutely no help,' she said. 'I really don't know where you'd find that sort of information.'

'It was very kind of you to try. I'm staying down in the docks area, so I'll wander back down and have a look through the museum anyway. I'm sure I'll find other things of interest there.'

As she traipsed down towards the docks again she wondered why she was trying to find out where Raphael was a prisoner of war. He was part of such a distant past. If she hadn't met Elena's cousin Marco, she wouldn't be bothering at all. Deciding to give the museum a miss she consulted her map. She wasn't far from Salamanca Place, where the receptionist had told her there were souvenir and coffee shops. She found a seat outside a pleasant café on a corner. After sipping from a steaming cup of coffee, she continued along the row of sandstone buildings until she came to a shop selling Tasmanian woollen items. Inside was a friendly woman behind the counter, who chatted about the weather as Angela perused the shelves.

'And where are you going after Hobart?' she asked, wrapping two pairs of woollen gloves Angela had selected, one pair for Emily and one for herself.

'The Tasman Peninsula.'

'It's beautiful down there.' She handed Angela the wrapped gloves. 'Are you going to Port Arthur?'

Angela nodded. 'Yes we are.'

'It's amazing now. They've done such a great job since that dreadful massacre. They've even got a new visitor centre and restaurant.'

'I very much look forward to seeing it all,' Angela said, placing the gloves into her handbag and trying not to think of the terrible mass shooting that took so many lives in 1996.

She then wandered back to her hotel and after a light lunch, feeling quite tired, she lay on her bed for a short siesta. She had not long woken up when she heard a gentle knock on the door.

'Gosh, I hope I didn't wake you,' Emily said, when Angela opened the door.

'Not at all. I was just lying on that wonderful bed being lazy.'

'So, what did you do this morning?' Emily asked, stepping into the room.

Angela filled her in before handing her the gloves she had bought for her.

'Wow, Nonna. Thank you. They're perfect for this weather.' She tried them on and touched her face with the soft wool. 'I'll treasure them forever.'

'I'm glad you like them.'

'I'll leave them on as I've got another shoot at four up below the mountain at what they call the Female Factory, where female convicts were held in the 1800s. This evening the fellow from the tourist bureau and the photographer are coming to join us for a drink downstairs, if that's okay.'

'Of course it is, darling.'

'What say we meet downstairs in that lovely bar at six.'

'That sounds fun.'

'Are you sure you're not too tired?'

'I'll rest a bit more and won't have a late night.'

Just on six, Angela was comfortably ensconced in a leather armchair in the hotel's Long Bar down below. Next to her sat the photographer and then Emily and another man, who Emily told Angela was with the Tourist Bureau. She smiled as she watched Emily laughing with them both. No matter whether she found out anything about where Raphael was held as a prisoner during the war, she was very glad that she had come with Emily on this trip. Although she was tired, she was enjoying herself immensely. On the table in front of her was a bowl of mixed nuts. Picking a walnut up she put it in her mouth.

'We seem to grow more walnuts than apples these days,' the photographer said as he watched her take another one from the bowl. 'I was up the east coast photographing a huge grove last week for a promotion.'

'Yes, I believe most apple orchards have been pulled out,' Angela said. 'Sad, but no doubt a sign of the times.'

'You're right about that. The EU destroyed our overseas market badly when England stopped taking a lot of our apples. Mind you, I photographed a couple of small remaining orchards up the Tamar when they were in full blossom this year, and over the years I've taken a few great shots down the Huon. Nothing like an orchard in bloom.'

'Talking of orchards,' Angela said. 'I know it's a long shot, but if you've photographed a few do you happen by chance to know of any that had convict buildings on the sea and with a waterfall?'

'Gosh,' the cameraman laughed. 'Now, that's a big ask.'

'This one was south of Hobart. But not in the Huon Valley.'

He thought for a moment. 'Maybe round Sorell. They had orchards there. But you said it was on the water.'

'Yes,' Angela nodded. 'I think a bay rather than the open sea.'

He scratched his head and looked to the other photographer. 'Could be Norfolk Bay ... what you think?'

'Could well be.'

'Oh!' Emily said. 'Where is that?'

'Down on the Tasman Peninsula, where we're going tomorrow.' Another pause. 'Do you know what? I reckon I might know just the place it could be.'

'Really!' Emily said.

'Yes,' he said. 'Could well be there. I was doing the filming for that TV show, *Gourmet Farmer.* We went to this great place to film a segment on the demise of orcharding, but also to talk to the fishermen down there. They go as far south as Maatsuyker Island in the Southern Ocean to fish for crays. We had a bonza cray bake on the shores of Norfolk Bay at the foot of this bloke's property. Great character he was. Has a terrific museum with some beaut historic pieces from when it was an orchard. Sadly, there's only a few rows of apples and some pears there now. Mostly, they farm cattle with a scattering of sheep. It's called *Waterfall Bay* and has been in the same family for generations. I didn't see the waterfall, as we were filming in the convict buildings by the bay, but, if it's called *Waterfall Bay,* it'd have to have a waterfall, wouldn't it? There's two *Waterfall Bays* on the Peninsula. The other one's an isolated cove, mighty hard to get to along a steep track from Eaglehawk Neck. Not sure which one got the name first.'

'I wonder if there were any Italian prisoners on the orchard you were filming?' Angela asked.

'There sure was,' the cameraman said. 'In fact, the owner showed me a photo he had on the wall of his museum with the prisoners picking apples there, and there he was sitting right in their midst looking as pleased as pie. Only a kid he was.'

Angela's face lit up. 'A photograph!'

'Yes.' The cameraman paused, scratching his head again. 'I'm trying to remember the owner's name. Ah yes, I remember now. Doug Larkham. He said the prisoners were damn hard workers and got on well with the locals. He reckoned his family were sad to see them go. And a couple of them were loath to leave.' He looked at Angela. 'Is it of special interest to you, Mrs Erskine? The Italian prisoners, that is.'

Angela paused before answering. 'I originally came from an island in Italy, near Naples. I knew a couple of our soldiers were taken prisoner at Tobruk and brought here to work on the land as many of the Australian farm workers had gone to serve in the war. So yes, it is of interest.'

'I could ring Doug Larkham and see if you could pop in when we're down there.'

Angela felt a rush of excitement. 'I'd like that very much,' she said, giving him a grateful smile. 'If it's not too much trouble, that is. It's just that one particular soldier made it sound rather nice. And seeing as we're in Tasmania we might as well have a look.'

'Gosh,' Emily said. 'Do you think that's where your friend Raphael worked as a prisoner?'

'I have no idea,' Angela said. 'But it might be worth a visit.'

Angela's excitement grew as they finished their drinks. If *Waterfall Bay* did turn out to be where Raphael worked as a prisoner, she would be able to remember enough of what he told Maria, Aunt Sophia and herself to be able to build a picture of what it was like back in the 1940s. Particularly, if there was someone who was a child at the time who might remember the prisoners.

And there was a photograph of them!

***

The next morning, Angela and Emily drove out of Hobart, through the town of Sorrell and along the Arthur Highway to the tiny hamlet of Murdunna and down to the seaside village of Dunalley where, seeing that the bridge had been lifted to let a yacht go through, and attracted by a sign proclaiming 'the best scallop pies in Tassie' outside a ramshackle café, they decided to pull over.

'Don't know about you, but I'm starving,' Emily said, hopping out of the car in front of the cafe. 'And as they reckon they have the best Tassie scallop pies we really should try one.'

Angela wasn't that hungry, but when Emily came back and she smelt the delicious aroma of pastry and seafood she suddenly found her appetite.

'That was delicious,' Emily said, licking her lips as they drove over the bridge a few minutes later with the yacht now disappearing into the wide bay.

Angela smiled and wrapped away the small paper bag her pie had been in. 'It was certainly worth stopping for. Do you know I think that's the first scallop pie I've ever eaten?'

'Not even on Procida?'

'Fish pie, but not scallop.'

'Well, there you go. And I've never had a Tassie one. They're yummy.'

Further on, they came to the steep hill running down to the narrow isthmus that was Eaglehawk Neck, joining the Tasman Peninsula to the rest of Tasmania. Angela gasped when she saw the sparkling stretch of white sand with thunderous waves rolling in from the ocean and the wide bay stretching across to the sandstone cliffs on the far headlands, a startling mix of brown, ochres and reds.

'Now that would have to be one of the best views in Australia,' Emily exclaimed, slowing down.

'It certainly is. So this narrow neck of land is where they had the guard dogs stationed to stop the convicts escaping.'

'You've done your research.' Emily laughed.

'I watched a *Getaway* episode many years ago. It showed where we are right now.'

'Those unlucky convicts must have been desperate. Poor sods.'

'Poor sods is precisely what they were.'

'Anyway,' Emily added, glancing at Angela, 'wasn't it great how that cameraman happened to be the one doing our shoot down here? And that he told us about the orchard at *Waterfall Bay?*'

'It certainly was, darling.'

'It'd be so amazing if it was where Raphael was held prisoner, wouldn't it? I can't wait to find out.'

'I'm surprised he didn't describe this view when he was telling Aunt Sophia, Maria and me about coming here.' She sighed. 'So perhaps this peninsula isn't where he was after all.'

'He was probably cramped in the back of an army truck, a van or such and couldn't see out.'

Angela smiled. 'You're probably right.'

Looking at the rumbling expanse of ocean on one side and the calm stretch of water on the other side, which she presumed was Norfolk Bay, she tried to imagine what Raphael would have been thinking if he *was* in an army truck coming down here? Although he would have been pleased to leave the horrors of Libya and Tobruk behind, surely he would have been anxious as to what lay ahead.

Now the road hugged the bay and out on the water a few small boats bobbed up and down with people fishing in them. She remembered how Raphael said they used to fish in a bay. Was it this bay?

'I bet that building's really old,' Emily said, looking to where a large stone house stood close to a jetty. 'Mind you, I reckon it'd be freezing cold in winter.'

Angela remembered Raphael telling her how cold it was on the orchard where he was, even colder than Procida in winter.

'I'm sure they'd have huge fireplaces,' she said, hoping there had been one where Raphael was held prisoner, even if it turned out not to be down here.

Emily checked her watch and glanced across at Angela. 'Are you sure you don't want to go to *Waterfall Bay* now? I know we have an appointment tomorrow with Doug Larkham to look at the photograph and talk to him.' She looked at the GPS map on the dashboard. 'The road branches off not far on and I'm sure we can drive through *Waterfall Bay* and right around the Peninsula and still get to our hotel before dinner. It's such a lovely afternoon it might be nice to have a quick look. And I believe the drive's very picturesque.'

Angela hesitated for a moment and then smiled. 'Why not?'

A few minutes later, they branched off and followed the road up a steep hill with the bay on one side and rolling hills and treed mountains on the other. When they got to the summit there was a wonderful view down over a valley. Angela had rarely seen such a pretty valley before. It was even prettier than the valley where *Riverside* was situated up the Hunter. Compared to the rest of Tasmania, it was green and fertile. To their left was a row of poplars lining a dirt road and then the road went up another hill. And from the top of the hill, you could see for miles out over the bay where small islands were dotted here and there, as if they had been carefully placed there by a talented architect of such beauty.

Driving down into the next valley it was even lovelier than the last one. On the slope of the hill above the bay was a quaint wooden church nestled within tall trees and with a small cemetery surrounding it. Next door was a pale green weatherboard cottage with deep verandas on all sides. Undulating paddocks rose up against a pine forest in the distance.

In the heart of the valley was a small cluster of houses set among a thick arbour of trees, which looked like oak. And there were a few rows of apple trees, perhaps the remainder of an orchard. In front of that was a run-down stone cottage, which looked as though it was from convict times.

'Oh, look! This is *Waterfall Bay*,' Emily said, pointing out the sign post a little further on before they came to another house from a bygone era, two storey this time with a red roof. On the other side of the road were a group of sandstone buildings.

'So it is,' Angela said as Emily slowed down. She felt a surge of delight.

'Do you want to stop now?' Emily asked. 'See if Doug Larkham is there and can tell us if Raphael was here?'

Angela waited a while before answering. She looked around. If this was where Raphael and his fellow prisoners had been held captive it was certainly a beautiful spot. For a moment, she imagined him living in that old house. Walking across this road, which would probably have been a dirt road back then, across to the bay on the other side. Was that where he said he went looking for cockles and fishing for small fish? Flathead. Was that hill to their left the hill he said he used to walk up because the view from the top reminded him of Procida and the view to Ischia and Capri? She was dying to know the answers, but she didn't want to arrive on Doug Larkham's doorstep unannounced. She had waited so long tomorrow would be time enough.

No,' she said. 'Let's leave it until tomorrow. The poor man is probably regretting already saying he would see us, let alone turning up a day early.'

Emily nodded. 'Even though I'd love to stop, you're probably quite right.'

Just as they got to the top of the hill on the other side of the village, Emily's phone rang. She pulled aside onto the verge of the road to answer it.

'It's Angus,' she said to Angela as she looked at the screen.

Angela smiled. 'Go sit on that log over there on the other side of the road and talk to him. If he's gone to the trouble to ring you down here, he must be keen to talk to you.' She opened the window. 'I'll enjoy just breathing in this beautiful country air. And looking at those contented cows under that tree over there.'

Emily smiled. 'Goodo.'

She got out of the car and walked across the road with the phone held to her ear. Angela watched her sit down on the log of wood, beyond which the paddocks rolled down to the sparkling waters of the bay. She felt a contentment she hadn't felt for a long time. She realised that she hadn't even thought of the reporter from the *Sydney Mail*, and what he might unearth. And even if this wasn't the place where Raphael had lived during the war, it was still a beautiful part of the world to enjoy.

No matter what happened, she was so glad she had decided to come with Emily to see it.

***

'Just wondering how things are going down in Tassie?' Angus asked Emily.

'Great,' she said. 'We're down the Tasman Peninsula at a place called *Waterfall Bay*. It's where we think the fellow Nonna knew in Italy may have been held prisoner during the war. It's the strangest thing,' she told him. 'I have a huge suspicion he must have meant a great deal to her.' She looked out over the bay to where a yacht was sailing close to the island. 'It's such a lovely spot. In a way the farm here reminds me of *Kilmarnock*. There are lots of English style trees, poplars and firs, but it's much greener. I think it gets a lot more rain than you do. Apart from the beautiful bay, which it fronts onto, there's supposedly a river and a lovely waterfall. We're meeting the owner tomorrow, so we'll get to see a bit more.'

'I'm glad it reminds you of *Kilmarnock,*' he said with a smile in his voice.

'It must be older than *Kilmarnock,* as there's lots of convict buildings. But tell me, any news on your dad?'

'He seems to be coming on okay.' She heard him chuckle. 'They're enjoying the break so much I reckon they might stay up there for a while.' There was a pause and she heard him clear his throat. 'What's say when you come back you drive down here for a weekend. It gets a bit lonely rambling around here on my own.' Another pause, longer this time. 'Actually, it's not just that. I'd like to see you again, Emily.'

She smiled, feeling a jolt of pleasure. 'How about I come down the weekend after I get back?'

'That'd be great. I'll book us into *Grazings* for a meal. And we can do a bit of riding round the place. Maybe take a picnic to the river.'

'That sounds terrific.' She looked back across the road to where Nonna waited. 'Anyway, I'd best get back to Nonna. I've left her in the car.'

'I'm looking forward to meeting her one day.'

She laughed. 'I think she's looking forward to meeting you as well.'

After she hung up, she sat there for a moment, contemplating their conversation. It sounded as though Angus was looking to take things further. And Emily had to admit that she was keen to do so as well. All she had to do now was put Mathew right out of her mind. She smiled to herself. As time went on, and the more she got to know Angus, it was getting a lot easier to do that.

Chapter Twenty-One

The next day Angela sat on a bench in the sunshine among the sandstone ruins at Port Arthur. Her seat overlooked a sheltered bay where a boat ferried tourists out to the Isle of the Dead. She wondered about the many convicts who had been exiled to this tragic, yet in its own way, beautiful, place. And how did the local community move on from the 1996 horror, particularly as so many of their own were massacred? It was as if Tasmania's innocence had been destroyed forever.

'Are you ready, Nonna?' Emily asked, bouncing across the lawn after finishing filming the advertisement.

Angela smiled at her. 'I'm sure tourists will double in numbers when people see that ad with you in it on TV.'

'Don't know about that, Nonna.' She glanced around and smiled. 'But I'm glad I might in a small way help the economy of such a beautiful peninsula. I'm told so many of those who were working here at the time have never recovered.'

'I'm not surprised,' Angela said. 'It's something that would stay with you forever.'

Emily nodded. 'Now that I'm finished work for the day, why don't we go and pay our respects to the memorial for the victims over there? I'd like to sit in front of it for a moment, and then we can head to *Waterfall Bay.* See what we can find there.'

'That sounds lovely, darling.'

They stood in silence for some time by the memorial for the massacre victims, a beautiful garden with a tranquil pond glimmering in the sunshine. Angela felt such sadness for all of those poor people, who had happily come here to Port Arthur on that beautiful sunny day not knowing that they were about to lose their lives.

'Many of the dead were so young,' Emily said, as they walked to the car parked under a sprawling beech tree afterwards. 'Two were just little girls with their mother.'

'It was unimaginably tragic. Sadly, maniacs like that don't differentiate between who they shoot.' Angela sighed. 'It was the same during the war.'

'You were only very young yourself at that time, weren't you?'

'I was lucky to be on Procida. In Naples, it was so much worse.'

'How old were you when you met your Raphael?'

Angela smiled. 'I was just thirteen. And eighteen when he came back from the war.'

'Wow! And here we are all these years later, looking to see if we can find where he was held a prisoner here in Tassie.'

'As I've said, it's just that he made it sound rather nice.'

'Well, if he was holed up in *Waterfall Bay* he wasn't wrong.' Emily looked back down to the where part of the penitentiary was lit up by a shaft of sunshine. 'I wonder if he came here to Port Arthur?'

'I've no idea. He mentioned convict buildings; however, I think that was on the orchard where he was a prisoner.'

'It's gotta be *Waterfall Bay*,' Emily said, grabbing the car keys out of her handbag.

'Well, we'll find out shortly.'

They drove up through the tiny village at the top of the hill and past the Fox and Hounds Hotel where they had spent the previous night and along the road which looped through the heavily treed hills and dales until they came to the turnoff for *Waterfall Bay*. As they passed the small weatherboard church on the hill, Angela thought again what a beautiful spot it was. And although there were only the remains of an orchard in *Waterfall Bay,* she could envisage what it would have looked like back in 1941 when Raphael was first brought here, if in fact he was. There would have been thousands of apple trees with horses carting the huge bins, which Raphael and his fellow apple pickers had filled, across the road to the packing sheds. If there was a market for the apples they would then be hauled down to the jetty where they were loaded on ships for Hobart—just as Raphael had told her that day as they sat on the beach on Procida. How disappointed she would be to discover he wasn't one of the men in the photograph Doug Larkham had in his museum, and this wasn't the orchard after all.

After Emily pulled the car to a halt under the large oak on the side of the road she turned to Angela. 'You wait here, Nonna. I'll see if I can find Doug Larkham.'

Angela looked around as she waited for her to return. On one side of the road a verdant valley spread upwards towards the forest and on the other side green fields rolled down to the pretty bay where waves broke on the shore. If this *was* the place where Raphael was held prisoner, he and his fellow prisoners had indeed been lucky. So many Italian prisoners were treated appallingly in the abhorrent prisoner's camps in Europe. She opened her window and remembered Raphael telling her how when he was working in the orchard it was the smells of the Australian bush, the eucalypts, wattle, grass and the sheep and cattle mixed with the salty air of the bay that he loved so much. Was this the same piquant aroma he savoured all those years ago? She looked around for a wattle tree and saw two by the stone cottage perched on the side of the road.

Now she saw Emily walking towards the car. And by her side was a tall man with a shot of white hair and huge, expressive eyes. He was wearing a pair of blue jeans and a green pullover, which was spattered with leaves and pieces of dried grass and had a hole in the arm. His boots were caked in mud and by his side was a sheep dog, wagging its tail enthusiastically to welcome the visitors. Although Doug Larkham would have to be in his mid-seventies, he looked remarkably fit and able for his age.

'Young Fred and I were up the back doing a bit of fencing,' he said, shooing the dog away before he opened Angela's door. 'Time ran away. I'm afraid I didn't have time to get changed.'

'Thank you so much for seeing us,' Angela said. 'It's very kind of you. I hope we haven't disrupted your day too much.'

'Ah, not at all.' He took Angela's hand to help her out of the car. 'I believe you may know one of the Italian prisoners who were here during the war.'

'I'm not sure if this was the place, but it does sound as though it could be—'

Before she had a chance to add any more he beckoned. 'Come, I'll take you down to the museum that I've put together. It isn't much, but it gives me a hell of a lot of pleasure. I'm lucky enough to have unearthed a great deal of stuff left behind by my ancestors. Larkhams have been working the land here for generations.'

He steered Emily and Angela along a pathway lined with blue gums and poplar trees until it opened up and there was a clear view of the bay, stretching out as if it was a vast seascape watercolour. On either side of the path was a line of sandstone buildings, which looked as though they had been here since convict times.

As if reading Angela's mind, he said. *'Waterfall Bay* was one of the outstations to Port Arthur. My family and I have restored the buildings over time.'

He then gestured for them to follow him past what he said was a convict solitary confinement cell hidden below a huge walnut tree.

'That's the old apple sheds and cool room,' he said as they passed a gigantic wooden shed, 'now chock a block full of farm machinery, tractors, old cars and everything else we can't work out what to do with.' He chuckled as he gestured to a rusted plough and a derelict tractor beside the sheds. 'We try and have a clearance sale every now and then, but each time I put something out to sell I think I might use it and drag it back here. And, Anne, my wife, is even worse.'

Further on they came to another sandstone building where half a dozen chickens pecked in the dirt by the front door. Inside it was obvious to Angela that it was the museum he had mentioned. There were a number of old photographs lining the thick stone walls and numerous small relics of farm machinery and other bits and pieces, which must have been used in the apple industry over time, were spread around the wooden floor. Angela stood beside Emily, taking it all in. She glanced at the photographs to her left, many of which were obviously of Doug Larkham's ancestors. Looking at the clothes they were wearing, the photos appeared to have been taken in the 1800s or early 1900s.

Doug walked over to the wall on his right and took down a photo, wiping away the dust from the glass frame.

'This is the photo I've got of the Italian prisoners,' he said. 'Some of them still come back to visit.' He laughed. 'So we mustn't have treated them too badly, eh? They're getting on a bit now, and the long trip from Italy is a bit much for them to handle. But over the years, reckon we've had four or five visit us.'

He handed Angela the photo. As she looked at the young men standing there, dressed in their dark uniforms in front of the stone cottage they had passed on the way in, her heart lurched and her face became flushed.

Crouching down beside a small boy, whom she imagined was Doug Larkham, was Raphael. There was no mistaking him. It was the same floppy dark hair, open face and mischievous dark eyes that she remembered so well from Procida.

'Do you recognise any of them?' Doug Larkham asked.

Angela waited sometime before answering, all the time holding Raphael's eyes with hers.

'Yes,' she said. 'I do.'

Emily leaned forward to look at the photo. 'Gosh, Nonna. Which one is Raphael?'

'Raphael,' Doug Larkham exclaimed. 'Raphael Lombardi?'

'Yes,' Angela said. 'That's him.'

'Well, I'll be blowed,' he said. 'Raphael, eh?'

'You remember him?' Angela asked.

'Bloody oath, I do. When I was a kid we used to call him "the flute man". Never heard anyone play like him.' He chuckled heartily as if recalling that time. 'Mind you, I'd never heard anyone play the flute before he came here. Still haven't heard a better player. Then and now.'

Angela gasped. 'You've seen him since?'

'Sure have. He's one of the best doctors the Peninsula has had in a long time.'

'He came back here as a doctor?' Angela exclaimed, finding it difficult to believe what she was hearing.

'Sure did.'

'How on earth did that happen?'

Doug looked at the photo Angela was holding. 'He reckoned he always wanted to be a doctor. So when he was in his forties he took himself to medical school in Italy and applied to come to Australia, then here to Tassie after he completed the necessary study to qualify in Australia. Said he was happy here during the war and wanted to get away from Naples. He started down here as a locum. However, the locals liked him so much he ended up being here more or less full-time. In fact, he retired down here.'

'He was married with children,' Angela said, recalling his wife and twins on the beach at Procida. 'Did they come here too?'

'Nah. Just him. We often chew the cud together, particularly on a Friday night over at the club. He reckoned his wife wasn't too keen on him becoming a doctor, so that's pretty much why they broke up. He was in some sort of business in Naples. His wife's family owned half of it. Said his kids were grown up and left home, but were in the business too. He left most of what he owned in Italy to his wife and kids when he came over here. So they were well looked after.'

Emily looked at Angela and back to Doug. 'Did he remarry when here?'

'No. Never.' He laughed. 'Not that he wasn't sought after by the women-folk round here. Figured he'd been married once and that was enough. Somehow, I got the impression there was someone else in his life. When I asked he was kind of cagey, but one night after a few beers I dragged out of him that there was once a girl back in Italy he was pretty fond of. She had come to Australia after the war with her sister, but he had no idea where she was living now. He tried to find her many times without any success, no matter how hard he tried. Thought she had probably married and changed her name.' He grinned. 'I suspect that woman was the main reason why he came back to Australia.'

So he tried to find me, Angela thought with an inward jump of joy. If only I had known. 'Did his children ever come and visit him?' she asked.

'They both visited him quite a few times over the years. He'd bought himself a small farm down here, which they liked to come to. Nice place looking down over the bay along a bit.' He paused and cleared his throat. 'You knew him well in Italy, Mrs Erskine?'

Emily was about to break in, when Angela lifted her hand. 'We were very young. But I do recall him telling me about this place. That's why I wanted to have a look.'

'He and his fellow prisoners were darn hard workers,' Doug said. 'I remember my father telling me he was pretty cut up when they were sent back to Italy. Most of them became part of the family, more or less. I was only very young when they were here.

331

But I remembered Raphael particularly. Apart from playing the flute, he made me a toy wooden horse and cart. Still got it. My kids had it and now the grandkids. That's why I was so chuffed when he turned up back here. He didn't speak much English when he arrived during the war, by the time he left he could speak a fair bit. He also made a darn good pasta. Said there was a lady back on his island who was a great cook and had let him help her sometimes.'

'Do you think that was Aunt Sophia?' Emily asked.

Angela nodded. 'Yes. I think it probably was. She was very fond of him.'

'How lovely,' Emily said, smiling at them both.

Angela was fearful to ask the next question that was jumping up and down impatiently in her mind. But after a moment she gave a small cough and ventured tentatively. 'Is he still here, by any chance?'

'Not right now. He's gone to Antarctica on an expedition ship.'

'Antarctica!' Emily exclaimed. 'Gosh, how old would he be, Nonna?'

'In his mid-eighties.'

'He's as fit as a fiddle,' Doug said. 'Took up hang-gliding when he was eighty. I know he had trouble at first getting a passage down south, but he somehow convinced them. Reckoned he signed something to say if he died on the trip they were to throw him overboard.' He laughed. 'There's a doctor still practicing up Newtown way and he's ninety-three. So he told them that if that bloke was still practicing why couldn't he go to Antarctica as their ship's doctor's assistant? Anyway, they bought it. Last email I had from Raphael, the ship was on its way home and he was having a ball. He reckons they have him playing the flute every night.' He pointed to the cottage Angela and Emily had seen by the roadside. 'I'll show you the place where he and his fellow prisoners lived during the war. We've done it up as a farm stay, but as you can see on the outside we left it looking pretty much as it did back in its day.'

'I'd like that very much,' Angela said.

'How incredible that this is the place, Nonna,' Emily said, placing her arm around Angela.

'Yes,' Angela said, squeezing her hand. 'It is, isn't it?'

Chapter Twenty- Two

On the way to the cottage, with Fred bounding in and out of the paddocks beside them, Angela smiled happily to herself. Not only did Raphael fulfil his dream of becoming a doctor, he had also tried to find her. Listening to Emily and Doug Larkham chatting companionably she had an image of Raphael walking along this road during the war and beside that image was one of an elderly man walking this very same road, possibly with Doug Larkham by his side.

Crossing a stone bridge, Doug pointed out a tall waterfall burbling over rugged brown rocks further up the river.

'That's the waterfall that gave this place its name,' he said. 'Sometimes it's a bit like Niagara. Other times, in the middle of summer, there's hardly a drop. Depends on the rainfall. Down here, we've had a bit lately so it's not too bad.'

'It looks so pretty,' Emily said.

Angela nodded. 'I remember Raphael telling me he used to swim below the waterfall.'

Doug smiled. 'I still have a dip up there. Might be a bit cold, but I prefer it to the sea.'

When they reached the cottage, Angela was amazed at what a pretty garden surrounded it. A brilliant plethora of roses, flowering begonias and lavender dotted the green lawn and in between there were dollops of unruly wildflowers merrily dancing in the breeze.

In the corner was a pear tree where someone had made a children's swing out of rope and wood. Next to the pear was a large wattle, the branches spread out grandly above a wooden fence. She smiled as she wondered if this was one of the wattle trees Raphael loved so much when he was a prisoner here? Around a small fountain there were roses and carnations. As they stood on the stone-flagged back verandah, she admired the tranquil view over the dam and beyond to the rolling hills and forest. In the dam, ducks and a few geese swam among the reeds and there was a small wooden rowboat pulled up on the grassy bank. Across the other side of the dam, cattle grazed contentedly and further on there were more clusters of sheep.

'All that used to be orchard,' Doug said, following her gaze. 'We pulled it out twenty odd years ago. We make more money farming than we would with apples these days. Sad to see the orchards go, but no good flogging a dead horse, eh?' He pointed to a herd of cattle grazing by the river. 'We've had pretty mean times with the cattle and sheep too, but thank God they're doing okay now.'

Angela rested her eyes on the view. She thought of Raphael standing on this same verandah during the war looking at this scene each morning before he went to work in the orchard or apple sheds. Or at the end of the day's work.

335

Doug rustled around for the key, which was hidden behind a loose stone on the wall. 'Come in and I'll show you around,' he beckoned.

The kitchen was at the back of the house and also flagstone. Although there were modern appliances and fitted Huon Pine benches and cupboards, Angela imagined how it may have been when Raphael was here all those years ago. The window over the sink looked out on the same view as from the verandah. To the front of the cottage there was a living room with a large stone fireplace and three bedrooms.

'We had bunks in here for Raphael and his mates,' Doug said. 'It looked nothing like this, but they made it comfortable enough.'

'You've done such a great job doing it up, yet retaining the character,' Emily said, after they moved back to the living room and stood in front of the fireplace.

'Yes,' Angela agreed. 'You certainly have.'

Doug pointed to a brick. 'See that mark there? Shows it was made by a convict. We've managed to unearth many of those bricks over the years, and, of course, there's the ones which the other buildings are built of.' He touched the mantelpiece above the fireplace. 'In Raphael's day they had an old plough disk they used to hang on a chain over the fire to cook on. I remember it as a kid. When Anne and I first got married we made one much the same. Worked well.'

Angela looked around. She wondered if Raphael and his fellow prisoners all got on. It wasn't a large space, so they would have been on top of each other a lot.

As if reading her mind, Doug said, 'My father reckoned they had the odd brawl among themselves. Was bound to happen, but they seemed to work through it.' He chuckled. 'No one killed anyone. All who arrived went home to Italy in '46 or '47. And, as I said, they were missed a great deal when they went.'

Angela smiled and looked around. 'It sounds as though Raphael had never forgotten his time here, if he came back after all those years.'

'He reckoned he didn't,' Doug said, ushering them back outside to the stone verandah where he raised his hand against the sun and peered along the near paddock below the dam. 'I'd best go check on that sheep on its back up there. Why don't you sit here and wait for me, then we can go on up to the house and have a cup of tea. Anne is expecting you.'

'That sounds lovely,' Angela said.

'Can I come with you to check the sheep out?' Emily asked. 'I'd love a walk in the country and,' she added, smiling at Angela, 'I'm sure Nonna would like to spend some time here at the cottage, wouldn't you?'

Angela smiled. 'That seems like a lovely idea.'

Doug looked at Emily. 'Sure then. Why not? We'll leave your grandmother here to imagine what it was like when Raphael and his fellow prisoners were here.' He laughed. 'We sometimes sit here together and down a few beers. I like to hear what it was like for him back then. Being a kid, I didn't fully appreciate why they were here. To me they were just the Italians who lived here and worked in the orchard and played with us kids. He'd often tell me they were darn lucky to escape the war and come here, even though they missed Italy.'

Angela smiled. 'It would have been a haven here compared to the brutality of the war in Europe. And particularly at Tobruk.' She sighed. 'He told me it was while he was in Libya among all that carnage that he decided to become a doctor.'

'Yes,' Doug said. 'He told me that as well.'

As she watched Emily walk by Doug Larkham's side through the green field to where the sheep lay on its back, she thought again how wonderful it was that Raphael had been able to live out his dream of becoming a doctor. A dream he had told her about again and again when they were young and in love that long hot summer when he came back to Procida after the war.

And how long did he try to find her? No wonder he didn't succeed, as he would have been searching for Angeline Vincento. If Gina, their next door neighbour on Procida had lived, maybe he would have been aware that Maria had died giving birth and that Angela had married her widower. Angela had no doubt that she would have kept in touch with Gina, who was sure to have seen Raphael and told him the girls' news. But sadly, Gina and her husband Phillipe had both died in quick succession six months after the girls left, having contracted a deadly influenza which swept the island. Neither she nor Maria had kept in touch with anyone else.

'What's the silly point?' Maria had scoffed, when Angela suggested they write to a couple of their island friends. 'No one would give a hoot what we're up to. And even if they were in the slightest bit interested, they'd somehow manage to turn it into gossip.'

In the end, Angela had gone along with Maria's suggestion. As much as she would have loved to have known how Raphael was, there was no way in the world that she could have written to him when he was married to someone else and the father of two children. But if she had known he had come to Australia, how differently things may have turned out.

She wondered what to do now. Should she ask Doug Larkham to tell Raphael in an email that a silly, little old lady, who had known him a lifetime ago, had come to see where he had been held prisoner during the war? Should she give Doug her home address and if Raphael wanted to contact her, he could. Or should she ask him for Raphael's email and get Emily to email him on her behalf? But after all these years, what was the stupid point of two doddery old people (well, Raphael gallivanting in Antarctica was obviously not that doddery) trying to recapture what they had when they were young and beautiful, living on an island the other side of the world? Then again, it would be very nice just to see him again. Or should she remember him as he was? As he was in that photo Doug Larkham had in his museum? And surely it would be much kinder to Angela if Raphael remembered her as she was back then rather than seeing her as she was now. He would surely get a shock, as, of course, she might too. It could be a bit like seeing a cherished book left outside for decades, where the harsh elements had ruined its pages. What was once new and exciting was now rather sad and decrepit, even though what was written on those pages remained with the reader forever.

She was still thinking of what to do when Emily called out from where she was hopping over a wooden stye. 'Isn't this place to die for, Nonna?'

Angela smiled at her. 'It's not hard to imagine why people would want to come back.' She laughed. 'Even, if they *were* prisoners of war.'

'Come,' said Doug. 'Anne will have tea and her famous rock cakes ready. And,' he added, looking at Emily. 'She's sure to want to meet the beautiful model who's selling our state to tourists. Particularly, if it means more business for our farm stays.'

They strolled back along the road until they reached Doug's house, which was set in a magnificent garden dotted with flowering shrubs, beds of petunias, daisies and geraniums. A magnificent rose garden surrounded a stone fountain and the lawn was bordered by pear and apple trees, together with a cluster of raspberry, plum, apricot, and even a mulberry tree. On the banks of the river, Angela could see an enclosed vegetable patch.

'We have to enclose it because of the wildlife,' Doug said.

'Oh, yes. I remember Raphael telling me if they didn't enclose the one they had during the war the possums and wallabies would destroy it.'

'He still curses and swears about them up at his place.' He paused. 'Would you like to have a look at it afterwards? I've got to go and check on his pot plants anyway. When we've had a cuppa, we could head along.'

Angela paused for a moment. 'Surely that would be an invasion of Raphael's privacy.'

'Nonna, I'm sure he wouldn't mind,' Emily jumped in.

'I could take a photo of you both and email it to Raphael,' Doug said. 'Wouldn't that give him a chuckle, eh!'

In the end, Angela nodded. 'If you don't think it's intruding, I'd like to see his house very much.'

***

It was a small weatherboard house perched on top of a hill with a wonderful view of the bay. There was a vegetable patch behind a high fence and beyond that, maybe on the next-door neighbour's property, was a vineyard running down to the water. Directly in front of Raphael's house, a few cattle grazed contentedly.

'He lets Mick, who owns the vineyard, run his cattle here,' Doug said. 'They keep old Mungo company.'

'Mungo?' Emily asked, looking around.

'He's down there under that willow by the creek. His favourite spot.'

As Angela glanced to where he pointed, she smiled. Standing regal under a weeping willow tree was a long-haired brown goat, not unlike the one Raphael had stopped to pet on his way down to Pozzo Vecchio Beach where a young Angeline and Maria were swimming naked that steaming hot afternoon the day they first met.

'He's had him for years,' Doug said. 'I told him it's too damn wet here for goats, but he got him all the same. And old Mungo made a fool of me as he's still going strong after all these years. That weeping willow's his favourite spot.'

Around the house was a neat garden of flowers and shrubs, and on the verandah there were pots of gardenias and geraniums. Next to the door was a cane lounge with comfy cushions.

'We often sit here together,' Doug said. 'You can never get sick of that view, eh!'

As Angela gazed across the expanse of water to the islands and beyond to little bays and inlets, she thought how much this view must remind Raphael of the view from Procida across to the islands of Capri and Ischa.

'Come on inside,' Doug said. 'The few pot plants I need to check are in his sunroom.'

When they stood in the living room, Angela looked around. Although it was neat, it was a room well-lived in. There were comfy chairs, a foot stool, a coffee table with a few medical magazines on top and a couple of paperback novels. In the corner, there was a small television and full bookshelves lined two of the walls. Walking over, she picked up one of two cane flutes lying on a shelf next to the books. She remembered Raphael telling her how during the war he had found some cane here in *Waterfall Bay* to craft his own flutes. She held it in one hand and then the other, envisaging him sitting on the verandah here playing, the haunting notes rising in the wind and floating down to the bay.

Emily smiled as she watched her. 'One day I'd love to hear him play,' she said, coming alongside and touching the flute.

Placing it back down, Angela nodded. 'It would be wonderful to be able to listen to him again.'

Above the fireplace there was a painting of what she imagined was a local scene with a beach overhung with native trees. Below that there was a mantelpiece, which held bits and pieces. And it was there that she saw it. Sitting right in the middle was the very same tourmaline stone that Raphael had shown her when he gave her the one she still cherished.

I have one too, Angeline. When I look at it I will think of you.

She walked over and picked it up, fondling it in her hand. She felt her eyes water and quickly blinked them away.

'What a beautiful stone,' Emily said coming over and putting her hand out to take it.

'It's called a tourmaline stone,' Angela said. 'I have one very similar in my jewellery case.'

'Is it a stone from Italy? Is that why you both have one?'

Angela nodded. 'You can find them in other places, though I suspect this one is from Italy.'

She put the stone back on the mantelpiece and smiled. 'Now, I really feel as though we should go. Poor Raphael would have a fit if he knew we were going through his things.'

'I'm finished with the pots now anyway,' Doug said, coming back into the living room. 'Let's head outside and I'll take a photo of you both in front of the house.'

When he had finished clicking his phone, he laughed. 'Well, if that doesn't give Raphael a kick, I don't know what will.'

'You'll have to tell him that it's Angeline Vincento,' Angela said. 'I don't think Angela Erskine would mean much to him at all.'

Doug smiled. 'Ah, but I'm sure he wouldn't have forgotten your face, Mrs Erskine.'

Angela now realised that Doug suspected she was the girl who Raphael had never forgotten. And, as they walked back towards Doug's house, where a herd of cattle lazed under the poplars by the river at the bottom of the garden, Angela decided she would give Doug her address after all. When he sent that photo to Raphael he could pass it on. If Raphael, on seeing that photo of her as she is now, wanted to find her so be it. If he didn't, she would quite understand. At least she'd discovered he was happy, living in this beautiful part of the world, and had realised his dream of becoming a doctor.

That happy thought was enough for Angela to take to her grave.

***

Later, as they drove back to Hobart and as Emily quizzed Angela more about Raphael, she told her how she and Maria had first met him on the beach all those years ago. How they had formed a tight friendship and when he went to fight in the war they had prayed for him, hoping he was safe. She even told her of the day he came back to Procida and walked into the tiny shop on Marina Grande where she was working so he could buy cigarettes. What a shock she got to see him. She told her how they used to explore the island together on his bicycle, stroll through the laneways and fields, and swim at the beaches. How despite the two of them being very much in love, he was forced to marry the girl his parents had chosen for him in order to save the family business.

After she finished talking, there was a long silence before Emily pulled the car to the side of the road. She pushed her sunglasses back on her forehead and leant over, taking her in her arms. 'Oh darling, Nonna,' she said, stroking her hair, 'thank you for sharing that with me. I can't wait to meet him.'

Angela nodded, and felt her eyes fill with tears. Wiping them away with her hand, she smiled. 'It would be lovely if one day you could.'

And as she said that, she thought how much Raphael would love to meet Maria's granddaughter, who she had absolutely no doubt he would adore.

Chapter Twenty-Three

When she got out of her car the following week at *Kilmarnock,* Emily looked around, breathing the fresh country air deep into her lungs. She really did love this place. There must have been some rain, as the paddocks were slightly greener. She was about to open the door to the back seat to get her overnight bag out when she saw Angus walking towards her and her heart gave a little jump. He was wearing a pair of blue jeans and a green pullover. By his side, Rex wagged his tail excitedly before bounding over to greet her.

'I reckon he remembers you,' Angus said, beaming her a welcoming smile.

Emily put her handbag down and knelt beside Rex, tickling him behind the ear.

'I really must get a dog,' she said, as Rex licked her all over. 'Maybe I'll talk to Nonna about getting one.'

'A good idea,' Angus said, kneeling down beside her and pulling Rex gently by the collar to stop him licking her. 'I missed not having one up in Sydney.'

All of a sudden, Emily felt quite shy. She wasn't really quite sure how to handle this weekend. Although she had thought he was keen to take their relationship further, she wondered if she had overestimated his feelings for her. Had he just wanted her here as he was lonely on his own and wanted company? Or, as she hoped, *was* there more to it? To detract from how she was feeling, she raised an eyebrow. 'Any news on your dad?'

'They're now talking of going overseas. Maybe have a look for a yacht in the Med after all.'

'Oh. So you'll stay on here then?'

'That's the plan.'

'And what do you think of that?'

'I'm getting more and more used to the idea.'

'You don't miss the bright city lights?'

'Not really. Besides,' he said with a chuckle, 'there's always the dazzling lights of Gundaroo down the road.'

'Quite true,' she said with a smile and went to the front seat where she pulled out a paper bag. 'I almost forgot. I got these meat pies at Marulan for our lunch. I needed petrol and the pies looked so good I couldn't resist them. They just need heating up.'

'That sounds great. I went into Gundaroo this morning and got some bread and a few other things.' He grabbed her overnight bag out of the back seat. 'I was going to make you a sandwich, but a pie sounds much more up my alley.'

As they walked through the garden with Rex cavorting by her side, Emily couldn't help noticing how it had been let go to a certain extent. With his parents away, Angus no doubt had enough to do without worrying about the garden, but at least the lawns had been mowed and looked as though they had been watered. Stepping onto the verandah, she glanced to her right and could see the horses in the near paddock, and beyond that a herd of cattle grazed contentedly under a stand of gums.

'Here,' Angus said, pulling open the flyscreen door.

Walking inside, she felt as if she had come home. Everything seemed so familiar. Yet she couldn't help thinking of what had happened last time she was here. How Bill had nearly died.

'I've put you in Duncan's room,' Angus said. 'Hope that's okay?'

'Absolutely.' She handed him the pies. 'You put these in the oven and I'll only be a sec.'

'Would you like a wine or beer with lunch?'

'Thanks, but not if we're going for a ride as you said on the phone. Tonight though. I put a bottle of *Pinot Gris* in my bag.'

When she went into Duncan's room, she stood there for a second. It did seem strange to be here with Angus without his parents being here. When she had a few weekends away with Mathew up the Blue Mountains and down the coast, they, of course, shared a bedroom. But here she was with Angus, sleeping in his brother's bedroom, not sure what their relationship was going to be. She put her bag on the bed and after taking the bottle of wine out and also placing it on the bed, she went along to the loo. Looking at herself in the mirror as she washed her hands, she fiddled with her messy hair and smoothed her white shirt down, tucking the front into the belt around the waist of her blue jeans.

In the kitchen she handed Angus the wine. 'Should be okay. It's from a vineyard around here.'

'Thanks,' he said, gratefully, looking at the label. 'I'll put it in the fridge for later.'

Emily glanced around the neat kitchen. 'Gosh, you've got it looking great.'

'You should have seen it early this morning. Nothing like a visitor to get things in order.' When they sat at the table, he filled their water glasses up from a jug from the fridge. 'So Tassie was fun? I've only been there once, on a school rugby trip to Hobart.'

'We had a terrific time.'

Although they had spoken on the phone, she filled him in more about their time in Port Arthur, their trip up the east coast to Swansea where they stayed in a wonderful B&B, which both her and Nonna had loved. She then told him all about their time at *Waterfall Bay*. How happy Nonna was to discover that Raphael was still alive.

'I hope he contacts her,' she said. 'Doug Larkham, who owns the farm, took a photo of us outside Raphael's house. He was going to email it to Raphael on the ship he's coming home from Antarctica on.' She refilled her glass from the jug and chuckled. 'It sounds as though they were very much in love when they were young until they were forced apart by his family. Then, as you know she and Maria, my grandmother, came to Australia and Nonna ended up marrying my grandfather.'

At the mention of her grandfather, Angus got up from where he was sitting. 'I presume you saw the article in the *Sydney Mail* this morning? About your grandfather.'

Emily's heart missed a beat. It was what she'd been dreading. Her grandfather outed as corrupt. 'No,' she said with a slight shake to her voice. 'I went for an early run and then took Nonna a cup of tea and the newspapers, but I was rushing so hadn't read them.'

'Well, it's an interesting article,' he said, handing her the paper. 'It's on page five.'

'Oh!'

She took hold of the paper and fiddled with it in her hand, which she noticed was shaking.

'Are you okay?' he asked, looking at her with concern.

'Yes, yes. I'm fine.'

She glanced at his face trying to read his expression. Was it one of pity? 'Surely your family's used to publicity,' he said, eyeing her curiously.

Not this sort of publicity!

Nodding slowly, she opened the newspaper to page five where she saw a large photo of her grandfather staring out at her. She had never seen this photo of him as a young man before. He looked so handsome, his earnest eyes staring straight at the camera. She glanced at the headline.

Titans of the Restaurant Trade.

The emergence of Italian restaurants in the 1950s, particularly Beppi's, which is the longest standing Italian restaurant in Darlinghurst, has sparked the curiosity of our Greg Ashton. Read how the late Stewart Erskine began his Erskine's restaurant empire after working at Cesare's restaurant in Stanley Street, across the road from Beppi's and once owned by the late Cesare Carpani, who was murdered outside his restaurant forty years ago.

Emily quickly scanned the article, looking for any mention of Glasgow Mine, but all she could see was one sentence near the end of the article, saying how her grandfather had branched out into other businesses, including mining. The rest of the article was mainly about how in the 1950s Italian restaurants were just coming into fashion in Australia. How *Beppi's* was still trading in the same spot as back then and that Dimitri Carpani, the son of Cesare, had now taken over the *Erskine's* chain, after purchasing it from Stewart Erskine's son, Gavin. She let out an inward sigh, as she looked at photographs of the restaurants, *Beppi's*, *Cesare's* and the first *Erskine's*. Next to her grandfather was a photo of Cesare Carpani. Emily couldn't help notice what an unattractive man he was, with his fleshy, pillowy cheeks and bulbous nose, whilst

Beppi Pelosi had a lovely face. But there was no doubt that her grandfather was the handsomest of the three.

She put down the paper and glanced at Angus. 'Nonna would like that article. No doubt she's seen it in the paper this morning.'

He eyed her worriedly. 'Looking at your reaction, it's almost as though you were expecting something else to be written about your grandfather.'

Now was not the time to tell him about Glasgow Mine. Maybe later if their relationship progressed she would tell him, she thought.

'Did I? Sorry, I think I'm just tired after the trip down. The traffic around the airport and going into the tunnel was horrendous.'

'So would you like a rest before we go for a ride?'

'Gosh, no. A ride will do me the world of good.'

'You can ride Cassidy. I'll take Dad's horse. He needs a bit of a run.'

'Well, let's hope there's no snakes around. Don't want a repeat performance like with your dad.'

'Don't worry. I'll keep an eye out.'

Later, after finishing their pies and washing up, they saddled up the horses and rode down to the large wooden sheds where Angus showed her where they sheared the sheep. Inside the shed there was a tangy smell of wool and manure, not unpleasant at all. And hanging from the rafters were some electric shears.

'We shear the sheep that have the coarser wool, which is mostly used for carpets now. We then shear them again in spring, together with the other sheep with the finer wool.'

'Oh. I didn't realise you bred two sorts.'

'Yeah. Works well. Means together with the cattle and sheep we breed for consumption we've a good income coming in regularly during the year.'

Outside in the holding pen there were a couple of stragglers, who must have got left behind when the shearers let the others out. Angus opened the gate and they rushed through. After that, he and Emily rode down through the paddocks to the river where they let the horses drink.

As Emily sat in the saddle with the reins loose around Cassidy's neck, she sighed. 'I didn't realise how much I missed the country and horse riding until coming down here with Chrissy,' she said, sighing happily. 'It gets better each time.'

Angus's eyes met hers. 'When I first met you at the Coogee Bay Hotel I couldn't imagine you as a rider, but there you go. How wrong was I?'

'Well, I *was* sort of dolled up for a night out.'

'Both suit you,' he said with a warm smile. 'Dolled up and here as you are now.'

She held his eyes before he pulled his father's horse up by the reins and walked him over to where she was. 'Emily, I can't tell you how great it is to have you here at *Kilmarnock*.' He threw her a lopsided grin. 'The old place feels a lot brighter with you here.'

'Thanks, Angus,' she said, returning his grin. 'It's terrific to be here.'

He pointed to where a rock jutted out over the river. 'Let's go sit on that rock and listen to the water for a moment. We can tie the horses to that branch over there.'

Emily nodded. 'That sounds a lovely idea.'

When they were sitting on the rock he took her hand and held it in his, lifting it to his lips, dispelling any doubts in Emily's mind about where their relationship was heading. He then leant over and kissed her on the lips, tentatively at first, but as Emily responded it became long and passionate. Although she had enjoyed kissing Mathew, she realised that with him she had never experienced the absolute tingling thrill that shot through her body right now. It was something she had never experienced with anyone before.

However, just as she felt her body totally yielding to his with desire, Angus pulled back. 'Sorry,' he said with a smile. 'I shouldn't have moved so quickly.'

'And why not?'

She pulled him close and placed her lips on his. And as they kissed again, the same uncontrollable thrill rushed through her. It was sometime later when they pulled apart and sat in silence, holding hands and listening to the sound of the water trickling over the rocks and the happy chirp of crickets.

'Thank you,' he said, kissing her hand. 'I've dreamt of doing that for so long.'

She smiled and touched his lips with her fingers. 'It was beautiful.' She looked across the river to the far bank where a rope hung down from a tree with a black rubber tyre attached. 'That must be the rubber tyre you and Duncan played on as kids,' she said, pointing.

Silence stretched out and she felt his pain. 'I haven't been on it … not since …'

She squeezed his hand. 'Maybe one day you and I could do that.'

'I'd like that very much,' he said, smiling at her. The silence was warm around them as they watched a red and green rosella fly from one branch to another on a blue gum across the water where it made a high pitched whistle, which attracted two more rosellas. Soon there were at least six of them perched there, making a colourful display.

'Where is Duncan buried?' Emily asked.

'Here on *Kilmarnock.*'

'Oh.'

'We have a small graveyard where McBrides have been buried for centuries. 'Come,' he beckoned, standing up and dragging her to her feet, 'let's ride along and I'll show you where he is. If we stay here like this I'm sure to do something I might regret. And you've only been here for a few hours.' He looked at his watch.

'By the time we go visit Duncan, ride back, fix the horses and have a shower, it'll be time for a drink before heading into Gundaroo.' He gave her a wink. 'I booked the best table at *Grazings* for us.'

'Wow. Thank you.'

To Emily, Duncan's resting spot was one of the loveliest burial places she had seen. Even lovelier than where her grandmother, Maria, was buried at Waverley Cemetery on a hill looking down over the sea. Perched halfway down the riverbank under an arbor of red gums it had a view across the water to the paddocks on the far side, where cattle and sheep grazed. Betty had obviously been working her garden magic down here, for Duncan's grave was a mass of yellow and white daisies, wildflowers and native shrubs, and a profusion of wild river roses, lined the white wooden fence around the graveyard.

'They brought him home from Afghanistan?' she said, as they sat on the horses looking down from above.

'Yeah. To Fairbairn in Canberra.' He coughed and looked away. 'They gave him a full military funeral at Duntroon.' He turned slowly back to her and then down to Duncan's grave. 'After that, we brought him here.' There was a long pause. 'What a bloody waste. He was one of the best.'

She leant over and took his hand. 'I'm so sorry for you and your parents.'

'Yeah, well, we know it was his choice to go into the army ... even so ...'

'Shall we go down to his grave?'

He waited awhile before answering 'Not right now. I was there yesterday.'

'Maybe I'll go? Will you wait, while I do?'

'Sure,' he said, looking down sadly. 'I'll watch you from here.'

She nodded before dismounting and handing him Cassidy's reins. Carefully, she scrambled down to Duncan's grave, which was slightly away from the other graves of McBrides who had been buried there over the centuries. She stood there for a moment looking at his headstone before leaning down and pulling a couple of weeds from the soil, which she threw on the ground nearby. She then wiped bird droppings from his headstone with a twig.

I never knew you, she said silently to him, wiping a tear from her eye. But if you were anything like your brother I'm sure I'd have liked you a lot.

And just as Angus had said to her before, she thought miserably of what an utter waste it was to have such a young man lying here in the ground on the wonderful property that had been his home..

Stopping at the wooden fence on the way back up to Angus and the horses, she picked a bright red rose in full bloom.

'I'll put this in some water back at the house,' she said, threading it through the clasp on Cassidy's saddle before giving him a pat. 'That way Duncan can feel part of us being here.'

Angus nodded. 'Thank you. He'd like that a lot.'

Once she was mounted back on Cassidy, they rode home to the yards, where they dismounted and put the horses away in the adjoining paddock. As they strolled towards the homestead, Angus took her hand in his. With her other hand she brought the red rose to her nose and smelt the glorious aroma.

'It's beautiful,' she said, letting Angus smell it too.

Just before they reached the verandah he pulled her close and gave her another long, arduous kiss, which she couldn't help feel had a sad sort of desperation to it. 'That was for Duncan, in case he's spying from above.' He smiled, stroking his hand through her hair before standing back and looking up at the sky. 'Reckon he'd be more than happy to see me here right now with you.'

She saw his eyes water up and a tear dribbled out. She lifted her hand and wiped it away. 'And I know two others who'll be very happy for us.' She laughed, lightly, thinking of two of her favourite people.

He looked at her quizzically. 'And who might they be?'

'Chrissy and darling Nonna.'

He pulled her close to him. 'You know I fell in love with you the moment I saw you at the Coogee Bay Hotel.'

'Did you now?' She laughed and touched his lips with her hand. 'Well then, Angus McBride. You might just have convinced me to feel the very same way about you.'

He chuckled. 'So it's not just *Kilmarnock* and riding horses that you love?'

'Ah, yes. Well, now that you mention it—'

He grabbed hold of her and kissed her again. 'Go,' he eventually said, standing back and giving her a wink, 'go put your glad rags on and after a drink in the garden we'll head into the thriving metropolis of Gundaroo and paint the town red.'

As she had a shower and got dressed, she felt the happiest she had in ages. Not only because she was here at *Kilmarnock* with Angus, but surely the reporter, Greg Ashton, was unlikely to continue his investigations into her grandfather's dealings in Glasgow Mine after writing that positive article about him in today's paper. Nonna would be pleased about that. She seemed really good during their trip to Tasmania and she and Emily had even gone to an early movie the previous night and had a quick meal afterwards. And this morning, when she took her in the newspapers, she had seemed quite chirpy. Emily knew that half the battle in fighting cancer was having a positive attitude and Nonna seemed to have spadefuls of that. She hoped desperately that her cancer had slowed down and that she would be around for quite a while. Not only for Emily and her family, but also for Raphael, if he was to contact her.

Chapter Twenty-Four

After Emily left for Kilmarnock, Angela lay in bed for a while, reading the newspapers. She always got the *Australian,* but she had asked the newsagency to also send her the *Sydney Mail* just in case an article on Stewart appeared and she could prepare herself to deal with it. Why she bothered reading the news she wasn't sure, for as usual it was full of doom and gloom. Global warming was sure to destroy the earth and if that didn't do it, then terrorism and planes dropping out of the sky were going a long way to getting rid of mankind.

She picked up the *Sydney Mail* and started to thumb through. When she turned to page five she got a huge shock to see Stewart staring out at her, together with Cesare Carpani. But as she read on and saw the other photos in the article, including one of Beppi Pelosi of *Beppi's* fame, her shock turned to relief. Although Greg Ashton mentioned that Stewart had worked for Cesare Caparni in the 1950s and wrote about the current friendship between Dimitri and Gavin, including buying a racehorse together, he clearly had no idea that Cesare had raped Maria and that Gavin was Cesare's son. He had described Cesare's murder, but he was obviously unaware that Stewart was the one who murdered him and that Angela had helped to cover it up.

She let out a long, relieved sigh as she held the newspaper in her hand. She hadn't seen that photo of Stewart before. It must be one that was on file at the newspaper. It was a black and white photo, but as always she remembered the vivid colour of those eyes so well. His photo looked just like the man she met at Villawood, so it must have been taken not long after he opened his first *Erskine's*. Before Maria's death shattered him so utterly, and he had learned the truth of Gavin's conception and Angela's vow to her sister's secret. She sighed as she thought how those soft and caring eyes had turned from what they were in this photo to hard and calculating. She then looked at Cesare Carpani. It was a very old photo, possibly even before Maria, Angela and Stewart went to work for him at *Cesare's*, but even back then his eyes appeared quite evil. Or was it just that Angela now knew so well what he was capable of?

She sighed again and got out of bed. In the kitchen she made some toast and sat at the bench, reading and re-reading the story. Although there was a small mention of Maria and Angela having worked at Cesare's, the main thrust of the story was about the emergence of Italian restaurants in Sydney back in the 1950s and how Stewart had gone on to make a huge success of *Erskine's*. Although it didn't actually say so in the article, one could believe that Stewart should have been grateful to Cesare Carpani for giving him a great start in the restaurant business when he first arrived in Australia from Scotland.

What a total lie and sham that was, she fumed as she put the paper down and took her breakfast things to the sink, where she rinsed them under the tap before placing them in the dishwasher.

She decided to spend the morning going through some of her papers. It was high time that she got rid of final bits and pieces before she died. In the bedroom, she pulled out the cardboard box where she kept her papers and put it on her bed, making two piles. One to throw out and one to keep.

She suddenly heard the phone in the hallway ring and got up to answer it.

'Have you seen the article on Dad?' Gavin asked her down the line, 'About working at Cesare's and starting *Erskine's.*'

'Yes,' Angela said. 'I did.'

'Good article, isn't it?'

A long silence ensued before Angela said. 'Yes, it is. Although it made it sound as though Cesare Carpani gave your father the start he needed to commence *Erskine's.* Your father didn't need anyone to help give him a start.'

'You never liked Dimitri's father, did you?'

She swallowed a deep breath to try and control her emotions. 'I suppose Cesare did give him a start in a roundabout sort of way,' she eventually said.

'He must have taught Dad how to cook.'

'Stewart *knew* how to cook. That's why Cesare employed him.'

'Dimitri told me he and his mother contributed to the article, hence Greg Ashton knew he and I are friends and have bought that racehorse together.' He paused for a moment. 'I'm surprised, Mother, that he didn't involve you more in researching the piece.'

'I did tell you he came around one day, having seen that article in *Trove* about us working at *Cesare's*. However, as I was very busy at the time, I had to give him short shift,' she lied.

'Oh yeah. I remember now you saying he came back. And I was right, wasn't I? About it being Beppi's award that may have inspired the article. Anyway, the whole Glasgow Mine thing has been dropped for good by the government.'

Angela took an inward breath. 'Really! How can you be sure of that?'

'Because,' he said, sounding a bit sheepish, 'let's say some money changed hands.'

'You mean you paid someone off in the government to hush it up?' Angela gasped.

'I'm not the only shareholder in Glasgow Mine, Mother. Dimitri Carpani also has a number of shares, which Dad used as part of the payment when he bought his mother out of *Cesare's* after his father's death.'

Angela shook her head. She had forgotten that Stewart had partly paid for *Cesare's* with shares in Glasgow Mine. Now, of course, those shares belonged to Dimitri and his mother, and if the mine was shut down they could become worthless.

'He doesn't want to risk having the mine closed,' Gavin went on, 'but most of all having his *Erskine's* franchise dragged through the mud. It's in his interest as well as ours to ensure the inquiry gets stopped. Let's just say being well-heeled and a full-bred Italian, unlike me, he's got influential friends in the right places who gladly accepted compensation in return for turning a blind eye.'

If only you knew, Gavin. That's you too. Full-bred Italian to the core.

She sighed. How ironic that the transaction Stewart made all those years ago with Cesare's widow might save him from being outed as having obtained his mining lease more or less illegally. And how incongruous that the sons of Cesare Carpani have played a part in saving the name of the man who murdered the man who sired them. She looked across to where the photo of Maria and Stewart sat on the sideboard and held Maria's laughing eyes with hers. Although her sister would be pleased that Stewart's name would remain unsullied, how desolate she would be to know how it had been saved.

'But,' Gavin said, his voice hard and hostile down the phone, 'if it wasn't going to be the Erskine name that'd be sullied, I would've been more than happy if they'd got the bastard. Even if he has been dead for years. And, by God,' he added, with such bitterness that it startled Angela, 'if that reporter knew how the great Stewart

Erskine died having it off with my wife, the mother of his grandchildren, he'd really have a goddam story, wouldn't he?'

But they're not his grandchildren.

Listening to Gavin raving, it was almost as though it was Cesare Carpani come to life again, the time he vowed to annihilate Stewart all those years ago when he opened a restaurant in competition with his own, his vengeance knowing no end. She took a deep breath to try and douse the fire raging inside of her, making her heart race as if she had run a hundred mile marathon.

'Anyway,' Gavin said, his voice sounding calmer now, 'that's how the cookie crumbles, Mother. And you, I and the rest of the family should be grateful to Dimitri for saving our name being dragged through the mud.' There was a long pause and in it Angela again tried to come to terms with what she had just learnt. She knew there was corruption in all governments, with a couple of NSW politicians languishing in jail, but to think that in this day and age it was still possible to buy a politician off was mind-boggling.

'But enough of that business, I'd best be off,' said Gavin. 'I'm taking Bianca for a drive up the Blue Mountains. We'll have lunch up there somewhere.'

'So you're still seeing her?' Angela asked, trying to bring a normality to her voice, even though inside she was still shaking.

'I really think she could be the one, Mother.'

'That's good,' Angela said. 'I'm very pleased for you, Gavin.'

And in a way she was. Through no fault of his own Gavin's life had been scarred by circumstances well beyond his control. Although Stewart had ensured, by his business successes and then by his betrayal with Gavin's wife which caused his own demise, that Gavin had become a rich, rich man, at what cost had it come?

After hanging up, she went back with a heaviness in her step to the bedroom and continued sorting her papers. She then put the box back into the cupboard and moved to the bathroom for a shower.

Standing under the scalding water, she sighed. Odd as it seemed, she was glad she was dying. She was tired of living a lie. She desperately wanted someone to confide in, but there was no one to ease her burden, not without destroying many lives, including her own.

As the water eased the pain in her hip, she thought of Raphael on his way back from Antarctica. Surely he would be home by now? And would Doug Larkham have given him Angela's address? If so, would he write to her? Silly as it was, yesterday she had checked the letterbox. Just in case. She smiled to herself, realising she was behaving like a love-sick teenager. She had no doubt that Raphael would have taken one look at the photo Doug had taken in front of his house and decided that the last thing he wanted to do was make contact after all these years. Yet, there was the tourmaline stone on his mantelpiece. Did that mean he still thought of her? When she came home from Tasmania, she had gone to her jewellery case and taken out her own stone and fondled it gently, remembering so clearly the day he gave it to her. She then put it in her handbag, ensuring it would be with her always.

After her shower she checked the letterbox again. On finding it empty, she spent some time in her garden before walking up to the shops to get some fresh bread for her lunch. After lunch, she paced to and fro, thinking over and over of the conversation she had had with Gavin. Trying once again to come to terms with it all. Later, she tried to concentrate on a novel, opening and shutting the pages, but finding she was unable to remember anything she had read. She got up and went into the kitchen to decide what to have for dinner. She was looking through the freezer for something easy to prepare when the phone rang.

'Just checking you're okay,' Emily said.

'I'm fine, darling. So you got there safely?'

'Yes, and we had a lovely ride this afternoon. Later we're going into *Grazings* in Gundaroo for dinner. Did you see that article in the *Sydney Mail* about Grandpa? And how you all worked at *Cesare's?*'

'Yes, I did.'

'Do you think now that reporter has written all that about Grandpa he won't bother with following up about Glasgow Mine?'

Angela waited a while before answering. There was no way she was going to tell Emily how Gavin and Dimitri Carpani had sorted it out. 'I hope so,' she eventually said, 'and your father seemed to think that's the case when he rang.'

'Gosh, Nonna, I hope he's right.'

'How's Angus?' Angela asked, not wanting to dwell on the subject any longer.

Emily told her how his parents were thinking of flying to the Med and buying a yacht and how Angus was going to stay on and manage *Kilmarnock.*

'And how is he coping?'

'He's doing really well.'

'That's great, darling.'

'I truly do like him, Nonna. And he told me he's fancied me since we first met.'

Angela smiled to herself. 'Fancied?'

'He actually used stronger words than that. He said he's loved me from the moment we met at the Coogee Bay Hotel.'

'Darling, that's wonderful. I'm so pleased. And I can't wait to meet him.'

'He said he'll be up in Sydney next week to do an exam for his uni course. Maybe we could have him around for dinner.'

'That would be lovely.'

'Anyway, glad you're okay. I'll be home tomorrow after lunch.'

'Well, drive safely, darling.'

'I will. See you then, darling Nonna. Take care.'

On hanging up, Angela decided to cook herself an omelette. She ate it at the kitchen bench and then cleared up. After watching television for a short while she went to bed. As she lay there, she thought how lovely it was that Emily had found Angus McBride. It sounded as though he was very much in love with her and Emily was feeling the same way about him. When Angela departed this world she felt contented to know Emily would have Angus to look after her.

She turned off the light and tried to go to sleep; however, much as she tried, sleep evaded her. It was two hours later when she opened the drawer by her bed and took out a box of sleeping tablets and took one. An hour after that she fell into a deep slumber.

***

Although it was a bit nippy for a swim the next morning Angela felt a walk would do her good and clear her mind. She had taken an extra painkiller earlier, and for the first time in quite a while she was in little pain from her hip. She had a slight ache in her chest, which she put down to indigestion, but she felt quite strong. She decided she wouldn't even take her walking stick, but she would take her phone and her handbag as she thought she might stop at the fish and chip shop opposite the beach and buy herself some squid for lunch as a treat. She would sit on the wall overlooking

the beach and share it with the seagulls. She'd leave Emily a note
to say where she was going, just in case she came back before
Angela did.

When she got down to the beach it was fairly deserted, as the
wind was up and it was quite cold. At first, Angela paddled in the
waves with her shoes in hand, relishing the cool water on her bare
feet and watching the waves wash a myriad of colourful shells in
and out. She then sat for a moment on the sand before walking
along the beach until she came to the end, where the waves were
pounding against the cliffs.

Suddenly, she felt quite faint from the exertion and sat down on
the sand beside a wide rock, where the waves had not yet reached.
She lay back, loving the sun on her face. Before long she closed
her eyes and drifted in and out of sleep.

She saw Raphael. It was a memory clear as a bell. It was on a
hot and humid afternoon as they loitered happily among the
wildflowers in a field on Procida during that glorious summer of
love after he came back from the war. With the ruffles of her
blouse rippling in the warm breeze, and with the jingling of goat
bells in a nearby field, Raphael took her hand and led her to where
their favourite weeping willow tree spread its thick branches in a
splendid hanging canopy, dappling the ground beneath in shifting
glimmers of sun and shade. Plopping onto the ground, he pulled
her down on top of him, all the time laughing his happy, jingling
laugh as the sweet smell of hot grass tickled her nostrils and a soft

breeze shifted the leaves of the willow. On the pond, two white swans nestled among the reeds. Rustling in his bag, Raphael pulled out his flute and played a tune, the glorious notes mingling with the warm breeze. Angela had never heard such a beautiful tune.

'Did you just make that up?' she asked when he had finished.

'Yes,' he said with a gentle wink. 'It can be our tune, Angeline. I will give it a name.' He was silent for a moment with just the whispering of the wind around them. 'I know what it will be.'

'And what is that?'

'Amore.'

'That's beautiful,' she said, smiling at him tenderly.

Placing his flute on the ground he kissed her hair, her forehead, the lobes of her ears, her cheeks and then placed his lips on her lips, undid her bra and kissed her tanned breasts. Angela knew without doubt that she was about to lose her virginity. Even though it would be a mortal sin and she'd just been to communion, she didn't care one little bit. All she felt was love, delicious skin-tingling love. Taking hold of his hand she moved it down to her belly where the buttons on her slacks were done up. When the last button was undone she wriggled out, one leg at a time, took his hand and placed it inside her pants.

'Angeline, we should stop,' Raphael whispered. 'It is not right.'

'It is right,' Angela murmured, her heart beating so fast she thought it might run out of beats. 'We belong together, so how can it be wrong?'

Raphael placed his lips on hers and kissed her with such ardour that she almost lost her breath. Soon they were both naked. Touching her skin softly, he slid his hand over her belly and across her breasts and down to where she felt sticky and moist between her legs. And, as the mottled rays cast shapes and shadows upon their writhing bodies, Angela had no idea it was possible to reach such heights of ecstasy; that she could lose control of her body to such a degree that it solely belonged to another person. And always would.

With a jolt she awoke from her reverie and looked around, and heard the crash of the waves on the shore. She felt a pain behind her breast bone. It was a sort of ache that spread across her chest and down her arm. The incoming tide now touched her toes.

I really should drag myself up and go and get my squid and chips at the café across the road, she thought to herself. I must have a compressed nerve in my chest so standing up will relieve that. And something to eat will make me feel stronger and put an end to the stupid, romantic dreams of an old lady.

But when she tried to lift her body from the sand, her chest hurt even more and she was unable to sit up. It was as though she had become part of the sand, which refused to yield her. Now the water touched her knees, then her thighs. It wasn't unpleasant in the least, even though it was quite cold.

So she lay there, looking up at the sky where the clouds seemed to be bumping into each other as they vied for front position. After a moment, the pain in her chest intensified more and more and she closed her eyes, willing it to go away.

Chapter Twenty-Five

When Emily got back to Bronte that afternoon she found Nonna's note on the table. She looked out of the window and saw how windy it was. She hoped that Nonna had rugged up well. She had no idea what time it was when she had gone down there, but if she was going to have lunch in the café as her note said she was going to do, it must have been morning. Emily thought she would unpack and then go down and join her.

Just as she had put the kettle on and taken her overnight bag to her bedroom, there was a knock on the door. It couldn't be Nonna as she had a key. Maybe it was Jonathon, or her father even.

When she opened the door there was an elderly man standing on the doorstep. The moment she saw him she knew who he was. Although he was obviously quite old, he was tall and he still had a good head of hair. When Nonna had known him it would have been dark brown, now it was white, as if it were a thick sprinkling of newly fallen snow. When he smiled, his warm brown eyes glinted with humour and his whole face seemed to join in the merriment.

'You're the girl in the photograph with Angeline,' he said with a beaming smile. 'Her granddaughter.'

'Raphael? Raphael Lombardi.'

He laughed. 'That was the name I was given.'

Emily couldn't stop herself. She rushed forward and gave him a hug. 'Nonna will be so pleased you're here. She couldn't believe that you came back to Australia and achieved your dream of being a doctor.'

'Was a doctor,' he grinned.

'Once a doctor, always a doctor.' Emily laughed and urged him inside. 'Nonna has gone for a walk on the beach. I was just going down to join her.' She looked around for a suitcase, for surely he would have one if he'd flown up from Tasmania.

'How was Antarctica?' she asked. 'We were amazed to hear you had gone there.'

'And why would that be?'

'Well … because …'

He laughed out loud and his whole face lit up. For a second, Emily could see the handsome young man in Doug Larkham's photograph with his fellow prisoners at *Waterfall Bay*. 'Because someone as ancient as me doesn't do such things. Tasmania is close to Antarctica and when I got the opportunity why would I refuse? After all, at my *ancient* age there might not be a next time.'

Emily smiled. 'I'm sure Nonna will insist that you stay.'

'I'm not so sure, so I booked into a hotel. I dropped my suitcase there on the way.'

'Well, come in anyway. I've put the kettle on so we can have a cup of tea or coffee and then we'll go down and find Nonna. She probably met up with some of her friends down there. They often meet by the rockpool. In fact, one of her friends, Elena, had a cousin come and stay a while back who knew you. He said he met you on the ship going back to Italy after the war. He also worked on an orchard in Tassie. I can only remember his first name. Marco.'

Raphael smiled as he followed Emily to the kitchen. 'Marco Agostine. I remember him well. We made quite a team. He singing and I playing the flute.'

'Nonna said you're very good.'

'I like playing. But good, well…not so sure about that.'

'Marco said you are as well.'

Raphael looked out of the window. 'Do you think your grandmother should be out in this wind? It seems to have come up quite a bit.'

'Oh, I'm sure she'll be okay. But you're right the wind has come up, so let's put off tea until we find her. Then she can join us.'

'That sounds like a good idea. I'm looking forward to seeing her very much. It is a long time since we last saw each other.'

'She will be so excited.'

Just as they were heading to the door, Emily's phone rang. 'I won't be a moment,' she said to Raphael.

'Is that Emily?' a woman's voice asked.

'Yes, that's me.'

'I found this phone I'm using in an elderly woman's handbag down here on the beach at Bronte. Her whole bag is soaked and I'm surprised the phone works. Your number was the last number that came up.'

'What do you mean her handbag got soaked?' Emily asked in alarm.

'I was jogging along the beach and when I came to the end I saw this woman lying here. The waves were coming in. I managed to pull her to safety. I've called the ambulance and they're on their way.'

Emily felt her heart sink. 'Oh my God!'

'She's not too good, but I've been able to keep her talking a bit. She keeps saying Raphael, Raphael. Does that name mean anything to you?'

Emily looked at Raphael. 'Yes, it does. We're on our way now, she's my Nonna. Can you please tell her that Raphael is with me? And that she must hold on. We're coming right now.'

When she got off the phone she told Raphael what had happened and she saw the colour drain from his cheeks. Together they got in her car and drove quickly to the other end of the beach where there was a crowd gathering. Emily could see an ambulance parked up on the road. Although Raphael was fit enough to go to Antarctica, he was not up to sprinting across the sand.

'I'll run to her,' she said, 'and tell her you're on your way.'

Emily left him in her wake as she raced across the beach to where Nonna was now lying on a stretcher, covered with a blanket. Her eyes were closed and she looked very small and pale. After telling the medicos who she was, Emily knelt down and took hold of Nonna's hand.

'Nonna. It's me. Emily. Raphael is with me. He's back from Antarctica. He came looking for you, Nonna. He's found you. Isn't that wonderful?'

***

Angela opened her eyes and saw the blurry figure of Emily against the sky. And next to her was an elderly man. When he smiled she knew it was Raphael, for even at his great age she would recognise those earnest brown eyes anywhere.

'You came,' she said, a rogue tear sliding down her cheek onto the sand.

'Yes, I came,' he said, kneeling down to take her hand. 'It has taken me a long time to find you, Angeline, and look at you here, lying on this stretcher like this.' He grinned. 'What on earth were you thinking, coming down to the beach in this weather?'

Angela smiled up at him. 'I love the beach. But you know that.'

Raphael lifted her hand to his lips and she could feel the warmth of his skin against her cold flesh. She felt herself drift upwards. It was if she was floating. High, high up into the sky among the shifting clouds. Now she was one of them with the wind blowing her this way and that.

'Angeline, Angeline,' she heard Raphael say, 'stay with us.'

She still kept floating … high … high …

She was never one for heights, but she didn't mind floating like this one little bit because Raphael was now with her. And so too was Emily. Just as she reached where she knew the stars would be hiding until it was dark, when they would come out to play, she heard another voice.

'Mrs Erskine, Mrs Erskine …'

Now she was no longer a floating cloud. She was lying on a stretcher on the beach with Raphael and Emily looking on worriedly beside a medic, who was calling her name.

'Mrs Erskine.'

'Yes,' she murmured, hardly audible, 'that's me.'

'We're going to take you in the ambulance to the hospital,' the medic said. 'We need to check your heart.'

'But … but I'd rather stay on the beach. With Raphael. With Emily.'

'I know,' the medic said. 'They can meet us at the hospital.'

She nodded and murmured, 'My handbag … where is it?'

'It's here,' the medic said. 'Sadly, it got saturated by the waves.'

'There … there's a gemstone in there,' she said. 'Raphael will know it.' She gave Raphael a weak smile. 'You gave it to me.'

Raphael smiled and touched her on the forehead. '*Si*, Angeline. I remember. I have mine still.'

Angela nodded but found she was unable to say anything as her chest felt heavy and her voice seemed to have disappeared.

'Your granddaughter will look after your bag while we get you to hospital,' the medic said, as they extended the legs of the stretcher and headed up to the street.

Raphael knelt down and picked up her hand, holding it all the way until they reached the ambulance parked on the road. 'It'll be a much less bumpy ride than on the back of my bicycle on Procida, Angeline. But hold on tightly, just as you did back then.'

Angela smiled weakly. '*Si*, of course. I remember. And … and you … you became a doctor …'

Raphael nodded. 'I did. And now I found you, Angeline.'

And they were the last words Angela heard as she was placed in the ambulance. As the sirens screamed loudly, she smiled to herself. After all these years Raphael had come. He had found her.

***

When Emily and Raphael arrived at the hospital they were ushered into a waiting room where Emily told him about Nonna's cancer diagnosis.

'That would have made her very weak and affected her heart,' he said, looking worried. He then glanced at Nonna's handbag, which Emily had brought with her. 'Angeline said there was a gemstone in her handbag.'

'Oh yes, she did say that, didn't she?'

She felt around for the stone and found it in the side pocket. She looked at it for a moment admiring the wonderful dazzling colours before handing it to Raphael. 'It's beautiful. I heard you say to Nonna that you had one the same as hers. I saw it at your house in *Waterfall Bay*.' She watched him take hold of the stone and fondle it gently in his hand. 'Nonna said it came from Italy.'

'Yes,' he said. 'It is called a tourmaline stone. I gave it to Angeline before she left Procida to come to Australia. I kept one the same. I told her every time I looked at it I would think of her.'

Emily felt herself choke up. She swallowed hard to try and contain a hidden sob. 'And did you?'

He smiled and his whole face lit up. 'Yes, I did. Every time.'

'You meant a lot to each other, didn't you?'

He nodded. 'They were happy times.'

'And you knew her sister, Maria. My grandmother.'

'Your grandmother?'

'It's a long story. Maria died having my father. Nonna then married her widower, my grandfather. His name was Stewart Erskine. He's dead too.'

'That is very sad.' There was a long silence as Raphael played with the stone in his hand. He held it up to the shaft of sunshine filtering through the window and Emily could see the magnificent colours shining brightly. 'Yes, I knew Maria,' he said, nodding. 'She was a great character and very beautiful.'

'But it was Nonna, Angeline, who you loved?'

He smiled sadly. 'She was very special to me.' Emily could see he was trying hard to contain his emotions. 'And I stupidly let her go.'

At that moment the doctor came out and told them that Nonna wasn't doing too well. As Raphael had said, the cancer had weakened her body and her heart was failing. The doctor told Emily she should ring any other family members who might want to see her.

She looked at him in horror, and without thinking picked up Raphael's hand. 'Is she dying? she asked the doctor, her eyes imploring a different answer than the one she was fearful of getting.

'We're doing our best, but she is very weak,' he said, adjusting the stethoscope around his neck.

Raphael squeezed Emily's hand and looked at her. 'What about your parents?'

She was about to say she didn't really have a mother. Instead, she nodded. 'My father should be here. And my brothers.'

He put her hand back in her lap. 'Maybe you should go and ring them now.'

'Yes,' the doctor said. 'That would be a good idea.'

Giving them both a sad smile, Emily walked out to the corridor and made the phone calls.

'She must have had a heart attack,' she told each one. 'A woman found her lying on the beach. The doctor said she's very weak and you should come before … before …'

'I'll catch the next bus from Byron,' Allen said.

And both Jonathon and her father said they'd come as soon as possible, although her father was down at Wollongong on business and Jonathon was out on the harbour on a client's yacht.

She had not long come back into the waiting room when a nurse came out to tell them they could be with Nonna. When Emily walked with Raphael into the ward where Nonna was, she got a dreadful shock to see her lying on the bed with machines beeping and a nurse hovering. She looked so pale against the pillow.

When Emily picked up her hand she stirred.

'Please … please, my darling,' Nonna whispered, hardly audible '… don't be sad. I am happy to go. I have met up with Raphael again … and you are here with me.' She touched the gold lira pendant around her neck. 'When I am gone to join Maria,' she said to Emily, 'wear this pendant always and it will keep me close to you.'

'Darling, Nonna …'

'Rest, Angeline,' Raphael said, his voice breaking.

'Yes … doctor,' Nonna said, looking feebly at him. She then closed her eyes and Emily saw a look of contentment appear on her face. It was as if she had come to the end of a much-cherished film she was watching and although sad it had finished, she was happy with the way it had ended.

For an hour she hovered between life and death, and all the time Raphael and Emily sat with her. Seeing Raphael fuss over her as a doctor and a very special friend, Emily felt such tenderness as she had never felt before. At one stage she had to get up and leave the room for she felt she was intruding.

On checking her messages, she saw Angus had texted to see if she had got home safely. Wanting to hear his voice, she rang back and told him what had happened.

'To see them together is so beautiful,' she said to him. 'I think Nonna's perfectly happy to go now that she has found him and realises he never forgot her.'

'I'll come up in the morning,' he said.

'Thank you,' Emily said. 'I'd like that very much.'

Back in the room, she was absolutely positive that just before Nonna took her last ragged breath her eyes flickered and she smiled at Raphael. As Emily looked to where he held Nonna's hand in his, tears dropped from his caring brown eyes down the deep lines on his craggy cheeks.

Now that Nonna was no longer able to see her cry, Emily's own tears streamed down her face onto the sheets. In her heart, she felt it was a mercy Nonna had died this way, rather than the cancer causing her dreadful pain in the coming months. Still, she couldn't believe that she had gone forever.

For as far back as Emily could remember, Nonna was such an essential part of her life. She had *been* her life. Without Nonna, Emily's life would have been so different. She looked across at Raphael again. What if Nonna had stayed on Procida and married him? If she and Maria had stayed there, Emily would not exist. Maria would never have met her grandfather.

Both she and Raphael were still sitting by Nonna's bed when the doctor came back in, and after confirming Nonna had died, he gently asked them to leave so that he could do what he needed to do. Reluctantly, she stood up and with one last, lingering kiss on Nonna's now cold forehead, she undid the gold lira pendant from around Nonna's neck and placed it around her own neck, kissing the lira with her lips. She then left the room, leaving Raphael to say his final goodbyes.

Afterwards, as they waited for her father and Jonathon to arrive, despite her own devastation, she went to Raphael and put her arms around him.

'Oh, Raphael,' she said. 'I'm so sorry for you after all this time. Just when you found her.'

Raphael smiled. 'It is best that she went this way. Cancer is a cruel disease and she would have suffered,'

'Yes, I know, but even so.'

'I was lucky. I got to see her,' he said. 'I might have been too late.'

'And she got to see you. She died happy. knowing you had found her.'

As she sat beside him. she knew what she would do. After pouring them both a glass of Nonna's favourite *Pinot Grigio,* she and Raphael would sit on the verandah in Nonna's much-loved spot under the clematis vine, looking over her beloved garden to the wide stretch of sea beyond. While sitting there, she would ask him to tell her about a young Raphael Lombardi and an even younger Angeline Vincento when they all lived on the island of Procida with Emily's grandmother, Maria.

Epilogue

One Year Later
Kilmarnock

Although the sun was now shining brightly, a substantial summer storm had come last week followed by days of torrential rains. The dam at *Kilmarnock* was almost full and the paddocks were the greenest they had been in many years. Down in the shearing sheds, the shearers were hard at work, backs bent, sheep bleating. On the stove in the kitchen, Emily had a large pot of stew simmering. It was one of Nonna's favourite recipes, *braciole in ragu sauce,* which she had taught Emily years ago.

'Aunt Sophia taught it to me and Maria,' she told Emily the first time they made it together when Emily was a teenager.

She smiled as she mused how it had become one of Angus's favourite dishes. She thought of the night he had asked her to marry him. They were having dinner at *Grazings* in Gundaroo on a cold and blustery early spring evening. With the flames from the log fire casting warm shadows onto his loving face, he placed a blue velvet box on the table between them. Inside was a beautiful sapphire ring. Slipping it on her finger Emily thought her heart would burst with joy, much like the trees that were bursting into bloom throughout the countryside.

'So …' he asked with a large grin. 'Do you like it?'

'Oh Angus, it's stunning.'

'And will you marry me?'

She leant across the table and placed a long, arduous kiss on his lips. Sitting back in her chair she smiled broadly. 'I could think of nothing I'd like more.'

As she watched him smile with happiness, her only sadness was that Nonna wasn't there to help them celebrate that happiness. And that neither Nonna or her grandfather, who Emily had long since decided she would remember as the kindly and loving man he was to her, rather than what had been suggested he might have been in his business dealings, had met Angus. She was sure they would have loved him, as would have Maria, her grandmother.

She placed a tablecloth on the wooden table below the wattle tree in *Kilmarnock's* garden, where a brightly coloured rosella perched on a branch covered in golden blossom. She knew the shearers and Angus would come up shortly. Few things gave Emily more pride than to see the shearers do justice to her lunches. Although she mostly spent the first part of each week living in Sydney, where she still did the odd modelling job and had re-enrolled at uni to finish her English Literature degree, she looked forward to Thursdays when she would hop in her car and drive down to *Kilmarnock* to spend the weekend with Angus. Or he would come up to Sydney where they would stay at Nonna's house in Bronte, which she had left to Emily, having provided for her brothers elsewhere. But when the shearers were here, she chose to stay down for the whole week to help Angus.

His parents had decided to leave the running of *Kilmarnock* to him, and having shelved the idea of getting a yacht in the Med, they had decided to buy a small farm in the hinterland behind the Gold Coast in Queensland, close to where Betty's sister lived and they would keep a yacht at Runaway Bay and sail the Queensland coast, and maybe further afield, perhaps as far as Vanuatu or New Zealand.

'Even though they'll always be part of *Kilmarnock* and come and stay when they want, Mum thought Dad would do better to make a fresh start away from the memories of Duncan, which *Kilmarnock* invokes,' Angus told her.

Last week, Allen had driven down from Sydney with Emily. She was chuffed to see how well he got on with Angus. Angus even got him up on Jess and the three of them had gone down to check the sheep in the far river paddock.

Her father and his now fiancé, Bianca, hadn't been down to *Kilmarnock,* although last month she and Angus had gone to lunch with them and Dimitri Carpani and his wife at his restaurant, *Erskine's* at Rushcutters Bay. And despite her misgivings about 'another' woman in her father's life, Emily realised that while she and Bianca would never be firm buddies she was happy to see how contented her father had become in her company. She couldn't get over how much her father looked like Dimitri Carpani, but she supposed that was the Italian coming out in them both. She also found it strange to be dining in an *Erskine's* restaurant now owned by Dimitri and not her grandfather.

As she waited for the shearers to wander up to the garden for lunch she grabbed the hose and watered the weeping willow tree in the corner, which she and Angus had planted a couple of months previously as a memorial to Nonna. She smiled as she thought of the weekend they did that. How Raphael had come to stay and had helped them plant it. Although she knew Nonna had always loved the willow tree in her front garden at Bronte, where she often sat on the wooden seat in the shade beneath it, she had no idea that it was so significant. Not until Raphael told her that night after Nonna had died, and they were sitting under the clematis vine at Nonna's house having a glass of wine, that it was a tree that meant a lot to both he and Nonna.

'There was a beautiful weeping willow tree in a meadow of wildflowers on the island of Procida,' he said. 'Angeline and I liked to sit in its shade.' Then he smiled. 'It was under that tree that I played her a tune on my flute which we decided to call *Amore*.'

'Love?'

'Yes … love. And,' he winked mischievously, 'it was where I first kissed her.'

It was the way he said 'kissed' that made Emily suspect there might have been more than just a kiss that went on under that tree. But if there was, it was something between Raphael and Nonna.

When he came to *Kilmarnock* to plant the willow tree, Raphael bought a few packets of wildflower seeds, which they mixed with some of Nonna's ashes, and spread beneath the tree. Afterwards, they opened a bottle of Nonna's favourite *Pinot Grigio* and, as Raphael played a spine-tingling rendition of his and Nonna's tune, *Amore,* on his flute, they toasted a wonderful lady who was so cherished.

'That is such a beautiful tune,' Emily said. 'Nonna must have loved it.'

He gave her a tender smile. 'We both did. But, now … we must not be maudlin. She wouldn't like it. So, I will play you another tune. Maria and Angeline used to dance to this on Procida. They will enjoy listening from up above. And you two must dance and clap your hands, just as they did.'

As he played a rousing rendition of *Tarantella,* Angus and Emily danced around the garden, Emily blissfully happy in Angus's arms. She had no doubt that Raphael was right. Her grandmother, Maria, who she never met, and Nonna, who had taken her place so wonderfully, would be dancing with joy above. Even her beloved grandfather might be joining in, happy that his wife had met up with her old friend from Procida before she died. She also hoped that Duncan was looking down as his brother twirled her around the garden before stopping and clapping their hands to *Tarantella.*

Now, after watering the tree, which was growing taller and stronger each day, she leant down and picked a bunch of the wildflowers, today a riot of colour waving freely in the breeze. She took them inside and put them in a glass vase where she placed them next to a photograph of herself and Nonna, which she kept on the pine dresser in the kitchen.

Since that day when they planted the willow tree, Raphael had been up from Tasmania to stay with Emily a couple of times at Bronte. Together they sat on the verandah, chatting of far distant times. Sometimes he would play his flute, and, as Emily listened to the floating notes, she thought how fortunate she was to have this man, who meant so much to Nonna, in her life. Once, when Raphael was there she had invited Nonna's friend Elena around and for some time she and Raphael had talked of Italy. Elena even gave Raphael Marco's address and since then they had written to each other a couple of times, reminiscing on their times as prisoners of war in Tasmania.

She worried about Raphael on his own in his house at *Waterfall Bay* in Tasmania, but he assured her that he was more than happy to be there on his own and that if anything should happen to him Doug and Anne Larkham were not far away.

Emily heard the shearers coming up from the sheds and went inside. She pulled out a wooden tray, placing the knives, forks and plates on top. When she took them outside Angus was there, with Rex bounding by his side, to take the tray from her. Soon, they were all sitting around the table, laughing and talking. A couple of the shearers, with their faces lined and marked by the sun, were quite old for such a strenuous job, even though they used electric shears, but two of the other shearers were fairly new on the job. They told Emily they loved what they did, mainly as it took them all over the country. Even to New Zealand.

She burst with pride when Jack, the youngest, said, 'Gees, Emily, I've never had food as bonza as this before. No matter where I've sheared.'

She looked across at Angus and smiled. When he winked at her, she touched her stomach and felt her heart flutter. She wished Nonna was here to see how happy she was.

That night as she sat on the verandah, waiting for Angus to join her after his shower, she looked out over the paddocks to where the line of tall poplars edged the riverbank. In the near paddock, the horses grazed contentedly and beyond that the newly shorn sheep were gathered under the large gum tree in the corner.

'How about a glass of wine?' Angus asked, when he came out to join her.

Emily smiled and touched her stomach. 'I'd best not.'

Angus's face burst into a huge smile. 'And why would that be?'

Emily grinned. 'Because … well … … inside here,' she said with a dreamy smile, touching her stomach again, 'is a wee McBride.'

'So it was positive,' he said, his eyes glinting in happiness.

Emily laughed. 'It certainly was.' She then gave a mock sigh. 'God knows what I'll wear to our wedding.'

They planned a late summer wedding, here at *Kilmarnock*. Bill and Betty said they would come down and help organise it all, and hopefully the weather would be lovely so they could have it in the garden. Chrissy was to be her bridesmaid and Raphael was to be a treasured guest.

Sitting here on the verandah, with Rex lying by Angus's chair, she mused how lucky she was to have this man by her side, and how happy Nonna would have been to know that she and Angus were finally together.

Glancing over, she threw him a bright smile. 'Go get yourself a beer and I'd love an apple juice. Then we can take it to the willow tree and tell Nonna our happy news.'

Later, when they stood under the branches of the weeping willow, a light breeze came up from the east and a sweet honey scent from the wattle tree in the corner of the garden filled the air. As flecks of golden blossom floated across the lawn, she remembered how pleased Raphael had been when he saw that tree for the first time.

'When I said goodbye to your Nonna on Procida before she left for Australia, I told her to think of me and smile when the wattle blooms,' he said. 'I wonder if she did?'

'I'm sure she did,' Emily said.

Smiling with the memory, Emily looked up at Angus. 'All we need now is for Raphael to be here to play a tune on his flute.'

Lifting her face to his Angus kissed her long and ardently. When the usual tingle travelled her body she felt such happiness that she didn't think was possible. He then stood back and smiled, the creases on his farmer's sunburnt face making him more handsome than ever. 'Let's pretend we can hear Raphael playing his tune, *Amore*,' he said, before making an exaggerated bow. 'Would you, my beautiful lady … and,' he added, placing his hand gently on her stomach, 'our wee McBride-to-be, give me the honour of this dance?'

Emily threw her head back and laughed out loud. 'But of course,' she said, touching the gold lira pendant around her neck, a pendant which had made the long trip to Australia from that far place on the other side of the world where Nonna had found love all those years ago.

Amore.

'We'd both be delighted,' she said with a smile, folding into his arms.

ACKNOWLEDGEMENTS

I could not have written this book without the help of a number of people.

Firstly I would like to thank Selwa Anthony who has represented me for many years. Her guidance, acumen and friendship have meant so much to me.

When I first started writing in Tasmania after many years in the hectic world of business it was the author and tutor Rosie Dub who encouraged me to keep going.

I thank Nicola O'Shea for her wonderful editorial advice with my last novel, *The Homestead on the River*, and this book. Also Rebecca Wylie for her copy edit.

The renowned award-winning author, Annie Seaton has been an inspiration to me and guided me through the layout and cover design of this book as well as making editorial suggestions.

Every day I give thanks for my daughters, Charlotte and Georgie, and my five beautiful grandchildren who have given me inspiration to write.

I was with my soulmate, Rob Peterswald, on our yacht in the Mediterranean when we first discovered the tiny island of Procida featured in this book. We also discovered Tasmania together and the apple orchard where Italian prisoners-of-war worked, and is the setting for part of this book. We have had the greatest fun side by side for many, many years and have published eight photographic coffee table books about the wonderful sailing destinations we have discovered across the world.

See www.ballynastraghbooks.com.au

About the Author

Rosie Mackenzie was born in Ireland and moved to Australia when she was seven years old. After a successful business career in Tasmania, she now spends her time, writing, sailing and with her family. She is married to Rob Peterswald and they have two daughters and five grandchildren. She and Rob have published eight photographic coffee table books on sailing, seafood and wine together. She has adopted the pen name, Rosie Mackenzie for her historical fiction to honour her mother. Her previous Rosie Mackenzie novel, The *Homestead on the River* was published by Harper Collins. When not in Australia, she and Rob are on their boat exploring the world. The island of Procida in the Bay of Naples is one of their favourite anchorages in the Mediterranean. Rosie has also published a memoir, *Can My Pony Come Too?* under her name, Rosemary Esmonde Peterswald, and *Bird of Paradise,* a novel set in Papua New Guinea.

The second edition of *The Homestead on the River*, previously published by Harper Collins Australia, will be released shortly.

www.ingramcontent.com/pod-product-compliance
Lightning Source LLC
Chambersburg PA
CBHW050112120726
47904CB00004B/1322